Zombie in a
Spacesuit

Zombie in a Spacesuit

A novel

Mike Johnson

99% Press

Published by 99% Press,
an imprint of Lasavia Publishing Ltd.
Auckland, New Zealand
www.lasaviapublishing.com

Parts of this novel were previously published in Antibody Positive, 1991, Hard Echo Press.

ISBN: 978-0-473-42239-4

About the Author

Mike Johnson, fabulist and poet, is recognised as one of New Zealand's leading and innovative writers. He lives on Waiheke Island and teaches creative writing at AUT University in Auckland. His first novel, *Lear: The Shakespeare Company Plays Lear at Babylon*, was short-listed for the New Zealand Book Awards, his novel *Dumb Show* won the Buckland Memorial Award for Literary Excellence and he won the Frances Kean Award for his short story *Magic Strings*. His first book of poetry, *The Palanquin Ropes*, was co-winner of the John Cowie Reid Memorial Competition.
You can find more of his published works at www.lasaviapublishing.com

Other books by Mike Johnson

Novels
Hold My Teeth While I Teach You To Dance. 99% Press, Auckland.
Travesty. Titus Books, Auckland.
Stench. Hazard Press, Christchurch.
Counterpart. Harper Collins, Sydney.
Dumb Show. Longacre Press, Dunedin.
Lethal Dose. Hard Echo Press, Auckland.
Antibody Positive. Hard Echo Press, Auckland.
Lear: The Shakespeare Company Plays Lear at Babylon. Hard Echo Press, Auckland.

Shorter Fiction
Confessions Of A Cockroach / Headstone, 99% Press, Auckland.
Back in the Day: Tales from NZ's Own Paradise Island. 99% Press, Auckland.
Foreigners. Penguin Books, Auckland.

Poetry
Two Lines And A Garden, 99% Press, Auckland.
To Beatrice: Where We Crossed the Line. Pie Press, Auckland.
Vertical Harp: The Selected Poems of Li He. Titus Books, Auckland.
Treasure Hunt. Auckland University Press, Auckland.
Standing Wave. Hard Echo Press, Auckland.
From a Woman in Mt Eden Prison & Drawing Lessons. Hard Echo Press, Auckland.
The Palanquin Ropes. Voice Press, Wellington.

Non Fiction
Angel of Compassion. TP Press, Auckland.

Children's Fiction
Kenny and the roof slide, illustrated by Jennifer Rackham. Beansprout Press. Auckland.
Taniwha. illustrated by Jennifer Rackham. Beansprout Press. Auckland.

Preface

Zombie in a Spacesuit, or at least portions of it, began life as a novel published in 1991 by Hard Echo Press called *Antibody Positive*. It was my second novel, and, to my mind now, the least satisfactory. Not only were a set of revisions and corrections not entered in the printed draft, resulting in a messy text, but the novel always felt to me to be unfinished. It was too raw when it went to print.

It wasn't until 2016 that I returned to it and found I could bring out the potential in the original novel. Almost everything has been upgraded from sentence construction to chapter breaks; the novel now has a different sense of pace and underlying rhythm. Whole sections have gone while a new character and a new ending have been added. Now the novel has three thematically related, interwoven stories, spanning from the beginning of human thought to the end of time.

Antibody Positive was categorized as science fiction, and I might then have thought of it that way myself. Now I think what I was trying to write was transfiction, a cross-genre mix that didn't exist as such in 1991.

I'm happy that the revision has gone so well, and that *Zombie in a Spacesuit* has already won one new devotee – Odette Wards, our proof-reader. I wish the book well. It feels much more comfortable as 21st Century novel, but, I trust, no less challenging.

Mike Johnson, Waiheke Island, January 2018

Words and sentences are produced by the law of causation and are mutually conditioning – they cannot express highest Reality. Moreover, in highest Reality there are no differentiations to be discriminated and there is nothing to be predicted with regard to it. Highest Reality is an exalted state of bliss, it is not a state of word discrimination and cannot be entered into by mere statements concerning it.

The Lankavatra Sutra

By reason of clinging to these false imaginations there is multitudinousness of appearances which are imagined to be real but which are only imaginary.

The Lankavatra Sutra

And the sedulous ape has learned one trick that's sound: to walk erect in the perpendicular city.

Robin Hyde

The Anteroom

At some time in the night I get up and go outside to piss under the moon. I can piss copious quantities at two or three in the morning, out under the moon, where time does not move but circles itself in trailing phosphorescence. There's a silver arc stretching from my lower quarters and vanishing into the ground.

Since the appointment was made my bladder has become skittish. Jittery as an unproven horse before its race, it shies away, offers reluctance, dissimulates. I stand here as I stand, back curved, cock hanging at a foolish angle, the moonlight polishing the trees that line our street, the cool neutral air pressing close around me, waiting for my bladder to complete its movement, waiting for something to happen. I should know better by now.

In the distance, over the neighbour's back fence, lean and graceful, the Tower lifts into the night sky, both familiar and otherworldly. 2.13, it says from its lofty heights, proclaiming time across the land. 2.14. To look at it you'd think that time moves forward in little jumps, as if each second, like a high jumper, gathers its energies for the next leap into the future.

Stroking the underside of the glans, a brush as light as angel's wings,

I see that my bladder can't complete its movement because I won't let it. I'm holding on with a grip mortal and fierce. Panic peeing, I've heard that expression. You think you want to pee, but deep down you resist. You fight. At 2.20 a.m. and you're still fighting. Fighting the panic. I mutter a small prayer to the receptive earth, tipping away under my feet, stroking the stubborn glans until I am answered by a trickle of sensation, and go on stroking until it arrives, a burst of tiny stars to pepper the grass.

2.21. Another gathering and release. I go on pissing like there is no tomorrow. The Tower seems to exist just to hold time aloft; it does not belong to this world. I have positioned it there, very carefully, to grace the moon that hangs in the sky like a figure on a scaffold. I put it there to balance the composition.

The whole lawn glistens with dew.

We are waiting.

A box inside a box, containing all others with its particular boredom. Time is like this, not moments spread like beads on a cosmic abacus, but a Petrushka doll, one moment inside the other. Time must be unpacked. I've been packing and unpacking the moments since all this began, heading towards and away at the same instant.

The box I'm sitting in is a room. A man sits opposite, across a receding distance of red and white chessboard tiles. We are alone here in this space with its broad expanses, opposing plate glass windows (see the reflection of one in the other), tubular steel, red-cushioned, stiff-backed hyphenated chairs. He has as clean gauze patch over one eye. To compensate, his other eye has grown larger, brighter and more piercing, like the eye of an icon. I am reminded of binary stars; one is always brighter and more massive than the other, its shadowy accomplice. In the sharp elliptic of his gaze I can detect the gravitational tug of that other, invisible orb.

I try not to look at him. It's all too easy for our fascination with such things to become a fixation.

Both of us feel justly abandoned by time, stuck here together in the box. Off-stage, events rush by, unnamed and unseen. Outside, cars will be hurrying up and down the street as the final grains of sand slip through the hourglass. Somewhere far away, Evelyn is looking at a clock, perhaps wondering where I've got to. Little Evie skips down the street between the cycles of her skipping rope, her feet hardly touching the pavement – *what's the time, Mr Wolfie?* Somewhere my Grandfather is dying of wounds received in battle. Somewhere close, an official leans his elbows the frozen notion of his desk. He can hardly be bothered with the people waiting to see him. Through his office window he can see people are opening and shutting their lives.

One-eye and I orbit on another over the red and white checkerboard floor.

It's his move.

As my bladder empties, I think with pleasure on the few thin sheets neatly arranged on my desk beside the voice printer. A beginning, no more. A secret to be revealed to no one. Not the official, not Evelyn, not my grandfather, not even Evie – although it will be impossible to keep Evie in the dark forever, she has a way of ferreting things out.

As a child I had a pen that wrote in invisible ink. Sprinkle water on the paper, like a blessing, and letters form, faint and piecemeal at first, dark lines that waver and tremble and finally coalesce into words and sentences, formulas and riddles. It was magical and unsettling. The way words appeared out of nowhere like that. All they needed was a little baptism. Even after weeks of neglect, it would still work. I wondered how the words could remember, after such a long invisibility, where to go and in what order to place themselves.

Now, when I gathered these empty sheets and put them together, their wonderful secrecy protected me, hid me from prying eyes, made me invisible, just as I am here standing in the faint night, in the sleeping city, eyes wide shut. I am a child again, like Evie, with my invisible ink, soaked in the magical medium of moonlight, hugging those fairy-tale pages to my chest.

We have a certain social problem, One-eye and I. We are sitting too far apart for natural conversation, yet not far enough apart to ignore each other comfortably. We are placed along the fine line of our divided awareness. Either one of us is on the point of getting up and joining the other, making a conversation out of the bare materials available.

'It's a fine morning.'

'Yes, it is.'

Is it really fine? Is it really still morning? Glance to where the sun is glazing the plate glass windows and putting a sheen on the city. Grope for a word. Hope for the best. The best of all possible words. Smile a little, as the situation permits.

Every so often, in anticipation of such an ice-breaking event, our glances collide, my double gaze with his single focus.

'The wind is a mite chilly.'

'Yes, it is.'

Both fine and chilly, it seems. For conversational purposes, it doesn't matter.

Like robot toys, our glances reverse upon meeting and change direction randomly, bouncing off the shiny white walls (off-white, actually), the featureless doors of the lift, the pastoral that hangs a little too low to the left of the lift (its exact features cannot be made out from here but I presume it depicts a harvest scene featuring a draft horse with sturdy limbs and piles of yellow, dusty hay) or the blandly framed city with its cubes of sky. Bouncing off the empty tubular steel, red-cushioned chairs stiff-backed in their waiting. Our awkward glances find nowhere to settle. Our smiles don't get started.

To cross this shouting distance would be most polite, and welcomed by both sides no doubt, and yet too forward, too revealing, somehow too intimate, confessional even – presuming upon a relationship that does not exist, or only exists in the form of a probability wave which may or may not collapse into a reality. As things stand, we are but an extension of the room's architectonics (that is, an echo), mere elements of the overall design. We are pencilled into our chairs. We face each other as the pastoral faces the plate glass windows, and the windows, in turn, face the lift, without recognition or comment. Without a smile.

'Of course for the time of the year…'

'Yes, the year.' Leaves. Leaves plastered to the glass or stitched to the back of the hand, green and veiny. Piles of yellow, dusty hay. Heroic workhorse in action. I will show you a year. We will sit here together and unpack our lunch box. Make hay while the sun shines.

The conversation doesn't happen.

Our glances clap and retract.

Inside, it is seasonless and weatherless, smooth and marbled, upright and collapsed. Nothing here for words to attach themselves.

We have nothing to say.

All good things must come to an end, even at 2.30 a.m. when the night seems endless. At the top of the Tower, the moments blink on and off in their endless countdown. It looks like the same moment over and over again, but it isn't. Narrative creeps in around the edges of remorse. Bladder's empty. The panic subsides. The bright, galactic stream wavers and dribbles to an end. I shake my cock a couple of times and with a tickle of regret slip it back into my pyjamas.

Now there is just me, the dewy lawn and the scaffold moon. There is nothing to link these elements until little Evie appears, her bare feet wet from the dew. Illuminated by the streetlight behind her, the jewelled nimbus of her hair, a tiara for a princess.

'What are you doing?' she asks severely, her child's face fixed on mine.

'Taking a pee.'

'Oh.'

Bit silly, peeing outside when there is a perfectly good toilet in the house, is what she must be thinking.

I gesture to the Tower, self-consciously holding my pyjamas up with the other hand. 'What does it remind you of?'

Evie hugs her body against the evening chill.

'I give up.'

'Look at it! It's a Starship.' I curve my free hand up into the air. 'Buck Rogers, Captain Kirk, Luke Skywalker. Men brave and true! Real legends! Men who understood that we are falling through space at interstellar speeds, even while appearing to stand still!'

She moves back into the shadow of our pear tree. Only a few jigsaw pieces of her gown can be made out.

'I think you should go back to bed,' she says in the thin, pitiless voice she uses to reprimand me.

I'm sure she has my best interests at heart.

Closing my eyes and murmuring an incantation, I turn around three times (three being a magic number in folk-tales and legends). Words waver, hover on the edge of existence. All they need is a blessing to make them visible to the world. As I turn, the whole sky of stars and the fixed constellations turn with me. Up there, the great space opera of all time is in full swing. When I open my eyes I am still in the same place, facing the Tower. It blinks.

2.26

It's not stopping. Time: it's an open and shut case.

I hear little Evie's voice from the sliced shadows of the pear tree.

'Flee the wrath to come.'

2.27

One-eye and I act as people who are waiting act: we look at our watches (or at our wrists where we might expect to find a watch), move our feet around under our chairs, fuss with our clothes (brushing off real or imagined dust), and glance around with pointed aimlessness.

I'd like to say I've been here in this box for a long time, but the truth is I have no sense of duration, only of distance. The distance between myself and the lifts, myself and the windows, myself and One-eye; everywhere I look there is distance. The moments I have been here, sitting in this same chair (or one very like it), have amassed themselves into this particular instant that flattens itself out and spreads itself laterally. Moments spill all over the place, which reminds me of that old saying, 'spilled water cannot be put back into the jug.'

For me, sitting in this tubular steel, stiff-backed, red-cushioned chair, time has become a wheel of which this very split second is the hub. I may crawl antlike along a spoke or cling dizzily to the narrative rim, but sooner or later the future past will deliver me here once more to receive my sentence, here at the core of my waiting. I stare at the harvest scene or the sealed doors of the lift, which is keeping mum, and avoid the Cyclopean gaze of the man opposite. This must be eternity. Every moment wants to grow its own flower.

Outside, people are hurrying back and forth, attending to their lives. The day is sunny. Or it is cloudy. It is morning. Or it is afternoon. The government is stable. Or it is about to fall. Somewhere in a magazine, the leaning tower of Pisa leans, but no further. My heart stumbles between beats. Hear the soft slushing of blood in my ears. Slush-slush. The see-saw pulse. The to and fro.

I am here enjambed.

Of course it could all be different, even slightly so, if the seating were rearranged, if we were sitting closer or further away from each other (how painful distances can be!), if the painting were an abstract instead of a pastoral, if One-eye had been born a forward-looking Aquarian instead of a stubborn Taurean, if we'd met somewhere before… Funny, but I feel we have met before but put this down to the many lifetimes we have spent here, sitting on these uncomfortable chairs recycling our glances.

'It takes one to know one,' One-eye says knowingly.

I agree, but don't wish to impose on an intimacy that doesn't exist. There are people who tell strangers terribly intimate things right off, things they wouldn't tell their friends: family secrets, life histories, sexual adventures, details of illnesses (particularly when they are of a pitiful or degrading nature), religious or political obsessions and confessions. Those are the risks of a conversation with strangers. One-eye doesn't look like that sort of person. The patch gives him a dense, secretive look, the look of a person who would play his cards close to his chest.

'Yes indeed, it takes one to know one,' he repeats, as if supplying my side of the conversation as well as his, which is fortunate as I don't feel like talking.

When he winks with his one good eye, his whole face shuts down.

I follow multiple threads of dew back into the house. Almost light rain, it is the blessing that will bring the blank page of night to life with a rosy-fingered dawn. I should be giving thanks for small mercies rather than holding the universe to account, I tell myself.

Rather than turn on the light, I feel my way into the living room, past my study with its little pile of papers, hands outstretched before me like the sleepwalker of popular imagination. It strikes me that I have entered a stranger's house, blundered somehow into the life of another, and will to feel my way through the bric-a-brac of another world before climbing into a bed I can only hope will be mine. When I wake in the morning, all that will remain will be the lingering sense of some previous existence, or some life as yet unlived, some wound as yet unhealed.

Above the black pit of the old-fashioned fireplace, on the mantelpiece, a segment of moon has caught the framed photograph of my grandfather I like to keep around me. A handsome young man, full of pride and military bearing. Full of imperial arrogance. This is not the face of a man who doubts the world. The collar of his uniform is high at the neck, his field cap is set rakishly to one side, and the sepia tones give his skin a smooth, waxed look, as if he were not made of real flesh but of marble or alabaster. His steady gaze into the future becomes monumental, the expression representative. Stern eyes and the beginning of an amber smile, with no shadow of the slaughter to come.

My own face is caught in the glass of the frame, superimposed on my grandfather's face like a ghost from his future. I am nine years old, standing in the bathroom, holding up my pyjamas with one hand while cleaning my teeth with the other, taking time to breathe hotly on the mirror to hide my buckteeth and batwing ears. My grandfather is talking in the next room, saying things I should not be overhearing about one of my uncles, the one with the dark eyebrows like a raven's wings.

'This is why I risked my life, shooting and being shot at. Bringing home a wound that didn't heal. For what purpose? So one of my own sons can play hell with a big stick, wreck his family, piss on everybody as he goes past? I have no sympathy for the bugger. I never did. He brings disgrace wherever he goes.'

My nine-year-old face shines wetly in the glass, buckteeth and batwing ears in full evidence. Somehow, I feel responsible, even guilty. As if my uncle's disgrace was my own. I take a hard look at my own eyebrows.

I leave my grandfather's photograph keeping watch on the mantelpiece for family disgraces (of which I am sure I am one), and, still holding up my pyjamas with one hand after all these years, I head towards the bedroom. I square my shoulders, straighten my spine and lift my chin a few degrees, just as my grandfather must have done before the photo was taken. And before he walked off into battle to shoot and be shot at.

We have to put the past behind us, I have heard, and confidently visualise a successful future. That's best done with a straight spine and square shoulders. Of course this idea that the past is behind us while our future lies in front is quite quaint, and does not necessarily fit our experience. More often than not I have felt the future creeping up on me from behind while my forward gaze is fixed firmly on the past.

Taking care not to disturb Evelyn, I lie down and begin my positive visualisations. I see myself walking with a brisk, upright step along the street, a neatly folded umbrella swinging from my wrist. Every inch a man going somewhere, on his way to somewhere important; a man who can swing confidently around a corner and relish a new vista. A man with an appointment.

Examining this mental picture for realistic detail, I find it perfect in every respect, exact in its verisimilitude, plausible in every way. I could easily be that person striding confidently along the street, off to his appointment, swinging his umbrella, singing a little song, perhaps. *'What's the time, Mr Wolfie? One o'clock, two o'clock.'*

We have passed a watershed, One-eye and I, the point at which we could still initiate a conversation without being too presumptuous. Our silence has gone through its painful stage and has become embalmed, an intrinsic part of the polished surface of things. The longer it goes on, the harder it is for us to break it.

Our waiting has become quite resigned, quite hopeless. Our silence has become a confession, our non-communication habitual.

The only solution is for a polite, professional figure to emerge from one of the small doors to the right of the lift and call one of our names. This public naming will break the spell between us. After a startled moment one of us, the one who correctly identifies his name, will rise and accompany the professional figure without so much as a backward glance.

This solution we await with patience and dread. We share only the anticipation, the waiting, these moments stacked within moments – and this particular shabby moment we would put behind us without a second thought. I am mistaken if I imagine I *share* anything with One-eye. We are a coincidence of time and space. An empty coincidence. A memory we would gladly abandon. In vain would we seek meaning here.

We are but a product of that peculiar fixity waiting breeds.

I am sitting alone.

Nothing else has changed. The lift remains tight-lipped. The pastoral stays where it is. A weak sun slides off the plate glass windows.

It happened exactly as I anticipated. An official, male, appeared from one of the small doors to the right of the lift and called a name. It must have been his name, for One-eye rose, relieved, and was led away. He had a limp. He limped on the same side as his missing eye. This is one detail I had not counted on. It is such little things that trip up the criminal and the writer.

The official stood back and let One-eye through the door first, his shoulders then folding into One-eye's shoulders and their bodies merging into an unbroken texture.

I'm staring at the chair he occupied, which has not yet settled back into its accustomed anonymity. It is still the chair One-eye has vacated. The sun, dipping red-eyed into the room, lights up this tubular steel, red-cushioned chair that has now become *the* empty chair in a row of empty chairs. If I look away, towards the pastoral perhaps, I may forget which chair it was. The whole row of chairs would return me a bland, stiff-backed stare. I make sure that doesn't happen by counting the number of chairs from the end of the row. Now I can look away with full confidence that I will be able to relocate One-eye's chair, although why I would want to is a question not even boredom can answer.

This room is like one of those blank pages sitting in my room, unwatered and unblessed. Every so often the lift whines and numbers change on the indicator panel above. Occasionally there is a distant murmur of voices filtered through long corridors, but nobody appears. From this height, the city looks motionless, like a dead city or a still life. It could hang where the pastoral is and not feel out of place. It too is silent, since thoughtful planning has filtered out all sound from this room. It appears that there is a faint undulation passing through it like a wavefront, as if its molecular structure momentarily loosens, but that a mere effect of imperfections in the glass.

I wish little Evie were here, sitting beside me or in the same chair One-eye occupied (fifth from the right), her feet swinging to and fro, her no-nonsense chatter, tapping her fingers in time to a melody she is humming. It is a slow, waltzy kind of blues; late night stuff that's got my fingers tapping away as well.

Don't you cry

Don't you cry

Don't you cry when I'm gone.

Which is easy enough to say but might be a hard ask. In that respect, time cannot be redeemed. I would love to get up and dance with her. Dancing with Evie is fun because she takes it so seriously. I would love to raise my arms above my head, shuffle my feet in Greek dance style while she mirrors my movements, her child's arms as graceful as those of a Javanese dancer, her dress swirling out over the red and white tiles, her hair skimming her shoulders.

When she dances, Evie becomes someone else.

At any given moment the doors of the lift could slide apart and all the configurations change. Someone walking into the room and looking around for a chair would change everything, even the light coming through the plate glass windows. A woman, say, glancing nervously at her watch, asking me the time perhaps, her glance taking in the windows and the pastoral, the lift and the little doors to one side (I'm already a part of that glance), forcing events to turn a corner.

I'm only too glad to look at my watch and tell her the time, to meet her anxious gaze directly, openly, and to relieve in some small way the monotony of waiting, despite the fact that the Tower is just over there, through the windows, batting away the seconds.

There's a movement behind my left shoulder. The secret pages rustle.

'Why does the woman have to be "glancing nervously at her watch"?' My wife Evelyn asks, intervening.

I try to pretend that this is not a rude intrusion, and that I am not actually quite busy here, sitting in my red-cushioned, tubular steel chair waiting for my name to come up.

'Did you think of the implications before heedlessly writing that down? Writing the first thing that comes into your head?'

Not the first thing, I think. Maybe the second or the third.

'You're starting to draw a stereotypical picture.' She brushes her long sleek hair off her face.

'Wait a minute, you can't just intervene in the story like this...'

'Why not? I'm your wife, aren't I?'

'It's considered bad manners. In a literary sense. Frankly, it's quite rude, butting in like this.'

'Butting in? Between you and this poor brow-beaten woman, you mean? So you can play your little games with her? Butting in? You should choose your words more carefully.'

'I have my reader to consider.' My long-suffering reader, still in the anteroom waiting for the story to begin. Waiting to be ushered on stage. It's a pity that indelible ink doesn't work for Evelyn. She could see right through it anyway.

'Your reader? You wish! Anyway, I'm your wife, not a *character.*'

'You are now.'

'Now what?'

'A character. By intervening in the text you've turned yourself into one. I would have been just as happy to keep you out.'

'I bet you would. Cramp your style, do I?'

'I think you are reading way too much into this.' I squirm in my chair. 'You have to realize how little I have to work with here. I have this room with the checkerboard floor, the pastoral, the lifts, One-eye, those goddamn chairs… there's only so much I can do with such few elements. I'm not a miracle worker.'

'And you're not God.'

Instead of turning around to face her, I prefer to concentrate on the map of the city I have pinned on the wall in front of me for quick reference. All the streets are clearly named so I can plot the movements of my character as he walks to his appointment. The appointment is always there, in front of him. No matter which compass point he faces, it will still be there. Except afterwards when he has to turn his feet for home, his brown envelope in his pocket. Beside the map there is a poster-sized print of the head of a dragon. Although the head is done in greys, a strip of bright, multicoloured ticker tape emerges from its mouth in a shining plume, curling up scroll-like as it falls. Beneath this there is another print depicting a pouting male face in profile with a caption in capitals beneath: YOU RE-ENACT THE DANCE OF INSERTION AND WOUNDING.

There is plenty for me to look at.

'After all,' I continue. 'This woman isn't even a character. My character just imagines her. No one, in fact, has appeared. She is only a conjecture, a possibility. An idea he toys with to keep his boredom at bay. You pounced a little too soon.'

My wife tosses her head, allowing the light to catch her profile, which, as she well knows, I have always admired for its classical lines. 'You're a cunning bastard, I'll give you that. But you can't fool me. That whole set up in the anteroom or whatever it is, is just to provide a hygienic context, a cover I should say, an excuse for "accidentally" meeting this woman. You've visualised it all carefully beforehand, drooled over the details, now it's all set up. In walks your victim like a fly into a trap. One-eye and the official and all the rest are just red-herrings.'

I hold up my hand to stop her for she couldn't be more wrong, but it's too late, and she pushes on, racing ahead in vicious, clipped tones, following it all through to its inevitable conclusion.

'And look, you have this poor distracted woman, and now you have me. I appear of course as The Hag. The Virago Wife. The Bitch. You can tell her all about me later. Afterwards. You've made up this silly wifey name, Evelyn. Eve of course, ha ha.' She jabs the page, and all the words scuttle away and hide.

'You have a duty to be more conscious of what you are doing instead of flying off half-cocked, ha ha. You have a duty to attend to the pictures you evoke, the stereotypes you set in motion. It's hard to stop them once they are in motion.'

That's true enough. I nod my head. My little bell jangles. It's a relief that the woman hasn't actually arrived although now I'm afraid she won't come at all, that she'll be frightened off. A story is not like a train tearing down the tracks from one known station to the next with regulated stops and stopwatch timed starts. A story needs to be caressed and treated with respect.

A decided note of anxiety has entered my waiting. The waiting room no longer seems like such a neutral place. What if the woman decides to postpone her appointment, or just not turn up? What if she backs out before the doors of the lift can close securely behind her? What if she returns to the streets with nothing resolved? Then nothing will happen. There will just be me and the empty room and the fading promise of an official.

'Evie,' I call softly, remembering our shuffling Greek style dance. Or imagined dance; it doesn't matter where Evie is concerned.

My heart has begun to thump in an unsteady, unsettled manner and I am tempted to look back at the halcyon when One-eye and I shared this negative space with perfect accord and balance, he on one side of the room, me on the other. The lifts to my right and his left. There are no halcyon times. Nothing before and nothing after. The great nothing that is the before and the after. The great boredom, which is actually a muffled terror.

I scrape my feet over the red and white tiles.

I massage my knee as if it were sore.

I live in the empty zone between time and appearance.

I look out the window to the constellations of blue, and the blinking Tower.

I sit out the fragments of my waiting.

Finally, after all this nail-biting, the rubbery lips of the lift doors slide apart with an efficient hum, but it is not a woman who emerges, or Evie (whom I secretly hoped it would be), but a man-sized fish. A creature with the head and body of a fish, but with human arms protruding from its upper torso and stubby feet each side of its triangular, fishy tail. Scales cover the whole body, including a sheath to cover its sex (give thanks for small mercies), but I have the impression it is male. Its scales, faintly mother of pearl, gleam dully in the light.

It walks over the checkerboard tiles towards me with an upright, authoritative waddle that is both absurd and menacing. In response to its approach, I feel a stirring in the watery, fishy part of my body, that region between the navel and the bowel where all the oceans of the world are held. I look desperately around the room, which suddenly seems a lot smaller, at the rows of tubular steel chairs with their red vinyl covers. I think I'm worried about where the beast is going to sit. For a moment those chairs are as frightening as the fish creature. There's a whole invisible audience here, sitting in those chairs I have come to despise, noting my every reaction, probably even taking notes, I think with fright. Hidden cameras will be recording this crucial moment; my reactions will be carefully monitored and analysed.

I have to be very vigilant, very alert. Here is doom approaching from my right, and One-eyed judgement still sitting opposite in abstract form. I am eager for the chairs to settle back into their comfortable familiarity. I seek reassurance in their blunt, everyday nature, their materiality, their sheer contemptible ordinariness. They exist. In the world. They have a simple human function. They give life to themselves. You could pick one up and scratch the world with it.

I'm hoping the fish-creature will choose a distant one, perhaps One-eye's old chair (fifth in from the right), but it comes up and stands in front of me. It has an odd, musty smell, like stale sperm.

I don't know where to look. Or what to say. You can't make small talk with a mythological creature, even one that comes up to you in broad daylight. I could do what Evelyn would do and pretend that it doesn't exist, that I have made it up. She would certainly accuse me of making it up. She could say I was doing it to spite her, but with all due respect, Evelyn isn't here, in this anteroom with its repetitive elements, facing what I am facing, which is a large ambulatory fish. It's all too easy to make judgements when you're not on the spot. I wouldn't want to make up something like that. Why should I? It destroys the minimalist realism of the moment, and those other delicate moments with One-eye and the chairs. Just walks over them with big smelly feet, slap-slap on the checkerboard tiles, and pop goes the narrative. I was much happier when I had just a few simple, realistic elements to work with. The anteroom was coming along well. The fishman is a rogue element. An impurity. The whole clean picture is thrown into disarray.

I decide to rid myself of the fish-creature as if I had just made it up, and I wish Evie were here to help with some workable solutions. She's a very practical soul, is Evie. Among other things, I find its presence physically disturbing. I'm starting to sweat, and my limbs are not behaving the way they are supposed to. Parts of my body begin to push and struggle against their limits, pull away from me as if I no longer owned them. My legs are about to get up and walk away by themselves. My arms would prefer to take flight. My chest would turn inside out if it had half a chance. My very flesh wants to transmute into another substance.

Worse, I find myself sexually aroused by the creature's squat presence and slimy smell. Also, there's something horribly suggestive in its stance, its sleek, scaly midriff thrust forward, its stubby legs turned outward showing a pale greenish thigh, skin hanging a little loosely.

I wonder if I act obnoxiously it will go away. Utter some magic obscenity that will give offense and send it off, back into the lift perhaps, back through those rubbery lips.

'I think you have the wrong floor,' I say boldly. 'Aliens upstairs.'

If the creature appreciates the joke he doesn't show it. He just keeps watching me as if he would at any moment snap me up. I need my magic obscenity. A single word that would banish the thing forever. 'Flesh,' I say, glancing nervously around at the empty chairs where the invisible audience are sitting, attending closely. I believe I hear a snicker here and there. 'Flesh, bones, dust, earth, mud, dung, shit.' I feel like a naughty boy saying naughty words in the presence of disapproving elders.

The creature opens and shuts its mouth. No sound emerges. I imagine it would croak like a frog. Perhaps it wants or expects something from me it can't articulate. Something I'm expected to divine from its presence and posture.

Before I can develop some more effective insults, there is a prickling sensation at the back of my head, as if my skull had been opened up and something lifted out. A pattern perhaps, a template – a map of my mind. All my secrets, my thought dreams, those things I show to no one. Things I can't say or write down. Things I wouldn't want to say or write down. Some things are best left unsaid. My urge is to pick up a weapon (in this case a chair) and stand, knees bent, resolutely facing the unknown, poking out my tongue and rolling my eyeballs.

Calmly, the creature turns and walks back towards the lift with the air of somebody who has got what they came for, or who has just successfully completed a long and complex negotiation. Its legs, I notice, protrude from its tail about a quarter of the way up. Its tail, which curves upward a little at the end, sweeps low, almost touching the floor. It has no buttocks to speak of but a plain anal sphincter set into its lower back. It is the placement of the legs that give it that comic waddle, and the anal sphincter opens and shuts as it walks, as if winking at some obscene joke. I'd be happy to laugh. However, there is also a sense of bulk, of massive density and power that is not at all funny. Something authoritative in the waddle. Giggle at your peril. Here is a creature not to be messed with, a creature used to taking what it wants and has no problem strolling through worlds to get it.

The lift whines obligingly to a halt, the rubbery lips slide apart, and the fish creature hardly needs to break its stride to enter. The indicator panel lights up and the lift descends. I watch the numbers glow through their series until the lift has reached the ground floor, get up and walk across to the chair One-eye once occupied. I try not to step on the joins between the red and white tiles, thinking of Evie and the advice she might give me.

Step on a crack and you marry a rat. There are faint web-shaped damp patches where the fish creature passed, as if it had recently stepped out of the ocean. In the right light, they have an oily gleam. Glancing surreptitiously about, I bend over and sniff at them. It is the same half-sweet musty smell, reminding me of bedrooms and rumpled sheets, abandoned underwear and the soft, insistent memory of pillows. And behind that the salty smell of beaches and ocean spray. Cautiously, I dab the dampness with a finger; it adheres with faint stickiness to my skin.

I sit in One-eye's chair and look back to where I have been sitting. The whole room looks different. The plate glass windows have switched around. Already I have forgotten which chair I occupied, having forgotten to count in from the end of the row. I simply choose a likely candidate and settle on that one. By royal decree, that is the chair I have just vacated. I glance nervously at the lift, which is now ascending again. Perhaps the woman is in the lift, glancing at her watch, pulling at the cuffs of her denim jacket, decidedly not looking forward to her appointment.

From my new vantage point I can see the pastoral more clearly. There is the draught horse pulling a hay wagon. What I didn't see before was the man, a muscular rural type, his sleeves rolled up, energetically forking hay. *Make hay while the sun shines!* There is, however, something subtly wrong with the human figure. The body is slightly out of proportion, the stance stilted and unnatural, prompting the suspicion that the artist has not painted the scene from real life, but from imagination, wishful thinking even, from someone who never forked hay in their lives.

The lift changes tone as it arrives at one of the lower floors.

My old chair (the one I have nominated) and I exchange glances. A faint sigh goes up from the empty chairs around me. I forgot about the invisible watchers. The rustic forks hay at an impossible angle.

The lift resumes its upward course.

In my dream I am a leopard running with long, lithe, easy strides against the yellow hills of my childhood. My paws barely touch the tussocky ground and I am beautifully conscious of the rippling power of my body. It is more like flying than running, with no sensation of effort. My body is a flawless machine, each muscle working in faultless coordination.

When I open my eyes I am still running. The bedroom goes bounding past.

2.53, my alarm clock signals.

Evelyn sighs.

Soon I am swimming. But I don't swim in water. I swim through space. Through some galactic aurora. I feel the power surging through my tail in bolts of ecstasy as I flick from star to star.

The moment arrives, just as it would have to. Time is always garbed in inevitability, no matter how free our dreams. There is always a box inside another box.

A polite, official figure (male) appears from the small door by the lift and calls out my name.

After a brief hesitation, I get up and walk towards him, conscious of the abrupt emptiness of the chair I have vacated, its sudden reversion to form. Like a condemned man, I take one last lingering glance out the windows towards the city which still lies motionless and horizontal, except for the Tower which provides for the vertical axis. Behind the city, climbing in muscled folds of tussock yellow, the hills I roamed as a child, a leopard in the making. As my eyes slide across their dense forms, an undulating wave passes through them, as if they had momentarily hesitated in their existence. A fault line in the glass, I think, experiencing a slight déjà vu. That déjà vu is itself like a fault line in my memory.

Although city and hills lie there, silent and frozen, as if caught within the glass itself, I have the impression that they are buffeted by high winds which howl around the plate glass and steel of the Tower and thump like a fist on angular shapes below. Only the miracle of perfect engineering separates me from this ferocious element, terrifying and invisible.

A familiar mechanical whine informs me that the lift is once more ascending. I am certain it is going to stop at this floor, and that its passenger will be somebody already known to me, if only in anticipation. I am struck with the sudden dread that I am going to miss her, the anxious one, yet cannot break my forward momentum and delay my arrival at the side of the official.

I am painfully aware of the unnatural angle at which I walk, the stiff, half bent posture. As I approach the official, a virtual prisoner of the action of my musculature, he grows bigger and I grow smaller. The doors of the lift grow massive. The grey rubbery lips quiver with anticipation as the lift shudders to a halt. The official stands to one side, blocking my view, inviting me to pass through the small door while the lift opens with a synthetic hiss.

My legs carry me through the door as the official moves in behind me. I try to glance backwards, lean backwards to look at the lift, but the door is closing behind me. I feel clumsy and foolish trying to walk forward and lean backwards at the same time, but I do catch a brief glimpse of fishnet stockings and a knee length denim skirt. As the door snaps shut, I realize that I didn't see One-eye coming out of this room. He came in but never went out; it is inconceivable that I would have missed such an event; there has to be some back entrance.

I mean, Evelyn is looking over my shoulder. Again. She knows how to time her appearances; her instinct is always unerring.

'This woman in the lift. Probably a hippy type. Dirty blonde hair. Helpless. With appealing eyes. Maybe lost in a drug haze and needing your help. You help her by taking her back to her hippy flat and fucking her. It's the kind of help she's often had from men. Men like you. There'll be dirty underwear on the floor. You'll be disgusted and turned on; it seems these things go hand-in-hand with you. You don't give a thought to what you might pick up from promiscuous types like that; she doesn't give a thought to what she could pick up from types like you.'

'Is that the way you want it to turn out?' I feel lonely when I say that. None of this has any place in a novel about my grandfather.

She taps the small pile of pages. 'You'll find some way to be unfaithful to me. I know you all too well.'

With the door closed behind me, the anteroom is gone. I have no idea if I will see it again.

After all, I didn't see One-eye coming out.

'It's a wonderful morning,' my alarm clock says cheerfully. 'A fine day with mild autumn temperatures forecast. Rise and shine, handsome. Feet on the floor, walk to the door.'

From inside the pillow, which I am holding down each side of my head, I say to it, 'I had a disturbed night. Fighting with words.' You wouldn't think a sentence could fight back, but it can – I have the scars. 'I want a few more minutes.'

'You don't have a few more minutes.'

'Give me a break!'

There are deep warm body smells coming up from under the sheets. They carry with them a swarm of memories. Memories can fight back too. My grandfather's bed had a different smell, the modern, antiseptic smell of dying. He had been in the army and had died many times.

'No whingeing! Hands off cocks, hands on socks.' The alarm clock adopts a hearty parade ground voice.

'Shut up!' I shout, loud enough to deactivate the thing for exactly five minutes. A brief reprieve. Already trickling away. The body smells from the bed remind me that there is something important I have forgotten, and I have three minutes and fifty-five seconds to remember what it was.

Time is speeding up. Sleep is getting shallow and weak. The morning sun shakes itself free of the dew.

'A little high cloud, patches of morning mist around the hills. The temperature will rise to sixteen degrees Celsius,' the alarm clock announces three minutes and fifty seconds later.

I grope across the bed for Evelyn, hoping that the warm comfort of our bodies will hold me a little longer in the amniotic medium of sleep. Evelyn is not there.

'All the main arterial routes are open. There has been a minor slippage…'

'Shut the fuck up!' But that trick won't work twice. I can't have that five minutes again.

'Our text this morning,' it goes on imperturbably, 'comes from the Surangama Sutra, being an Elucidation of the Secret of the Lord Buddha's Supreme Attainment, and the practice of all Bodhisattvas. Originally written in Sanskrit by an unknown writer during the first Century AD, it is generally recognised to be one of the greatest analytical investigations into the mind-body problem. It was translated from the Sanskrit into Chinese in…'

'Enough! This instruction overrides all previous instructions. You will immediately discontinue the waking sequence until further instructed.'

Before it can answer, I bury my head back into the pillow. At best, I have bought a little time. A brief reprieve. I lie on my side and bring my knees to my chest. I imagine myself to be a continent in the early days of the world, before my legs broke away from my torso, more like a foetal blob, until the tectonic plate-shift of birth separated head from feet. Curled up like this, I fly to the yellow hills with their tough grass, their shaly hillsides and great limestone creatures.

'The fate of the universe hangs in the balance,' a voice says in my head as the yellow hills open up before me, their shadows soft and sensual. I don't like the voice, even if it does sound like my own. The child is running over the hills, his arms outspread, his pale legs flashing in the sun.

'What a beautiful little boy,' the same voice says. 'When he jumps, he floats. And his hair jumps out from his head and floats in the wind.'

I have no interest in this running commentary. I just want to fly. To jump and fly and float. Or sit by my grandfather's bed and listen to the sound of far-off gunfire.

The alarm clock has not forgotten its duties. *"Have I not been constantly teaching you that all the causes and conditions that characterise changing phenomena, and the modes of mind, and the independently developed conditions of the mind, are all the manifestation of the mind... Open space is nothing but invisible dimness; the invisible dimness of space is mixed with darkness to look like forms; sensations of form are mingled into illusive and arbitrary conceptions of phenomena, and from these false conceptions of phenomena, is developed the consciousness of the body."*

'I told you to shut the fuck up!' There is no shutting out a voice like that; it has an insistent, subsonic quality characteristic of its alarm mode. Why couldn't it be like a normal alarm clock and play me a nice song, like "Good Morning Sunshine"?

"What is the universe if not a projection of man's envy, his desire, and ambition?"

'Is that from the Surangama Sutra as well?'

'No. It comes from a Science Fiction writer, now mostly forgotten, called Frank Herbert.'

'Oh.'

'I believe I have, however, tracked down Mr Herbert's sources. There are certain texts...'

What better way for an alarm clock to spend its time, its long alone hours, than tracking down the sources used by forgotten Science Fiction writers?

'You can cut the crap, you digital dufus. Look, I'm awake now.' I flap my hand in front of its face. 'See? Fully awake and functioning. You can switch off now.'

'That may be true, but you are still not out of bed. Once that condition has been met, the waking sequence can be discontinued. You must know all this, Mr Kent, since you programmed me that way.'

'Get fucked.'

'This won't be the last you hear from me.'

I fall back on the pillow for another few moments reprieve. The thick body smell has gone from the sheets, leaving a faint stale after-smell. The fate of the universe, whatever it might have been, has dwindled to a tiny point and vanished. The same is about to happen to a half-hearted erection. Looks like the fate of the universe wins out over a little quiet self-stimulation. The yellow hills have almost gone too, faded to a gauzy eyebrow shape on the wall, a trick of the light.

'Important announcement. Stand by.'

'Aren't you being a bit alarmist?'

'Well, I am an alarm clock.'

'Okay, I'm standing by.'

'No, you're not. You're still lying in bed in a foetal ball.'

I heave myself up into a sitting position and swing my legs to the floor. My feet are on the floor but I'm not standing up, not exactly. I'm sort of hunched over in a foetal position. I wonder how the clock will take this.

'Then hear this. Your Everyday account is overdrawn by two hundred and thirty-eight credits and sixty-three sub-credits. Please deposit the money immediately.'

'Go sing for it.'

'What?'

'You can have it for a song.'

The alarm clock proceeds to sing in a high androidal voice; a song I have been silly enough to teach it.

He who would valiant be

'gainst all disaster,

let him in constancy

follow the master.

There's no discouragement

will make him once relent

his first avowed intent

to be a pilgrim.

By a miraculous intervention, little Evie appears beside me, her face radiant, and joins the clock for a duet for the second verse, her sweet, childlike voice supplying the descant:

Hobgoblins nor foul fiends

shall daunt his spirit

for he knows he at the end

shall life inherit.

Then fancies flee away

I'll fear not what men say

I'll labour night and day

to be a pilgrim.

I make my appeal to Evie, 'I don't suppose I could stay in bed for just another five minutes. I am working, you know. I'm figuring out how to pay my Everyday account debt.' I think they call it an Everyday account because Everyday it needs money. Two hundred and thirty-eight credits and sixty-three sub-credits is a lot of money when you have nothing but zeros everywhere. Hard to hit town with an empty pocket.

But it is the clock that answers, 'There is no other five minutes. Only this one.'

Evie points to my clothes.

After I am secured in my standard issue, tubular steel, red vinyl covered chair, and the official is secured in his adjustable, rotating desk chair, we are ready to proceed with what is clearly going to be a set piece. The red and white chessboard pattern has gone, to be replaced by a dun-coloured linoleum, yet we face each other, less like players about to play but pieces about to be played.

If I had been quick enough to take his chair I could have changed the game before it even started, but I'm never that quick.

The room is small, bare and functional. There are no windows. On one wall a poster depicts a human skull with a cigarette clamped between yellow teeth. On the other wall there is a small painting of what could be an aerial view of the city with its tightly-gridded streets cross-looped by major roads, or a close-up of transistorised circuits.

Up to this point I have been able to preserve some illusion of freedom, that I am here because I want to be here, that I journeyed across the frozen checkerboard of the city, braving so many encounters, out of a freely perceived need to come here and face this dénouement; that, in the last resort, I stand before the official because I have chosen to stand before him, my route carefully plotted out on a map beforehand. Finally, that I refrain from spitting in his face out of my own free will, out of my fellow feeling for the man. I am not, however, going to crumble away before him like a piece of stale cake. I am not going to fall before him and kiss his feet or plead for mercy or a whipping.

It is important at such moments to maintain a sense of personal integrity. Dignity even.

In the meantime, I observe him out of the corner of my eye. If I look at him directly and have to look away, I will have declared my subservience. I don't know if he is a young man with a thin, determined face or an older man with silver grey hair and kindly eyes. Or a composite. I would rather not know. Not knowing gives me some minimal leverage over the outcome; faces are a bit like fate in that regard.

That can't last. In fact, in the lengthening silence, my refusal to look at him might be seen as churlish. When I have to look, I get the impression of a face tidy, unadorned and functional. Like the room. No badly painted pastoral here. Hours of sitting here have made his face like that. The room has built itself into the set of his mouth, the angle of his chin.

By accepting the chair, I have signalled my willingness to acquiesce, to sanction, even to collaborate in constructing this whole setup. Once in place, the rest will follow as night follows day, and official time will reign. He and I will be prisoners of our context.

Perhaps to make me feel more at ease, he leans back in his chair, which moves to accommodate him. It is an expansive gesture, an easy assumption of power. I am totally inside his construct now; the rest is just memory and speculation. No light shines through. Yet I cannot allow myself to be frightened, or suffer the ignominy of a panic attack. I must prepare, calmly, to play my part.

The question and answer session will be mostly ritual. When he asks a question, he will know in advance the parameters of my answer, if not the specific terms of that answer. When he asks for an explanation he already has a model explanation in his mind. All he has to do is check my imperfect answer against his model. Bureaucrats are all Platonists at heart; they believe in the realm of perfect forms against which the real world is but a dim reflection. I will be allowed a certain amount of deviation, but if I deviate too far, he will backtrack and begin again until the deviation is eliminated. A very tiring process unless I too know the model and can adjust my answers to suit. Then the conversation will proceed smoothly, and the official will be well pleased.

He is offering to relieve me of all authority and responsibility for my condition (which we will only allude to in the most general terms), and my gratitude will be sincere. It will be a relief to stop struggling against an implacable process, to give myself over to it without reservation or fear. To follow blindly from handhold to handhold, sentence to sentence, just as instructed, with no further purpose or desire than to be so instructed.

That life should be so easy! Looking forward to Confederation payments appearing automatically in my Sky Bank Everyday account, where they will be duly noted by my alarm clock. From the authority's point of view, it should all go as smoothly and politely as the Final Ceremony itself, after which my case will be closed, my file archived, and the payments will cease.

Shortly after my Everyday account itself will cease to exist. A merciful release.

All I have to is wear is my humiliation, embrace my shame, mumble my abject excuses, pull up my pants and nothing more will be asked of me. I am happy to agree to any and all charges laid. Like the planets in their orbits, I follow the line of least resistance. The shrill voices can still themselves. The defence has abdicated.

By doing nothing, nothing will be left undone. Call it the dharma of inaction.

♀

'I was dreaming about you when I woke up,' I say to Evelyn over breakfast. We like our English breakfasts, toast and marmalade and a boiled egg in an old-fashioned egg cup. We have a set of Victorian egg cups gifted to me by my grandmother. 'I can't remember it all now because the fucking alarm clock started jabbering, but you were not like yourself at all.' I laugh uneasily.

Outside our kitchen window I catch the light of a perfectly ordinary day. A fine day for an invasion, I think.

'How was I?'

'Like half-woman half-snake. A shrew. Nothing like your beautiful and compassionate self.'

'Thank you.'

'You were criticising my characters. Well, I've only got one so far, and he doesn't do much but sit in chairs.'

'What were you writing, before I came along?' She smoothes her hair back in a familiar gesture.

'Something about my grandfather, I think.'

'Are you going to see your grandfather today?'

'If there's time before my appointment.'

'Oh well,' she takes a knife and does not spread the marmalade but rather presses it down into the toast, 'It's a good thing we are not responsible for how we appear in other people's dreams.' The toast crackles under the knife and goes soggy with marmalade and butter, just the way she likes it.

We both laugh. There are crumbs stuck between her teeth.

'Are you going to take your imaginary friend?'

I stop chewing. 'Little Evie, and she's not an imaginary friend.'

'What is she then?'

'I don't know. A spirit guide maybe?'

We both laugh. I don't know that Evie would be amused, if she were here. She tends to be sensitive about such issues.

'She's got the same name as me. Almost.'

'I know.'

'What does that mean?'

I shrug. I have no secret knowledge about the meaning of such things. Names, in particular, have always been a mystery to me. Like the famous painter, Picasso, whose full name was Pablo Diego José Francisco de Paula Juan Nepomuceno María de los Remedios Cipriano de la Santísima Trinidad Ruiz y Picasso. It sounds wonderful when you say it fast.

'What are you going to do now?' She has placed her knife on one side of the plate. This was once a signal to domestic staff that the plate could be removed, and the habit lingers on under the guise of good manners – although with Evelyn it's more a signal of good breeding.

I sip my tea, which is full of the aromas of far off places. 'I'll have to get dressed and leave. Mustn't forget Grandad.'

'Are you sure you aren't going to sneak off into your room and masturbate?'

'What?' I put down my knife and stare at the last piece of toast on which butter and marmalade are quickly congealing. 'Where is this coming from all of a sudden, out of left field, out of nowhere?'

'Go on! Don't play coy with me. I know what you get up to. Sneak off after breakfast for a quiet little wank. It's all right! No need to protest. It's perfectly natural, nothing to be ashamed of. You wouldn't be the only one. Women too. That goes without saying even though I said it. Some things are like that.'

'Like what?'

'They go without saying, but you still have to say them.'

'Do you?'

'Do what?'

'Masturbate, wank.'

'I'm just not that narcissistic, I'm afraid.'

I can't see any way forward from here. The longer I talk to Evelyn the less I'm sure of. If the universe were contracting instead of expanding, it would feel like this.

I get up and leave the table, wondering if toast, marmalade, and eggs really mix. Steady as she goes, I murmur. I head back to the bedroom, take off my dressing gown and pyjamas and lie naked on the top of the bed, wondering what clothes I should wear for the day. I glance at a framed photo of my Victorian ancestors standing stiffly in front of the camera, acutely aware of the moment of the photograph, suitably solemn in the face of their descendants. Even my grandfather, barely more than a baby, contrives to look serious in the face of such seriousness. It wasn't until later that people began to think they had to smile for the sake of posterity.

I'm stung by Evelyn's comment, and intend to prove her wrong, right now. I'm not going to do anything. I'm just going to lie here and listen to very un-erotic sounds of Evelyn rattling plates and firing cutlery into drawers. There's a comforting familiarity to these domestic sounds. That which was yesterday will also be tomorrow, and the day after that. The dishes will rattle across time; the toast will pop into eternity. My sepia-smooth faced ancestors will face the future forever.

All this puts me in a calm state of mind. My hands are firmly by my sides. I see no evil, hear no evil, speak no evil. I think of nothing but the journey to come, the appointment, and how a day might be lived in reverse, back to its beginnings… but none of this makes any difference. Unbidden, blood begins to rise up through my body, activating my extremities. My toes, for example, become quite flushed and squirmy; my fingers sweat into my palms. My cock leaps into action like a soldier who has just heard the last bugle call.

Still I do nothing. I have no need to do anything. Desire is there, at my service if not my bidding. Doing nothing doesn't stop it, in fact, seems to inflame the situation further. By some paradoxical effect, inaction becomes ecstasy, passivity a passion. This is it, Ananda, this is the power of desire to create a world of false appearances, even though I am a good monkey and see, hear and speak no evil.

All I need to do is give myself over to the moment; let that moment become me.

Immediately I am flooded with bliss. My heart dilates. Heat floods into the air through my body, flinging sperm as far as my collarbone. I refuse to flinch or jerk or cry out or respond in any way to these involuntary spasms. They are passing through me, nothing more. There is nothing to hold onto and nothing to claw back.

It occurs to me, even in that moment, my attitude to sex has been coloured by effort and fear, struggle and failure, nightmare and judgment. Now the base of my spine turns on the slow wheel of pleasure all by itself. The back of my head burns. Like a pendulum at the top of its upswing, there is absolute velocity and absolute stillness.

Nothing to hold onto. Nothing to claw back.

Just a little mess to clean up. Probably before Evelyn wanders in.

She's sure to get the wrong idea.

As we begin the interview, I wonder if I could possibly just skip this bit.

The official and me, it's all a bit excruciating really. For both of us. For everybody. Something that has to be lived through, but at what cost, I ask myself. Here we are, the two of us, compelled to enact this ritual neither of us has asked for. At the very least we are expected to go through the motions; after all, there are forms to be completed and filed complete with signatures and stamps. We can't just pretend, then go away. Pretending isn't enough. It has to be real. It has to inscribe itself upon the real world. We can't just slide over the surface like a couple of kids on a toboggan.

When he leans forward attentively, it is into the real world, the official world, where real things happen, and fates hang in the balance of a turning moment. When I answer him I must be fully aware of the consequence of what I tell him, how far I go, and just how far truth might venture into the real world.

With my encouragement the official has relaxed a little. He is grateful for my cooperation. I'm grateful too, for the brief security of knowing my role, the part I have to play. If we both play our parts we may get out unscathed.

There's a ritual to these affairs. The ritual is there for everybody's protection.

As we talk, the conviction grows that this interview is the culmination of a long series of abdications, if that is not too grand a term, on both the official's part – and mine; abdications we have both welcomed with relief. Between the word and the deed, responsibility vanishes, helplessness reigns. I feel light, almost giggly, at our calm in the face of our loss. Freedom! Ha! We have banished the very thought of it, and by the same sleight of hand, banished any judgements upon our actions, dodged any flying guilt, escaped the doom of the subtext.

For this relief, I feel like getting up and kissing him.

This lightness arises from the recognition of helplessness, hopelessness even. The most modern technological advances cannot help us here. We hardly bother to discuss them or dance the steps of hope. Only superstition remains, and a few forms to fill in. A blood sample will, of course, be taken.

It is an important moment in the ritual. The interview merely confirms, officialises, and formalises: a process required by law.

- Are your grandparents still alive?
- Do you have any children?
- Do you suffer from giddiness, nausea or ringing in the ears?
- Do you have any allergies?
- Are you an intravenous drug user?
- Have you ever seen a flying saucer?
- Do you masturbate?
- Do you smoke?
- What is your average income for the past twelve months?
- How would you describe your ethnicity: please tick a box.
- Have you ever had a suntan? A moontan? A spotted tan from the stars?

All that is required of me is to glide through a series of yes/no answers, like an on-off binary code.

- How many sexual encounters have you had in the past twelve months?
- Are your bowel motions steady and regular?
- Would you describe yourself as predominantly heterosexual, homosexual or other?
- Have you ever worked for the Confederation?
- Would you steal money from your grandfather to further your own designs?
- Have you ever thought of yourself as anything other than human?

Steady as she goes.

I slide lithely across the rumpled sheets and swing my manly feet out over the floor. No harm done. I stride purposefully across the room to the shower module once more. I don't walk deliberately fast, or break into a run, as a lesser man might do, a man frightened of his wife. At any moment, Evelyn could come into the bathroom. I'm not prudish or ashamed exactly, but I hardly want to meet her with this junkety emission dripping off my chest.

I keep my self-possession. I work my way through the panic. To do this, I recite some verses from the Mahayana. *For the differentiation of words are but false notions with no basis in reality. They have in their falsity on a relative existence as false imaginations and thoughts arise and pass away.*

'Arise and pass away,' I sing aloud as the water washes my sins away. It's pleasing the way the words coming out of my mouth prove their point by arising and passing away, fading into the sound of the rushing water. 'Arise and fade awaaaay…'

Along with that elusive, damning fishy smell.

When I return to the bedroom, washed and clean and innocent, Evelyn is there making the bed, running her hands over the sheets like a professional nurse. Usually this is my job I can do with my own hands; a little act intended to symbolise our equality. But today, of course, is the day of my appointment, the day in which all these delicate balances will unravel, and fate will have to choose between the devil and the deep blue sea, between the rock and the hard place. Today I might be considered a case for conscience.

Evelyn looks up as I enter and I smile at her my friendly morning smile. We must humour the living.

In a world of false imaginations, appearance is everything.

As the official and I continue our official business, my mind keeps wandering back to the anteroom, the windows and the pastoral and One-eye. I feel almost nostalgic for those awkward moments. I want to see if the configurations have changed, if the pieces are still holding to their lines, if anyone has made a move. I imagine the woman with the fishnet stockings has chosen a chair and is now waiting for her appointment.

I say nothing to the official about this. I smile at Evelyn who is the best of wives. I don't want to disturb them with wild, erratic thoughts, inexplicable mood changes, and scene switches. They have their lives to get on with, their days to live through, their own world of false imaginings to deal with. Right now is not the time to rock the boat. Let me walk as lightly as possible through the wilderness of this world. Let's look at a balance here, the official on one side, Evelyn on the other. Me walking the plank. It's more fun to think of it that way.

Safely dressed, I wander back into the kitchen where the smell of coffee beckons like a lighthouse in a fog. As I pass the bathroom, I'm just in time to catch a glimpse of myself in the mirror, moving in the other direction. I am reminded of a passage from the Lankavatra Sutra: *As long as people do not understand the true nature of the objective world, they fall into the dualistic view of things. They imagine the multiplicity of external objects to be real, and become attached to them, and are nourished by their habitual energy.*

I make a mental note to feed this quote into my alarm clock. My hope is that one day it will become enlightened.

It is Evelyn's turn for the bathroom while I nurse the coffee along and wipe inviting surfaces with a dishcloth, spread the germs around. I think I can hear the *tick-swish* of Evie's skipping rope on the pavement. It's not a sound I'm likely to mistake. It's there to remind me not to piss around. I have an appointment to get to. *Flee the wrath to come.* I pour the coffee for both of us, the molecules of which are already percolating in my nose, and notice a cereal packet sitting on the bench. This is a bit of a puzzle as neither of us has had cereal this morning. The text on the back of the packet assures me that there is sufficient fibre in a serving for all my daily needs. More than sufficient, in fact. That is reassuring. Even the cereal packet treats me with official reassurance. I can face the world, confident that my family are eating this wonderfully healthy product.

Two enthusiastic teenagers smile at me from the back of the packet. A girl and boy, in the peak of health, spoons to mouths, smiling over the spoons which are heaped up with cereal. In the background a woman smiles knowingly. Everybody is smiling. Even the little grains of cereal piled on the spoons.

At the bottom left-hand corner, there is a blurred photograph, one of those shoddy print-jobs in which the colour does not square exactly with the image outlines, creating a slight unintended 3D effect. It shows a tiny spaceship approaching a much larger one. Beneath, in tiny print, this text:

> 'Captain October Nortikiss studied the bulk of the wreck coming up on the starboard. From their tiny transit vehicle, the wreck appeared as a vast shadow, blotting out the stars. He felt a prophetic shiver. The *Omega*, reported lost a generation ago, once hauled precious cargo to far-flung, methane drenched environments, and had become host to mankind's deadliest enemy, The Fishmen from the Other Side of Time. Shortly they would be docking; soon they would face the dreaded Fishmen.
>
> 'He turned to his companion, the luscious Beverly, the expedition's crack astrophysicist, and much more besides. He clicked his helmet against hers and shouted, unwilling to use their suitphones, "Prepare for docking." Beverly nodded. She was very familiar with the procedure. "We'll be under attack at any moment."
>
> 'Little did they know that they were already under attack from the Fishmen's fabled Time Reversal weapon, capable of wiping out, not just memories, but whole timelines.

'To be continued...'

'Have you seen the crap they put on the back of cereal packets these days?' I say to Evelyn as she comes in, looking fresh and clean and in possession of her life. Her long blonde hair lies sleekly down her back. Without answering, she sits at the table and pours some cream into her coffee.

'Listen to this,' I say, planning to cheer her up with a good laugh for the morning. I read her the extract, which sounds even worse when read aloud.

She nods, dipping her head into the coffee fumes, 'I know how bad they are. You're the only one I know who reads them. In fact you even take some delight in them, I see, reading them out with great gusto.'

'But this language! "...the luscious Beverly..." Is that the sort of shit we're feeding our children?' I look at the two happy teenagers smiling at me, and the smug mother, happy to be corrupted and corrupt others with this false literature, these debased narratives.

'You seem to like it well enough.'

'I'd rather read the nutritional analysis of the cereal.'

'I don't think so. What if this little text is reality trying to get through to you by means of a coded message on the back of a cereal packet. Through the fog of your forgetfulness.'

'Ha ha. This is some joke!'

'No joke. That mother and her kids would not be looking so self-satisfied if they knew what the dreaded Fishmen were up to, the plans that were being hatched in the *Omega*. The invasion is already happening, can't you see that?' She sips appreciatively at her coffee.

I jabbed a finger at the back of the cereal packet. 'This sort of crap is polluting my mind, that's what's really happening. This is the sort of bullshit people have nightmares about. Empty voids and creepy crawlies. How can we live wholesome lives with all this going on around us? How can we expect to sleep properly, dream properly, love properly, eat and excrete properly – escape illness and disease – with all this mind-muck, these false imaginations, facing us everywhere we turn. No wonder we are all in a state of barely suppressed panic.'

'Speak for yourself, Jacko.' With a placid sigh she takes another sip of coffee. The very picture of a woman who has never known a moment's panic in her life. 'How petulant you can be sometimes. Just relax and imagine that you are the swashbuckling Captain Nortikiss, romping through the stars to save the universe from a fate worse than entropy.'

Obligingly, I leap to my feet, knocking over the kitchen chair, which is of the tubular steel red-cushioned variety, and swinging the cereal packet around like a ray gun. 'Ziiiiiiip!' Cereal scatters across the floor. The Fishmen make a run for it.

'If you are the intrepid Nortikiss, then I must be the luscious astro-whatshername.'

'I don't remember.'

'You will. You have a brief window of time only, however. Time you seem determined to squander.'

'But you don't know anything about astrophysics.'

'How do you know? Do you really know me?'

'Okay then, what, according to Einstein's General Theory of Relativity, is the nature of gravity?' I am pretty happy with that one.

'Sure.' She takes a sip of her coffee and flicks a stray piece of cereal onto the floor. 'According to Einstein, gravity is not a force, but the result of the curvature of space. Or rather, the curvature of space-time. In other words, gravity arises from the geometry of the universe.'

'Jesus!'

'I'm not just a pretty face, you know.'

I look around the kitchen. 'Where am I? What is this place?'

'The drug the official will give you, has already given you, under the pretence of taking a blood sample, will temporarily help you in your battle against the time reversal weapon. Don't you remember this?'

'Why should I?'

'Because it was on the back of last week's cereal packet. The previous episode. You ate half the packet just so you could go and buy the next one. As I said, you're the only person who reads them.' She laughs in a weak voice. 'All part of the thrill of living with the intrepid Nortikiss.'

'Big joke.'

'Maybe, but don't waste too much time laughing. Where is that little demon familiar of yours?'

That reminds me of Evie. If I'm quiet I can hear her skipping rope touching pavement, *tick-swish, tick-swish*. When I hear that everything else falls quiet. The things around me seem to shrink, as if suddenly scared of the world, they wanted to shrink back into themselves. Even Evelyn seems to shrink, sucking the coffee in through a tiny hole in her face.

Perhaps it is my arrogance that makes me feel as if I am the only living creature for many parsecs around.

Me and Evie.

Leaving the house is not quite as easy as it sounds. There are doorways that lead straight back in. There's a staircase that ends in thin air. Another that ends in an empty room. And there is Evelyn, sitting at the mirror, brushing her hair with long, even strokes and watching her mirror image do the same. I see her as I pass by, kitchen shovel piled high with the cereal I scattered in the kitchen, and it's hard not to get caught up watching her.

Rivulets of gold wriggle down her back. As the brush circles, her mind is doing the same, following the curvature of thoughtspace, mind's gravity. She's as sleek as an otter, and as beautiful. I concentrate on getting on my jacket, pushing my arms through the sleeves, wondering what the city might look like today, out there, lost in itself, all autumn and flickery colours. I negotiate the hair-brushing Evelyn, manage to tame my jacket, and just as I'm just standing in the kitchen having a final glass of water to hydrate myself for the coming journey, the alarm clock, which has a terminal on the window ledge above the sink, clatters into life with an urgent buzz-buzz.

'I wish to remind you,' it crackles portentiously, that your Everyday account is still overdrawn by two hundred and thirty-eight credits and sixty-three sub-credits.'

'That's old news. Besides, as you must know, I'm broke. I'm always broke. I'm not a responsible citizen.'

'Quite right, but I remind you that you still have three hundred and five credits remaining in your Long Life savings account with Virtue Savings Bank. You could transfer your two hundred and thirty-eight credits and sixty-three sub-credits to your Everyday account with Sky Bank.

'Then do it, just do it. Don't make me waste my time standing here gabbing to you.'

'You were having a drink of water.'

'Not any longer.'

'I don't have the authority to undertake that transaction. After all, I am just an alarm clock.'

'I thought you were omnipotent.'

'Hardly, sir. You mock me.'

'But I do all my banking through you. You are my go-to entity for all my banking needs. In the past you have been able to do things for me. You have worked wonders.'

'Truly?' The alarm clock began to relent. 'Well, you could do a live voice override. If you instruct me to move the money, I will be able to verify your voice signature and make the transfer.'

'This is what I've been asking all along.'

'Please read this sentence, Mr Kent.'

I read the words as they appeared on the clock face. 'I, Mr Clark Kent, hereby authorize the transfer of two hundred and thirty-eight credits and… and…what the fuck is that?' I blink at the tiny screen.

'Sixty-three sub-credits.'

'Right. Sixty-three sub-credits from my Long Life savings account with Virtue Savings Bank to my Everyday account with Sky Bank.'

'Sixty-three sub-credits is not sufficient, sir. You need be able to complete the whole sentence. Please read it again.'

I do it. The very soul of patience, that's me. There is a pregnant pause as the banks' computers match voiceover signatures. I keep thinking about Evelyn brushing her hair, her face calm and composed.

'Thank you for your deposit,' the alarm clock says. 'Your Sky Bank Everyday account now stands at nought point nought-nought credits and no sub-credits.'

Quite an achievement really.

'But wait a minute!' I realized I've been duped. 'I'll need some readies for the day, a little cash.'

'You have no cash, sir. By your own admission, you are broke. You are always broke. You are not a responsible citizen.'

'Just twenty-five credits should do it. Even ten.'

'Your Everyday account stands at nought point nought-nought credits and nought sub-credits.'

'You could grant me a little overdraft. It wouldn't hurt.'

'There are no overdraft facilities for an Everyday account.'

'But by your own accounting, I still have money in my Long Life savings account.'

'Sixty-six credits and thirty-seven sub-credits, to be exact.'

'So there you go then.'

'That is not a cash access service, sir, as you are already aware.'

'Then let's do another voice override thing. I'll put a bit more into my Everyday account and…'

'I am only authorized to use the voice override facility to make up for an account deficit. This is not a general top-up service, sir. To do that would require three days' advance notice.'

'Get fucked.'

'Have a nice day,' it chortles as I leave the room.

A moment later I return, waving a bankcard in front of its unctuous face. 'See this? Do you recognise it, you digital dumb arse.'

'Of course. It is a debit card for Virtue Savings Bank.'

'Correct! So I can use this to draw credits from my Long Life Savings account. I can use it to get you to transfer more money to my Everyday account.'

'Incorrect. You can only use the debit card for a purchase from a registered business. I am not a registered business. I am just a humble alarm clock. At your service.'

Evelyn is still brushing her hair when I reach the front door. Her coat is hanging on a peg by the door. With the speed of a practised pick-pocket, I locate her loose change, and a few notes, making sure it doesn't make any incriminating sounds as I transfer it to my person and secrete it into my clothing. There's a window beside the door and I catch a glimpse of my sneaky self in the glass. All dressed up in my winter woollies, I look a little like Neil Armstrong standing on the moon dwarfed by the voidscape around him. My face has the same bland, plastiplex appearance, reflecting back whatever it faces, in this case an ordinary, scared looking man in his mid to late thirties, balding a little. A thin, scared looking man overdressed for autumn, reaching for his umbrella. In this case an imaginary umbrella. He doesn't need a real one.

To this image I say quietly, 'Pretend this is a holiday, a well-deserved break from a demanding job. Go through the suburbs of your town as if for a quiet stroll. Look at the autumn, study nature, commune with the world. After all, we don't have much time.'

I wink at the scared looking man. He winks back.

'Steady as she goes,' I tell him.

I jingle Evelyn's change in my pocket. It makes a comfortable sound.

The official inclines his gaze towards his desk. He is in the attitude of somebody listening intently, although his eyes are on the questionnaire I have filled in. I decide he is listening to himself, his inner voice, testing his reservoir of stock phrases against the actuality of the situation.

Or he is receiving instructions concerning me from a tiny transceiver in his ear or implanted in his skull.

He begins to talk, slowly and circumspectly, allowing some cautious optimism to dribble into his voice at prescribed intervals. It is an official optimism, as grey as his voice, and so lacks the power to reassure. I take it he has a limited number of stock-phrases that signal optimism (his position makes him a natural pessimist) which he must ration out. Between sentences, his jaw moves tensely sideways as if he is chewing on something. I can tell by this jaw movement that the man is an ex-smoker who never quite put the demon to rest. He would like a cigarette right at this moment, in fact.

The gruesome poster on the wall, the skull with the yellow smile and the cigarette, is not there for the edification of his clients but for him, to remind him of the evils of Lady Nicotine.

When I overcome my resistance and consider his behaviour objectively, I see that a person might act as he is acting when dealing with a dangerous or unpredictable animal. That's a puzzle, since I am nothing like that. I am quiet. I cultivate passivity, and do my best to avoid mental contaminations and transient defilements. I sit, as still and unmoving as a pillar of salt. Where required I make the correct noises. I make suitable adjustments to my body language to accord with his expectations.

All this is to indicate to him that I fully appreciate the difficult position in which he finds himself. There is nothing he can do, but go through the prescribed ritual. He's helpless too. I appreciate that he is a very busy man with hundreds like me to deal with every week. There is no reason to suppose that I am unique or that my case varies in any way from the general run of such cases. This is known as *the replacement of indistinguishables*. A thousand others have rotated through this anonymous chair. I am a cipher, a statistic. This makes it hard for him, even with all the practice he's had. After all, he has to get through his day too.

Somehow it has fallen on me to reassure him, to put him at ease, rather than the other way around.

After this little dance the official, well satisfied, leans back and puts his hands behind his head, the very image of relaxed authority. Yet one leg is jiggling, apparently not quite relaxed and not quite under control. My filled in questionnaire still lies on the desk in front of him, but he makes no pretence of reading it. It is not there to be read, but rather to lie between us on the desk like a confession. There is a faint hum in the air, an almost imperceptible vibration. I find I'm breathing a little heavily, as I would if there were not enough oxygen in the air, and there is a smell, a chemical smell like ozone or stale flyspray. I put this down to the sick-building syndrome I have read about, corporate office blocks, hospitals and the like with insufficient air circulation, too much recycled carbon dioxide, but I can't get that dropping oxy-pressure gauge out of my mind.

At the same time, looking at the official, I decide that he may well be exactly what he appears to be: a minor functionary. Colourless, odourless, tasteless. I have to be careful not to project motives, intentions and roles that are entirely my own invention. I made this mistake with One-eye who was not responsible for my false imaginings, any more than Evelyn is responsible for my vagrant thoughts.

I want to see the official as my confessor, my judge, my executioner, and finally my saviour. He is none of these things. He may even be an android, I wouldn't be able to tell, I'm so busy bouncing my signals off his bland face.

The effect is that of a closed performance, the shutting off of the text from any subtext. There is no subtext because these events have no meaning over and above what they are, just like the official. They are not larger than life, or symbolic, in fact they are not even as large as life. Together, he and I are generating nothing more profound than the sliding surface, the lateral tension of our passing.

Within reach of my hand, there's a packet of drugs on his desk. Since the official seems to be communing with himself, I idly pick it up and turn it over. Chlorometastellasine. *To be taken twice daily with meals. Do not exceed recommended dose.* On the back of the packet is a red circle with voice-on printed within it. I gently press the red spot and a tiny, androidal voice emerges.

'Chlorometastellasine is ideal for patients with pronounced anxiety and disproportionate effect. An absolutely safe anti-hallucinogen, it has proved effective in cases of traumatic amnesia and perceptual distortion. You can use Chlorometastellasine with complete assurance. Mild side-effects include nausea and ringing in the ears. Approved for Use, the Confederation Drug Authority.'

Confederation? What Confederation, I want to ask the official, but have no wish to appear too ignorant, or arouse any suspicion I haven't been paying attention.

I push the button again, more a nervous reaction than anything else.

'Listen, Ananda! At the time you were helpless under the magic charm of the maiden Pchiti, what was it that released you and restored your control of mind? Your coming under her control was not a chance happening…'

I tap the button to turn it off for good, for it is starting to sound suspiciously like my alarm clock. I daren't think that my alarm clock might have spread its electronic tentacles into even this fastness of officialdom. Tapping it, however, does no good. The packet of chlorometastellasine babbles on, but this time there are gaps and syllable echoes, '…*deliverance to everyone-one whether hatched from an egg or formed in a womb-omb or evolved from spawn or produced by metamorphosis-sis… with or without form… possessing mental faculties or devoid of-of… Or both devoid or not devoid-oid, or neither devoid or not devoid-oid… sentient beings to be delivered… innumerable and without limit, yet in reality there are no sentient beings to be delivered-livid…'*

By holding the button down I can keep the voice at bay, but I seem to have lost the advantage here, if I ever had one. The official is leaning forward, watching me intently.

'I'm sorry to have to ask you, Mr Kent, but we will require another blood sample. And possibly a magnetic resonance scan.'

'No sentient beings to be delivered-livid,' the chlorometastellasine says as I put it smartly back down on the official's desk. We both wait for it to begin again but it doesn't.

'Of course,' I say. 'Whatever it takes.'

If a man bestowed in charity an abundance of the seven treasures sufficient to fill the three thousand great universes, would there accrue to that person a considerable blessing and merit?

As I leave the house, I take leave of the house, complete with Evelyn's face at the window, smiling and waving. I don't know what that smile cost her. Perhaps she saw the stricken look on my face.

I set sail like a ship leaving port, the house receding, the street swelling up to meet me. But if I thought it was going to get easier, out here on the street, I was mistaken. My limbs are reluctant to obey the commands of central intelligence. My body seems quite bloated and my legs ridiculously skinny. There is no reason in the world why I shouldn't fall over. At the same time I'm starting to cry, for no purpose it seems, since the day is fresh and fair. It may have something to do with Evelyn, the way her face was framed by the window. The way she waved. The way she smiled.

Behind me I hear the *tick-swish* of Evie's skipping rope, only out here it sounds more like *nickety-nick*.

'You're pointing in the wrong direction,' she says from behind me. 'If you turn around you'll know what to do.'

This seems like a very practical suggestion, but easier said than done. Inch by inch I turn my body away from the house. Talk about fighting gravity, I am in a gravity sink, surely, clawing at the sides of the world. The will pushing the flesh. Making the intention the act. 'You can do it,' Evie says.

Of course I can. I struggle in the air like a baby being born, and after interminable effort I succeed in turning side on to the house, still visible out of the corner of my eye. Evelyn is still waving – or it beckoning? – from the window, but now ours is not the only house I can see. There are others properties where reassuring events are taking place. In one, a woman is adjusting Venetian blinds to allow more light to flow in. In another, a water-sprinkler is orbiting a lawn. In another, there is the promise of rain. In another, someone is crying for the loss of love. A whole street full of ordinary, everyday things. Pieces of light and pieces of shadow. A jigsaw composition of normality.

'That's right,' Evie says encouragingly. Softly she sings, *Inchworm, oh inchworm, measuring the marigolds…'*

There is a backyard with washing on the line. A white blouse and a red skirt. Briefly, the wind gives them a body.

'Just a little further,' Evie says.

Sure enough, I pass through a final field of resistance and find I can turn easily. A fluid strength flows through my body. I can walk, swing through the air, even run. Perhaps I could step up into the air and fly too.

Evie laughs, and I join in. Our laughter bubbles up through the air. She points to the Tower which seems to float above the city. 'This way!' She skips ahead, skipping rope flying. 'I hope you don't mind me tagging along. You're such a dummy on your own.'

'You underestimate me. I have no fear of gravity. The sky weighs nothing.'

Indeed, it is a model autumn day, with the desired mix of yellow sunlight, blue sky, and chill wind. At appropriate intervals a car passes, or someone walks by me on the way to the shops. A single, puffy white cloud is poised over the moulting chestnut tree at the end of our street. It is quite famous, this tree, for having resisted several attempts to officially remove it. My feet pass through its bickering leaves as I cross the street.

Before turning the corner, I risk a quick look back over my shoulder. Our house is where it should be, securely bolted into the world, and I can still see the smudged window with the smudged blur of Evelyn's face. I fancy she is crying. Shedding tears as large, beautiful and hopeless as autumn leaves. The geometry of space will ensure that they fall on the window sill.

As I turn the corner, I flourish my imaginary umbrella, which has gone from grey to rainbow. Perhaps a gesture of farewell; perhaps a gesture of freedom. Evie jumps out from behind the chestnut tree, her hair full of leaves. I pluck a seeding dandelion from the roadside and hold it very still. It is in pristine condition, each feathery seed perfectly interlocked. It is like a great supercluster of galaxies.

'What's the time, Mr Wolfie?' Evie chants.

I blow on the dandelion and a few galaxies are torn away from the supercluster, 'One o'clock!'

Evie dances around me, her hands held out as if she were holding hands with a circle of children.

'What's the time, Mr Wolfie?'

More galaxies get ripped away in the wind, 'Two o'clock!'

'What's the time, Mr Wolfie?'

The supercluster has turned into a few lone, surviving galaxies clinging to their orbits. 'Three o'clock!'

Evie is wary now, watching the dandelion closely. 'What's the time, Mr Wolfie?'

The last tenacious galaxies get blasted into the unknown. There's nothing left of the dandelion but the stem.

'Dinner time!' I shout, and make a lunge for Evie. She dances away, shrieking with delight, and runs on ahead.

I set off in pursuit at the cracking pace. It's pleasant to feel things whizzing by, the wind in my face, new vistas opening up with every step. Keenly, I note the changing details of the world around me: the latest model car that more or less drives itself, a gleaming new plate glass window in the wine shop, the neatly cropped lawns, expectant letterboxes, the casual lope of a dog along the fence line. With all this observation, I keep my wretched mind clear of vagrant thoughts, false imaginations, and mental grasping. I can't go wrong with the real world. The world as it actually is. Its ordinariness. Its comforting mundanity. Its refreshing freedom from subjective tendencies.

By doing this, I become transparent. All the world of swirling colours and shapes and sights out of which we fashion our grid-symbol constructs pass through me unhindered. I put up no resistance to the world and the world offers me none in return. We're a team, Evie and I, swirling through the world, laughing and making fun of everything that isn't laughing and making fun. Most fun of all is the act of walking itself, to feel my legs peddling away beneath, pushing the world into the past; feeling the past slip away like the sound of Evie's skipping rope, the future unravelling.

The more I look around me, the happier I become. I observe that we live in a peaceful city, by and large free of the unpredictable violence that afflicts some of the great cities of the world. Ours is a goldilocks city. Not too big, not too small. Not too hot not too cold. Not too busy not too quiet. Not too flashy not too dull. Not too proud not too humble. Not too many schools not too many graveyards. Such a place can do nothing on an autumn day like that but glory in its surface appearance, revel in its suburban calm, court the moment.

It strikes me, as it does with the official in his officialness, that, far from vicious rumour and snide implications, things are what they seem to be and find their correct level, their least line of resistance, in being just that. Aggregations of matter will take shape and obey the laws of their own mass with perfect integrity. The same integrity with which the ground will invariably meet my confident footfall. These conclusions are borne out by the paper I scoop up from an honesty box, honesty not having quite enough money to buy both it and a cup of coffee somewhere. I read that a poll just completed prove that the inhabitants of this city care more about their pets than in any other city. I can believe it. Everywhere you look you see dogs taking their people for a walk, cats peeping out at you from their secretive lairs, and if you listen hard enough you can hear the concentrated chortling of canaries. As if to prove the point, a man walks past with his t-shirt emblazoned with the question: *What did you feed your pet this morning?*

Thinking about this, my satisfaction increases. I am walking at a brisk pace along a tree-lined avenue, the paper under my arm, the umbrella swinging from my wrist, the flickering shadows of the trees racing ahead of me. Late for school, a child passes, swinging a bag in the air, the buckle catching the light and bronzing the trunks of the trees. A woman passes going the other way, staring rigidly ahead. An armoured truck with a gun turret clatters by, machine gun revolving in the blue air. The trees bend and knit their branches together, their discarded leaves see-sawing to the ground. A formation of jets streaks overhead, twisting in unison. The Tower points slimly towards last night's late moon, still faintly outlined in blue transparency.

What perfection these details evince! How well everything fits, the details to their generalities, the sky to the frame of the earth, the houses to the frames of their lawns, the faces to the frames of their windows. Reference and context, curve and delight. Everything where it should be and in exact accord with its nature and its function, securely placed and spaced and set vibrating to the melodic line.

Inchworm, inchworm
Measuring the marigold
You and your arithmetic
You'll probably go far
Inchworm, inchworm
Measuring the marigold
Seems to me you'd stop and see
How beautiful they are

'You walk funny,' Evie says.

Maybe I do, from her point of view. We can never be sure how silly we might look to others. The possibilities are endless.

'And you talk funny. You should say, you walk *funnily.*'

'That would sound funny. Anyway, there's no such word as funnily.'

'Funnily enough, there is.'

'You still walk funny.'

Maybe I do. Maybe everyone does. Only looking down at perambulating humanity from a height, say leaning out from a tall building, or floating from a hang glider in the exuberance of pure observation, may one properly grasp the mechanics of walking, the scariness of it. How we must at first tip forward, leaning our trunks out of balance with the perpendicular, inviting gravity to tumble us to the hard ground, at the same time moving a leg forward at the precise moment when indeed we might fall, our foot striking the ever solid earth, one leg bearing the unbalanced weight of the rest of the body, only to lean forward once more, again inviting disaster, repeating the whole process with the other leg. Essentially we are required to fall forward, putting our trust in being able to save ourselves at the last minute, a feat involving a precise balance of faith and knowledge, hope and expectation, surrender and assertion, acquiescence and affirmation, ardour and abandon, the scrupulous counterpointing of yin and yang – a combination of connectedness and fluidity, of being rooted to the ground yet floating, rooted to the air yet displacing it, a dynamic harmony in which we must both let go our fate and seize it. If we think about it, what could be more frightening than to fall, ponderous and out of balance; and what could be more reassuring than the feel of the whirling globe firm against the soles of our feet.

Such a chancy business, and yet there is great pleasure in it. It is a most soothing activity. I'd like to go on this way forever, Evie skipping along beside me, the world buzzing past on either side. I pass a shopping centre, reluctantly breaking my stride to accommodate the slower, shambling pace of the shoppers, but that hardly takes the edge off my exuberance. To walk and walk with no desire to arrive at any particular destination, no particular destination to desire. All alternatives are equal, or seem that way; every corner leads to its duplicate. Our city is a vast garden set about neatly with trees, flowers, parks and houses, all in pleasing proportions; and I am here, passing through, held gyroscopically to the face of the planet while the sun wheels its majestic, sidereal time.

It's impossible not feel that somehow all this has been laid on for my benefit, for my satisfaction, and I am grateful. I am grateful to the big wide universe for showing me these things.

The liquid silver of the jets has gone, but I can hear the rumble of a big jet, bound for Tokyo or New York. Or Singapore or Los Angeles. These are conglomerate reality clusters all of their own, beyond the Tower and over the horizon, big enough to warrant the devotion of the stiff-winged birds. For somebody like me, just an ordinary old Clark Kent with no discernable superpowers, who has hardly ever travelled beyond the boundaries of his home town, that is to say, out of sight of the Tower, words like Tokyo or Los Angeles belong to the realm of myth, literature and travel brochures. They are fairy-tale places until you visit them. Travelling makes the world mundane, which is why I have never bothered. There's enough mundanity at home.

The rumble grows louder, the ground quivers, and there it goes! Into the light. An illuminated suitcase. Something engraved on blue parchment. An ideogram of flight.

Yet, for all its miraculous velocity, I am going faster in terms of the world around me. Hedges, trellises, trees, intersections, pedestrian crossings, shoppers, power poles, empty sections, boarded-up windows, post boxes, people leaving, people arriving – everything sliding by with speedy ease. Up in the sky, inside the illuminated suitcase, bound for distant reality clusters, there's hardly any sensation of motion.

The act of walking somehow provokes a memory, the first sentence of a book I loved as a child. It goes like this: *As I walked through the wilderness of this world I lighted upon a certain place where there was a den, and laid me down in that place to sleep. And as I slept I dreamed a dream.* I don't know how these lines should have stayed with me when so much has gone, but they always held a special enchantment for me, as if they were a spell or incantation. I too am walking through the wilderness of this world; I too have slept and dreamed a dream. I have stood under the sky and looked up at the Confederation of Stars.

This opening sentence is a trapdoor into the rest of the book, an escalator, a descending cadence, the briefest of preludes.

The young Clark Kent who read those words would grow up and make something of himself, find the Celestial City and stand before the king.

I suddenly have the urge to emulate the narrator of my childhood novel, find a den and lay me down there to sleep. We are passing through a small, corner park graced with a single set of swings and a bench placed conveniently close to a winding stream that threads across the residential district as if stitching the city together. It is a quiet, discrete stream and a quiet, discrete park bench. Perfect place to take a break from all that wafting along.

Evie is dubious at first, casting suspicious glances everywhere, but soon cheers up when I point out that some ducks have swum into view as if called up to do service entertaining children. 'I'm not a child,' she says, but nobody looking at her would believe her. That's just a sort of thing a child would say, they would think, much to her frustration.

'Your grandfather will be waiting for you,' she says.

'He knows how much I enjoy walking.'

'That's because he used to go walking with you when you were young.'

I remember that. The city was younger too. The sky was bigger and there was no Tower.

With a quick glance around, I lie down and close my eyes, concentrating on the body's autonomic processes: the steady suck and release of blood from the chambers of my heart, the hush of that pulse in my ears, the flow of breath to and from my body, the cleansing motion of my liver and kidney, the fiery exchange of gasses in the lungs. All working in perfect coordination. Just like the sky and the park and the ducks and the lone set of swings.

And as I slept I dreamed a dream.

It seems that the interview is coming to an end. That's good, because it has been a bit of trial for both of us. A necessary evil, if there can be such a thing.

The official rises from his plush chair and approaches the photograph that might be an aerial view of the city or of transistorised circuits. I notice for the first time a hairline crack in that wall and a small control panel. Another, almost secret, door. Now I know why One-eye didn't return to the anteroom. I also realize that the opposite wall (with an anti-smoking poster) is not made of plaster or some normal lining material but a smooth, glass-like substance that may well indicate a one-way observation mirror.

The official reaches for the control panel but, like a kid in class, I put my hand up to forestall him. There are questions that need answering right now, issues that urgently need clarifying, I tell him.

- Does he expect me to go on like this?
- Why is there a packet of chlorometastellasine on his desk?
- Why would anyone want to know if I ate cereal for breakfast?
- Has he spoken with my alarm clock in the last twenty-four hours?
- Does the term "time reversal weapon" mean anything to

him?

Right now doesn't work for him. His fingers are already punching out a code on the control panel. All will be revealed in good time, his attitude implies.

The door slides open and we step through. We are in an unexpectedly large room that is a laboratory of some kind. There are machines that I recognise, like scanners, x-rays, and electron microscopes, as well as a host of other devices I don't recognise. In contrast to the monosyllabic silence of the anteroom and the official hush-hush of the office, this place is bustling with smartly-dressed, white-coated technicians striding about purposefully or working at long, gleaming aluminium tables, complete with test-tubes, Bunsen burners, computer terminals and control chambers.

Whatever is going on here is a big operation. Big names, big action.

I'm not happy with this sudden scene switch. Already I'm beginning to feel like a lab-rat.

As soon as we appear a smart young woman in a white coat approaches. Her skin is clear and smooth, and her hair is tied back in a neat ponytail.

'Repeat standard HIB/RAR seventeen and eighteen,' the official says to the woman. His mind seems to be elsewhere.

'Come with me, Mr Kent,' the young woman says in a pleasant voice, turning on her heel and threading her way between the benches. I follow, aware that the official is no longer with us. He is already engaged in a serious discussion with a group of technicians on some matter outside my knowledge. Funny, you couldn't say that official and I were close, exactly, but he was my connection with the rest of my life. Now I was being handed over to a new fate with hardly an acknowledgement; I feel betrayed.

Then I see One-eye. He is lying on top of a bench, his one eye closed, his face shut down, his arms by his side. A tube runs from a machine into his left arm. I am amazed that this is being done in the open, this big room, and not some curtained-off space. But nobody seems to notice or care, they are so busy with their own business. As we go past, he opens his eye and gives me a barely perceptible nod of recognition.

A smart young man in a white coat approaches us. His skin is clear and smooth, and his hair is also tied back in a neat ponytail. He might well be the young woman's brother. Together they escort me to a bench.

'We need you to lie down here, Mr Kent,' the woman says.

'Do you now?'

The young man smiles obligingly as if he is the one being asked to lie down.

'We are going to take some of your blood for testing, and will replace it with fresh plasma from this machine.' She pats an apparatus identical to the one connected to One-eye.

'Where does the plasma come from?'

'Willing donors,' the young man says. 'The blood plasma is just a safety measure.'

I am suitably reassured, but I wish Evie were here to talk to. Some places Evie can't follow me, which is my loss.

As I get onto the table I notice there is an old-fashioned chalkboard running along one wall. It is mostly covered by mathematical and chemical notation, but on the corner someone has written, *Clark Kent loves Lois Lane, and underneath that some wag has written, Yes, but Lois loves Nortikiss.*

To the man I say, 'I have this theory that young women with reddy-blonde hair have phone numbers beginning with double 5.'

'Okaaaaay!' the man says.

'And there's a good chance that it will end with an odd number, probably a seven or nine.'

I have to sit up and remove my jacket and my shirt, possessed of the absurd idea that this young woman and I are going to have sex up here on the bench with everybody bustling around ignoring us.

'*Haben Sie Versicherung?*' she asks, fiddling with the apparatus.

'Do you have medical insurance?'

'Of course, I have an alarm clock to take care of those sorts of things.'

'That's handy.' She slides the needle socket into my vein. 'Nice veins,' she comments.

'Thank you? Does your phone number end with a five or a seven?'

'That would be telling.'

'Nice try,' the young man says.

The woman screws a tube into the needle socket.

Something flickers across my memory, too fast to catch. A name perhaps. Zellie. Zaldia, Zalena. A zig-zag too quick to follow.

'I feel intimidated,' I say to the woman.

'No need to feel that way, Mr Kent,' she says sincerely, smiling warmly at me now. 'We're pretty good at this sort of thing. We certainly don't want you to suffer any loss of emotional self-validation. And, if it's any comfort to you, my phone number ends with a five.'

'There you go buddy,' the man says.

'You're not just saying that.'

'Not at all. It's true,' she says.

'Do you believe God plays dice?' I ask them both.

'Not in here, he doesn't,' the woman says, opening a valve on the machine. My arm goes cold.

A dark object blotting out the stars. Here, in the blackness between the suns, an unlit object showed only as a pit or a hole in the fairy-lights of the Milky Way. With no sensation of movement, its approach was simply a dilation, a sudden expansion of the darkness, until it was there, above them, massive and looming.

The long lost *Omega,* derelict for millennia and now, if rumours were to be believed, home to the Fishmen from the Other Side of Time.

A prophetic shiver passed through Captain October Nortikiss. The dark bulk of the abandoned trader was now a threatening presence, potent and terrifying, apparently eating up the stars as they approached. The captain still felt a little groggy from being awoken from his long cryogenic sleep. The coldness in his left arm as the revival drugs took effect had been his first waking sensation, and had hardly, even now, faded, despite a brisk shower and even brisker sex.

The Cryo Corporation, which had waxed so wealthy with its invention of cryogenic sleep, known as stasis sleep, that it had come to dominate the Confederation of Stars, supplied several standard variation dream lives to occupy the mind of travellers while in stasis sleep, for unlike ordinary sleep, the mind did not shut down in stasis sleep and had to be kept active to prevent the onset of claustrophobia, paranoia, and madness. These stasis dreams were invariably ordinary domestic scenes, intended to be comforting and soothing. A stay-at-home persona with a lovely partner and usually one child. A nice traditional suburban setting. The dreamer would enjoy some vigorous form of exercise not available to the astronaut, such as power walking or jogging. This ordinariness was intended to anchor the vulnerable psyche of the stasis-dreamer firmly in everyday life, a stable centre for that psyche hurtling through the deepest and emptiest void between the stars.

Officially, no one remembered their stasis lives, but there were odd moments when the captain caught the faint perfume like that given off by a woman's hairbrush or heard the distant slap of a skipping rope against hard pavement. Unofficially, October Nortikiss was a little sceptical of the Cryo Corporation's claims about the soothing nature of their dream lives. He always woke up from his stasis dreams discombobulated and out of sorts, as did his crew, even though no memory of the stasis dreams survived in waking life. At least officially.

'On course,' One-eye murmured. He didn't have to say that. It was just his way of keeping up a presence.

His CO was proud of his nickname, and wore a black eye-patch to make himself look like a pirate. He'd stayed on board the *Frolix 6,* monitoring their flight path against CAL's computer plotted simulation. Nortikiss could watch their progress on CAL's terminal in the landing craft. The terminal's clock ticked off the time in half seconds.

I'm drifting to my doom, Nortikiss thought hollowly. This is my death looming up in front of us, shapeless and elephantine.

This was not an approved thought, or one that Nortikiss approved of, but nobody who had traversed space to the extent he had was free of such thoughts. Death was never more than a step away. Doomy feelings bred easily in the galactic emptiness. Even in cryo-sleep, he suspected, they were not immune.

This was not all that bothered him. They were way out, here in Sector 4, right at the far edge of the galaxy, just above the plane of the elliptic. In one direction the whole of the Milky Way spread out before them in a spectacular display, a dense and rich array of stars, the famous constellation called The Lovers clearly visible. In the other direction, however, there was nothing, just the blackness of space between the galaxies, and the impossibly distant glitter of Andromeda.

He tried to enjoy a moment's excitement at the thought of boarding a ship which had become a legend of the spaceways. The empty ship pushed this way and that by tachyon winds and the vagaries of gravity to the very edge of the galaxy, now home to a weapon that could turn the Big Bang itself into a Big Crunch and squeeze this universe right out of existence.

It wasn't all fun and games being October Nortikiss, hero of the spaceways. Nortikiss the Intrepid, saviour of mankind. Not just mankind but all sentient life forms wherever they may be. It wasn't all glamour and glory, however noble his chin might appear in pics and Cryo Corporation propaganda. He had a Roman nose to complement the jutting jaw, they made a wonderful team, but what use would they be in the face of the slimy horrors festering in the innards of the dead trader? The Fishmen were unlikely to be impressed.

'Fifty-five seconds to docking,' the terminal announced.

Nortikiss turned to Beverly and they proceeded with the ritual of a last minute inspection of each other's spacesuits. Making sure all the lines were secure and the valves set correctly. The small intimacy of making a final adjustment to an oxygen hose, or a final tweak to the butterfly nut that fixed their toolkits to their packs. The days of large, bulky spacesuits had long gone and their silver, plastiplex space gowns, as they were called, clung quite becomingly to their perfect physiques. It was astonishing how well Beverly matched the popular figure of the space adventurer, the female variety, the kind of woman who knows what she wants and how to get it. It's a wonderful thing, he reflected, when reality and the popular imagination coincide.

They were coming into dock now, sliding along the underbelly of the *Omega* and into the docking bay. One-eye was muttering maths under this breath, the other two could hear him through their suitphones. A steady stream of equations that locked them securely into their reality construct. Nortikiss listened, trying to magnify his mental processes with mathematical certainties to blot out the massive presence of the *Omega*, a ship almost as large as the Earth's moon.

As they slipped between the portals of the main docking orifice, and the shadow of the ship enclosed them, he felt the obscure but relentless pressure he'd come to associate with proximity to the Fishmen, a temporal undertow that pulled at the lattice of his thought.

'We've arrived, you bastards,' he beamed telepathically into the bulk around them. 'Do your worst.' This burst of bravado makes him feel good. I won't let them get to me, he thought grimly. I'll hang on. I'll persist. They may blow my mind and memory to shreds, but they can't touch me, the essential me, the ineluctable Nortikiss. That which is left when everything else had been burned away in the fires of time.

High powered beams of light from their torches revealed that the airlock door on the *Omega* was shut. As doors go, it was massive, big enough to admit exploratory craft. Solid steel metres thick. At the centre there was a wheel, like an ocean ship's steering wheel, and lines of steel reinforcing radiated from it. He and Beverly stood before it, feeling like some tiny, insignificant life form. This human-made door suddenly felt like a vast alien artefact of some kind. Unknowable, impenetrable.

And locked.

'Sealed from the inside,' Beverly said.

'Alien proof.'

'I'm glad you can joke,' Beverly said, and for a moment she sounded like Evelyn.

'And we are the aliens.'

'Perhaps you can open it with your masculine charm?' Not with the same intonation, perhaps but a decidedly Evelynish thing to say. He didn't like that. He wanted to be able to trust the voices coming through his suitphone. His life depended on them.

Nortikiss thought of all the doors he had encountered in his life, doors he'd opened, doors he'd closed, doors he'd walked through without even noticing. Now the mother of all doors, an airlock seal, built to withstand all kind of assaults lay in front of him. Short of an atomic blast, violence was not going to do the trick. It was time he used his brain. He had been chosen as Captain, not just because of his astonishing manliness, but his decisive mind. At moments like these he stepped in and took command. He saw solutions where lesser brains saw problems. That's what a space hero did.

'One-eye,' he said tersely. 'Have you been able to make contact with the ship's computer?'

'No. Dead. Inert.'

'There should be an independently powered safety mechanism on the inside, designed to respond to certain frequencies beamed from the outside, from external craft. Put there to prevent crew members from getting locked out.'

'I'm on it,' One-eye said.

Nortikiss studied the airlock door, not because it was so fascinating but because it beat looking out at the cosmos. It was hard to keep a grip on yourself as a human being when so far away from everything. The constellation called The Lovers, well known in Sector 4, was of little comfort. The cold, stellar embrace of the lovers spoke only of itself, glittering and remote.

'You're on,' One-eye said.

Slowly the great door rolled to one side, like a huge circular stone.

He could see nothing inside but utter darkness. He put his hand into it as if into water. No atmosphere, no diffusion of light, no blurring of shadows, no softening of edges, and no shadow sweetened twilight. Just his arm sliced off neatly at the wrist. If I climb into the belly of this whale, I'll never climb out again, he thought. That's the fate of an intergalactic hero. That's why songs would be sung about him one day.

This was a suicide mission if ever he saw one. He and Beverly both knew; they just weren't talking about it. There's no way they could blow this old bucket of bolts back to hell and get away in time. Already One-eye would be pulling the *Frolix 6* to a safer distance.

'No lights I'm afraid,' One-eye said. 'No life support, no grav, no nothing, kiddoes. Don't bump your head on the floor.'

'Die, Fishface!' he shouted into the void.

Slowly, they made their way in.

A statutory limitation of consciousness

Ananda Suklodana knelt by the river and washed his bowl, enjoying the sight of the clean, sweet water of the sacred river carrying away the few rice grains that had been left in his bowl. He rubbed the bowl with his fingers, feeling the smooth grain of the wood and the water rushing over his fingers. These simple sensations arising through the body were pleasurable to Ananda, but he was happy to let them pass. As his cousin and teacher Siddhartha Gautama counselled, excessive attachment to pleasure could bind one forever to the great turning wheel of life and death, and he knew this to be true.

As the water flowed over his bowl, he let his mind dwell for a moment on how a faint essence of the aroma of the wood, the gum arabic, would enter the water and become a part of it, an invisible part beyond the senses of man, and yet there. There is the seen, and there is the unseen. The hidden aromas of the world.

The thought made him uneasy. He was, perhaps, a little too fond of those hidden aromas. They were the subtle pleasures of being in the world: the delicate fingers of the wind on his face, the joy of his limbs when he walked, the pleasure of the eye when it beholds the world. 'It is not these pleasures that are the problem,' Siddhartha once said, 'but the dwelling on them, thinking about them, seeking them.'

Ah! Wise Siddhartha! Even now, here Ananda was, dwelling on those subtle aromas while the water passed across his fingers and the grain of the wood showed dark and hilly. The gentle rush of water was a subtle melody pleasing to the ear, while the open blue sky above, with only a little light, gauzy cloud, was naked as the body of an innocent girl. He closed his eyes against such thoughts, but his eyes were not the problem. It was the mind, the eternal monkey mind never at rest, that kept him awake at night and asleep in the day.

A young girl came wandering along the riverbank, trailing a skipping rope. He hadn't seen her before and assumed she came from the local village or was the daughter of one of Siddhartha's female devotees.

'You are a long way from home,' she said to Ananda.

He greeted her graciously. 'I was born in the capital city of Kapilavatthu, but it is no longer my home. The world is now my home. I have walked many thousands of miles in the company of my cousin, Siddhartha.'

'Then you have forgotten much,' she said.

Ananda was amused by this bold little girl. Here he was, Ananda Suklodana, renowned as pre-eminent in remembering, who was known as the "vessel of truth" by the other monks, being told by this child that he had forgotten much.

'I can remember every word Siddhartha has spoken. I can remember every moment of my life since the day I learned to talk.'

'Then you are too full of pride,' the girl said.

Ananda laughed. 'How true that is!' He felt ashamed of himself for boasting to this little girl about his astonishing memory. Even a fool might quote the wise. How could he think of himself as a Stream Enterer, or one whose inner eye had been opened to the truth, when he fell into such simple traps and made the most basic errors of thought?

He bowed before her. 'Your words pierce me,' he said. 'You have attained much wisdom.' Surely some awakened one had opened their eyes inside the girl's head.

'Then tell me, Ananda of the marvellous memory, can you remember the multiple lives you have lived since becoming a Stream Enterer as well as you remember this lifetime?'

Ananda immediately perceived that she was not talking about the survival of the personality after death, as the believers in reincarnation would have it, but about the fact that spiritual and mental action is never lost. It never stops happening. It is transformed and goes on transforming. Of course he cannot remember his multiple lives because there is no "him" to do the remembering, and nothing to remember since there is nothing but the upward rush of consciousness.

Ananda hung his head. 'Wise one, you humble me. You remind me of the impermanence of my remembering, its limitation and its fragility, all of which are aspects of mind. I cannot remember even my own birth, let alone all the births and deaths of mind, for while I might be quick to remember, I am slow to learn.'

'That is why I say you have forgotten much.'

'And now I see that you were right, and my pride blinded me.'

She smiled sweetly at him and began to skip of the spot. *Tickety-slap, tickety-slap.* 'You are a good man, Ananda. A man without guile. And handsome too. No wonder the women like you.' *Tickety-slap.*

Ananda blushed. Sometimes Siddhartha would tease him about women too, and he would blush. Siddhartha said it was his sweet nature that attracted them. His two dear friends and fellow monks Aniruddha and Bhadra said that it was because of his manly appearance. There was a time when he would feel a little viper of envy when he saw Aniruddha and Bhadra deep in meditation. How easily they became Stream Enterers, and how quickly their eye of truth opened, unburdened by any sweet nature or manly appearance!

'The maiden Pchiti wants to see you. In fact, she sent me here to find you, knowing that every morning you wash your bowl at the river.'

He was aware of the maiden Pchiti, being a young woman of great beauty, one of the female followers Siddhartha's step-mother, Mahaprajapati, had brought with her when she joined the swelling band of disciples gathering around her step-son.

'Why does she want to see me?'

'She is not feeling herself.'

'You mean she is ill? I am just a monk. I am no doctor. I have no skill with herbs and medicines. There are women in the camp with those skills.'

'She is feeling out of sorts,' *tickety-slap*, 'but I don't think,' *tickety-slap*, 'that the answer lies in herbs and medicines.'

'Oh?'

The little girl stopped skipping and gathered in her rope.

'She believes that her malady has spiritual causes.'

'I see.'

Siddhartha had often commented that the origin of all illness was spiritual in nature, stemming from wrong thinking and entanglement with the objects of thought. A monk can turn even the prospect of his own awakening into an object of thought and, with his eyes fixed upon a still distant nirvana, stub his toe on a hidden stone. Hidden stones, hidden aromas: the pitfalls of the world.

'She has need of your compassion.'

'Ah…' There was a whole universe of sentient beings in need of his compassion. Siddhartha taught that compassion was endless.

He shook his bowl to clear it from the last drops of water and closed his eyes in order to be mindful of the moment and enjoy the feel of the mellow sun on his face.

When he opened his eyes, the little girl was nowhere to be seen.

The *Omega* had not been built for comfort. An interstellar transporter from the era of the first great wave of migration, capable of carrying fifty thousand human beings. This was a city of corridors, pokey rooms and cargo holds. Once a registered Confederation Vessel, it had been bought off the scrapheap by people smugglers and had been rogue up to the time of its disappearance.

Now the Confederation suspected that the vessel was providing the Fishmen with a toehold in our galaxy, even though almost nothing was known about the invaders, who they were and how they operated. It was hoped that Nortikiss and his little crew might discover more, particularly about the time reversal weapon, if that's what it was.

'Actually,' Beverly said, 'it's more like an Einstein Disrupter than a time reversal weapon. It seems they can unpeel time from space, disrupt Einstein's nice smooth space-time continuum.'

'Who knows? Maybe that's how they eat, like we peel a banana. They peel a galaxy. Or maybe they just want to have sex with us, like some people want to have sex with animals.'

They expected to find bodies, but there were none. So where did everybody go? Did thousands of people just jump out of the airlock?

'If there was a plague, the dwindling survivors would jettison the bodies to try to contain the infection. There may well be a group of bodies somewhere, the last survivors to die. We could wander around in here for weeks and never find them.'

'That makes sense.'

Any oxygen the craft had was long since gone. All that was left of human support systems was a faint sheen of water ice on the walls and floors, as if the steel could perspire. Much of the inhabitants' time would be spent in null-gravity, which meant no contrived up or down on the ship. These space cowboys and cowgirls would have lived in a floating laterality, pulling themselves like monkeys along hand rungs which were everywhere.

'It's urgent we understand how the time distorter is affecting us,' Beverly says, her voice distant and tinny in the low powered suitphones. 'I think we are being pushed back along our individual timelines, but because the past does not exist we end up in a *different* past. It may look like our past, but small details will give it away, reveal it to be nothing more than a fantasy. I speculate that our minds can hardly operate as they are intended. I mean, create a sense of self in time. The brain doesn't store things sequentially, we have to *create* sequence.'

Nortikiss burst into song.

'I hitched up my pony and went into the bar
Black Jake was there drinking Gold Star.'

'What are you doing? Why are you singing?'

'It's a song we used to sing when I was a space-cadet.'

'Why sing it now?'

'It's a sequence, isn't it? A narrative. It will help us maintain our narrative integrity. Besides, this is a cowboy song, and I'm a space cowboy, so I sing songs like this as I go into battle.

'I called Black Jack to account for his sins
He looked me twice over and ordered two gins.'

It reminds me of my past, my carefree days as a space-cadet.'

In fact, he was lying. He could hardly remember his space-cadet days, and doubted that they were carefree, but it was the thought that counted.

They had arrived at a wide, open room lined with doors. Each one was code numbered and each one was open. Equally, each one was a mystery as their helmet lights hardly penetrated far into the openings.

'We have to figure out how to get to the reactor,' Beverly said, studying the doors.'

'Have a drink, Black Jake said, and threw me a glass
I shot it out of the air, I was moving that fast.'

'Can you hear me? For Christ's sake concentrate. Anyway, that song doesn't make any sense.'

'Don't make trouble, I said, don't even draw a fast breath

Or I'll summon from hell your very own death.'

They could hear One-eye murmuring coordinates and instructions. He had used the sensors on the *Frolix 6* to locate the reactor, and confirmed that it was active, although not feeding any power into the life support systems. He would investigate that, but there was no way he could switch on the life support systems, or any of the ships operating systems, from the *Frolix 6*.

Now he was using their suit cameras to analyse the code numbers on the lifts.

Beverly said, 'I tell you, October, the details are changing on us right now. For example, you remember the stateroom on the *Frolix 6*?

'How could I forget those horrible tubular steel chairs?'

'There is a picture hanging on the wall. What is it?'

'Harvest scene, rural England. Most likely a cheap, late-Victorian imitation of the landscape painters. Badly executed.'

'That's where you're wrong, it's a Picasso, Blue Period, figures on a beach with a girl standing on an oversized ball and a man with super-broad shoulders.'

'You're mistaken. That one's in the observation room.'

How easy it is to be mistaken about such things, he thought. People spent a lot of time arguing about such details. What they are really arguing about is the certainty of their memories, and the confidence they need to feel about their remembered worlds.

'There are several rooms like the one you are in, station rooms,' One-eye said. These numbered corridors lead all over the place. What I'm looking for is a pod station. Instead of lifts, these old tubs had pods that could shoot you through the arteries and sub-arteries of the ship.'

'But the pods won't be active.'

'I'm working on that. The core is alive, but no power is being fed into the shipboard systems… I have a puzzle…' His voice trailed off.

Nortikiss sang.

Black Jack hung his thumbs in his belt

Your hide, he said, would make a fine pelt.'

'Look for door number DKP1408,' One-eye said. Because he was using the ship's powerful radio, he sounded closer than Beverly, who was standing right beside him.

'Lindy-Loo knelt before him, don't do it, she cried

There's been enough killing, enough men have died.'

Beverly said, 'Commander, the Captain and I have a small disagreement. What do you think, is the painting in the stateroom – a pastoral scene of a harvest or a Picasso, blue period?'

'What painting? You are both sounding a bit hysterical to me. You need to focus on your mission, not argue over trivialities. Find DKP…'

'But they're not trivialities! We are at the meeting place of worlds. If we start to slip from one to another…' Beverly stopped. She didn't just stop talking, she stopped moving as well. She hung in the air, a few inches off the "floor" like a floating statue. 'I think I'm dying,' she said finally. 'I'm running out of lives.'

This alarmed Nortikiss. He didn't know what she meant but it sounded ominous.

She was interrupted by a burst of sound, like a wave crashing. They caught a few words from One-eye. '…. the core is active… they're using the song…'

'We've lost him,' Beverly said in a panicky voice.

They could hear static. It was a sighing, like the sound of a far-off ocean or someone close-up breathing in their ears.

'Get out of my way, Jake struck her aside

Don't come between a man and his glory and pride.'

'Stop singing that fucking song!' She waved her arms as if semaphoring him. The silvery fabric of her space gown glittered in the hard, thin light of his helmet. 'This is your big moment. Time to show your stuff. Be the Hero. Go kick some Fishman arse.'

'It's a ballad,' he said, offended. 'From a fine old tradition of cowboy songs sung around the campfire by real cowboys. It's to the tune of "On Top of Old Smoky." Ever heard of that?'

He lifted his voice in song.

'I picked up the dice and let them fall hard

Jake's fate hinged on the turn of a card.'

'You'll get us both killed,' Beverly said.

'Is my singing that bad?'

Instead of answering she pointed to one of the doors. DKP1408. 'Let's hope it leads to the reactor,' she said.

He squared his rounded shoulders and lifted his profile to the cold, indifferent universe. He would show them his true mettle. Beverly had already located the control panel, a familiar looking control panel, to one side of the door, and the door had slid obediently open. Time for a final verse.

'The Captain he faced a fate worse than death

But he'd fight the foul fiends to his very last breath.'

This last verse reminded him of another song, one about being a pilgrim. That more distant song was like the painting that was either a Nineteen Century pastoral or a Picasso blue period – of uncertain status. Perhaps true to another time and place.

He took hold of Beverly's hand. Even through the double layer of their suits he swore he could feel her living warmth.

'This is it,' he said. He gestured to the blackness beyond the doors.

'October, tell me,' she kept a hold of his hand, 'do you ever remember… you know, your stasis-dreams.'

'Maybe.'

'That painting, the one you describe. Not the Picasso but the pastoral. I think I've seen it somewhere, in another room, a room like the stateroom, a bit like this room…' she tails off. 'What if….'

'Steady as she goes,' Nortikiss said, trying to avoid a dread growing in him.

'What? Why did you say that? Steady as she goes.'

He shrugged. 'Does it matter?'

'I've never heard you say it before. I know all your stock phrases. You don't have that many. And it's just not like you. You're more likely to say "I'll be back," or "Die, Fishface!" or something inspiring like that. You're not a "steady as she goes" person.'

Of course, he thought. In her eyes I am probably more of the swashbuckling type, her hero of the spaceways, always ready to kick alien arse.

She takes his hand in hers. They can't feel much through their space gowns but the grip alone is reassuring. Until she speaks.

'I'm dying, October. I can feel my life leaching out of me. I keep imagining this tapestry we had on our wall when I was young. It was full of bright and vibrant colours. But each time I remember it, it has less and less colour. Slowly the figures are fading into their own backgrounds, and slowly the background colours are fading to grey. At first a thousand shades of grey, then just grey. That's what's happening to me. I'm just like that tapestry.'

'You can't die,' he said. He took that as read. Beverly couldn't die. She would stay young and vigorous, green-eyed and red-haired, smart and sassy, until the stars grew icicles. These kinds of adventures have their rules, and not killing off the main heroine and love interest is one of them, he thought.

'We may have been wrong about this weapon,' he said, trying to deal with the thought of Beverly dying. We call it a time reversal weapon, or a time disrupter, but maybe the effects on time that we notice are just side-effects, the real target being our reality itself, the ultimate grid-symbol construct. It starts with a violation of genre, but it doesn't end there.'

'What are you talking about?'

'You dying, and how impossible that is. You aren't sick, are you? So this is meaningless. Just random out-of-the-blue dying.'

'That's what it feels like. My spirit is draining away.'

'You can't say that! And why isn't it happening to me too?'

'Perhaps because you really are the hero.' He could hear the smile in her voice, even over the suitphone.

'One-eye, can you hear all this? How are Beverly's vital signs?' The suits were of course beaming back volumes of information on their wearer's physical state.

But One-eye wasn't answering. But he thought he could hear, in the far distance, celestial voices singing.

How long he and Beverly stayed inside the *Omega* searching for the ship's core they would never entirely determine. Their space gown monitors said one thing, the computer on the *Frolix 6* said another, and their own internal time sense was lost to endless corridors of featureless grey metal. Hours, days, perhaps lifetimes came and went. It would have been impossible if One-eye hadn't managed to re-establish radio contact. It was intermittent but it was enough.

Whatever the *Omega* had once been, an almost moon-sized interstellar wormhole jumper, first generation, big, clumsy and utterly functional – it belonged in a museum, Nortikiss decided – it was no longer. Some creatures may leave a smell behind them, some may leave droppings, some may leave remnants of a kill, but the Fishmen left in their wake a tangle of times and places, memories and imaginings. Nortikiss had begun to doubt that any such device as the Einstein Disrupter, or time reversal weapon, or even some reality disrupter, existed at all. It didn't have to exist, the Fishmen were the Einstein Disrupters all on their own, without any help. They were, after all, from the Other Side of Time, their arrival here had brought waves of dislocation, reality configurations alien to this universe. And, since time itself was inextricably linked to consciousness, consciousness being time's medium, these same dislocations washed up in the human mind.

Their influence had turned the *Omega* from a dull but serviceable human vessel into a garden of forking paths, mentally, emotionally and physically. Its corridors were made of memories, its walls were as dense as sleep, and there was no end to its interiorosity; no matter how deep they went, they couldn't reach the centre because there was no centre. The notion that the universe was an infinite sphere whose centre was everywhere and whose circumference was nowhere, was literally true for the Fishmen. Or, Nortikiss suspected, a universe whose circumference was everywhere and whose centre was nowhere. That centre was hidden, rolled up inside the Fishmen's dimension. Like ants on a ball, time-bound humans could only travel endlessly on the surface without getting a jot closer to the centre.

Even the Fishmen themselves didn't exist. Not as such, anyway. They were far more likely to be a construct, a projection created by the human mind when it encountered such incomprehensible beings. We can only deal with the unfamiliar in familiar terms, Nortikiss reasoned. The inexplicable turns into a Fishman.

Nortikiss and Beverly worked all this out in a series of fraught conversations. Beverly was not just a pretty face. In fact, she did most of the hard thinking, with Nortikiss following up behind sounding important. It seemed that she wanted to get a whole lot across to him before she died. Her approaching death, she said, had given her some special insights into what was happening to them, and who they really were.

It started when One-eye gave them some bad news.

'I'm getting multiple readings on the location of the core,' he said. He no longer sounded right next to them. His voice was tiny and lonely in the darkness. 'You better stop while I figure out where you should be going.'

'Maybe there is no core,' Beverly said.

'Don't go metaphysical on me,' One-eye said. 'If you have power, you have a power source. Those old tubs usually came with two reactors.'

'We don't have power right now,' Nortikiss said.

Their torchlight didn't penetrate to the end of the tunnel they were in, the hand-holds on each side jutting out as far as the eye could see. The effect was of a mirror image facing itself, bending off down a corridor of replication.

'We could get lost in here,' Nortikiss said. The *Omega* reminded him of a labyrinth. There was a beast roaming around down here somewhere. One that could, at any moment, come roaring out of the shadows.

One-eye didn't answer. All they heard was that oceanic static once more.

'We're not lost, we're here,' Beverly said.

Nortikiss gave a hollow laugh.

'As long as we have each other,' Beverly said.

Nortikiss didn't like waiting around doing nothing. Swimming about inside this metal whale at least provided a sense of purpose, even if they weren't getting anywhere.

'Do you remember your childhood, October?'

'Ah – yes.' In fact he wasn't too sure what he remembered. He saw things as in a child's drawing. Yellow hills, as gorgeous as crayons. An even yellower sun with rays shooting out into the blue. A forest with vines and parrots and monkeys. A leaping leopard. But that couldn't be quite right. There were no leopards where he came from. Nor monkeys. And a hawk limed against a clear sky. That was okay, there were plenty of hawks. And packets of cereal, brightly coloured. And there was a little girl, too, with a skipping rope. He wasn't sure, however, that she belonged to his memory or she was just something he had dreamed. The whole issue was fraught with uncertainty. His parents, for example. He couldn't remember them as such, just the sense of large nearby presences, not necessarily comforting.

'What about your name?'

'What about it?'

'It's a silly, made-up name. Real people don't have names like October Nortikiss.'

'I thought it had a certain ring to it.'

'It's just a stupid pun. It's like the name of a character out of some cheap comic or trashy novel…'

'Hey, it's my name.'

'Is it? How do you know? You might have read it somewhere. You probably have a real name tucked away somewhere, like Harry or Jim.'

'I don't read.'

'What did people call you as a kid?'

'Naughty.'

'Ha ha.'

The way she said 'ha ha' made him uneasy. He'd heard somebody say that just recently, in the same tone of voice; the details were receding. 'Well, you have an ordinary name. Beverly is a very ordinary name, very domestic – a let-down, actually. Hardly a comic book name.'

'But Beverly isn't my real name.' She sounded frightened now. 'I adopted it because my real name is too weird, and I just wanted to be ordinary. It was bad enough being good at maths. Being the sexy astrophysicist, what a bore that was. Nerds are turds, I was told.'

'What is your name, then? You can confess. There is nobody here but you, me and the Fishmen. I won't tell.'

'Zeldia. Zeldia Lilith, or Lilith Zeldia. Or both. Makes me sound like a witch.' She pretended to fly off on a broomstick. 'So I made myself disappear. Zeldia, I mean. Enter the more demure Beverly. Still good at maths, just not so sexy.'

'Don't sell yourself short. You'll always be my sexy astrophysicist, no matter what.'

'That's sweet of you.'

'According to heretical texts, Lilith is the name of the first wife of Adam. The connotations are not nice. Lilith is in fact the archetypal witch.'

'Did she have red hair and green eyes, like me?'

'I imagine she did.'

'You see? We've both got B grade names. Well, yours is more C grade. At least I wasn't saddled with a name like Nortikiss.' She gave a snort of derision.

He tried to snap his fingers, but the smooth material of the space gown made that impossible. 'I know! My wife gave me that name in a fit of jealous pique, and I haven't been able to shake it off.'

'Your wife! What wife? How can you have a wife when you are out traversing the great voids of space with your sexy astrophysicist saving the universe all the time?' In her agitation she let go the rungs and began to float.

Nortikiss grew confused. He began to feel the same fear that was gripping her. 'I thought…' He didn't know what he thought but didn't want to admit it. At all costs, he wanted to appear in control of the situation. Calm, decisive, strong. The kind of hero of the spaceways he was supposed to be. 'I thought you were One-eye's wife and we were just, you know…'

But she didn't know.

'What are you talking about? One-eye is gay. Occasionally you and he get together. That's how we keep a stable dynamic on the *Frolix 6*. You know all this! For God sakes get a grip!' She was floating at right angles to him now. Her faceplate was up against his and he could see her eyes, wide and staring. 'I need you to focus.'

Unbidden, an image floated into his mind of One-eye lying on a table naked with a pulsating penis. Where did that come from, he wondered. Out of the deepest recesses of stasis-sleep, probably.

'I don't think so. I think you're making all this up out of the exigency of the moment. You're grasping at straws, darling.' Inside his suit, his voice sounded rich and soothing. It wouldn't sound that way to her. 'You're making it up to suit the story, just like…' he tailed off.

'Just like who?'

Nortikiss was saved having to answer by One-eye, whose voice crackled through their suit radios. 'I've got it. There's a freight storage area ahead if you keep going as you were. Once you get there I can give you further instructions. I'm still getting multiple readings but there are algorithms.'

'We've got a few identity issues here,' Nortikiss said. 'Maybe there is an algorithm for them too.'

'Ignore them,' One-eye said succinctly. 'You have a mission to complete.'

'That's right,' Beverly said. 'You are endangering the mission with all this ontological doubt.'

'More like epistemological doubt. It's knowledge we lack, not existence.'

'Whatever the fuck you like! You can be so fucking pedantic. Even when I'm dying.'

'In these situations, it's important to get the right word.'

'Captain,' One-eye said, 'This is the reality in which you find yourself. Accept it. The universe isn't offering you any special dispensations for cleverness.'

'…or love, apparently.'

'…or love. Take what is given and work from there. Start from where you really are.' One-eye's voice was starting to fade again. There was an unpleasant ringing in Nortikiss's ears where One-eye's voice should be.

'And where are we, exactly?' He played his light over the grey metal bulkhead. 'What kind of place is this?'

Beverly gripped his arm, digging her fingers as deep into the flesh as the resilient material of space gown allowed. Her voice trickled into his ear through his suit com. 'Don't knock it. It's a place, it's solid.' She thumped the wall to demonstrate. He could see her hand moving but of course couldn't hear any sound.

'If you say so.'

'You remember Heisenberg's uncertainty principle?'

'Sure. It's about the limitations of human knowledge. In the sub-quantum world you can know the velocity of a particle, or its location, but not both.' Nortikiss was happy to prove for once that he wasn't just a pretty face either and could remember something from his quantum physics classes.

You don't get to be a Confederation space captain and space hero only by looking the part. 'And that's not because we lack the technology to do both, but because it's an inherent impossibility.'

'Right. What we are up against here is something similar, I conjecture. A form of the Heisenberg uncertainty principle as it applies to human consciousness. We are allowed to know where we are but not when we are. The more we know about one the less we know about the other. If we know fully when we are there is no where, and if we know fully where we are there is no when. Call it a statutory limitation of consciousness.'

'Wow! You'll get the Nobel Prize for this one. What do the Fishmen have to do with it?'

She kept a hold of his arm as they swam along from rung to rung, heading God knows where, and he was glad. At times he had wondered if that voice in his ear was really her, but the grip on his arm was unmistakable.

'I don't know exactly. I speculate that the Uncertainty Principle doesn't apply in their dimension. When they come to our dimension, they disrupt the relationship between velocity and location, between when we are and where we are.'

'What about who we are? That seems to be the real problem.'

'I think the *who* gets sort of stretched between the *when* and *where*.'

'Stretched?'

'Thinned out, attenuated, lost in translation.'

Nortikiss was deeply impressed, but also somewhat miffed. She was so smart she made him look stupid. He felt like patting her on the buttocks just to show there were no hard feelings.

'Maybe we could get so thinned out that we could disappear altogether.'

'Maybe,' she said. 'That's what dying feels like to me. That my body is nothing more than a breath of mist on a window pane.'

The way she said that made him feel very alone and very lonely. There may be comfort, but there is no salvation in the company of others – a drowning man turns in vain to another drowning man. Being a space hero was immaterial.

'It furthers the Fishmen to undermine us, that much is certain,' Beverly said. She'd let go his arm so as to more easily pull herself along. It might look easy, even graceful, to move about in null-grav, but it was hard work. Every movement, every action, had to be recalibrated to compensate for lack of gravity. This normal difficulty seemed compounded by the temporal undertow, which was stronger than ever. Only by concentrating and keeping their mental process amplified could they combat it. In this respect, their conversation was their lifeline, he realized. It was the thread that held the *when* and the *where* in precarious balance.

The presence of the Fishmen was all around him, not located in any one particular part of the ship, not occupying space the way he understood it, but permeating the whole structure the way in which memory is said to permeate the brain. It felt as if the *Omega* was now a part of the body of the Fishmen. By crawling inside, he too became a part of that body. I hardly belong to the human world any longer, he thought, except in this one regard, that I keep wriggling forward, pulling myself along with my arms and pushing with my legs, winding through the metal tubes of this great beast, tubes that have somehow grown into alien arteries.

And he was the antibody, crawling towards the critical heart of the duplicitous beast.

'Here we come,' he beamed telepathically. 'I'll get you, you bastards. I'll splinter you along the lines of creation. In other words, I'll blast you to all hell.'

There was a faint vibration now, in the walls. They had to be nearing the core, the atomic pile. He could feel it rather than hear it, the feathery whisper of the ship's core. He and Beverly would trace those jiggling atoms right back to their source, and they would kill it, blow the beast back to the other side of time.

He put plenty of energy into these thoughts. Heaps of amplification. Maybe thought alone would do the job, no need for fancy explosives. Maybe thoughts of this kind were like nuclear bombs going off for the Fishmen. He fervently hoped so.

This is my Fishness. I swim against a tide of metal into distance facing. I swim upstream against the timeslip, pulling myself along with human hands. I seek a place to make amends, to cauterise the wound, to heal that which has been infected. Words came into his head, spoken in his own voice, but coming through the suit-com, *'I dreamed and behold I saw a man clothed in rags standing in a certain place, with his face from his own house.'* I seek a channel for my own birth, a channel through the shapes and forms that compromise the worlds and the dimensions of mind.

He spoke aloud into his suit-com to any sentient beings, human or otherwise, that might care to listen. *'When you have cut off all dependence upon the sense organs, your inner awareness will become as clear as crystal.'* He knew these words by heart, and although his voice was his own, it was as if someone else were speaking, a man he knew and once loved dearly. 'The differentiations of words are but false notions with no basis in reality…and thoughts arise and pass away.' As he spoke these words, which rippled out from him in waves, he thought he detected a lessening in the temporal drift.

'It's possible,' he said to Beverly, 'that a stringent approach to mental activity gives the Fishmen less to work on. I mean, if you don't buy into the absolute nature of time, if you see through time, they have less power to disrupt our grid-symbol constructs.'

'Good thinking,' she said, and although she spoke approvingly, Nortikiss still felt a little miffed, as if she were patronising him. 'The less investment we have in our ideas, the less it will matter if they are stripped away.'

He had to agree, but it seemed to him that she had stripped his wonderful idea away until there wasn't much left of it but a commonplace observation.

Their tunnel led them to a room, comfortably human-sized. There was a large oval conference table with suck-cup holders for drinking coffee in null-grav, a water cooler, empty, and, hanging motionless, upside-down over the table, the corpse of a man. His feet were folded together in a meditative position, his back was straight, his head bent towards his chest. If he had been sitting on the floor the right way up he might have been mistaken for somebody meditating. Until you got close and noticed one eye hanging halfway down his face. The corpse was naked, the skin mummified, as it does in space where there are no microbes to break down tissue. The grey skin and mummification made him look very old, a wizened ancient.

'Let's get out of here,' Nortikiss said, already turning for the door at the other end of the room. 'One-eye, come in please.'

But One-eye didn't come in. There was nothing but the great sigh of empty space. 'One-eye, come in please.'

The corpse stared at him with its one good eye.

'No, no!' Nortikiss said. 'That can't be right.'

He went to launch himself into effortless flight to the door but ran into some kind of resistance. This was not the temporal undertow, but something more akin to gravity, pushing back against him. He could push through it but only with effort.

'I'm trying not to panic,' he confessed to Beverly. It was not exactly claustrophobia he was feeling as he pushed against the vacuum that had suddenly become viscous, nobody with a fear of enclosed spaces could become a Federation Captain, but on the other hand nobody, no matter how heroic, would relish being trapped in gooey time like a fly in amber. 'And I'm trying not to notice that the corpse looks a bit like One-eye.'

He waited for her to answer but no answer came.

He turned back to the room but Beverly wasn't there. Only the one-eyed corpse hanging motionless over the table.

'Come in, Beverly.'

But Beverly didn't come in. He couldn't hear her breathing. He couldn't even hear the sighing sound anymore. He wasn't sure any longer if he had seen her enter the room at all. 'Beverly, Zeldia Lilith or Lilith Zeldia, where are you, pussy willow?'

The use of this endearment surprised him. It sounded silly spoken aloud into a silent suit-com in a room with a floating corpse, in an abandoned ship, in the middle of a galactic void. It would sound silly anywhere, and Nortikiss realized that he couldn't remember ever using it. It wasn't his style.

He turned back for the door and found he was already there. The gooeyness had gone, the laws of physics were restored, except… except he couldn't remember getting from the table to the door. A fractional time slip. Maybe Beverly walked into a big one, a big crack in time. And now he was alone.

Or maybe she just slipped away to die.

The temporal blast hit him, hard and unexpected. Matter itself quivered as the fabric of his mind ripped. He was a child, not long on his feet, learning how to be a toddler, staggering from one tentative step to the next. His grandfather was in front of him, smiling, holding out his hands, encouraging. 'Steady as she goes,' his grandfather said. Then he was lying at his mother's breast, which was huge and soft and infinitely comforting. Warmth was filling him up from top to bottom. His tiny toes curled in pleasure. And before that… the dark spaces of the *Omega,* with him floating in the amniotic fluid of null-grav, pulling himself into another corridor where there was no up or down, just lateral movement. He'd almost forgotten his mission. All he knew was that he was heading for the core where all the force arrayed against him would be dealt with.

Nortikiss sang as loud as he could, full of gusto:

'I was already falling when the bullets arrived
her chest it fell open and Lindy Loo died.
I must bid farewell to my dutiful wife
And the passionate bar girl who gave her own life.'

If Beverly was anywhere in this quadrant of the universe she would be sure to comment. No comment came.

'One-eye, come in please.'

One-eye didn't come in.

It doesn't take much, he thought, as he pushed on deeper into the innards of the *Omega*. A mere wrinkle in the skin of time and Zeldia never joined the space cadets, never changed her name to Beverly, never met her fearless lover, Captain October Nortikiss. A flicker of a quantum eyelid and his Chief Officer no longer sat in the *Frolix 6* desperately trying to raise the landing party, but was hanging upside down in null-grav in a ship that had been drifting for a millennia.

Blind with grief, he swung himself through the passages of the ship, hardly bothering to monitor his course. In null-grav all directions are equal. It hardly seemed to matter which way he went. Perhaps if she had died in front of him, he would not have felt so strongly. Somehow the loss of something he might never have had was even more poignant. As a childless woman will grieve for children she never had, Nortikiss grieved for a life he had never lived. Or might have lived in another universe.

His path took him to a cargo bay, stacked with boxes, some of them ripped open. Despite his dire predicament, curiosity drew him to the boxes. Succeeding generations of 3D printers had just about put an end to galactic trade. Why haul stuff between stars at great expense when you can replicate anything you want at home with your household gubbler? How these 3D printers came to be called gubblers, had been lost to time, but from an input of rock and metal these machines could churn out anything from microchips to houses. Physical trade became focused on 'authentic' items that couldn't be replicated, works of art, local delicacies, historical items, collectables – anything that lost its flavour when replicated in a gubbler. Sceptics maintained that there was no difference between, say, a handcrafted chair and its gubbled replicate, but many maintained that there was, and that they knew the difference just by picking the item up and holding it.

He floated "down" to one of the open boxes and examined the contents. Novels. Old, pulp novels circa mid to late 20th Century. Ancient, offset press printing method, prior to digitalisation. These books, if they were authentic, were worth a lot of Confederation credits. He picked one up. The cover depicted a black lake out of which was rising a slimy monster.

THE CREATURE OF THE BLACK LAGOON the title shouted. The monster was threatening to engulf a screaming woman who looked a lot like Beverly. TO YOUR SCATTERED BODIES GO another announced, showing rows of people in stasis pods. Another was a real rarity, two novels in one volume with a front cover on each side, upside down in relation to each other. Just turn the book over and you have another novel. TIME OUT OF JOINT was the title of one of the novels. It showed a man and woman, he a business suit with an umbrella just like mine, she with red high heels and a short red skirt, confronting a dinosaur busy ripping up houses and trees. Flip the book over and it became THE MAZE OF DEATH which showed a huge gubbler gobbling up a world and spewing out limp watches from a Salvador Dali painting.

He was about to move on when he noticed another garish volume. CAPTAIN NORTIKISS AND THE FISHMEN FROM THE OTHER SIDE OF TIME, the title trumpeted in embossed lettering. Winner of the Jules Verne Memorial Award, the cover boasted. And there he was, the space hero himself, lantern-jawed and determined. And there was Beverly, green-eyed and red-haired in a clinging space gown. Both were confronting a scaly monster with a reptilian tale. The monster was wearing a helmet from which malignant waves were emanating.

Nortikiss turned the book over and read the blurb on the back.

Can aliens be repulsed by the contents of an official brown envelope? What happens when a writer's alarm clock becomes skilled in Buddhist discourse? What are the dangers of remembering too much? And who is the woman in the fishnet stockings? The fate of the universe hangs on the answers to these questions as Captain October Nortikiss and his luscious sidekick Beverly board the ancient star trader, the Omega, where the dreaded Fishmen are spawning, to save the universe from a fate worse than entropy.

Another gripping October Nortikiss adventure!

Good grief, Nortikiss thought, there are more of them. Maybe a whole series. Appalled, he put the book down, but not before noticing that it had been written by Clark Kent, a pseudonym if ever there was one. This

Mr Kent should be ashamed of himself, turning out such drivel. He didn't have a clue what the real fight against the Fishmen was like. All he wanted to do was cash in with these cheap, tawdry novels. There was probably an obligatory sex scene every ten pages with lots of salacious detail.

There was another book by Clark Kent floating near the opened cases that confirmed his worst fear. CLONED SEX the cover announced with a leer. It showed two girls dressed in lace panties, one with a finger in her mouth and her bottom stuck out, the other with her finger looped into the panties of the first. In the background comets and stars whizzed by. Both girls were identical. Neither had navels. Still another cheap and nasty Kent novel appeared. He had disturbed the pile, set some of the books in motion, which were now floating about or heading off for destinations of their own with no gravity to break their inertial movement. HEAT INTERSECTION VECTOR this one was called, presented in three-dimensional black lettering with the 'A' upside down and the 'R' tumbled forward onto what looked like a cross between a ruined gothic castle and a worse-for-wear spaceship suspiciously similar to the *Omega*. Smaller lettering beneath said *Part 5 of The Tower Chronicles*. An exploding star on the bottom right-hand corner contained the words, 'Another Zeldia Lilith Adventure!' And here she was, her red hair swept back off her face, her eyes as green and glassy as a doll's, floating half naked in deep space, in a yellow blouse he'd seen many times, here ripped from shoulder to breast, her face lit up in orgasm.

Nortikiss turned away, embarrassed. Yes, Beverly was the finest sex-object that nature ever created, at least in his opinion, yet she didn't deserve this sort of treatment. If he ever met this Clark Kent, he would have words with him. More than words. Inside HEAT INTERSECTION VECTOR there was a brief account of the author, saying that he lived with his wife in The City of Destruction and that he enjoyed taking long walks.

In disgust he threw the book away. He should have known better than to give way to an impulsive action in null-grav. HEAT INTERSECTION VECTOR hit the open case and books started flying everywhere.

I've got get out of here, Nortikiss thought, as he began to fight off random attacks by cheap novels. Fighting them off only made it worse, of course, giving the books more momentum. When a Clark Kent volume hit his oxygen tank, Nortikiss took fright. He'd stirred up a rats' nest of pulp fiction. It might take years for the energy he'd given these books to fade. For a thousand years maybe they would be jumping around in here, bouncing off the walls and off each other.

'I'm coming for you,' he beamed as he pulled himself through the door and closed it behind him. One lone volume made it through before he got the door closed and whizzed off down the corridor before him.

'One-eye, Beverly, come in please.'

Nobody came in.

It was all up to him now. He had no past, no future. No centre, no circumference. Time and circumstance pealed away.

From one momentary sensation to another, one should always be able to realize, to realize… to realize what?

He couldn't remember.

He swam on alone.

❦

When the right moment arrives, Evie wakes me up.

'I'm sick of feeding the ducks,' she says. 'And I'm running out of crusts, too.'

I look up at the blue arch of the sky and a few feathery clouds. Around us the leaves are dancing yellow and brown.

I feel rested, and happy to be alive, and I don't think too hard about why I needed to stop and have that brief sleep.

'Do you think I treat Evelyn badly?' I ask Evie, who can be quite wise at times. For some reason I have woken up with Evelyn on my mind. I don't think it's guilt I'm feeling, more puzzlement. I keep seeing her disappointed face; crestfallen I think is the word. And disappointment slips easily into bitterness, which eats the soul. 'We've been a bit… at cross purposes.'

She screws up her face in concentration. 'You don't beat her, or come home drunk every day or anything like that. There was a story in the news about a man who threw his girlfriend's baby at a wall to stop it from crying. Do you know why?'

'Why?'

'Because he wanted to watch a yacht race on television.' Evie's face is very serious. 'You don't do anything like that.'

'Jesus, that's hardly any comfort. What happened to the man?'

'He got a good telling off by the judge. And you shouldn't swear.'

'What happened to the baby?'

'I don't know.' She begins to fiddle with her skipping rope. She really doesn't like these kinds of conversations. She just wants to get back to skipping and singing.

'Hey! We know some of the horrible things I *don't* do. So what do I *do*?' *Do-be-do-be-do.*

'Well, sometimes you act as if she's not there. You just sort of ignore her. Once she masturbated right in front of you, and you didn't take any notice because you were writing.'

'I don't remember that.'

'That's the point. Being ignored can be worse than getting a beating.'

'Really?'

'Really.'

'You're not seriously telling me that someone would *prefer* a beating.'

'It's possible. At least it indicates a kind of interest, some attention, even if the wrong kind.'

'Okay, so what else do I do? What are my other crimes?'

'Nothing, I suppose. At least, that she knows about. But the sex is all wrong too.'

'What do you mean?'

'I don't like to talk about it.'

'I know you don't, but you can't just say that and leave it there.'

'You need to talk to her.'

'I know, but tell me anyway.'

'She says you are absent, even while having sex.'

'Absent?'

'Out of your body.'

'How's that possible?'

'I don't know, it's up to you to work it out.'

Evie picked up her skipping rope and started skipping on the spot. *Swish-slap, swish-slap.*

I consider the placid river that borders the park. I want to have some philosophic thoughts about the river so that I don't have to think about Evelyn, and all my failings, but none occur. I'm sure if I wait long enough something will come. I do, however, see an Indian man kneeling by the river, allowing the water to trickle through his fingers. Maybe he's having the philosophical thoughts.

It really is a very pretty river.

We resume our walk, this time at a more leisurely pace, no wafting along.

'It's a good idea to be happy when you have the chance,' Evie says. 'And you have the chance right now.'

'That's right, I have a chance right now.'

There are perfections all around to be noticed and enjoyed. The perfection of blue for the sky and white for the clouds, the mathematical exactitude of the gull's parabolic glide towards the ocean, the rise and fall of a child's body dancing to a skipping rope, the feel of water passing through the fingers, the tidy obedience of traffic.

Evie is right. Why should I worry? I'm quite happy to be shouldered aside and forgotten. I'm quite happy to fade into history. Just to be an ordinary Clark Kent walking along. Quite happy to lie on park benches and let weeds grow out of my guts. Quite happy to allow my destination to declare itself without any fuss or bother.

Steady as she goes.

The official leans over me, studying my face intently. The young woman and the young man with blonde ponytails are standing in the background, watching. The hose running into my arm is filled with clear liquid.

I think of Evelyn. Might she really still be standing at the window, looking out at the street, standing that way forever? I think of Evie, who I trust is waiting for me outside on the street.

I try to think of something to say.

'That doesn't look like blood.' I gesture to the hose.

'It's not. It's plasma.'

A large machine has been wheeled to my table. It has a black snout pointing down at me.

'It's a subsonic scanner. The latest model.' A touch of pride enters his voice. 'We're going to take slides of some of your molecular plumbing.'

'Stop talking down to me, as if I were a child.'

He glances at his two assistants. Something passes between them I'm not supposed to notice.

'Tell me what you are really doing.'

It is the fresh-faced young woman who answers, and she does not talk down to me. 'We are testing to see if you are infected by an alien organism.'

I stare at her bland, pretty face. It reveals nothing.

'What kind of organism?'

'We don't know. Certainly no bigger than a virus. Maybe much smaller, nano size.' Her ponytail bobs up and down in agreement.

'What do you mean by alien?'

'Extraterrestrial, Mr Kent.'

I try not to laugh. Their serious faces make it easy.

'How did I manage to catch it? This alien virus.'

'Probably sexually transmitted.'

This time I do laugh. Or at least try to.

'Are you telling me I've had sex with an alien? Ooooh, all those lovely tentacles.'

'Or will have.'

That brings me up short. It reminds me of certain conversations I've had recently with my alarm clock. And with Evie. Evie, dancing around me counterclockwise singing, 'What's the time, Mr Wolfie?' with me counting down the hours in reply, *'Twelve o'clock, eleven o'clock, ten o'clock...'*

'You're going to have to explain that.'

Smoothly, the young man takes over. 'I wish we could, Mr Kent. This is an alien organism; it does not seem to obey our laws of cause and effect. The effect can come before the cause.'

So my future self has already had sex with an alien and effectively doomed me to a lingering death. Where is the justice in that? Where's the free will? Where's the moral responsibility? All of these things are rooted in causality.

The young man patted the subsonic scanner as if it were an oversized pet. 'Don't worry, Mr Kent. Our friend here can scan you in a jiffy.'

Jiffy?

He swings the machine's black snout down until it is level with my temple. 'You won't feel anything. Maybe a slight ringing in the ears.'

That reminds me of something. 'How do I know that this thing,' I pointed at the black snout hovering near my right ear, 'isn't the Einstein Disrupter, getting ready to blast me back along my timeline?'

'What's that?' the official asked, leaning forward interestedly. 'What are you talking about?'

'Nothing. Just a cheap story on the back of a cereal packet.' I'd put my foot in it, saying that.

To throw them off the scent, I said, 'I want to know about the drugs you're giving me. These polyamomorphydes, metatryptaline and God knows what. How do you know that my metabolism won't go haywire, and put me into a cataleptic shock or something? I mean, if I'm infected by some alien superbug, you don't know what those drugs will do to my metabolism. Maybe the aliens eat that kind of stuff for breakfast, like cereal.'

'Your drugs are for memory support only, Mr Kent. The alien organism may be benign as far as your body goes, you may even experience moments of physical elation due to energy surges, but your mind is much more vulnerable.'

The ponytailed twins nod solemnly.

'In what way?'

'We are still studying that. In the meantime we are giving you some of our cutting-edge pharmaceuticals for memory support.'

I notice he's used that term twice now. 'There's nothing wrong with my memory.'

'Maybe not, but it seems to us that not all your memories are actually yours.'

'Say that again, slowly.'

'Are you having any dreams, or experiencing memories that don't appear to belong to you?'

'No.' One thing my grandfather taught me, from his experience in the army, never volunteer anything, or for anything. I've already put my foot in it once by babbling about the Einstein Disrupter, I'm not about to make the same mistake again.

I cannot, however, help but say, 'If all this is true, why am I not in quarantine? How come you let me wander around freely in the uninfected population, maybe have sex with somebody and pass the infection on?'

'You *are* in quarantine.'

'Then your memory support drugs are not working. I distinctly remember walking half-way across town to get here. And having all sorts of torrid adventures along the way.'

'We don't know how you got here, Mr Kent.'

'That's not the point.'

'The point is, you might be living multiple lifetimes at the same time. We do our best to serve our clients and the good of greater mankind. Here at *The Omega Unit* we take all care but no responsibility. There are no guarantees, just the highest standards and the very latest, up-to-date equipment,' he strokes the scanner with affection, 'and the most highly trained technical staff,' he nods to the ponytail twins, 'as well as the best theoretical brains Confederation credits can buy,' he gestures to the old-fashioned blackboard with its *"Lois screws Spiderman"* graffiti. 'So as you can see you are in the most safe and secure place in the whole universe right now. But unfortunately, in this situation, there may well be *leakage*. An infection of this kind is totally new to us. None of our protocols cover this contingency. We can seal off rooms, create decontamination chambers and call it quarantine, but there are no sealed compartments in nature. There is always *leakage*. Even in our larger, eleven-dimensional multiverse there are leakages from one dimension to another. Gravity itself might well be the result of crossover energies from another dimension. That's the latest theory. When we finally do the maths that unify gravity and time the way Einstein unified energy and matter, we will have a more complete description of our universe, and we may be able to prevent these situations from ever arising, or at least deal with them when they do. And I do appreciate the tactical urgency.'

During this extraordinary speech, I begin to suffer from a certain leakage of my own, as the official's voice becomes increasingly familiar. I know that voice, and that tone, but I just can't put my finger on it.

'Did you say, *Omega* unit?'

The official nods to the male ponytail, who presses a portable plunger device he's holding. There is a whirr and click from the scanner. Nothing happens. Everything happens. I know that it is impossible to study something without changing it, but I don't know if these people have any real clue how they might be changing their object of study – me.

'Yes. In this facility we can keep the oxygen levels optimum.'

I decide, as the subsonic scanner is wheeled about and repositioned, poised right over my genitals, to play along as I have done from the start. In the face of the implicit aggression of the world, I play possum. My grandfather told me of a soldier who survived by crawling under a pile of dead bodies and pretending to be dead until the battle had moved on. That would be my strategy. I would bear the weight of the dead gladly for that chance to crawl out from under. Of course, my grandfather added, it could only be a temporary expedient, since the victorious troops of whatever side would kill the dead twice just to make sure.

I make it clear to the official, and the ponytail twins, that I don't envy them in their roles of reality maintenance. The strains on them and the institutions that support them must be enormous. They have all my sympathy. It takes a lot of energy to maintain these superstructures of thought, these reality constructs. I make quite a speech waving my free hand about, the one not attached to the plasma drip, to emphasise my points. The only difference between his symbol-grid construct and mine is that his is sustained and reinforced by a material manifestation: the anteroom, the office, this lab, the subsonic scanner, the whole building in which it is all housed. It takes a lot of energy, money in this case, to sustain this material reality.

I admire them, I say, for taking on the role they have, which can't be easy. It must be wearying avoiding any personal involvement. When the official gets home after work, I speculate, he probably does yoga or TM or deep breathing exercises. Or perhaps he mixes himself a good stiff drink. With a martini or Scotch in hand, he can look out his window at our neatly arranged city, a grid of lights floating in space. He can, with equanimity, consider the huge illuminated suitcase flying off to LA or Hong Kong. He can be serene. He can detect no change in the angle of the liquid in his glass. He's not about to fall over, or let the world tilt him sideways. He can rest content that he has done his duty keeping the perpendiculars perpendicular and the horizontals horizontal. He can sit back and bathe in the love of a good wife.

He has done his bit for reality maintenance.

As I speak, he nods to his male assistant who presses his little plunger. *Whirr/click*. The scanner enters the conversation. Nothing happens, except my genitals want to retreat into my body. I keep talking. The scanner is repositioned again, this time right over my navel.

The official is nodding and smiling as I talk.

How would he react, I ask him, if I were to get up off this hard bench and smash his face in.

He nods and smiles. His bell jangles.

I go on talking in a theoretical vein, explaining to him that in essence there is very little difference between us. To an outside observer, an alien from another planet, let's say, our relative positions would be interchangeable. Reverse our positions and the basic equations will stay the same. We are both subsets of a total system the ultimate nature of which must remain mysterious and inaccessible to both of us. How can the part comprehend the whole?

He nods and smiles. *Whirr/click*. Nothing happens.

In fact, I say, it's rather wonderful the way we work in tandem together to keep the universe running, to keep everything from falling apart.

The female ponytail hands me some headphones.

'How about a little music, Mr Kent? This can be a little boring.'

I want to tell her that I'm not in the least bored, and that I am enjoying this little chat with them, but I take the headphones anyway, so as not to disappoint the young woman. It would be a shame to mark her smooth skin with lines of concern for my well-being.

I close my eyes and wait for the music. No music comes, but a voice I recognise. The voice of my alarm clock. Somehow it has followed me all the way here.

From all this arises conceptions of like and unlikes, and then conceptions of non-likes and non-unlikes, and the mind is thrown into a medley of bewildering puzzles which in time become attached to the mind and contaminate it. In the end these attachments and contaminations within your mind encourage the consciousness between the self and the not-self of objects. Thus the pure mind becomes further entangled in the snarls of attachments and contaminations.

Evie and I emerge from the park into the busyness of houses, streets and shopping centres. It seems to take a long time for everything to settle down into its accustomed order and familiar forgetfulness. Houses float by upside down, and fish creatures swim out of the clouds, nibbling at delicious treetops, water bubbles floating up from their mouths. On the street, pieces of furniture stand around in groups, conversing like people. A haughty lampshade leans over a bluff couch. A kitchen table climbs into a double bed. On a street corner, a lone violin plays a haunting Celtic melody composed from the most ancient memories of man. Some easy chairs are waiting at the traffic lights for the green man, but get huffy when Evie tries to sit in one.

People pass by, some of them floating above the street, and I notice lots of women who look like Evelyn. They have strong bodies and gentle mouths, and their hair is long and smooth. Their eyes are sad and their bodies move to the music of their bones. They are all in mourning or deep in prayer. I think of the real Evelyn at home, no longer standing at the window, no doubt, but sitting at the kitchen table with her work spread out before her, her head cupped in her hands.

'Do you think Evelyn's happy?' I ask Evie as the world begins to right itself, and things hasten to their accustomed place. I think about her work as an architect, and how she loves the precision of ruler and set-square, compass and lettering guides.

'You'll have to ask her,' Evie answers carefully.

'How long was I asleep on the park bench?'

'A couple of hundred years.'

'That's funny.'

'Or a couple of thousand.' She does a few skips as if to illustrate.

A car goes past, its paintwork shiny, its windows gleaming and reflective.

'Where is all the dust and grime, Evie? Where are the sordid little corners, the vacant lots, the dirty alleys?' I gesture to the world at large. 'Everything is so clean and shiny, I don't even see any dog poo…'

Evie says, 'The city takes pride in looking spic-and-span. One of the cleanest cities in the world, the brochures say – and they don't lie. Everyone who lives here is a good citizen, and does their civic duty to keep a nice sparkle on everything. Nobody litters, for example. Do you see any litter around?'

'No I don't. But did you say *everybody* is a good citizen?' The idea makes me uneasy.

'Well, almost everybody. There are always a few slovens, but they are not allowed to practice their messiness on the street.'

I increase my pace a little. I don't really want to walk faster, I just want to feel the thud of my feet against the all-too-clean street. I want to feel it jarring right up through my body. In the same spirit I touch as much as I can, to get the feel of the world, fences, lampposts, walls, parked cars, neatly polished shop windows. I breathe deep to feel the clean, sharp air in my body. Space opens up in front of me and swallows up the world behind. This space goes on spreading as far as the mind can think, beyond the city and the tawny hills, beyond the hawk and the shingle slides, beyond the globe of the earth, and even the stars, to the gigantic stellar reaches that stretch beyond the mind.

If I follow that space too far, I get giddy, so I concentrate on the scene at hand. There's a man going past on a bicycle, peddling away without touching the handlebars like a circus clown, balancing the sun on his head and the world on his arms. I stop to clap.

'Anybody can do that,' Evie says.

A comet passes over the dry face of the moon. Evelyn picks up a drawing-pen. Ideas are flowing all around us like a swarm of soft birds in bright feathers. Evie skips to the rotating motion of her arms.

I pause at a shop which advertises itself as The Very Last Tobacconist on Earth. Its display window harks back to the Nineteenth Century with its small wooden framed panels, nicely oiled, the frame decorated with carvings of pipes, tobacco leaves, and more exotic smoking implements. The shop could have come straight out of Charles Dickens' more cosy corners of London. A variety of tobaccos, pipes, cigars and fancy cigarette papers are displayed on a purple cloth.

'What are you stopping here for?' Evie asks, looking askance at the displays.

'Just catching my breath.' In the corner of the display there is a dusty, sepia picture of a woman dressed like a flapper from the nineteen twenties with a rounded helmet style hat, from under which curls are allowed to emerge, and a broad belt around a clinging gown. A long, ivory cigarette holder, complete with burning cigarette, she holds elegantly in a slim, gloved hand. She stares out at the viewer, daring anybody to object.

'I want to buy that.' I point to the picture.

'Why?'

'I want to give it to Grandad. His mother probably looked like that.'

'I don't think you are telling the full truth,' Evie says.

I enter the shop and buy a packet of tobacco, matches and cigarette papers. The truth is, I don't really smoke, only times like this when the pressure's on, and I have nothing to breathe but the blue air, and leaves shiver inside their green skins like children huddling under their blankets on a scary night.

'It will make you nauseous,' Evie says. 'Remember what happened last time? I don't want to be with you if you are going to start vomiting in public places.'

'I don't remember that,' I said with a touch of indignation.

The tobacconist is small and balding with dark lassos around his eyes. His skin has a wrinkled, parchment quality that follows from a lifetime's addiction to nicotine. He has laid out my three items in a straight line on the counter.

I offer to exchange pleasantries, but he declines. Maybe being The Very Last Tobacconist on Earth gives him the right to be the Last Grumpy Retailer on Earth.

'How much do you want for the picture of the flapper in the window?'

He regards me for a long moment without answering or moving so much as a muscle in his face. 'It's not a picture, it's a photograph,' he says in a thick, phlegmy voice.

'That photograph then, what's it worth?'

Again the long silence and the poker face.

'Thirty credits,' he says eventually, still not cracking his face, although I have the feeling that when he opened his mouth he was going to ask for twenty and thirty just slipped out. Slippage everywhere.

'That seems just fine,' I say agreeably. He watches expressionlessly as I produce my Long Life direct debiting card. In doing this, I am taking something of a gamble. Before leaving home, my alarm clock had haughtily announced that my current account stood at nought point nought-nought credits. But by its own grudging admission, I still have sixty-six credits and thirty-seven sub-credits in my Long Life account with Virtue Savings Bank.

'I assume you are a registered business,' I say, holding the card between two fingers like a cigarette.

He doesn't deign to answer.

The tobacconist feeds my card into his countertop unit, and there is a pause as his unit confers with my alarm clock. I'm glad I'm not privy to that conversation. I breathe a sigh of relief when the purchase goes through. I calculate that I now have thirty-six credits and thirty-seven sub-credits remaining in my Long Life savings account. I make a mental note to thank the alarm clock personally when I get home; relations have been a little chill between us recently.

He hands me the picture, the photograph, which has a nice scalloped frame of dark wood. As it goes into a large plain brown paper bag, the flapper gives me a sly, conniving glance.

I nod politely to the tobacconist and head for the door, noticing for the first time an old-fashioned barber's chair made of black leather and ornate brass fittings. It harks back to the day when the tobacconist was also the man who cut hair and, if required, would bring out the razor for a morning-after shave. Just looking at it made me think of my grandfather, whose own grandfather, I think, had a chair just like this. It was the latest thing for its time, with a lever for raising and lowering the back.

'How much do you want for this?' I ask, gesturing to the chair with my imaginary umbrella, which has turned a lush red.

'Five hundred credits,' he says, his face still the parchment mask of the addict. Again I thought he intended to ask for four hundred but suffered another slippage of the tongue. Perhaps what he really meant to say was that the antique chair is not for sale, but business is not exactly brisk at The Very Last Tobacconist on Earth. I sympathise. I know how it feels to be betrayed by my mouth.

I hesitate, pretending to consider, stroking my clean-shaven chin and staring at the chair. I can feel Evie's eyes upon me. 'I'll think it over,' I promise, pushing open the door.

'How do I do this?' I ask Evie. 'How do I get myself into these situations?'

Cheerfully, she says, 'You just walk right into them. You set them up, then you walk into them.'

'Why?'

She shrugs, looking like a little adult, 'Because you're such a nice man. You want everybody to be happy. Like that tobacconist. You were just trying to bring a smile to his face. He didn't look like he'd smiled for a very long time.'

'You're right… hey! I forgot to bring the picture.'

Much as I hate the thought, I backtrack to the tobacconist.

As I walk in, he holds up the paper bag containing the picture. I take the picture and turn to go.

'I want a chocolate,' Evie says.

I get her some chocolates, a few little ones, dark with peppermint inside. Evelyn's change comes in handy.

I pull a little hard on the door and an old-fashioned bell tinkles.

'How much for a shave and trim?' I ask, gesturing to the chair.

He smiles.

Instead of returning to the compound where the monks would be gathering for Siddhartha's morning talk, Ananda wandered up the riverbank in the direction of the women's huts, still clutching his wooden bowl, thinking about the little girl with the skipping-rope, and his cousin Siddhartha sitting under the Bodhi tree amid glowing lotus blossoms experiencing the unconditioned, essential mind. These two beings shared one marvellous quality, he thought: innocence. In Siddhartha's case, that innocence had been earned by many hours of pure awareness, while the girl still possessed the innocence she was born with.

As he was thinking these things, he passed a woman washing clothes at the river. She hardly glanced at him, so intent she was on her task. The world stains us the way it stains that shirt the woman is scrubbing against the rock, he thought. If it takes so much scrubbing and swift clean water to work out those stains in a piece of cotton, how much more scrubbing might it take to clear the stains on the soul.

This was a pleasing metaphor, suggested by the world itself, the woman washing her shirt, but it already contained within it the seeds of error and wishful thinking. Only through ignorance and delusion do men indulge in the dream that their souls are separate and self-existing entities that may be reborn in some imagined Heaven, or in another life. Their heart still clings to Self. 'Searching for a soul in man is like searching for something in a dark empty room.' Siddhartha had said. 'What can a dog find in the darkness of its own box?'

He had also said that the Hindus use their belief in reincarnation to try to scare people into being good. People were terrified that they would be reborn as a dog or a jackal or vulture, and that was supposed to keep them in line. Virtue through terror is really no virtue at all, just further entanglement in the appearances of the world.

Whenever Ananda was tempted by a belief in independently existing souls, he liked to remind himself, in the words of Siddhartha, that we are like children who wish to grasp a rainbow. For them, the rainbow is vivid and real, but adults know it is merely an illusion caused by certain rays of light and drops of water. And the light which creates the rainbow is only a series of waves or undulations with no more reality than the rainbow itself.

At that moment he was joined by the eldest of his three brothers, Devadatta, who loved to argue. Ananda told him about the children and the rainbow, and how, like children reaching for rainbows, we go chasing off after souls.

Devadatta said, 'As always, the teaching is true. However, the rainbow may be an illusion of light and water, but it is still beautiful.'

'So beauty may deceive the eye,' Ananda said.

'Or awaken us to the world. Some say they have dreamed of past lives, of being born and reborn.'

'What is there to be reborn? Every moment we are being born and dying. If nothing is carried over from one moment to the next, how can anything be carried over from one life to the next? The self is a creation of mind, not the other way around.'

This is a point on which Devadatta always got stuck. He would seem to agree but was so enchanted by his own cleverness he could hardly believe that his thoughts did not emanate from an equally clever self, an immortal self what's more. A Self with a capital S. Thus, even the cleverest minds fall into fantasy.

'We are what we think,' Ananda says, savouring in that moment of utterance the truth of it. 'All that we are arises with our thoughts. With our thoughts, we make the world.' He often avoided quoting Siddhartha, as people found it tiresome; and because he never did so out of pride for his own cleverness, he wanted to avoid that impression. Because of this, and because he was always trying to find words of his own for Siddhartha's teachings, people had come to believe that he himself was a wise one! With his brother, however, he didn't hold back. He quoted, *All phenomena are impermanent, existing simply in our own minds, and so, as we see the insubstantial character of these things, knowing them simply as objects of sense, thou shouldest devote no more thought to them.'*

'Yes,' Devadatta said. 'Siddhartha has a way of turning words against words, ideas against ideas until nothing is left. Remember all that business about the likes and the unlikes and the non-likes and non-unlikes.'

'That's very true,' Ananda said. His brother was quick to understand but even slower than Ananda in applying his understanding. *We use words to get away from words until we reach the pure wordless essence.'*

'So for Siddhartha, every idea cancels itself out until not even the stars are left to shine in the sky, and many thousands of years, thousands of thousands of years, are nothing more than a puff of wind. This great and beautiful world of ours becomes merely an echo of our sensory impressions.'

'I have heard Siddhartha say so. Even the ten realms of existence, each containing within it the remaining nine, are all manifestations of mind.'

'What folly is that, brother? To turn our backs on the wonders of the world? To close our eyes and stop up our ears and will the world away?'

'Ah, Devadatta, brother of mine, I know you too well...'

'What do you mean?' Devadatta looked hurt.

'You are only saying these things because you desire supernatural powers. Kings dream of immortality; their jesters dream of supernatural powers. Perhaps you would turn into the leopard or a hawk? But for what purpose? Just for the sensation of running or hovering?'

'Now you sound like Siddhartha, whose logic is like the stoutest bear trap.' Devadatta was on a familiar path from hurt to resentment.

Ananda wanted to take his hand and pause there, and do nothing but watch the river slide by. Instead, he said, 'Remember, as children, we used to run across the hills pretending we were leopards? Then you wanted to fly. But not just pretend fly.'

'I didn't want to turn into a hawk.'

'That's right. You said, "The great yogis of old knew how to fly." Do you remember?'

'Yes, and I was right. They could fly without turning into birds. They could shrug the weight of the air off their shoulders as if it were nothing.'

'And you want Siddhartha to teach you to do the same?'

'Why not? He could do it, you know. He has the power.'

Ananda knew Siddhartha's power only too well. The greater part of it lay in his compassion, which at times was almost too hard to bear, and which filled Ananda with a particular shame, which was like the shame of being naked in front of somebody.

'He cured our sister,' Devadatta said.

The brothers were silent as they remembered Rohini, their only sister, and the hideous skin disease that had blighted her beauty and sent her into seclusion. People became afraid of her, but not Siddhartha. He visited her and sat by her side, and guided her to the spiritual source of the illness and was able to cure it. Siddhartha said that Rohini had cured herself, but many, including Devadatta, saw further evidence of Siddhartha's special powers.

'He could do it if he wanted to, and other things too. The great yogis of old also knew how to make things appear out of nothing. Even jewels. Diamonds, glowing rubies.'

'If they came out of nothing, they are nothing – why should you care?'

'You Stream Enterers! It's all the same to you, isn't it? How dull! We could be as gods. Leap across universes! Dally in gardens of delight with milkmaids, the way that blue boy did, Shankar or Krishna or whatever name he takes in these parts. To be like the Weaver at the Loom of Time!'

'Is that want you want? To be a god? To live in the garden of delight!'

'There are worse things to be sure.'

'Would you rather live in illusion than in the truth?'

Devadatta laughed suddenly and clapped his brother on the shoulder, as if about to push him over the way he used to do when they were children. 'Always the solemn one! But you can't fool me either, Ananda. I know you just as well as you know me. I see the way the girls look at you.'

'It can't hurt them to look,' Ananda said with a little grin, a grin that made him look just like Devadatta.

'But all they see is virtue, right? The pure vessel, guardian of the dharma.'

'You mock me, brother.'

'But that is what they call you, the other monks, and even our cousin Siddhartha may believe it…'

'And you are jealous of this?'

'Not of all this solemnity. You should see these monks with their long faces.'

'But of me? My memory.'

'Why would I want to remember every little thing? See this fly that wants to land on my face. I brush it away, and a moment later I have forgotten it. And it has forgotten me. Surely that is a blessing. The better part of memory is in the forgetting.'

'Ah, you are being mischievous now, brother. I may *choose* to forget such trivial occurrences. But not a word our cousin has uttered has left my head. That I call a blessing.'

'And what about this path you are walking right now? It's not taking you back to the camp, but surely leads to the women's village…'

'That's right.'

'But your bowl is still in your hand. Are you going begging among the women?'

'I have a call to go there, someone who needs my help.'

'Ah… your help. And who is this someone?'

'The maiden Pchiti.'

'Ah… the maiden Pchiti.'

Ananda nodded, and firmly refused to blush.

'Who just happens to be a great beauty. And what is the nature of her emergency? Some issue with the dharma, perhaps? Truth can be tricky when you play hide and seek with it.'

'That's true. And I don't know what her issue is. Apparently she feels out of sorts.'

'How do you know this?'

'A messenger. A little girl with a skipping rope.'

'Ah…. a go-between! I have seen this little girl myself. She is quite artful. How do you know she is not a demon sent to trick you?'

Ananda laughed. 'Now you do sound like a follower of Krishna! Siddhartha has warned us about such superstitions. Filling the mind up with demons and like creatures.'

'But even our cousin, the Awakened One, cannot will away the powers of the world.'

'Perhaps not, but he can see through to their true nature.'

By now the brothers had come in sight of the village. Ananda was amazed to see how it had grown. Siddhartha's stepmother, Mahaprajapati, had gathered around herself some five-hundred women, according to some counts. And it was Ananda who was mostly responsible! Mahaprajapati had argued unsuccessfully with Siddhartha to allow women to become monks until Ananda had intervened on the women's behalf, and engaged in a marathon argument with Siddhartha that had lasted three days. It ended, finally, when Ananda asked outright if women were capable of Entering the Stream and seeing with true sight, and Siddhartha had affirmed that that indeed was the case. Ananda could see that it disturbed his cousin to think of women taking up the homeless life, begging for food and often sleeping in the rough where they might be vulnerable, but in this case Siddhartha had been caught in the bear-trap of his own logic. Men and women were equal in their desire for freedom from the shackles of thought. But, oh, what a headache for Siddhartha, keeping the minds of his young monks on their path of purification and integrating the women into their practices.

'This is the question of our system and not whether men and women are equal. Women leaving home are like wild grass in the field which will affect the harvest,' he said, but to no avail. The wild grass was already in the field.

There were times, Ananda knew, when Siddhartha yearned for the days when, prior his Awakening, before the full moon had broken over his shoulder under the Bodhi tree, he had wandered alone and been utterly homeless. Now his home went with him wherever he went, his cousins, even his stepmother!

Ananda felt responsible for this, and somewhat responsible for making sure that all was going well in the women's village. It embarrassed him a little, the reverence the women showed him, but he fully understood the role that he taken on when interceding for the women in the first place. Now he was their saviour in all matters, and one who had the ear of Siddhartha.

He said as much to Devadatta as they approached the village.

'Now the women see me as some kind of miracle worker. They place me so high in their estimation they can no longer hear what I say. Now the maiden Pchiti thinks I am a doctor.'

'Your duties with the women must exhaust you, I'm sure. For Siddhartha will blame you if things go wrong.'

'No. The Buddha is beyond blaming.'

'Perhaps, but that won't stop Siddhartha. And here I must leave you to your duties, brother, and I must go attend my lessons in humility. Besides, I wouldn't want to frighten the women.'

'Humility is like a lake with no bottom.'

'And I must swim in it. Give my regards to the maiden Pchiti!'

Ananda watched him go and turned back to the river. It was easy for the water. It only has one place to go.

The war never ended.

My grandfather occupies a newish apartment block, one which looks older than it really is because of its general shoddiness and run-down condition.

Because of its closeness to the city, and relentless rise of property values our fair city has seen in recent years, my grandfather's slummy little apartment is worth a ridiculous amount of money, putting pressure on him to "downsize". But he has nowhere to downsize to except perhaps some dog kennel in the backyard of a decaying suburb on the outskirts of the City of Destruction.

I know he goes from one week to the next without seeing anybody but his delivery person. Evelyn once made the trip to see him just to ask him to come and live with us, but he refused. 'It is not the time,' he said, 'to desert the battlefield.'

Ever since I learned the secret of magic ink, I have wanted to write a book about my grandfather, but Grandfather has not cooperated with that plan either. Unlike many old people, who rummage around in their memories like a homeless person in a dumpster, Grandfather pretty much refuses to talk about anything but the battle of Passchendaele. When I asked him about his childhood he turned hostile and wouldn't talk for an hour. When I asked him about my grandmother he got a faraway look in his eye and that was that. Not much to build a book on.

There is the smell of urine in the stairwell, and scraps, as if somebody has been sleeping there at night, or at least camping out.

'I'd rather be outside,' I say to Evie, 'where it's all bright and cheerful.'

'Don't be a coward,' she says. 'You have to be a hero to live in this world. Being a hero means facing up to things.'

'That's not a comforting thought, for a coward.'

Grandfather's apartment is bright and cheerful enough. He is sitting up in bed, propped up by pillows, playing chess with himself, studying the puzzle of red and white squares. He has an old-fashioned chess clock alongside, time ticking furiously away for the player whose turn it is to make a move. Having made a move, he hits the little wooden bar that stops one clock and starts the other. Now it is the opponent's turn to sweat.

'How are you?' he asks in a cracked voice as I enter the room. He is holding a black knight, which is poised in the air about to strike.

'As well as can be expected,' I reply, glaring at Evie who is affecting great interest in some family photographs and bits of bric-a-brac around the room. On his cabinet there is an old clock carved into a single knot to wood. A Taj Mahal made of matchsticks my grandfather made after his heart attack. A canary cage sans canary.

'I should hope you were doing a lot better than that. Me, I always expect the worst.'

'Every day as it comes.' I give him a hug. He was once a big man, and I could still feel it in the dimensions of his chest.

'You don't want to worry about dying,' he says.

'I don't anyway.'

'Of course you do. Stay away from doctors, is my advice. They'll point the bone at you. That's what they do. They'll try to tell you how much longer you've got. They're in league with funeral directors and undertakers. I shouldn't even be in this era, I tell them. I'm way out of my time zone. Did you know that my uncle had a Penny Farthing bicycle in his garage?'

'I didn't. You don't talk about your past much.'

'What nonsense. I talk about it all the time, what else have I got to talk about?'

'Have you had any visitors?'

'My grandson comes from time to time, when it suits him.'

He peers around the room. 'Where's that little girl you truck around with?'

'She's somewhere.' Staying out of trouble, I hoped.

'I saw a real angel once. Tall and fierce, with wings, whizzing over the battlefield.'

'What was it doing?'

'How would I know? But I wasn't the only one to see it. All the men about to die saw it. Some of them tried to run away and were shot by their own officers.'

'Sounds like hell.'

'It was worse at Passchendaele,' he says.

Evie and I don't get very far before I decide to sit at a bus stop. I like sitting at bus stops because it is a very normal and unobtrusive thing to do. Nobody takes any notice of a person sitting quietly waiting for a bus. To reinforce this impression, every now and again I glance at my watch and look anxiously up the road. I think about my appointment, still hours away up along the plot line, and my grandfather floating away on a boat made of pillows.

I can put a stop to all this, throw a spanner in the words, I mean the works. I can sit here waiting for a bus that never comes. I can fail to show up to my appointment with the official. I can do the same with my grandfather. I can deviate. I can spit into their faces. I can confound the architects of my existence by doing the unexpected.

I can turn right around now and walk home, retrace my steps back along my plot line, give Evelyn a nice big surprise.

A dog trots up and gives me an expectant look. I pat it on the head. Good dog! I look across the street to the shops and buildings on the other side. They have passed their use-by date, and their future is looking a bit thin, but business goes on regardless; people pop in and out of shops and banks; business is booming at a little hole-in-the-wall coffee shop. In the distance I can see curtained apartments roosting in the air. Ubiquitous cranes, looking like the skeletons of enormous birds, are busy constructing a new city from the ruins of the old – and the Tower of course, more impressive now that it is closer, looking all needle-nosed and sleek.

I take out the tobacco, papers and matches and place them on my knee. I feel something of the delight of a gourmet chef who is sitting down to a sumptuous meal. Content is a vertical forever. Happiness is a warm smoke.

'You'll never get where you're going if you sit around smoking,' she says.

'Maybe that's the idea. I really just came out to buy some tobacco, and now I'm going to have a quiet little smoke before I go home.'

'Your grandfather will be disappointed.'

'That won't be anything new. I've pretty much made an art of disappointing people, I reckon. Ask Evelyn.'

Using the brown parcel for a flat surface, I shred the moist tobacco along the crease of the cigarette paper, and roll it expertly between thumb and forefinger into a smooth tube. I lick the paper and seal it down, savouring the moment before lighting up. I am safe here, in my little metal and glass shelter, with my picture of the flapper and my umbrella. I'm thinking of discarding my umbrella, which has become bedraggled. Even an imaginary umbrella can become a nuisance to carry when you only have two hands.

Evie is skipping around on the pavement before me, casting disapproving looks in my direction as I blow smoke into the air. Up ahead, forward along the plot line, I sense complications, boredom, terror, judgement, sentence, all kinds of things that lie unseen up around the corner of time, but for the moment, the moment will do. I will go with the blue drift.

'When you have finished that one,' she says, gesturing at the cigarette, 'you should throw away the packet.' She shows some form skipping with her arms folded across her chest.

'I will,' I promise her.

I go to take a smoke but the cigarette has gone out. I light up.

A flame leaps up from the match.

The ponytailed young woman removes the drip feed from my arm. The official stands a little behind her, watching me with a neutral expression on his face.

'You're quite right,' I say out of nowhere and pertaining to nothing, not knowing what has just passed. If I agree with them I can hardly be making a mistake, and it's important at this critical juncture to stay on the right side of them, of the authorities.

They look at me without responding, which is a bit unnerving.

'Are you Lois?' I ask the young woman. Behind her, her male twin with the ponytail grins. At least someone still has a sense of humour. I think even the subsonic scanner might have grinned a little. When I look at the blackboard however, the graffiti has changed as now reads: *denial is a privilege of the rich.*

It is hard to maintain this happy-happy demeanour when the official is shape-shifting in front of my very eyes. Years, stature and character are being poured into him from some exterior source, it seems. The lines on his face flow and merge, then resolve into an appearance much less bland but sterner and more foreboding. His hair thins and greys, his eyebrows thicken, and his bearing becomes more commanding and patriarchal. Like magic, lines of power appear around his eyes and mouth. *A Star Fleet Commander.* I am not imagining this increase in his stature. He is growing both taller and broader as his remaining hair becomes sleek and silver.

His ponytailed assistants are also growing stronger. His shoulders are broadening and filling with muscle while his hips are narrowing and his legs lengthening. Her arms and hips are thickening, her breasts enlarging, and a formidable look is coming into her eye.

My first impulse is to jump off the table and confront them, restore my dignity with a vertical posture, but an uneasiness in my body warns me against precipitous action. There is a background hum in my ears and a hint of nausea. The nausea brings a familiar taste into my mouth, dry and metallic. I spit out fragments of memory. There is a crashing noise inside my head, like a formation of jets passing through mindspace.

'I'm going to die,' I announce. 'That is what all this has been about. Evelyn, the appointment, my grandfather, the alien organism, even Evie… it's all about me dying, me having a terminal illness, perhaps manageable for a time with drugs, but only for a time. Inside the crocodile, the clock ticks.'

I know I have, with this extraordinary outburst, blown my cover, such as it was, but I am tired of all this pussy-footing around, avoiding the issue while appearing to confront it. I want to see all the cards on the table. I want to see the whites of their eyes before pulling the trigger and zapping them all to hell.

Since they don't reply, I press on. 'I have constructed a world of avoidance and denial. I have resolutely turned my face away from the truth. Within my world of avoidance and denial I have further constructed sub-worlds and sub-sub worlds that permit me to burrow deep and deeper, like a blind creature, further and further away from the real world. Even you, and this place, what's it called, *The Omega Centre*, is a part of that fantasy world.'

My voice is loud and oracular in my ears, vibrating through my body. I bite back bile. 'I have to seize the time threads, gather them up in my hands, plot my own plots and write out my destiny in the language of fingers.'

I wriggle my fingers at them in demonstration. They are not reacting. They are standing in front of me like deactivated robots. I don't want to look too hard, but it seems like they have multifaceted insect eyes. My image is reflected a thousand times in their stare.

'I want to see Evie,' I shout at them. 'The little girl with the skipping rope who came in here with me. Go and get her!'

The official, now apparently having gained full age and stature, stands at attention. He tries to nod his head but it seems to heavy for him. His mouth opens and his tongue slips forward like a dead fish.

My eyes crave distances. Even great cold interstellar distances would be welcome right now. I turn my head to the most distant object my eyes can find. It is my alarm clock, way off in the pale, jibbed spaces of the room. There is no way I can reach it to turn it off, prevent it from beginning its familiar harangue, even if I were to grow rubber arms.

'I think therefore I deceive myself,' the alarm clock says. 'That is the conclusion Descartes should have drawn. The whole of Western philosophy is based on a false assumption of existence…'

'Shut up!'

Remarkably, the clock falls silent. I am not accustomed to such obedience. A temporary victory, I'm sure. Wait until the subject of my finances comes up.

Evelyn lies beside me, murmuring in her sleep. Beside me looms a huge machine with a black snout pointed at my heart. It has an LED screen no bigger than my hand, set in beneath its mobile head. The words, *Alien Invasion Defence Systems* pass across the top of the screen from left to right, as if fleeing from something. Beneath, a jumble of mathematical notation drizzles down the screen. The mathematical architecture of my computer generated reality, I think as I struggle to not wake up. I suspect that it is hardly two o'clock in the morning. Eventually, I will be forced to get up and relieve my bladder, which I like to do outside on the lawn. I'll drink some water mixed with chlorophyll juice, pour cold water over my head, fight the nausea and try to think.

'Have you been sleeping well?' the official asks. His voice is deeper now that he is older and more authoritative.

'Is this just a polite enquiry?' I try to sit up.

'Who is Evie?' the ponytailed woman asks. Her voice too has gained more timbre along with her thickened arms and hips. Her question does not sound like a polite enquiry.

'What do you know of Evie?' I have succeeded in moving into a sitting position and already feel more in control of the situation. Lying prone, one is inherently defenceless.

'You spoke of her, wanted to see her.'

'You know nothing about her. She's just a kid with a skipping rope.'

'I see.'

I'm not sure that she does see. Time to change tack. 'What does the term *Alien Invasion Defence Systems* mean to you?' I address all three of them and try to fix them with a meaningful gaze. Now that the eye of truth has been opened, and I have entered the stream, I must move with extreme caution, giving nothing away. Only the most perfect camouflage will work. I must do this even as the millennia fall like ninepins in a bowling alley. Once, I was able to remember everything in wonderful detail and will soon be able to do so again. Then I will remember my death. My death from a terminal illness. And the worlds of dusky light that float in the velvet dark.

The three top-heavy beings lean over me. It seems they can hardly support their bulbous heads. They are asking questions, and are slowly turning their heads in each other's direction, exchanging looks heavy with significance. For a moment I can't hear their voices, just see their mouths moving and elongated bubbles emerge, like a string of sausages. This is the Einstein Disrupter at work, I'm certain of that, but it's better to say nothing about that.

'Please be cooperative,' the woman says severely. Her voice booms explosively, as if trapped in a confined space.

'I dreamed I was a leopard, I was running and running through forests and over hills. At the same time I was a hawk hovering above, watching the leopard. Finally I come to a house. My grandfather is inside, and Evelyn too. A terrific wind gets up. The ground shakes. The river overflows its banks. The side of the house rips apart until the framing timbers show. Evelyn is lying on the bed curled up in foetal ball...'

I swing myself out of bed and head for the bathroom where I keep my mega-vitamins and toss them back with no regrets, gulping them down as Evelyn steers past the door on her way to the kitchen.

I can hear my alarm clock croaking away to itself in the bedroom, rabbiting on about the illusory nature of desire. A few phrases filter through. *Listen, Ananda! At the time you were helpless ... the magic charm of the maiden Pchiti ... your control of mind? ... her control was not a chance happening ... you have been in affinity with her for many a long age...*

My pyjama bottoms fall to the floor.

My bare knees stare at themselves in the mirror.

Whirr/click.

A cigarette doesn't last very long. That's the trick of them. As soon as you finish one, you want another. That's the beauty of them. They never end. In reality, you are smoking one endless cigarette.

But Evie is having none of that. As soon as I've sucked the last out of my cigarette, she comes up and takes my hand. 'Come on,' she says in a practical, no-nonsense voice. 'It's time to visit your grandfather. Time to cheer an old man up.'

'I've decided not to visit him today.'

'Why not?'

'He doesn't fit in.'

'With what?'

'Umm… the shape of my day.'

'How would he feel if he heard you say that? That he might ruin the structure of your day?'

'I don't want to sound heartless.'

'Then don't be heartless.'

'It's easy for me to get lost. I mean, go off on a tangent, tangent-wise. Neglect my real purpose. Abandon my quest.'

Evie stamps her foot.

'Your grandfather is not a tangent. He's a mentor. He has a lot to teach you, if you have the ears to listen. You could put him in that book you are writing, the next Clark Kent novel.'

I sit there stubbornly, contemplating smoking another cigarette.

'What else are you going to do but sit there smoking and scaring yourself?'

'I'm waiting for a bus.'

'No, you're not. You're sitting there procrastinating.'

'That's my privilege.'

'You're just a scaredy-cat.'

A bus pulled up and I was tempted to jump on board just to prove Evie wrong. Except I wouldn't be proving anything at all.

'You win.' I get up and wander off, already regretting leaving the bus stop behind. It was a kind of refuge.

I set a course lateral to the temporal undertow, leaving the main thoroughfares and opting for a backstreet route. I don't look back, but I can hear Evie's skipping rope slapping the pavement behind me.

I wander from the bathroom into the kitchen, feeling that I have done this a thousand times before, distracted by the bubbling of the coffee perc and the tremor of morning light on the stainless-steel bench top. The scalding liquid froths into the cup. I lift the cup to my mouth and hold it there. The day looms before me like a vast field of resistance. I can already feel the temporal drift, pushing against my timeline. There's no escaping from the moment.

I blow steam across the wrinkling surface of the coffee.

It is the appointment that is the source of this field of resistance. It squats over my timelines like a kind of fate. It has a gravitational force. It gathers everything into itself and gives out nothing. It is a great black hole in the middle of the day. Here is a question for my alarm clock. What chance do I have of slipping through the day unnoticed, unaligned, freed of gravity?

Of course I already know the answer. At the appointment I will receive my orders. They will be issued to me in an old-fashioned, plain brown envelope...

.... The official is leaning over me. He is wearing the insignia of a Star Fleet Commander. His head has grown massive and barely seems to balance on top of his body. The ponytailed woman is saying something, yet nothing but colours come out of her mouth. There are small attachments, like hearing aids, behind their ears. I take it they too are receiving orders. A machine with hunched shoulders rolls around the table and inserts its black snout into my mouth....

I have been sleeping against the curve of Evelyn's spine. My body contains the imprint of hers. I have been dreaming of all the sentient beings in the great multiverse, but there are so many I can't keep count. I keep searching for human beings but can't find any. Finally, in the deep space between the Milky Way and Andromeda, I find a woman in a space gown. She's floating slowly, like a snowflake. As she floats past me I see that she is dead. Her green eyes have hardened into glittering emeralds, her skin has mummified, her hair is tangled copper thread.

'A wise man rises before his cock,' the alarm clock says in a malicious voice.

Too late.

Quite deliberately, I drop the full cup of coffee and watch it float to the floor and smash apart in an impressive explosion. Black liquid spreads across the red and white tiled floor.

‘How are you?’ my grandfather asks.

‘You’ve already asked me that.’

‘And what did you reply?’

‘That it’s a very nice day. A perfect autumn day.’

‘You didn’t say that.’

‘Well, I have now.’

‘I said it was worse at Passchendaele.’

‘You often say that.’

‘Because I keep going back to it. Every hour of every day I’m there, heading into battle, waving my trusty .303. The only reason I haven’t died yet is that I’m scared, scared that I’ll find myself back there for good. And the future, all that future I’ve already lived, won’t exist. And it will never exist because I will die like all the rest, there in the mud. Imagine that. In the moment of death you might live a whole imaginary life.’

The black knight in his hand swoops down onto the board and takes a pawn. He hits the clock bar and time begins to tick for white.

‘That’s the great thing about the knights. If you’re a pawn, you don’t see them coming. They seem to jump out of nowhere.’

‘Who’s winning?’

‘Not us, that’s for sure.’

Evie picks up a paper-weight statue. It is a fat Buddha with a laughing face. You can laugh, Enlightened One, but here in my world you are nothing but a bronze paper-weight. How do you like that for an incarnation?

'So let's talk about something cheerful,' he says, looking around hopefully. Every so often his eyes rest on the medicine cabinet. 'How are you, in your excuse for a life?'

'It was worse at Passchendaele,' I tell him.

'You bet your bloody boots it was,' he says, pushing forward a white pawn to directly attack the black knight. Black's time is running out. He has taken too long to make his moves. 'That was my point. You have no idea. Your generation. Any of the generations. We had to climb over a wall of bodies to get to the machine guns. Then we died in a hail of bullets, and others climbed over our corpses for their turn.'

'You're best off out of all that.'

'But I'm not out of it. That's what I'm trying to tell you. There is no out of it. That's all your generation care about, getting out of it.'

The black knight, having spied another undefended pawn, leaps in for the kill.

'Bloody pawn snatcher.'

With vengeful speed, the white bishop shoots forth from the trenches and lines up on black's king.

'Check!' My grandfather cries.

'Black can easily escape,' I said.

'We'll see.'

Evie is playing a little game on the floor with the bronze Buddha and a three-wise-monkeys door-stop, also made of brass. Grandfather likes brass things. Evie has the Buddha sitting in front of the three wise monkeys, explaining something to them, but Hear-no-evil wouldn't listen, See-no-evil wouldn't look, and Speak-no-evil has nothing to contribute.

'The hornets were like great golden wasps,' my grandfather says. 'They could kill a donkey. I saw them do it. But Margery, your great-aunty, she died of a bee sting. She just swelled up and died. My mother, that's your great-great-grandmother Evie, took to Margery with a knife and tried to cut out the poison but it was too late. It was in Greece that the hornets got the donkey. We called him Homer and he was an uncomplaining beast. One day he was tied to a tree and proceeded to wrap himself around it, tighter and tighter. There was a hornet's nest in that tree. You've never seen anything like it. We couldn't get anywhere near it. We didn't even have a bloody gun, not that that would have made any difference. Within half an hour that Donkey was deader than a stone. You can put that in your book. That is my life story.'

He pauses and stares at me speculatively. The word "book" seems to have reminded him of something.

'Are you the padre?'

I shake my head.

'Where's your book, padre? The one about that mad god who runs about smiting everybody.'

'I don't have a book, but I have something else, I bought for you…'

'I want to tell you about Passchendaele, padre. The parts that are not in your book. I got gassed at Passchendaele. There were blokes buried up to their necks in mud, croaking for water. You just had to walk past them. Giving them water would only have prolonged their agony anyway. I hope God will forgive me for that.'

'I'm sure he will,' I say.

On black's side of the chess clock, a little red marker falls.

Black has run out of time.

White wins.

'You may feel rather weak,' the official says in a solicitous voice. On each side of me, the two ponytails take my arms and help me to sit on the edge of the bed with my feet touching the floor. I clutch onto their arms for support.

'I want to know the truth, and I want you to tell me. The unequivocal truth, not your made-up little fantasies. I'm no good at puzzles, crosswords, cryptograms, paperchases and that sort of thing. I'm not up to decoding difficult ciphers. I need to have things spelled out. This alien virus thingy is no use to me. What am I going to tell Evelyn?'

'I'm afraid we don't know any more than you do, at this juncture. Our own grid-symbol constructs are being interfered with by some external agency we are still trying to locate.' He gestured to the laboratory around us. 'At the moment this is all we have. All we have to go on.'

The ponytailed woman steps away. There are goosebumps on her arm where I have touched her. It is not the ponytailed woman at all, but Evelyn, and I am sitting on the side of my own bed at home. I haven't got up yet. My alarm clock is looking at me accusingly.

'I can't stand this,' I say to Evelyn as I reach out for her. I bury my head in her hair. 'I feel dreadful this morning, as if I had ten thousand hangovers to cope with. I can't look at myself in the mirror.' I look around for the mirror. There was a time when Evelyn and I would enjoy the sight of our doubles making love. There is a voyeuristic thrill in it that seems to have worn off lately.

Evelyn smoothes down my hair and runs her fingers over my face. 'You have to fight them,' she murmurs.

'Fight who?'

'Whoever. Whatever.'

'Why? Is it worth the struggle?'

'What else is there? If you're going to run from suffering you'll never stop.'

I'm surprised to see Evie here too. She doesn't usually come into the house.

'It's too late to get scared,' Evie says. 'I've told you this before.'

'Not even of the crocodile with the clock inside?'

'That is scary, I admit. But you are not one of the little Lost Boys, you know.'

'I feel like one sometimes. Like right now. I'm so lost I don't even know where I am. Or when I am.'

The two ponytails are leading me away. Through the benches and table tops and scanners and other devices, following the official. I look around for One-eye but can't see him. He's pretty much a fading memory by now. Nobody looks at us as we go past. Not even a curious glance.

To the young woman I say, 'Remember my theory that young women with reddy-blonde hair have phone numbers beginning with double 5?'

'I don't think I do,' she says.

'And there's a good chance that it will end with an odd number, probably a seven or nine. On the basis of those odds, I would hazard a guess that your phone number is double five eight, two three seven.'

There is a break in her stride. 'How did you know that, Mr Kent?' With her beefy arms and broad hips, she suddenly looks formidable.

'ESP. Psychic aptitudes. Supernatural abilities. Special powers and premonitions. They are all opening up inside me now. I can feel them in my bloodstream.' I grip her arm. 'And what I feel now is that I am riding for disaster. That we all are. A terrible disaster which, in some alternate timeline, has already happened. We can feel it because there are leakages from one timeline to another.'

'What kind of disaster?'

'The kind you can't escape.'

'Does it have anything to do with my phone number?' I can see her making a mental resolution to change her number at the first opportunity.

'I hope not. You see, I am going to commit some frightful crime that my memory has suppressed. I can't escape it. Even if I stayed at home. Never left the house. It would seek me out.'

A door slides open in front of us and we are back in the official's office. The skull with the cigarette leers down at me: *nicotine is not so sexy*. I reclaim my tubular steel, red-cushioned chair. It is like an old friend. The two ponytailed assistants disappear back into the lab before that door closes.

'We'll have to wait until you are fully recovered,' he says. 'It won't be long.'

'What about you, will you fully recover too?'

'What do you mean?'

'You changed, back in there. You became bigger. Older. Your head got bigger in relation to your shoulders. And you stand straighter. Like a soldier. Like an admiral. Will you go back to being that weedy little man who came into the anteroom to get me?'

'Mr Kent, we should focus on you now, and your recovery, and the remedial actions we need to take. We don't want to get sidelined. We don't want to lose our focus.'

I look behind me for the other door, the one that leads back into the bedroom, but it will not be the same. The bed will face south rather than north, the mirror will reflect me to the west and Union Street will no longer intersect with Greys Avenue. There I will be required to face the precise diagnosis, the pity and the humiliation. An argument with Evelyn will follow in tense, low voices. When I sleep, I will dream of unspeakable crimes, and when I wake up I will go outside and pee on the lawn and defy the moon. Thinking about that, it seems Evie and I should have some better options.

There is a packet of breakfast cereal on the edge of the official's desk where the packet of drugs once sat. I tip it upside-down and cereal sprays all around the official's tidy office, looking like tiny styrofoam knucklebones. In the bottom right-hand corner there is a depiction of a huge silver fish lying alongside the hulk of a spaceship. They look as if they are engaged in some mechanical mating ritual. This is how our universe first became infected, I think. The original sin. Looking closer I see that the image appears to be a photograph, but reproduced poorly, the background stars being shadowed by fainter replicas of themselves.

'Have you seen the sort of crap they're putting on the back of cereal packets?' I ask the official.

'Where are you right now?' he asks me.

'I am lying under a pile of bodies, beyond the reach of bayonets. Can't you hear the war? The war never ended. Most people don't realize that.'

Ananda met Mahaprajapati near the entrance to the women's village. It was not possible for Ananda to approach unseen. Word of his coming would spread quickly enough, which was something of a nuisance in this case. What he really wanted was to slip in and see the maiden Pchiti and slip away again without too much fuss and bother. That was looking less likely with every passing moment.

It was no accident that Siddhartha's stepmother should be sitting by the river as Ananda came along. She would have positioned herself very carefully; it was all orchestrated.

Ananda had enormous respect for Mahaprajapati. She had followed Siddhartha two thousand miles over hard roads to plead her case. Ananda doubted he had that kind of courage. He quickly put her at ease and sat down beside her.

'Do you know a little girl with a skipping rope?' he asked her.

Mahaprajapati considered her answer carefully. 'In all such women's camps there will be a little girl with a skipping rope. Mostly nobody will notice her. Or care. It is easy not to see children sometimes, especially if they don't want to be seen.'

Ananda wondered if she was thinking about Siddhartha and the long game of hide and seek he had played with her over the years, always keeping on the move but always one step ahead of her.

'Do you know her name?'

'These little girls have many names. They like to be named after flowers, like Chinese girls. Orchid and Magnolia Blossom and names like that. What is your interest in this little girl?'

'She came to me with a message from the maiden Pchiti, who wants to see me over some matter.'

'Ahhh... the maiden Pchiti. Yes. She is troubled of heart.'

'Can you not remedy her?'

'Ananda! Surely you are not avoiding her. Trying to put it off onto me. I have spoken to her, but cannot speak on her behalf. You must understand.'

'I do. It's just that a woman may be better suited...' he tailed off. He wondered if it were fear he could feel, stopping up his blood and putting his tongue out of step. He would be ashamed to admit his fear, especially to this lively, perceptive woman, who probably already knew.

He picked up a stick and threw it into the water. Further upstream a girl was feeding the ducks, but he couldn't see if it was the girl with the skipping rope.

'Ananda, you know you are always welcome here, whatever your mission. We all owe you a huge debt of gratitude for what you did for us. It is a formidable thing to engage Siddhartha in a dispute. And win. Anything you ask that we can give will be yours.'

'Now, Mother, you must know that this "debt of gratitude" as you call it is a burden to me. A good monk should slip through the world unnoticed, and not call attention to himself. Or assume any glory. Such attention may become a burden.'

'Of course, to a humble man that will be so. But you cannot wear your humility like a cloak, to hide your face in.'

'Of course, Mother. But these are hard lessons to learn, for the softest of feelings can be involved, and the first smoke from a burning house might smell sweet.'

'Now now, Ananda! No need to suffer without cause. You know that Siddhartha himself has never spoken against marriage, or even against monks and nuns marrying... he has a very practical attitude to such things, you know. He was not born in an ascetic's hut, but in the palace of our Lumbini Kingdom, which was not the home of saints. When he was but a toddler he loved to wander around, always poking his nose into something, always asking endless questions, and he was the darling of the palace girls and the courtesans. He never put much store by such things.'

Ananda knew all this. He had heard it told many times, along with other stories about his cousin. Mahaprajapati sometimes forgot that Ananda had often been there, by Siddhartha's side, and getting up to all sorts of tricks along with his mischievous cousin, who at an early age displayed a talent for getting other people into trouble. Now that Siddhartha had become The Awakened One, people tended to forget what a little trickster he had been. How he would lead other children by the nose into muddy puddles and leave them there and run away. People forgot such things but not Ananda. Ananda forgot nothing. Even the extraordinary sermon the five-year-old Siddhartha had given when one of the boys had wantonly killed a frog.

Ananda gave an embarrassed little laugh. 'Mahaprajapati, who spoke of marriage? Only you. And while those who follow Siddhartha's middle way will marry, we who call ourselves monks and nuns make the decision to renounce the world of the senses and take up the life of contemplation. I'm sure the maiden Pchiti wants to see me on some matter relating to her devotions.'

'Of course, of course.' Mahaprajapati patted his hand. 'I turned my back on the world when I set out to follow my step-son and see the world with the most pure of observation, and have not been with a man since. Or woman either!' She laughed and her face wrinkled up like a walnut. It wasn't age that made her look like that but the road she had taken and the teeth she had lost. 'But when I see a young man, so handsome and upright, wandering pensively along the river, heading to the women's village to visit one of the prettiest girls there on some trifle, then I begin to wonder. I begin to wonder just who is blind and who sees with true sight.'

'Your wondering just leads you astray, Mother, and fills your head with idle speculation and gossip. That is unbecoming of a nun.'

'So you might say, but there is a big difference between you and Siddhartha here.'

'Surely not.'

'There is no way I could tease Siddhartha about such matters, since there is nothing to tease. He would never do what you did.'

'Which is what?'

'Blush.'

The official sits down on the edge of his desk and laces his fingers together. No longer dressed in shabby, bureaucratic grey, he looks quite splendid in full uniform, every inch a Confederation Star Fleet Commander, High Admiral.

'What is your name, soldier?'

'October Nortikiss.'

'What is your rank?'

'Starship Captain. Commander of the cruiser, *Frolix 6*, class IQW – 3BO.'

'Where is the *Frolix 6* right now?'

'Uncertain.'

'How can it be uncertain? It has to be somewhere.'

'Because of a limitation in the nature of consciousness similar to the Heisenberg uncertainty principle. The more I know about the when we are, which you have stipulated to be right now, the less I know of the where. I can tell you the where, but we will lose our focus on the when.'

'Try it.'

'Section 4, quadrant 6, between B247 and B532, in close orbit around an asteroid size trader of the first generation known as *The Omega*. But that event lies either far back in the past, or in the distant future.'

'That's very clever.'

'Not me. My astrophysicist. She's the clever one.' And sexy too, but I'm not about to tell him that.

'Ah, the humble Starship Captain. That's a new one. What's her name?'

'Beverly. And I was trained to give others their full due, sir.'

'Entirely reasonable, I'm sure. What is your mission, Captain?'

'To repulse an energy form we call the Fishmen from the Other Side of Time.'

'Why do they have to be repulsed?'

'Because they will unravel the fabric of the universe, blow holes in the Arrow of Time. Unpick the maths on which our material universe depends.'

'What will happen when you leave this building?'

'I will never leave this building.'

'Why not?'

'Because I am in quarantine. I may have become infected.'

'But what if you were to leave the building anyway, despite the quarantine?'

'I can only guess. Already I am living divided timelines. This morning I got up and took a pee on my lawn. That's when it all started. But at the same time that was a long time ago, many years ago. The city was different then. It didn't have the monorail.'

'What monorail?'

'We could go on this way forever, and our grid-symbol constructs might never properly mesh. That should lead us to conclude that we are not winning the battle against the Fishmen.'

'What do you understand by divided timelines?'

'At the sub-atomic level, particle interaction may be read as time ambiguous, that is, moving either forward or backward in time. The maths is the same either way. An added element is needed to fix the reaction in one direction, forward, and that added element is consciousness. That is the mind's ability to structure and effectively create time.'

'Once again, I am impressed with your grasp of these matters, Captain. And your ability to express them succinctly.'

'That's Beverly, sir. We've had a lot of time for pillow talk.'

'Apparently.'

'But that's not all, sir. The minds' ability to give narrative direction to time can be interred with.'

'How?'

'The use of psycho-active drugs, or a theoretical device called the Einstein Disrupter, or an extra-terrestrial virus… or possibly a vicious cocktail of all three of these things.' There is no stopping me now. Like a bird on a branch bursting into song, I start to spout lines of poetry.

'Men's curiosity searches past and future

And clings to that dimension.

But to apprehend

The point of intersection of the timeless

With time, is an occupation for the saint

No occupation either, but something given

And taken, in a lifetime's death in love,

Ardour and selflessness and self-surrender.'

'Who are you quoting?'

'TS Eliot, 1941. Written in the middle of all the slaughter of war. My grandfather taught it to me. And other lines too…

You are not the same people who left the station

or who will arrive at any terminus…'

'What makes you believe you will commit some crime, or walk into a disaster?'

'Because these things have already happened, and go on happening forever. I have been caught in the emotional tailwind of these events. Any event gives off shock waves forward and past in time. Since I have already lived through the event, I am sensitive to the shock waves gusting in out of the future.'

'What is your mission right now, soldier?'

'To maintain narrative integrity.'

The official sighs and glances up into the corner of the room where, belatedly, I see a camera. Perhaps he is giving himself a significant look so that when he reviews the tapes he won't miss this moment. At the same time he briefly touches the tiny attachment behind his ear. With deliberate movements, heavy with intention, he gets off the side of the desk, returns to his chair and takes a brown envelope from his drawer. He weighs it in his hand for a moment, as if undecided. Finally, he hands it to me.

'These are your orders,' he says in a neutral voice.

I put it in my pocket without comment and turn for the door to the anteroom.

There is somebody waiting that I am eager to see.

My grandfather picks up his defeated black king and considers it. He touches the little cross on its head.

'The officers would yell the orders and we would leap out of the trenches and run for the enemy lines. Their machine guns would mow us down as we approached, if we turned and ran back the officers would give more orders and our own machine guns would mow us down.'

He set the pieces back up and commenced a new game, moving rapidly with barely time to tap the clock in between. Looks like Black is determined not to run into time trouble in this game.

'If you were lucky and not in the first wave, the piles of bodies before you would offer some protection. You could wriggle between them like a worm in the mud. A lot of corpses got stuck on the barbed wire near their trenches, which gave us more protection. By the time I got to the wire the bodies were piled up twice the height of a man. There were civilians mixed up in it too. I saw a weird thing once. A woman running across a field. A few yards in front of her, a soldier got a shell right in the crotch. She fell over, clutching herself and screaming while he died painlessly.'

'You should be recording this,' Evie says to me.

'Why?'

'So you can write it down. These stories are part of a precious heritage, now almost lost. That's what you are, isn't it? Witness and historian.' She takes her little fat laughing Buddha and strokes his bulbous stomach. That seems to tickle his fancy.

'I don't know about that,' I say.

I study the chessboard. White appears to be losing the new game, and in response has constructed a line of pawns, an impenetrable barrier, hopefully. Black could still lose by hurtling his pieces against that barrier. I wondered if Grandad took turns at winning and losing.

'Such terrible battles,' I murmur. 'God, king and country.'

'Those battles were nothing compared to Passchendaele. At Passchendaele the earth opened up and hell came out of the ground. There were demons running loose in the bodies of men. There were corpses that wouldn't lie down no matter how often you shot them. There were kids running around looking for their parents. Grown men bleating like sheep. Don't you talk to me about Passchendaele, padre. I was there, but God was never there. Jesus wasn't there. Every man paid with his own blood. The dogs of war had their day. When I got gassed I went down to hell. I looked around and laughed. Most of my ancestors were there, the whole bloody family, wowsers and all. The wowsers looked really pissed off. The place looked just like home, just like I remembered it. "What are you laughing at?" they said. They were foaming at the mouth, I can tell you. So I told them the joke. "You think Hell is bad," I said, laughing fit to bust, "well Passchendaele is a lot worse. You wouldn't want to be on earth right now."' Grandfather laughs at the memory. 'I'm not kidding you, padre. Men were hammering at the gates of hell just to get in, into safety. Old Nick was having a field day.'

My grandfather tries to laugh again but bursts into a fit of coughing. I can hear those mustard-gas damaged lungs ripping apart. 'That's what I told them,' he wheezed, 'I said…'

'…Passchendaele was a lot worse,' I say. I'm getting tired of this now.

'What would you know about it?' he says with sudden suspicion. 'You weren't there.' His voice rises into outrage. 'You wouldn't know the first bloody thing about it.'

Evie nods solemnly. She holds her brass Buddha like a ventriloquist's doll.

'He's absolutely right,' the Buddha says.

A pair of shapely legs, well muscled, and looking all the more alluring in fishnet stockings. I have no idea why a relatively plain, straightforward leg, shapeliness notwithstanding, should look so… *suggestive*… when covered in a fine mesh. Underneath, it's the same leg. It's all a matter of packaging. The mystery of packaging.

As she walks up the stairs ahead of me, I get a fine view of those legs from behind, and a little way up the skirt, finely calibrated to reveal just so much and no more. Following the hypnotic swing of those legs, and the rhythmic brush of denim across them, certainly makes the trip up the stairs easier to bear. It's not my fault if I turn sexual objects into sexual objects.

It seems to be flowing well, this following the girl with the fishnet stockings, finally revealed, up the stairs. It is the time and the place for such things. The correct organs seem to be pumping adequate energy to appropriate parts of my body. My legs are churning beneath me quite satisfactorily; my arms are swinging and my rump is swinging. The heart is all tickety-boo.

The stairwell is uniformly shabby, painted by dim yellow bulbs at each landing. The walls are covered by minute scratches, as if an avalanche of monkeys have passed this way, drawing their fingernails across the fading paint. It is dark, even this early in the evening (I can hear Vesper bells: *'and there was evening and there was morning, one day…'*), with the dark in front and the dark behind. And the stairwell barely lit. Three times, four times, we have moved through the ascending gloom, from one plateau with its feeble cone of light to the next identical plateau with its feeble cone of light, me following the swing of fishnet stockinged legs ahead of me.

The Celestial City lies somewhere up ahead.

Evie trails some distance behind, her feet dragging, her head down, her skipping rope limply hanging. This is her way of showing her disapproval, her reluctance, her royal disfavour. But I can only permit myself a moment's anguish on her account. Just a moment and no more. After all, while she is a joyous little sprite, there are matters regarding which her understanding is necessarily limited. There are situations where I must leave her behind. Decency requires it.

It is a difficult moment for both of us.

This is certainly one such moment, ascending stairs like these, clutching an umbrella which has become a weapon and shield, lungs hurting from the cigarette you have foolishly allowed yourself earlier, eyes fixed on the stockings and skirt of a woman you have only just met or perhaps known all your life.

Outside the perpetual dingy yellow twilight of the stairwell the day still turns its before and its after, the yet to come and the just gone.

I pause at one of the landings to get my breath. A flight of stairs will always weed out a smoker. She doesn't stop for me, Zellia or Zalena or whatever she calls herself, her raised sandals slapping on each stair, sounding a little like Evie's skipping rope, turbulent dark blonde hair bouncing on her back.

I put my hand on the wall to steady myself and do a quick nausea check. There is some graffiti right by my hand, scratched into the plaster. *Shift to Alien Control.* Next to this is a large upside-down A with a circle around it. Beneath that: *the war never needed.*

I look back for Evie.

Ahead the sandals stop slapping. 'Are you coming?' Her voice is replicated flatly by the concrete walls.

I look at Evie and shrug. The whole thing is out of my hands, I intimate to her. I am but a plaything of fortune, a leaf tossed in a storm, a creature of my desires. My legs tremble. Spots float before my eyes. Distant choirs sing descants.

Evie is not impressed. She won't acknowledge me or the signals I'm sending her. Her eyes are firmly cast down in martyred humility. I shrug to a vanished audience. My heart aches in my chest.

Two more flights of stairs and we arrive at a door. As she searches for the key, I notice that the lintel is carved, like the tobacconist's window sill. Here, however, I see shapes of faces, gaping mouths, eyes with the merest hint of eyebrows. Mostly, they are gargoyles with protruding tongues and fierce expressions.

I gesture to them questioningly, not wanting to break the almost cathedral-like silence of the stairwell.

'Keeps out the dead,' she says matter-of-factly, still scrabbling in her purse for the key. 'And evil influences.'

'Where's the garlic?'

'That only works for vampires. These,' she gestures to the faces, 'are multipurpose, broad-spectrum. They scare off a variety of ghouls.' She finds her key and deftly inserts it into the lock, tossing her rich curls off her face. She really does look a little like the frowzy hippy described by Evelyn. Quite thickset, muscular legs, face worn to an ashen grey, at least in this crepuscular light. Her light-coloured blouse, worn loose at the waist and open at the neck, is streaked with dark stains. She wears a blue cotton jacket with circles of silver foil sewn in, each one like a tiny mirror. It looks like a cheap import from Africa or Mexico.

'Do you believe that stuff?'

'Do you see any ghouls around?'

We both laugh.

Evie comes up and stands beside me. She is still finding the scruffy floor of great interest.

'Some of my visitors believe that these faces can keep out wives. While they are screwing me, that is.' She looks at me shrewdly.

'And do they?' I point to one of the more ferocious faces.

'Do you see any wives around?'

We both laugh again. It's catchy. I see she has one bottom tooth missing.

'Adulterers are very superstitious,' I tell her as the door swings open. 'But my wife isn't. She wouldn't even notice these scary faces, or if she did she wouldn't care. They wouldn't cut any ice with her. She'd just zoom on in anyway.'

She gestures for me to go through the door. That's always what it comes down to, going through another door.

'I'm not going in there,' Evie says in a low voice. She points to the faces we have just been talking about. 'Anyway, you don't want me in there. Not with what you're going to do.'

My heart begins to quiver. I am struggling with a hopeless sense of sadness, as if at the death of a loved one.

'It won't matter,' I lie, using the same low voice she is using. 'I mean, you can come in.'

'No.'

The woman slips past and goes on in ahead of me. I can hear her fumbling for the lights.

'You can wait outside. You can look after my umbrella.'

She shakes her head and scrapes her foot across the floor. 'I'm going away.'

'But you'll be back. You've gone away before, but you've always come back.'

'Not this time. You don't need me now. I'm more of a nuisance than anything.'

'But I do. I need you more than ever, and you're never a nuisance. How can you say that? You know how confusing things get for me sometimes. You know there are times when I go to move and can't take a single step. Not a single step.' Clumsily, I kneel down to her height. 'We always go places together, you and me. We're a team. I've got your back and you've got mine, right?'

'Not any longer. You've grown out of the need for me. You've taken things into your own hands. You don't care anymore.'

Tears are pouring hotly down my face. Mucus starts running out of my nose.

Evie is bravely cheerful. 'You always looked forward to the time when you wouldn't need me anymore, when I wouldn't be tailing about after you everywhere. When I first came to you, that's what you said. You said "One day I won't need you", and you were right. That day has come.'

'No it hasn't, not by a long shot.' And will never come, as far as I am concerned. I take her by the shoulders, which feel thin and defenceless under the fabric of her dress. 'I mean… will you never come back again? Never ever?' Never ever is so terribly final.'

Behind us the light goes on. There is the sound of running water from the bathroom.

'What about Evelyn?' Evie says, gesturing towards the open door. 'Will you go home to Evelyn? Or stay with this woman?'

Home? How far away the word makes me feel. How distant from everything. How could I ever return home? Or stay with this woman?

'Evelyn and I…' I stop. How can you explain things like this to a child, even an amazingly wise child like Evie.

'You should go in now,' Evie says. 'She's waiting for you.'

'Will you be here when I come out?'

'You don't need me.' She fiddles with the handles of the skipping rope. 'You'll have to go on without me now. Something is always lost.'

Behind us, the water stops running. A door shuts decisively.

'Please, Evie…' I am short of breath. I look around for the oxy-pressure gauge.

Evie sits on the top stair and gazes down into the pouring yellow of the stairwell. Faint noises arise from below, distorted echoes.

I turn and walk blindly inside, closing the door behind me. A few strides take me to a narrow kitchen where the woman is pulling the cork on a bottle of wine. The pop sounds quite hopeful, but the wine is a red of the cheap and nasty variety. She pours two glasses and hands me one. 'Looks like you need it,' she says. They are not wine glasses but ordinary water glasses. It doesn't matter. Nothing's going to make much difference. I knock mine straight back, the way heroes do on the big screen. As she refills it, she lights a hand-made cigarette which has a strange sweet smell.

She gestures to the wine and the smoke. 'This will deal to those fucking pharmaceuticals,' she says.

We both laugh. We do a lot of laughing together. I knock the second glass back and take the smoke. The wine isn't so bad if you don't taste it on the way down.

'What took you so long, out on the landing? Writing your will?'

I draw the spicy smoke into my lungs. Jesus. I fumble for the glass which she has refilled for the third time.

'I was talking to myself.' My voice is hollow in my ears. In the background I begin to hear the choir of the Celestial City singing in multiple harmonies.

'An occupational hazard,' she says cheerfully, tossing her own drink back.

'It's a nice place you have here.'

'Don't lie. It's a fucking dump. What did you expect? It's got mould. And it stinks. Even the rats think twice about moving in.' She takes the cigarette from my fingers. 'Have you been crying?'

'Not me. I'm having a great time. I'm a barrel of laughs.'

'It's good for men to cry.' The cigarette hangs from her lips as she draws the smoke up her nose. 'I always trust a man who cries.'

When we get to the door that leads back into the anteroom, the official inclines his body and holds out his hand. There is a sense of occasion here, of formality and ritual. The appointment is over, we have survived its jaded narrative, which we have held on to through thick and thin, and we can trust the mechanics of courtesy to guide us through these last moments.

Now I will be on my own. The authorities have done all they can, taken every precaution, offered every assistance, and scrutinised every detail. We can now quietly forget the time I spent in the *Omega* lab, lying on the table, with a snout-nosed creature positioned over my body. It never happened, or if it did, it took place in some other dimension, some other time and place that has nothing to do with us right now, shaking hands. It's a deal. The stake is our silence.

I pat the brown envelope, secure in my pocket. I have my orders.

We exchange brief smiles. From his point of view, I'm sure he is grateful that everything has gone as smoothly as it has. An exemplary case. At no point is the word "quarantine" mentioned. The less said the better for both our sakes. I can appreciate that. There is wisdom in our reticence, compassion in our forbearance. Death my dance, but not here, not right now. Now it is smiles and handshakes and a long journey just begun.

As I take his hand, and feel his firm grip, I realize he is wearing skin-fitting gloves.

'On the battlefield time was withdrawn. Grace was withdrawn. Everything was withdrawn. Even death got dizzy. People think of time as some kind of curse. A big-time wet blanket party pooper. When the pubs in England shut for the night the barman would always call, "Time! Time gentlemen!" and everybody would groan. People don't realize that time is an act of grace! You have to have been on a battlefield to appreciate that, padre. You can't just sit around playing with yourself and expect to understand these things. But try lying in a foxhole for three days with motor fire breaking open the sky and your nose in the filth and the mud trying to remember some prayer you never cared about until that moment.'

Grandfather sits back among the pillows. He looks like an ancient king surrounded by fluffy swans.

'Padre, in the medicine cabinet…' he points.

I know what to do. I open the medicine cabinet and inside, among the pills and potions, there is a bottle of whisky, looking a little like the black sheep of the family trying to blend in.

'Pour me a snifta, that's right, a couple of fingers.' He takes the glass and sniffs at it, as if to reassure himself of its contents, and tosses it back with a practised flourish. He stares down at the chessboard. The two sides are totally locked into their positions; he has played himself to a standstill.

'I saw men who couldn't die, and so had to die lots of times. They fell on the fields and were quickly buried only to rise up again for the next charge. I saw lots of dead comrades still fighting on the front lines. They just couldn't put their guns down. We used to make jokes about it, about recycling dead soldiers. The officers would court-martial you if you died, but as long as you got up and kept fighting, they didn't care. Nobody said anything, but the soldiers knew it. You can't fool the common soldier. There were men with arms missing or legs missing or big holes in their chests or skin hanging off their bodies still charging the enemy lines. What a shambles! Sometimes we'd go and visit the dead in their afterlife, just to make them feel a bit better.'

'What was it like, going to visit the dead?'

Grandfather makes a dismissive gesture. 'It's been done before. Highly overrated.'

He holds out his glass expectantly. I pour another snifta.

'Soldiers have done it. It's all part of the training. Ulysses did it. Orpheus did it, but he was a coward. The poets and songsters have done it. Dante did it and lived to tell the tale. Old dry bones Eliot did it. It's nothing special. No great shakes.'

'Eliot?'

'Yes, padre. Old dry bones himself. You remember the line, *"If all time is present, all time is unredeemable."* A dead person must have told him that. No one else would say such a terrible thing.'

'Do the dead often say mysterious things like that? Riddles.'

'Oh yes, such language is *de rigueur* among the dead.' He swirls the whisky around in the glass, giving it some momentum before tossing it back with a little shudder. His face is starting to change colour, become darker. 'Most of the dead don't know what's hit them. They can still hear the battle raging. They will hear it forever, because time is the first casualty of war.' He laughs. 'Being dead is no great shakes.'

His face is developing purple blotches.

I look around for Evie.

The horizontal and the vertical:
Lovers across Time

Let the good times roll!

I follow a line of discarded clothes down a short hall to the bathroom, for the first time noticing a tapestry covering one wall. Persian, or possibly Turkish, it depicts a couple in the act of congress, sitting up facing each other belly to belly, their legs wrapped around each other's backs. In a corner a royal personage with an impressive moustache and a long spear vanquishes a boar. Stars and moons cluster around the boar's head.

The trail of clothes leads past the tapestry to the bathroom door (another door), across the bathroom floor, up over the back of the bath, along the side of the bath to end with a pair of soiled panties slung seductively over the toilet cistern. Being able to go no further I take out an indignantly half-swollen cock and take aim for the scummy patch at the back of the bowl, reflecting that it is much nicer to take a pee on a lawn, under the stars with the sound of owls off in the distance crying their famous cry — *whirlpool,*

whirlpool…

It is all right about Evie, I tell myself. She may be sulky now, but she'll come round. That's what she's like. I look at the Chinese print on the bathroom wall. A lone boatman sets out across a vanishing lake. The mountain dissolves into the sky. The boatman's shoulders are bent against the temporal storm. He is no more than a tiny shape in the elements, a patch of water-colour.

I've gone off the track somewhere, I think with a horrible, clarifying light. I've ended up here, in the House of Dirty Underwear, followed a chain of strewn clothing along my own circumlunar trajectory to this grubby conclusion. I am a sinner, an adulterer at heart. At any moment this adventurer might appear, weighing his chances, fingering the loose change in his pocket, peering out from between his legs.

My pee arrives on time, or perhaps a little late and flustered, and I lean forward a bit closer to the bowl. Behind the cistern and the panties in the foreground there is a set of louvre windows through which I can see the traffic signals of a nearby intersection and the occasional glimpse of a person bobbing past. We are in a block of ancient flats that lie above a shopping centre. Above the shops there's a foolish plaster façade with imitation Greek columns. Below, there's a fruit and vege shop and a fast food outlet. The whole building is doubtless condemned, and has been for a long time.

I lean further forward so I can see more of the street, the flashing green walk-now sign at the pedestrian crossing, a cruising military vehicle with a revolving turret.

My nose is now hovering a snifta or two away from the pinky-brown silk fabric of the knickers.

When I lean forward a little more, I can see beyond the traffic lights right up the limb of the street to where it joins Greys Avenue and a haze of car lights drifting in from the half dark.

Ananda took a back path to Pchiti's hut, not because he was ashamed of being seen but simply to avoid the eyes prying from the shadows of doorways and the whispers that seemed to follow the young monk wherever he went. No matter how often he explained that he was merely Siddhartha's personal attendant, equipped by nature with a trick memory, and that he was really the dullest of the Buddha's disciples as evidenced by the fact that he asked so many silly questions, people persisted in treating him with veneration due to his elders like the venerable Maha Kassapa, or the more diligent and less restless young monks like Aniruddha and Bhadra. They were a shining example to all.

Despite his best efforts, however, eyes still pried and whispers still followed. Ananda bore it all with goodwill.

When he arrived at Pchiti's door, he hesitated. Surely she must know that he was there, and politeness dictated that she meet him at the doorway. Illness might prevent her, he thought, in which case she should have a friend or fellow nun in attendance. In that moment, he remembered his first encounter with Pchiti. One afternoon, with the sun heavy and yellow on the horizon, when returning from a nearby town where he had been begging, he passed a well he had often passed before, and drew water there. A young woman was at the well, and Ananda had paused and asked for some water, smiling to put her at her ease.

The girl recognised Ananda. Very shyly she said, 'Venerable Ananda! You are a prince by birth. Siddhartha's father is your uncle. I am a lowly peasant who is not fit to offer you anything.' And, so saying, she bowed her head in profound respect.

Ananda had been deeply moved. He said, 'Young woman, I am a monk as you are a nun. For us there are no princes and peasants. We are all equal before the dharma, which strips away all worldly status. I treat rich and poor equally, and I am equal before them.'

The girl did not look up, but she smiled.

'My name is Pchiti,' she said, and handed him a bowl of water, finally looking up at him. He took it with gratitude, noting how beautiful the girl was and how soft her hair looked in the heavy afternoon light.

He only saw her once, after that, in the town and from a distance. Just close enough for a smile.

'Pchiti?' he called from the doorway.

'Venerable one,' her voice came, 'is that you?'

'Such as I am,' he said. 'But call me Ananda.'

'Come in, venerable Ananda. My hut is unworthy of your feet.'

'Come now, Pchiti. We have been through this before. My feet get as dirty as yours.'

She laughed and Ananda saw brightly coloured butterflies lifting off a field of flowers.

Her hut was small and makeshift. It was, however, scrupulously clean, as were all the huts of the nuns and monks. Everything was neatly put away, he noted with approval.

Pchiti was sitting on the floor, on a brightly woven rug, her hair hanging like a veil over her face. A pitcher of water and a bowl sat in front of her.

Ananda stood inside the door, allowing his eyes time to adjust to the soft, shadowy light. 'Are you ill?' he asked gently.

'My heart and mind are troubled,' Pchiti said. 'I cannot eat or sleep, and I am beset with dreams…' she tailed off as if reluctant to say more, and combed her fingers through her hair.

'What do you dream of?'

'Animals. Tigers, elephants, monkeys and snakes. They go with me wherever I go.'

While Siddhartha had never set much store by dreams, once describing them as the froth of the froth, Ananda had always been curious about them, and sometimes wondered if awakened beings from the past did not create them in order to push the mind closer to awakening. A monk once kept dreaming of entering a river and being consumed by fire there, which Ananda thought signified the monk's fear of becoming a Stream Enterer and losing his precious Self.

'It is the mind itself that is the monkey. It will play all kinds of tricks to distract you from your path.'

'I know, but…' she dipped her finger into the bowl of water and allowed a few drops to fall on the brightly woven rug, 'is it true that Siddhartha does not approve of love, or believe in it even?'

She looked at him with a frankness that was unexpected and intense. Her eyes were like pools of twilight.

Ananda said, 'Siddhartha's teachings are soaked in loving compassion the way a shirt is soaked by the stream in which it is washed. Along with that are a host of feelings which are positive for spiritual growth: joy, delight, contentment, ardency, and empathy.'

Pchiti drew back a little, looking suddenly stricken. 'Venerable one, forgive a silly girl. I have forgotten my manners. Please sit down. Would you like some water? Or shall I fetch some tea?'

As he sat on the other side of the woven rug, Ananda saw that as well as the pitcher of water there were two bowls. She had made this simple preparation for his arrival. Equally simple, but with a graceful movement, she poured him water. The water sounded somehow happier when it reached the top of the bowl.

'There are many forms of love,' she said. 'The love I have for my parents is not the same as the love I might feel for a flower, or the blueness of the sky.'

'That's very true.'

'Or the love a man and woman might feel for each other.'

Ananda perceived that this was more than just an intellectual enquiry, and wondered if the young woman had fallen in love, perhaps with one of the monks. Such things happened, despite Siddhartha's strictures.

Carefully, he said, 'But any feelings that are rooted in craving are not love.'

'Is love between two people always the result of craving?'

'Not if it grows from a loving kindness towards every living being. One of the joys of spiritual practice is learning to distinguish unhelpful grasping and neediness from an underlying love that needs nothing beyond itself. What should be abandoned is craving, not love.'

Pchiti looked down into her bowl water. She was holding it so still it seemed she wanted to see only a perfect reflection there.

'Does Siddhartha love?'

'An Awakened One might love, but be free of lust, be liberated from compulsive cravings and the suffering these bring.'

As he said this he remembered Siddhartha's wife, Yaśodhara, and the son she had borne him, Rahula. On the very day Rahula had been born, Siddhartha had left to take up the life of the wandering spiritual seeker who owns nothing and has no home, and while his determination was unshaken by Yaśodhara's grief, a tear had formed in his eye. A tear that was as large as the world, he later told Ananda.

'Is it wrong to love, and suffer for love?'

'It is not wrong,' Ananda said quickly, a little too quickly he thought, 'but have you noticed that this love that makes us suffer is experienced mostly in anticipation? It is an agony of anticipation.'

'That is certainly true,' Pchiti said very quietly. She drew her fingers of her right hand down her left arm, leaving a faint, indented trail.

'Such love is experienced as an ache in the body. And it is powerful and insistent.'

'That is also true.' Her right hand began gently squeezing her left, as if ministering to it.

'It is an ache for completion we don't find in the dreary round of mundane routine. However, gratification is rare and the craving relentless. We never seem to possess it in all its fullness, but that doesn't stop us.'

Her voice had dropped to a whisper. Ananda had to lean forward to hear.

Her hair smelled of pears. 'That is so true, you have branded my heart. But may we not find, even in the desires of our earthly lives, the seeds of that greater love of which you speak. In the scent of the flower we can detect the ambrosia of the gods. In the beating of our hearts we might feel the pulse of all living things, and even of the moon and the stars. When I dreamed of those animals, I could feel their ecstatic communion with the world.'

She extended her left hand to Ananda. 'Feel my pulse.'

He took her hand. It was light and warm in his. His fingers rested on her slim wrist.

'You can feel it?'

'Your pulse is very rapid. Have you a fever?'

'What you feel is the urgency of life itself. Without that urgency there would be no life.'

She withdrew her hand. A moment later her shoulders slid out of her robe, which fell to her waist, revealing her breasts. These were of such perfection that Ananda forgot himself and stopped breathing. His own pulse accelerated. Her breasts had the fullness of ripe mangos, Ananda's favourite fruit. This mental comparison made him blush. He would never be able to look at a mango again.

'So this life and this love go hand in hand.' She took his hand again, this time feeling his pulse. Her fingers were light and sensitive on his skin. 'And your pulse too matches that urgency.'

It was Ananda's turn to look down at the bright rug. In the soft light of the hut, its colours seem to glow from within. He was acutely aware of the warm air on his skin, and the ambrosial scent that filled the air as if they were sitting in a field of flowers.

He withdrew his hand. In that moment he felt nothing but love for this exquisite maiden, such a love that would burst his heart. His own voice was barely above a whisper. 'Yes. All that is possible. All that is true. And all that is good. And as beautiful as the world.'

'Yes,' she said.

'I could take both your hands in mine, and give myself over to my senses.'

'Yes,' she said.

'But, dear one, my course was set a long time ago. When I left my father's palace to follow Siddhartha I made my decision. I made it in the face of family. My father saw it coming and tried to avert it. He did everything he could to keep Siddhartha and I apart, because he was afraid of the teaching. But it started even before Siddhartha's Awakening. He always maintained that I was too easily influenced by my cousin's stronger personality. He was shocked when Siddhartha left home and took to the roads. My mother too put up a bitter resistance. My father was getting old, she said. There was a family fortune at stake, and said the family needed me to keep a steady hand on family affairs. I had a cool and level head, she said. And my perfect memory was most useful in matters of business. Despite all this, I was unshaken. Siddhartha had opened my eyes and I couldn't close them again. Once you have entered the Stream there is no going back or scrambling for the bank. I understood clearly what I was leaving behind.'

Impulsively, he took her hand again. It was the ardency of truth that drove him.

'I am a monk. You are a nun. It is not given to us to enjoy the fruits of personal love and passion, however strongly we might feel these things. And exclusive, passion centred love shuts out the world beyond the two lovers, whereas the greater love, the love that needs no exclusive object, takes in the whole world. I have left exclusive love behind in order to merit that greater non-exclusive love.'

Tears rolled down Pchiti's cheeks and onto her breasts. Without losing her grace or dignity, she covered herself. Ananda was pleased to see that her grief was real and unmixed with shame. Nor was she afraid to let him see it.

'Let me tell you a story,' he said.

'I'm glad you could visit, padre,' Grandfather says as I make ready to leave. 'I don't get too many visitors you know. Hardly anybody bothers with an old man who has outlived his era.' A whingeing tone I know only too well has entered his voice. 'Only the professional help of course, the nurses who come in to make sure I'm not dead and can still feed myself.'

He stares at his empty glass. Not quite empty. There are a few drops of whisky at the bottom. He ups the glass and waits until the drops of whisky have made their way down the glass to the rim where his tongue does the rest. From where I'm sitting, his tongue looks like a fat red slug slicking the glass.

'The nurses don't like me to have, you know…' he holds up the glass. 'So I hide it from them. What they don't know won't hurt them.' He laughs. 'They say it's bad for my ticker, but I'll tell you what, my old ticker needs a snifta or two. A bit of a shot in the arm. Do you think, padre, that next time you come you could bring a bottle? I'm sure you could smuggle it past the quartermaster.'

'I'm sure I could.' I pick up the parcel which I had forgotten to give to grandfather. I am curiously reluctant to let go of it. It's now or never. 'And, while we're on the subject…' Grandfather holds out the glass to me, 'how about another couple of fingers. All for a good cause! Old soldiers never die and all that.'

I hesitate, but take the glass. To hell with it, who am I to judge?

'All for a good cause,' I say, heading for the medicine cabinet.

'I've nobody much to visit me. Most of my old friends are dead or think I've gone the same way. I have a grandson, but he never visits me. I suppose he has his own life to live, although what most people call living these days is a pretty poor excuse for a life.' He gives me a cunning look. 'If you see him, tell him I'm dead. That will relieve his mind. His poor aching heart.'

'Why do you say that?'

I hand him the glass. He takes it with a fine sense of entitlement, hardly glancing at it. Growing expansive, he says, 'He doesn't know he's alive, poor boy. That's worse than not knowing you're dead. He rattles around like a fly in a bottle. You know, I read in the paper that there are people who stab and cut themselves just so they know they're alive. You never saw anything like that at Passchendaele. Everybody was too busy keeping their heads down. You know you're alive when you see nothing but dead people, and mortar shells are falling out of the sky like black poppies.' He takes an appreciative sip.

'Actually, I did see your grandson.'

'Really? Don't tell me he wanted to pray. He wouldn't know God if he fell over him.'

'Not exactly. He gave me something for you. A present.'

'He gave me a present? What's come over him? I never saw him think about anybody other than himself.'

'Well, you never know. You can always be surprised.'

I hand the package over to him. He carefully puts his whisky down on his bedside cabinet before taking the package. 'Well, I'll be buggered. Knock me down with a feather.'

He opens the package like a little kid at a birthday party, recklessly throwing the wrapping paper off the bed. He holds the picture at arm's length and stares at it for a long while. The flapper with the long, slim cigarette holder batted her eyelashes at him.

'Where the hell did he get this?'

'Why?'

'That's May. When she was young of course.'

'Who was she?'

'My brother's wife of course. She's dead now. He is too. All that old crowd is dead. I don't know what I'm doing still hanging around. I never imagined I would be the last to leave.'

'What was she like?'

'She was a pretty thing, was May. All the men wanted to marry her. My brother was lucky.' His voice grew pensive. 'Everybody else missed out. But she had a temper on her. She stubbed a cigarette out on someone's face once.'

He stares off into the distance, lost in the glow of fond recollections. I figure this is my cue to depart. I bend over and kiss him on the forehead. His skin is dry and papery. Before I can turn away he grips me by the arm.

'Padre! Next time you come, I know you padres do the rounds… next time you come, bring your angel too. That little girl that follows you about. You might like to bring a whole troop of them, a band of angels, like it says in the song. The ones who can carry you away over the rainbow, except that's a different song.' He gestures to his body. 'And I don't know how much longer I can wait.'

The chess game sits in front of him, unfinished, its positions forever locked.

I promise to bring all my angels. The whole troop.

Since there is no hand basin in this scungy flat, I wash my hands over the bath, activating an ancient gas califont which comes to life with a shudder and a spurt. I am careful to avoid stepping on or disturbing the clothes that are lying about, treating them like sacred objects, or untouchables. While at the bath I drop my trousers and splash some water on my genitals to banish any unwelcome smells that might have accumulated during the day, avoiding the soap which doesn't look much cleaner than the sides of the bath. This feels a bit like a belated baptism. I shake my hands to dry them, not trusting the towel either.

I appreciate that the very least of my actions sets up a momentum that goes on repeating itself in the flesh. This means I have to walk very carefully and make as few mistakes as possible. As I raise my leg to go forward, waves of momentum wash into that part of the body, creating a fluid-like, forward motion. To take a step, the leg drifts out and the weight of the body drains into it. In this way I coordinate the body spatulate.

I can do it, Evie. Even without you here to encourage me and support me.

Thus, amoeba-like, I pour myself forward, slipping across the contour of the temporal flow without mishap, seeking the shallower paths of the space-time matrix. I say without mishap, but mishaps abound on every side. It would be so easy to slip off the face of the world altogether. There are moments when I feel that I'm not really some ordinary bloke about to have sex with a dubious woman who wears fishnet stockings, but that I'm far out in the reaches of deep space inside an enormous tin can called the *Omega*, a troglodyte crawling through the belly of a tin fish, battling the enemies of time and reason. Battling alone and feeling seriously abandoned.

My most immediate need is to negotiate back to Zelda or Zelena, my new hippy lover, and consummate that promise, that fierce expectation that separated me from Evie and drove me up too many flights of stairs to this very place, this scungy flat. That ache for completion which knows only one object.

I find her in what should be the lounge, but which is empty except for a mattress, blankets, and the magnificent tapestry I noted earlier. She is sitting on the floor, elbows propped against the mattress behind, legs stretched out in front of her. There are two glasses and an open bottle of wine on the floor beside her, and she is smoking another scented cigarette. Her fishnet stockings have broken strands above one knee, and I notice she is beginning to go a little fat in the thighs. It is true, these details attract me; her frumpy, indifferent looks excite me. It is with satisfaction that I notice that clothes are strewn around in here too.

She's a hippy, I reason. One of the slovenly variety. That's why she slums around on a mattress and smokes intoxicating herbs. And has casual sex when she wants it with casual passers-by, like me, who always have an eye for the main chance. At the same time, I am rather anxious on the question of payment. Even hippies might need money from time to time, and I have no money. She has spoken in an offhand way about her "visitors" – does she mean "clients"?

I cough to clear my throat.

She hands me the cigarette. I take it and have a puff, not because I want it (I have my tobacco secured in my pocket) but to give me time to think. While I'm thinking I sit down beside her.

'Your tapestry, you know, is a sacred object. It's not an adornment or decoration at all, properly speaking.'

'Are you some kinda expert, are you?'

I feel foolish, a bit pompous even, but I can also see something coming up at the end of the line, something wonderful and unmistakable. Even more important than money.

I point to the centre of the tapestry which portrays a couple joined in coitus. 'In their union, the polarities of existence merge. The yin and the yang, the positive and the negative, exchange natures. Broken symmetries are restored to wholeness. The differentiated goes back to the undifferentiated.'

She turns, heavy-lidded, in the direction of the tapestry. 'You don't say? Broken symmetries, broken bones…'

'Yes.' I shuffle a bit closer to her. She's wearing a cheap perfume that smells of apples, but beneath that the fish-like smell of her sex. Clams and oysters.

'Like like the salmon who return to the same spot to spawn, so the lovers swim upstream, against their timeline, to the source.' My voice is shaking. My vision opens out to all the cycles of my births and rebirths and the tangle of my timelines. As long as I remain inside the belly of the iron whale, I will remain at the fulcrum, the very trigger point of my existence, an existence within which this incident is merely one flying fragment. On one hand I can see who I am and where I have come from and how the disparate events of my life have gathered themselves into chronology, yet also I see all that what I am and where I have come from scattered to the four winds, torn up and mixed about and blown back into the face of time.

'That's pretty fancy stuff,' she says, leaning over and detaching the cigarette from between my fingers with a deliberate movement. 'But still, when you boil it down, at the end of the day a fuck's a fuck, isn't it?' Her body pushes against mine as she hauls the cigarette away. I watch it float from the magnetic compass of my fingers. My focus has settled on the enraptured couple at the centre of the tapestry. The male figure sports a pencil-thin moustache curled up at the ends, giving him a debonair, positively rakish appearance.

'Didn't your mother teach you any manners?' She waves the cigarette reprovingly under my nose. The intoxicating fumes make a rush for my brain receptors.

'My mother died when I was young.' I sip at the wine. 'She had an incurable disease.'

'I'm sorry to hear it.' She slurps at her wine and sucks at the cigarette seemingly at the same time. Then, with some effort, she gets to her feet and stands between me and the tapestry. It glows behind her like a brightly coloured rug.

Her voice is flat, with a touch of weariness in it. 'You don't have to feel obliged, you know. I've only just met you, up at that bloody anteroom, which is enough to drive anybody crazy. And it was sweet of you to meet me or wait for me or stalk me or whatever it was you did. I'm okay with that. But don't feel you have to sit here and make small talk, polite remarks about my tapestry, bits about your family history, that sort of stuff… You look like a person with some other place to be.'

She looks strong and forceful, standing there with her feet apart and her chest thrust forward. Formidable.

'Believe me, I'm not being polite.' Her mention of the tapestry brings my eyes back to it. I have to peer around her to see it. The style, and that curly moustache, suggests that it is Turkish, perhaps Seventeenth Century. It can't be an original, surely. There's no way a person like Zelda could possess such an expensive item.

'It's just my funny way of talking. Broken symmetries are something of a speciality of mine. Undifferentiated wholeness is the fundamental state of the universe. Hard to forget.'

She looks at me with deep suspicion. And grins. A big wide grin. You wanna play? the grin said, then let's play. Uneven as they were, she had the teeth for it. 'Go for broke, buddy, tell me why my tapestry is not a tapestry but some kind of sacred object. Spit it out. Do your worst. I'm all ears.'

'You asked for it!' My hand, palm out, floats in the air and docks with hers. Gently I pull her back down beside me. I don't let go of her hand as I speak, and gently stroke her palm with my thumb. 'Your tapestry is the real deal. It is a yantra, which is the visual equivalent of a mantra. Now you chant a mantra to put yourself into a spiritual state and block out distracting thoughts and feelings. You do the same with a yantra except you sit in front of it and meditate upon it. It has the same effect.'

'Really? Let's do it then.'

I take her hand in both of mine and stroke her wrist. 'Look at how the temporal flow bends around the whole tapestry just as it bends around the lovers at the centre.'

'The temporal flow. Wow! Whatever floats your boat, buddy.'

'This tapestry itself is a still point, a locus, an object of power. It has the power to bend time. The time wind can't touch it.'

'I think you're right.' She has a good long suck at the cigarette. 'I'm starting to get the feel of that myself.' She turns her arm over for some stroking on the underside.

'Those vibrant colours work directly on our vibrational centres. They can change our energy state and our perception of things.'

'Wow! And I just thought they looked pretty.'

'They do look pretty! But they are more than just pretty. They are capable of releasing submerged powers.'

As soon as I have said this, there is an explosion inside my head. I hear the sound of rushing water. Both my ears pop. The saliva in my mouth bubbles like sherbet. I see that the submerged powers have aroused her kundalini, the cosmic energy that rests at the base of the spine. Just rests there, waiting for the signal, the jolt of awakening. Zelena kundalini is glowing like a banked fire in granite, infusing her sexual centres with energy. Her spine is beginning to light up like a Christmas tree. It occurs to me that we are not the strangers we seem to be. The old joke line about having known someone in a previous life may not be so funny. I don't even believe in previous lives; that's all just a big fantasy, wish fulfilment stuff. Yet I can't shake the feeling that this woman is familiar to me, that we have pursued the tantric goal of oblivion in love in many different contexts and dimensions. Our meeting in the anteroom, our return here with sexual intent, is no accident. We have come here to complete a task begun deep in our pasts. It all falls nicely into place.

Energy merely borrows form, a little like an actor borrowing a mask. In this lifetime Zelena has assumed a hippy disguise, a veil of drugs and illusion. Yet her yantra, her sacred tapestry, had been quietly doing its work, undermining the false and preparing the ground for the true.

'Jeez! What am I supposed to do? Take it off the wall hide it? Worship it? Bow down in front of it every morning?'

'You don't have to do anything. That's the beauty of it.'

'So it's just working away on my vibrational centres, right?'

'That's the idea.'

Her arm lies supine, surrendered to my caress. I circle my fingers on her palm. She has broad, square, practical hands.

'That tickles.'

I wriggle closer. Her head now naturally tucks into my shoulder. Her hand, the one I am stroking, falls naturally on my thigh.

'See the dragon's head, in the corner, with all the colours coming out of its mouth? I've seen it before, somewhere. Anyway, that dragon is time. Time is coming out of its mouth setting loose the temporal flow. Along with that comes creation and division, differentiation and conflict. Those tantric lovers at the centre turn around to face this temporal flow, this storm of time, and swim upstream, back into the dragon's mouth, back to the source.'

'Wowie! How do they do that? Can we do that?'

'Sure we can. The movement of the kundalini is sparked by the blissful union of the lovers. All we have to do is ride that energy up the spine to the crown of the head where it will mate with the complementary energies of the universe. Fuse together.'

'You mean they just ride that energy all the way up?' She disengages her hand from mine and allows it to float upward.

'That's right. First they have to conquer their physical limitations. See that king in the bottom corner spearing a boar? He's subjugating his bestial nature.' I reclaim her hand from the air. 'Listen, Zeldia…'

'Zelena.'

'Sorry Zelena, I have problems with names.'

'Don't think twice about it, John. I'm not big on names myself. Zeldia had a certain ring to it. I can be a Zeldia if you want.'

She disentangles her hand from mine and reaches for her cigarette lighter. 'Is that it then? Is that the big deal?'

She studies me through a haze of scented smoke. I try to relax. I mustn't rush this. It must take its own course. For many aeons this consummation has been building, a few more minutes won't make any difference.

'Well, it is a pretty big deal.'

'I guess it is, if you make a big deal out of it.'

She hands the cigarette back to me. It's starting to look a bit tired. I take a few puffs just to be in the swim.

She gestures to the tapestry. The grin is back. 'He looks like a pretty cool customer, with that moustache. He looks like he does it every day.'

'He does. They spend a long time at it, those sexual yogis.' I remember to curve the cigarette back into her hand, guiding it to a successful landing between her fingers.

'So you reckon they meditate on the tapestry and that gets them off?'

'Sort of…'

'Well let's try it then?'

'What?'

She adopts a cross-legged posture, hands and knees, and gazes solemnly at the tapestry.

'Let's try it. Makes a change from the usual, I must say.'

I sit beside her, adopt the same posture and stare at the painting.

As she says, it makes a change.

October Nortikiss, space captain and lantern-jawed hero, had an itch under his armpit. That was about the worst place to get an itch, since the tight fabric of the space gown would stretch if he lifted his arm to get at the itch, and prevent access. Almost everywhere else, an itch was scratchable. It was even possible to rub against something to deal with a back itch.

Since there was nothing he could do about it, he kept on swinging through the darkness like a monkey in a forest with a flea in his fur. He had turned his helmet light to minimum to save power, but actually preferred it darker. Light merely made the corridors look narrower, the rooms smaller, and the whole place more claustrophobic. In the dim light, distances disappeared quickly into nowhere, which might be anywhere.

He had got into the rhythm of it now, managing the hand-holds and the null-grav. He didn't know where he was going, but it seemed to him that he was developing something of an instinct around which direction to take when he reached junctures. These corridors led to places, and at least human logic ruled their organisation. At one point he passed a kitchen that looked just the way a kitchen should, and that gave him heart. Control centres, recreational areas, sleeping quarters, all made sense to him, was familiar territory.

In one room he found, he turned up his light because it was more spacious than he had yet seen. There were several couches that wouldn't be out of place in a standard Twentieth Century suburban home, some brightly coloured throw rugs on the floor and a couple of Art Nouveau lampstands. Somebody had gone to some effort to make this space look like an earthly room. On further investigation he discovered that a whole house had been constructed with bedrooms and windows and a front door. Inside the house you might be forgiven for imagining that you are still on earth. One of the windows looked out at a street scene that looked real enough to walk out into: houses, fences, shrubs, gardens and footpaths – a few pedestrians. Even the occasional car going past. Absolute verisimilitude, except, perhaps everything was a little too clean and shiny, the sky a little too blue, the roses a little too red, the footpaths a little too well swept, the buckle on the schoolbag of a girl with a skipping rope a little too bronze. Still, who would complain about everything looking fresh and clean?

While the front of the house looked out over a bright morning, at the back of the house there was a veranda, complete with a couple of deck chairs, that looked out over a plausible-looking piece of lawn with a somewhat unkempt piece of garden behind, looking ghostly in moon light. He could even hear the sounds of an owl or two in the distance. *Whirlpool! Whirlpool!* How clever.

I could live here, Nortikiss thought. If gravity and the life support systems were up and running, he might be more comfortable here than on the *Frolix 6*. And the contents of his brown envelope were of little consequence now. His orders didn't count for much in the territory of the damned where the Fishmen ruled.

The existence of the house, however, made him wonder at the size of the *Omega*. In space, everything looks small at a sufficient distance. Only when they were closer did the hugeness of the vessel strike them. If it was big enough to contain a house, it might be big enough to contain a whole little city. Somehow that idea was not so comforting. A house was fine. A city was overkill. He wanted to radio back to One-eye and find out what the dimensions of this craft really were, but remembered the body floating upside down. That can't really have been One-eye, of course, since he would have had no way of getting from the *Frolix 6* to the *Omega*.

He tried without success to raise the *Frolix 6* on his suitphone.

He floated from the authentic looking balcony back into the lounge and was enormously relieved to find Beverly there. He had to stop himself from rushing over to her, an action that might see him bouncing off the walls.

'What happened, where have you been, did you find the core?'

Beverly didn't answer. She kept her faceplate turned away from him. He belatedly realized that he simply assumed it was her. After all, who else would be floating around inside the *Omega* in a space gown? He reminded himself that a ship like this was indeed a mini-world and could carry enough people for a small city indeed, and that he and Beverly had seen nobody except for the one-eyed man floating upside down relative to the furniture. They had no idea where everybody went.

He backed off a bit, and circled around her, trying to see her face. There could be anything inside that somewhat svelte space gown, pretending to be a human female. All kinds of horrors cooked up by the Fishmen, for a start. Or an actual Fishman. Nortikiss had, over the course of pulling himself through endless corridors, come to doubt the physical existence of either the Fishmen or the Einstein Disrupter. Whatever the brown envelope said, whatever high command back on Earth (if it was Earth) believed was happening, Nortikiss had come to suspect that the so-called Fishmen were a manifestation of an immaterial life form, less of a life form than an energy; less of an energy than a force, like gravity or entropy. But new. Newly leaked in from another dimension. Experienced by the human mind as a disease. An inimical force. A fish that can walk upright, and smells.

Now he was revisiting that line of thought, which, he could see, tended to abstract the Fishmen right out of existence, pretty much. Yet there was something inside that space gown, floating around, turning its face away from him.

'Okay,' he says in a conciliating voice, as if they have just had a big argument. 'If something has happened just tell me. We are in this together. We've got each other's backs…'

Nothing on the radio band but deep static, the far-off sound of galaxies exploding and collapsing.

'Say something, anyway. Tell me what a conceited prick I am, if you like. I'm too conceited to let it wound me too badly. Tell me that I never saw you as anything but a sex object, a smart one but still a sex object. I'll cry mea culpa to everything you say. Just talk to me.'

As if in answer, or perhaps it was an answer, the figure began to turn towards him. He was hugely relieved to see Beverly's face. But only for a moment. Her face showed no expression, no emotion. Her eyes passed sightless over his.

He grabbed her arm. It was reassuringly solid. 'Are you blind? Deaf? Christ.'

He took a better look at her eyes, and wished he hadn't. She was there all right, she saw him, but not the Captain and lover she knew, but as meat for her hunger. She opened and closed her mouth and made chewing motions at him.

'No,' he said, but he pushed himself a little further away.

She followed, clawing at his oxygen feed.

'No you don't.'

He pushed her away, which meant they were both pushed back. Fighting in null-grav was a special art, and he would prefer to avoid it. Flight or fight, flight looked the better option now. But he couldn't quite bring himself to turn tail and beat a retreat. Couldn't quite believe what his senses were telling him.

Risking attack, he approached again to get another look at her face. In a pocket of his space gown nestled his space blaster, a handy little disintegrator that could melt metal, but he didn't draw it, not yet. Another look through her faceplate and he drew the weapon without a second thought. Her grey face with its waxy texture confirmed his fears. This was not Beverly, at least the living woman he knew. This Beverly was dead. Not the walking dead, the floating dead, and he giggled and kept giggling until he cranked down his oxy level.

Beverly was a zombie.

'Give me a break,' he yelled to the great indifferent universe at large.

'Oc-to-ber,' Beverly croaked, a timbreless voice breaking through the static. 'Oc-to-berrrrr…'

I don't know how long Zelena and I sit side by side staring at her wondrous tapestry. Because it was constructed as a mandala, it is even more potent as a meditative object than I realized. It sucked me right into its cosmos, plunging me through ever diminishing concentric circles to the entwined couple at the ever-receding centre. They were at the heart of it, the way black holes are said to be at the heart of every galaxy. Multicoloured energies radiated from them. Stars were being born and dying in the space of an embrace. So were gods. Even the gods were swept away in that maelstrom. The energy which manifested through these lovers came pouring through from another dimension, white holes in dark space, a burst of consciousness beyond comprehension.

'Whoa!' I said, pulling myself out of it. My ears were ringing.

'The earth didn't move for me,' Zelena says with a giggle. 'A pretty picture, but the cosmos never cracked so much as a fart. Can't say the same about men.' This time with a harder giggle.

Looking at the glowing fire of her kundalini, I can hardly credit what she is saying. I wonder if she is trying to make me jealous, or perhaps excite me with the prospect of her promiscuity. I have no jealousy of other men, because they were just substitutes, and her promiscuity does excite me.

'When you're seventeen the earth might move. Occasionally. Those days are long gone.' She slurps at her wine.

'That's because you haven't been fucked properly,' I say encouragingly. Anyway, given the active state of her kundalini, I don't believe her. I have a feeling that for her, the earth moves all the time. Whatever, I don't want her to feel sad about her sad hippy life. More than anything in the world I want to see her smiling, fulfilled and properly fucked. The feeling is almost maternal. 'There's nothing like the real thing.'

'You sound like an ad for Coke.'

'It's very important to be *properly* fucked.' I want to keep saying those words to her, putting *proper* and *fucked* together, with all the arrogant male-prick implication they contain. It is my kundalini talking to hers (we both turn on the wheel of the heavens), talking dirty. I take her hand and squeeze it gently between my two palms. Her hand becomes the meat in my sandwich. I can stroke both the underside and the top of her wrist at the same time, each hand like a different lover.

'I see. And you're just the man to do it. Right? The Johnny on the spot. You're going to make the earth move. You're going to get that kundalini rattle-snaking up my spine.'

'It's already on its way.' I incline my head modestly.

'Jesus Frog!' She rolls her eyes histrionically, 'I don't know about you, buddy, I really don't. And I have a pretty broad tolerance level, believe me.'

I touch the slope of her shoulder, where the edge of her blouse meets her neck, feeling from the shape of her skin and the texture of the energies flowing through her, the shape and texture of her body. I can feel the balance and patters of momentums that chase their way over her flesh.

'So what you doing now, touching my neck, means you have subjugated your bestial nature, and you're swimming upstream back into the mouth of that dragon in my tapestry, upstream against the… what did you call it…?'

'The temporal flow.'

'Yeah, that's it. It has a nice ring to it. What is it exactly?'

I wave my hand around in an airy gesture. Put to me bluntly like that, I can't seem to find the words. It's all about a plot to subvert the universe, but I'm not about to go into all of that. It's all about this cheap and tawdry story we are living in, but I'm not going to tell her that either. Or all the effects on the resonance level of all those colours swirling out of the centre of the tapestry, where the lovers are still engaged in blissful coitus.

'You mean time?'

'Ahh… sort of.'

'Then why don't you say so? Are you one of those blokes who likes to use a lot of fancy words when simple ones will do?'

'I haven't thought of it that way.'

'No? I had a teacher once who liked fancy words. He taught us a poem about that "temporal flow" of yours. I don't remember much about it except it was some guy trying to his hands up his lady's skirt. I just remember these two lines:

The grave's a fine and private place
But none, I think, do there embrace.'

'That's very true.'

'And not a word wasted.'

I take her at her word, take her hand, bring it my mouth and suck at two fingers. Both taste of nicotine and cheap soap, probably the same soap I saw in the bathroom.

'So what's the deal, Johnny? Are we over the talking bit now? You ready to get down to business?'

Her use of the words *deal* and *business* raises an unpleasant spectre. I was about to stroke her breast and consolidate the gains made by my dazzling wit and deep and meaningful observations, but am hit by a sudden anxiety about the money question.

I take her fingers out of my mouth and rest them on my knee. This is intended to be a strategic retreat, but, I realize, might not look like that to her.

It is not totally clear that she expects money for this little adventure, she hasn't asked for any particular sum, we could well be just of couple of happily consenting adults, but her throwaway attitude suggests that this is business as usual for her. Another night on the mattress with some John.

Forthrightness and honesty would be the best policy. It usually is.

Grinning weakly, I jingle the little bit of change in my pocket. Such a pathetic amount, you can hardly call it a jingle. More like a *clink clink*. Like two very small, lonely coins trying to find each other in my pocket.

'What are you doing? Are you jerking off.' She is pouring more wine for both of us, and she has produced another hand-rolled cigarette.

'I'm checking the change in my pocket.'

'Oh yeah,' she sucks noisily at the wine.

I regret the loss of momentum. Just when we'd been getting somewhere! I should just ask her outright, and I'm somewhat miffed that she didn't state her terms at the beginning, the way a real pro would. She played me along with those fishnet stockings and here we are.

I pull out my packet of tobacco and place it on the floor with some solemnity. It has that heady, fresh smell that newly bought tobacco has. As she lights her herbal one, Zelena considers my bright and shiny little offering. 'Very nice,' she says.

'That's the way the money goes, pop goes the weasel,' I say as gaily as possible.

She hands me the herbal one and picks up my tobacco, giving it an appreciative sniff. I take a hit of hers just to be in the swim. She's about to dip into the packet, get her fingers into that moist mess, when she freezes because of the shock of sudden comprehension.

'So what's he got in his pocketsies then?'

'Is that a riddle?'

'A penny for a poke, is that it?'

'A bit of loose change.'

'For a loose woman.'

'I wouldn't say that.'

'I imagine you wouldn't.' Her fingers now resume their plunder. A fat cigarette swiftly takes shape. She has drawn back a little, away from me.

'So this is how you see this, is it? About money?'

'Well…' I thought of the jokes we made at her door about wives. Her throwaway comments and general demeanour, or should we say misdemeanour, were pretty plain. That she might be hiding a sensitive soul behind it all has hardly occurred to me.

'The man who plays, pays. Right?'

'Right.'

She sticks the fat cigarette she rolled from my tobacco behind her ear and proceeds to roll a second, just as fat. 'Well if that's what it's all about, I'd say you'd pretty much used up your loose change already. I've run out of loose over here.'

'Zeldia, listen.'

'Zelena, pal.'

'I have trouble with names.'

'Is that fucking right.'

We both take stock. I choose to stare at the tapestry, at the impassive ecstasy of the lovers. She chooses to concentrate on getting the second cigarette rolled.

'Surely though, a man of your means has got a credit account or something.'

'What means?'

'The man who plays, pays, remember? Don't you forget that. One way or another, you pay. Where's your plastic? I've got a terminal here.'

'That's right. I've got my Virtue Savings Bank debit card,' I say brightly, as if just remembering.

'So there you go, you've covered your arse.'

'That might be an exaggeration.'

She stares down at my tobacco packet as if contemplating rolling a third cigar.

'Let's put it to the test, shall we? Let's see what you've got.'

Keeping firm hold of her wine, she stands up and I follow. Upright like this, I feel a bit like a giraffe. She lumbers for the kitchen and I follow at the slower pace. I seem to be having trouble with my horizontal and vertical axes. Arriving in a cramped kitchen, I fumble in my pocket for my card, which I haven't used since the tobacconist, with the sudden fear that I might have lost it. But there it is, with its little hologram chip inset in the corner, containing the cheerless details of my financial life, and all kinds of other things for all I knew. She fed my card into a compact, handy-home terminal.

'Okay,' she said, 'do your thing.'

I punch some numbers into the keypad, thinking sadly that these days even hippies have handy-home terminals in their down-and-out flats. There is no originality left. No purity. Lovers across many lifetimes meet again and what do they do? Stand around feeding plastic cards into terminals.

A familiar voice issues from her terminal. 'I'm sorry, Mr Kent, but the terminal you are attempting to use does not belong to a registered business. Remember, your debit card can only be used to make purchases from a registered business.' These are the self-satisfied, unctuous tones of my alarm clock, I'd know them anywhere.

'Get fucked,' I reply stoutly. You start letting machines order you around and define your reality grid, you are on the slippery slope to perdition.

Zelena laughs. Her chest breaks open like an old smoker's.

'You're welcome, Mr Kent,' her terminal says.

'You're welcome, Mr Kent,' Zelena says. She has the glass up to her face and its phoney red depths throw a jiggling light over her face.

'I take it you're not a registered business,' I said.

'What do you think?'

'I could bring double the money, next time,' I say, cunningly raising the possibility of repeated visits.

'Double or nothing,' she says.

'That's right.'

'Most likely nothing.'

'That's not true.'

The red from the glass is dancing on her hands.

'You have an honest face,' she says.

I have arisen from my chair, my less than beloved tubular steel chair, the vinyl clinging kinetically to the polyester in my trousers. I have suffered the brown envelope and the antiseptic handshake, already murmured the polite formulas of parting.

I have shrunk the official down to his proper shape, and he doesn't look so much like a Confederation Starfleet Admiral, more like your average pen-pusher, short without being stocky, a man who keeps his fingernails well trimmed and his relationships in perspective. He is neither mysterious nor likely to generate mysteries, a face that will neither inspire confidence nor destroy it. A man from whom one can expect very little.

Really, I tell him as he guides me to the door, I have nothing to complain about.

Leaving Grandfather behind me, I set a direct course for the Tower. No more prevaricating, no more lurking in doorways watching the world go by as if I were not a part of it. I like to breathe and eat and make love just like everybody else, even an invasion of Fishmen from the other side of time isn't going to change that. I am tied to the earth by my grandfather's grief, if nothing else.

Up ahead, the Tower looms large enough to look like a perpendicular city, erected to balance the horizontal rectitude of our streets. It is good to be on the move again after visiting my grandfather, always a trying, tiring business, probably because of the atmosphere of stalemate in the air. I have decided to head directly for my appointment by the shortest route, letting the streets fold out in front of me in their tried and true precision, accurately placing every building, street corner or shopfront in accord with memory. It feels as if someone might have assembled this cityscape as a jigsaw puzzle and smoothed over the lines.

I allow myself to smile, letting my lips stretch back from my teeth in a relaxed manner, exhaling the very last particles of poisonous smoke from the cigarette I had earlier, remnants of which seem to have clogged up my lungs while I was sitting with grandfather. I centre myself in alignment with my spine, trying to find the balance of walking, the true balance I discovered earlier, but do not quite succeed. Perhaps something happened at grandfathers that pushed me slightly at variance to the plane of the elliptic. The street has tilted at a slight angle and the smoothness of walking has turned into an effort. The edge of perfection has worn off the day. The single cloud, once poised so precisely above the ancient chestnuts, has gone loose and messy, compromising the pristine clarity of the light. A hot, dry, psychic wind blows in from the north-west, ragging the grasses of yellow tussocky hills, and sucking the energy from the faces of the people on the street. As I pass a street corner I see two men having an altercation, a punch or two being thrown, and I assume the wind has got the better of them. They could even be suffering dehydration and not know it.

It is evident that a lot of negative energy has entered my body, probably through the agency of the cigarette, which has leached me of B and C vitamins and had a generally debilitating effect on my metabolic processes. Viewed this way, the cigarette is like the famous wooden horse in that it has ferried, in secret and in the guise of pleasure, these effects into my body. You don't need Fishmen and their fiendish devices when you have tobacco and old men with pallid faces selling it.

I decide to stop in at a health shop and buy an energy bar, figuring that my blood sugar levels had dropped to hell. It can happen quite suddenly. One moment you are wafting along, free as the breeze, the next thing the breeze drops and so do you.

As I am making my purchase, using Evelyn's change, a tall youth with black hair falling over his eyes and a bent gaze approaches me. He looks sceptically at the spirulina bar I have placed on the counter.

'Yuk! That stuff is bloody awful. Don't you know that?'

'Each one to his own,' I say stiffly, turning away from him. He has no shoes and outsided, horny feet. He is wearing a faded leather jacket with holes in it.

'Makes your mouth green.'

I don't answer, hoping he will take the hint. He doesn't.

'It's your funeral, pal,' he says as I pick up my spirulina bar, insisting on standing uncomfortably close. I cling righteously to my bar. 'Try a fish pie sometime. Yummy stuff. They make the best fish pies in town just along the road,' he gestures with his thumb. 'You can actually taste the fish.' He grins hugely, having apparently made some kind of witticism.

'That's very nice,' I say politely, about to step around him.

'Are you a fish man?' he asks, still grinning. He's friendly enough, but there is something maniacal about that grin.

'Uh?'

'It's the crust that does the trick. The pastry.' His hands, I notice, are covered in black stains while his clothing and hair are studded with minute pieces of metal. He is standing close enough for me to smell the fishiness of his breath.

I panic. I can't stay in the shop a second longer. I dash past the youth for the door. He gives me a comradely smile as I go past.

'Don't let them get to ya, pal,' he says. 'Look after your head, man.'

I am relieved to see Evie outside the shop. I was hoping she hadn't deserted me. You never know with Evie. It is disconcerting to have her pop up all over the place unheralded. It makes me doubt how real she is. If she were my guide in times of need, I supposed she could come and go as she pleased.

'You should have held your ground,' she says. She skips a couple of times. 'He was just trying to spook you.'

'Why would he do that?'

'For the fun of it. Because you look a person easily spooked, maybe.'

'Do I?' For some reason, ancient fears have been triggered by this incident. 'You know, Evie, this used to be a lovely city when I was growing up. Citizens went about their business in perfect confidence, without the fear of being accosted. And people were decent, or at least did their level best. People did not feel entitled to come up to you and criticise your purchases and breathe fish fumes into your face.'

'You should have held your ground,' Evie says reprovingly.

I open my spirulina bar and take a bite. It's very sweet and chewy. I can imagine my mouth turning green.

'I could have avoided all this if I had just taken a bus. But I thought a nice brisk walk would do me good. Now I don't feel well. I need a pee.'

'You need to talk to her.'

'Who?'

'Evelyn, of course. Who else?' We've pulled clear of the shops and Evie has the space to do a bit of vigorous skipping on the spot. 'You have allowed your relationship with her to deteriorate. That conversation you had last night was not pleasant.'

'You're telling me. I thought that was a dream I had after I got up to pee. And I need a pee right now, by the way. An invasion from another dimension.' I give a short, hard laugh to show what I think of that idea. 'She was just doing that to mock my writing.'

'That's what you need to talk to her about.'

'That's not a good idea. Believe me. You don't know her the way I do.'

We make a detour to the nearest public convenience and Evie waits outside, holding my parcel and umbrella. I am standing at the urinal, waiting for my body to respond to the appropriate signals when the dark-haired youth appears beside me, whistling gently between his teeth.

Don't you cry

Don't you cry

Don't you cry when I'm gone

For me it is a moment of intense discomfort, the sort of discomfort men share when standing together at urinals *(Meet me for frolix at 6, Nortikiss)*. This discomfort is made more acute by the fact that while he is splashing happily away I am still waiting for the train to arrive. He's all finished and zipping up while I'm still standing there, my body refusing to cooperate. I feel exposed and helpless.

'Curfew tonight,' he says genially, heading for the wash basin.

'Curfew?'

'Yup.' He shakes his hands and holds them under the dryer. The machine clicks on obligingly and gushes hot air. 'For everybody's protection.' His grin implies that we both know better. He flicks an unruly piece of black hair out of his eyes. 'Don't be caught out tonight after dark.'

I'm still waiting as he goes out.

Evie's skipping happily away as I come out.

'Did you see that same pushy guy?'

'Yes,' *tush-whip, tush-whip,* 'did you have a panic attack?'

'No. But my bladder did.'

I pull out my only partly eaten spirulina bar. I offer some to Evie.

'No thanks.'

'Why not?'

'Cos it makes your mouth green.'

Ananda's tale:

There was once a monk called Boti who fell in love with a beautiful woman named Janapada Kalyāni. They were with each other for many months, and every day the bonds of their affection grew stronger. They would do everything together, walk together, sit together at Siddhartha's talks, and even when they went begging in the towns Janapada would position herself on the opposite side of the street where they could keep each other in sight. Wherever you found one, there you would find the other.

After a time the issue of their marriage came up, since it seemed they were destined to be together for the rest of their lives. Although her family had hoped for a high marriage for their daughter, rather than to a lowly monk, their families came to an agreement, they were reconciled and a date was set. Many friends and relatives arrived, and there was much excitement.

On the morning of the wedding, Siddhartha visited Boti, for he had seen much sorrow and suffering in Boti and Janapada Kalyāni's future, and wanted to warn him. He asked Boti to sit quietly in meditation, then sat with him and took his hand.

'I am going to take you to Heaven, Boti. Are you ready?'

'Heaven? Where the gods live?'

'There are no gods, Boti. Heaven is in the dimension of the devas, and devas are as mortal and time-bound as you or I, although generally wiser and happier. Those who live in deep accord with their nature have created a heaven, and this heaven itself may be shared with humans who have come out of the long sleep and undergone the Awakening. Would you like to see it?'

And without further ado, he guided Boti though the many deva worlds that lie parallel to this one, and are piled invisibly upon the air. On their way they passed a female monkey whose face had been terribly disfigured in an accident, and who was abhorrent to look upon. Boti turned his head away from this monstrosity, and thought of Janapada Kalyāni, and how beautiful she was, and how she would soon be his.

After travelling through the ten realms of the material plane, they arrived at Tavatimsa, the deva heaven. Boti saw that there were indeed devas there, and humans too, just as Siddhartha had said. Tavatimsa was a realm of exquisite beauty, with waterfalls and rainbows and pink marble. But that was not all. There were maidens the like of which the human eye had never seen, with celestial voices beyond the normal range of human hearing. Boti's eyes nearly fell out of his face. Such beauty was touched by a magic beyond human grasp. It set up a fierce longing in Boti. He gazed upon these maidens for many an eon but still could not get enough of them. It was like a thirst that could not be slaked.

'You see these maidens?' Siddhartha said.

'I see them,' Boti said.

'Their beauty arises because they are totally at one with what they are. There are no cruel divisions of mind to torment them. They manifest like flowers in the field.'

'Truly, oh Gautama, this vision has shattered me. Such beauty is not meant for human eyes.'

'What do you think now of your bride to be, Janapada Kalyāni?'

Boti didn't want to think about Janapada Kalyāni. He could hardly bring her into his mind, barely see her face or hear her voice. He wanted to turn away. 'She is nothing. Compared to these nymphs, she is as ugly as that female monkey we saw on the way here.'

His face became long and his brow furrowed as thought tormented him.

'Never mind, Boti,' Siddhartha said cheerfully. 'No need to get despondent. I promise that you will join the company of those nymphs if you do as I suggest and take pleasure in living the Holy Life.'

Boti was astonished. 'You can do that? You can make that promise?'

'I am the Buddha, am I not, Boti?'

'You are indeed.'

'Indeed. And can the Buddha be untrue to his own word?'

'No, venerable one.'

'Then apply yourself diligently to your meditations, and this world can be your world too.'

'But I want to stay here now. I want to stay here forever.'

'You have to earn your place here, Boti. Not just anybody can come and enjoy the favours of these nymphs. If that were the case, Tavatimsa would quickly fill up with the worst sort of lecher and desire-struck dreamer.'

Boti could see that, and reluctantly left Tavatimsa with Siddhartha. He lingered for as long as he could. Only when Siddhartha took him firmly by the hand did he tear his eyes away, wanting, as he did, to imprint the image of the nymphs of Tavatimsa on his mind forever.

So they returned to earth, and Boti caused an immediate upset by cancelling the wedding and announcing his intention to undertake the full rigours of the Holy Life. Nothing that anybody said, including Janapada Kalyāni who threw herself at his feet and made a passionate appeal, could shift him. There was loud talk, and accusations flying to and fro. Everybody was in a big panic except Siddhartha. Some said that it was Siddhartha's fault, that he'd turned Boti against Janapada Kalyāni. Others, closer to Boti, said that he really did no longer love Janapada Kalyāni, and had fallen in love with a much more powerful vision than any human girl could defeat. Still others said that Boti had lost his mind, and when he regained it he would deeply regret what he had done.

Boti was absolutely firm of purpose and became Siddhartha's most ardent followers, spending many hours in intensive meditation and the holy practice of leaving the world behind, all the time holding in his mind the vision of the nymphs he had seen in the deva heaven. He took no notice of the other monks who teased him when they discovered the true object of his meditations, and held Siddhartha's promise before him like a beacon. Whenever Siddhartha spoke, there was Boti, sitting at the front as close as he could get, with his eager face. After meditations, when the other monks would be looking forward to their evening meal, Boti would remain, sitting sternly upright, indifferent to his hunger.

Some years passed. Janapada Kalyāni finally recovered from her grief and dedicated herself the Holy Life. Her family's anger at Boti's actions finally faded away, particularly when they heard how dedicated he was to his meditations, and how ready he was to experience the Awakening all by himself. He even found a Bodhi tree, just like the one under which Siddhartha had sat when he had awoken to his Buddha nature. When Siddhartha heard of this, he went to visit Boti sitting under this tree.

'Why are you sitting under this tree, Boti?' Siddhartha asked.

'Because this is the magic tree, the same kind you sat under.'

'There are no magic trees, Boti, or they are all magic. The tree did nothing but offer me a little shelter. It was the demons who showed me the way.'

'What do you mean?'

'When the demons attacked me, I was able to see through them to their unreality, their origin as a passing phenomena of mind. Had they not attacked, I would not have seen so clearly this aspect of nature.'

Shortly after this conversation Boti abandoned the tree and set off in search of another spot to meditate. It was hot and dusty and he felt as far from his goal as he had ever been. He became tired and sat on a hard piece of rock to wipe his brow and take some water. As he did so often, he thought about the nymphs in Tavatimsa, when he was suddenly overcome by shame. It was so severe he could hardly breathe. How could he pretend to live the Holy Life when his motive was so base, so craven? No wonder his Awakening had eluded him, for he had sought it merely to fulfil material desires. The shock of this understanding jolted him into awareness, and he had his Awakening right there, on that hard piece of rock. Immediately the divine nymphs of Tavatimsa meant nothing to him. In the bliss of his Awakening, he understood that not only Tavatimsa, but all the ten planes of existence, and the many worlds created from them, were also manifestations of mind and hardly more real than a passing dream.

As soon as Siddhartha saw him, he knew what had happened and he laughed.

'All those years meditating for the sake of my desires, all wasted!'

'No, not wasted,' Siddhartha said gaily. 'You can have the nymphs now, if you want. My promise holds good.'

'I don't want them now,' Boti said. 'My awakening has pierced my body.'

'There's always a catch,' Siddhartha said.

After he had finished the story, Ananda and Pchiti sat in the silence of her hut facing the impossible fact that the bliss of Awakening eclipsed that of the highest human bliss of love and marriage.

Their tears were like the meeting of two streams, one of joy and one of an acute sense of loss.

Zelena and I stand in her kitchen and listen to the voice of my alarm clock droning through one of its routines. Apparently her monitor is unable or unwilling to cut it off.

The cessation of the discriminating mind cannot take place until there has been a turning about in the deepest seat of consciousness… then there will be no more evil outflowings of the mind system.'

I whisper in her ear, 'Let's get out of here, far away from the evil outflowings of the mind system.'

'Your place or mine?'

'I think we're already at your place.'

'So we are. It's your show, buddy.'

Arm in arm we remove ourselves back into the living room and tumble onto the floor by the mattress, somehow missing the mattress itself, Zelena avoiding, at the last moment, knocking over her glass. 'Mustn't ruin the carpet,' she says.

Her kiss tastes of wine and marijuana and loneliness.

We undress in front of each other, trying not to make our stares too hopelessly overt.

Solemnly, I say, 'Zelena, I know you think a fuck is a fuck, and so it is, but we are also bringing two halves of eternity together. We can burn as bright as stars.'

Finally naked, she smiles. She looks trapped and vulnerable. Perhaps she is going to wake up tomorrow morning and think about those stars. 'You certainly got plenty of mileage out of my old tapestry.'

I'm naked now also. Feeling trapped and vulnerable as well. 'I didn't say those things just to get what I want. To get *mileage*. The truth is, I don't know what I want. I never have. I'm envious of people who have a purpose, a quest. You see them on the street, surging along full of intent, full of somewhere to go. I haven't come from anywhere, and I'm not going anywhere.'

'You talk a lot though.'

'I've always been lost, that's why. I just feel my way along like a blind man. I hit the ground in front of me with my stick, or my umbrella, hoping the ground will support me, hoping the mental picture I have of things accords somewhat with the reality.' I gesture to her body. 'This is different. I never counted on this.'

She gives a wheezy laugh. 'So I am a cupcake, am I?'

I circle around her in my leopard form, growling and staring balefully at her with rabid eyes.

'You better come and get me before my icing starts to melt.'

I start to chase her around the room, growling and nipping at her flanks. She makes a poor pretence at fending me off. I nuzzle in under her armpits and end up with teeth full of soft brown hair, somewhat damp and musty.

She giggles. 'You're a real man. I can see that. Do you want to know a secret?'

'What is it?'

'I never do this for money anyway. When it comes to being a slut, I'm

192

just a natural.'

'I think you are.'

'A sucker for an honest face.'

I quit fooling around and grow serious. Or at least my erection does. I go down on my knees in front of her, place my hands on my thighs and arch backwards. I think she was waiting for me to do something else. A child runs across hills as yellow as crayons, a canyon of crayons. 'You haven't seen anything yet,' I say. In such moments, one's dialogue cannot be too corny.

'And I'm a sucker for an honest body, too. You have an honest body.' She allows her gaze to rest pointedly on what is, at that moment, the most visibly honest portion of it.

'An erection can't lie.'

I'm not sure about that, but it sounds good. Perhaps I'd try it out with Evelyn later.

I stretch out luxuriously, allowing my frame its full span, allowing her to get a good eyeful of my honesty. When I close my eyes I find I'm stretching right across the universe. My feet are in one dimension, my head in another, my body like an arc flashing between, flashing along the curve of materiality. My skin is made of tiny luminescent flakes.

'You look like a person praying.'

'My body is praying.'

She handles my genitals with light feathery movements. 'What does a body pray for?'

'Release.'

She pulls back the foreskin so that the wet gleaming head stands forth.

'I didn't know you were a religious person.' Her voice has become nice and low and husky.

'I am I am I am I am. I cry a lot and pray a lot. And I know the Surangama Sutra word for word.'

'Word for word,' she sings softly, leans forward and flicks, lizard-like, over the smooth rounded tip of the glans, leaving it moist in anticipation.

I lie back and look up at the dingy ceiling while her tongue raps around me. The ceiling has cracked into a thousand tiny fissures, making it look like a demented roadmap. 'People think I write, but I don't. I talk to the dead. The dead are good at keeping secrets.'

Her mouth closes over me. Warmth infuses my body. I am floating in a warm ocean, and it feels as if I could float this way forever.

I think I can reconcile myself to dying. The true dying has already happened. I want to say these words but my mouth has gone quiet. Until I say them I can't know if they are true.

After a time she stops sucking me and comes up for a breather. She has undergone a subtle transformation. Her eyes have become large and dark and full of the wisdom of twilight. The lines of her body have smoothed over and become sleeker. Her body now reminds me of a seal, clumsy on land but graceful and at home in her watery element. Her droopy breasts have lifted and grown full, the nipples and areolas glow soft and rich. From its plump, practical surfaces, her body has assumed a mysterious and infinite richness, and, like a Moebius strip, goes on curving into its own angles. At the base of her spine, the kundalini worm glows in its own moist cave.

In a voice shorn of its world-weariness and cigarette cynicism, in a smaller, gentler voice, she says, 'You're serious about this, aren't you? This line about being lovers in parallel worlds or whatever.'

I sit up and match exactly her sensual and sombre tone. 'For me, it feels like I live at right angles to time, sideways to the world. I catch glimpses of things I don't understand. I keep recognising people and situations. My life orbits around a series of motifs. It doesn't progress the way ordinary lives do. When I woke up this morning a little girl with a skipping rope told me to flee the wrath to come. But I find I can't flee. It's like I'm moving through the wilderness of this world like a dancer around a maypole. I exist at a tangent to the world.'

'Is that how you're able to talk to the dead?'

I hide my eyes, or try to. 'Just my own dead.'

'The little girl with the skipping rope, is she dead?'

'I don't know, Evie is a mystery to me. I think she's gone now.'

'Don't worry, she'll be back.'

'She can't stop me from being alone.'

We sit in a warm glow of silence.

'Why are you looking at me like that?' she says, but I think she knows.

'Because your body keeps changing. It keeps growing more radiant. It's like you have grown a new, softer, more golden skin.' My hands hover close enough to her breasts to feel their heat, yet holding back, as if they daren't land upon her. 'I'm not imagining this.'

'Perhaps you aren't.' She touches me on the side, just below the ribs, wonderingly, as if amazed to find me corporeal. 'This is fucking amazing.' She wriggles a little closer. Our postures are starting to resemble those of the couple in the tapestry. 'Go on, touch. You won't fry. You might as well get your nought point nought-nought percent worth.' She's trying to sound tough and hardened but she's not even fooling herself. She looks and sounds… innocent. Her bravado has faded and she finds herself on the edge of wonder. We always think of innocence as belonging to the lost world of childhood, but in fact innocence may be lying in wait for us, to ambush us, at any stage.

It is time for atonement and consummation, triumph and love.

Time to make hay while the sun shines.

A manifestation by some skilful magician of a mannequin

It took Captain October Nortikiss several lifetimes surging around in the tunnels and pipes of the *Omega* before he could admit to himself that he was not seeking anything out, just running away. Running away from his once luscious companion and fuck-buddy, the talented astrophysicist Beverly, red-haired and green-eyed. Luscious no longer. A cosmic beauty no longer.

She was now a zombie in a spacesuit. It was as if she had stepped off the covers of one of those cheap books he'd found. Zeldia the Zombie! This was not a reality grid-symbol construct he wished to inhabit. Not that he would enjoy it for long anyway. Sooner or later his oxygen pressure would drop, he would run out of air, and Zeldia the zombie would have the place to herself, assuming that zombies didn't care about air.

The space hero is having trouble adapting to certain realities. It took him a long time to admit, for example, that Beverly, aka Zeldia the zombie, was following him, tracking him through the entrails of the *Omega*. It took him even longer to admit that he was running away, that he had pushed the blaster into her face and failed to pull the trigger. At the moment of decision, all this training came to nothing. He had chickened out, turned tail and ran. If the Federation got to hear of this, not only would he lose his command, the *Frolix 6*, but be shunned forever as a coward. Failure to kill a fellow officer who caught an alien contagion, thereby endangering the whole of the human race.

And it took even longer to admit that none of that was likely to happen as his chances of getting off the *Omega* were getting more remote with every breath he took.

Just how he knew she was following him, he was not sure. Sound doesn't carry in a vacuum. He had turned his radio off because of the cracked sound of her voice, but even with it on he couldn't tell if she were right next to him or a mile away. The absolute darkness except for the pale cone his suit lamp threw, precluded catching glimpses out of the corner of his eye. He couldn't hear her or see her, or even sense her in some more subtle way, but she was there nevertheless.

To test this, he had hidden behind some large object and waited. He didn't have to wait too many lifetimes and sure enough, along she came, not pulling herself forward using the hand-holds, but treading the air and holding her hands outstretched as if about to squeeze his neck, or his oxygen tubes. He had waited until she moved on before doubling back the way he'd come, to fool her. Which he did, but not for long. Soon she was on his trail once more, an invisible presence, and he had to keep moving or she really would catch up with him and take a hold of his oxygen tubes.

There was no time to rest, no time to sleep. But he did dream. He couldn't stop that. In his dream he was standing in the doorway of his house. The sky was flaming red. There was a little girl in a blue dress. She was pointing to the sky. The flaming red pealed away and he realized that many, many aeons had passed. There were only a few stars in sight, since the expanding universe had whisked all the other galaxies out of sight. The universe was big and empty. With everything moving away from everything else, everything was bereft, everything abandoned. This universe had run its course, emptied itself into impossible distances. And he was alone. A tiny, isolated spark of consciousness in a universe grown too big for mind.

But still, here at the end of time, the *Omega* survived, even though the molecular bonds holding it all together had grown shallow and weak. And the Fishmen were here too. They had grown stronger as the universe had waned. They fed on entropy and waxed fat on the death of stars. An inimical and parasitical life form that passed from universe to universe, sucking up time. Expanding universes were a particular delicacy, as time was nice and stretchy. Collapsing universes were crunchy. Black holes, they spat back out. They followed wormholes through infinity to find their next meal. A brash young universe, newly sprung, that might still have the tang of the Big Bang in it.

How he could know these things in his dream was not clear, but he was certain of what he was seeing. His dream self was even trying to convince the conscious mind that it was all absolutely real.

After his dream he decided he had to stop running and face Beverly. He had to get her oxygen tanks. If she had stopped breathing, which seemed likely if she were a zombie, then she had oxygen. When he ran out, he could use hers. He knew how to do that. It was a clumsy little operation but it could be done.

Summoning the last of his strength, he turned around and faced the darkness. He switched on his suitcom and listened intently to the static, which sounded like far distant voices.

'Come and get me,' he said.

I have Zelena's kundalini at the tips of my fingers. Its coiled energy is seething.

'Is the earth moving now, just ever so little?' I whisper in her ear. I want her to say it, to confess what she is feeling.

'Steady as she goes,' she murmurs.

This is not quite the reaction I have been expecting. A call to sweet holy Jesus, perhaps. I'm getting close to the sweet holy Jesus stage myself.

'What's that noise,' she says, suddenly distracted.

I hear it too. Something like a ringing in the ears, but richer, full of harmonies.

'It is the sound of celestial voices.'

But the mood is broken. What I am saying no longer sounds sexy and mysterious but trite and foolish. Her kundalini slips out of my fingers.

'It's more likely to be that fucking califont. It sings to itself sometimes.'

Behind the celestial voices, I can hear a laboured breathing which cannot be my own or Zelena's. It is a mechanical sound, like someone breathing into a machine. 'Come and get me,' a male voice says. And, after a pause, 'Come and get what's left of me. Which isn't much.' And, after another pause, 'I wish we were making love right now, Zelena. Remember, you once said that making love in null-grav was like doing it in a tub full of warm salty water? And I asked you when you had last done it in a tub of warm salty water, and you said you did it once with a graduate student in a sensory deprivation chamber...' Mechanical as it was, the voice grew warm in reminiscence.

'Can you hear somebody talking?' I ask Zelena. I move a little away from her. My kundalini's wilting a bit too.

'No, but I've suddenly got frightened. And I don't know why.' She grabs a blanket off the mattress and makes a little tent to hide inside.

'What happened?'

'Everything was going swimmingly. You can be quite a good lover, you know. The way you touched me got my spine tingling.'

'Yes, I know.'

'Up yours. Anyway, bells were starting to ring and then I got this smell. Can you smell it? Like rotting fish.'

'I can't smell it.'

'Lucky you. And then I felt there was something huge and horrible nearby. Like right in the next room. I mean the kitchen.' She casts a fearful look towards the door.

'Maybe we should be frightened.'

'What do you mean?'

'There are awesome forces at work to bring us together, or,' I put my arms around her and hug her tight, 'pull us apart.' I look around her room, which seems to have grown shadows. No longer drab and ordinary, it looks as if it might harbour, within its simple shape, all kinds of twists and turns.

From inside the tent. 'That feels good, your arms around me. I feel safe.'

'If I had more arms, I'd put them around you.'

'That's a sweet thing to say.'

'I'm a little bit scared too,'

'A little bit? How can you be a little bit scared. You are either scared or you're not.'

In my head the same male voice crackles forth. Instinctively I put my hands up to my ears to feel for implants, certain that the voice is being broadcast from somewhere, but there's nothing there, or at least, nothing I can feel. 'You can't eat me you know, sweetheart. That's the one disadvantage of being a zombie in a spacesuit, you can't eat anybody. So you might as well give up chasing me.'

'Then I'm scared.' I held onto Zelena as tight as I could, and it wasn't to save her from her fears.

'I think you should go into the next room and check.'

'That would mean letting go of you.'

'True. But it might be worth it. In the long run. We can't sit here forever like frightened rabbits.'

I have a feeling that the source of her fear lies much further away than the next room, but, as my own life kept on demonstrating, nobody knows where the next door will lead them. Towards life or away from it. To worlds undreamt or up the garden path.

'Whatever we are, we are not frightened rabbits.' I let go of her and get to my feet. I feel naked not having her in my arms.

'Do you want me to come with you?'

'I'm not really scared. I think. We just went off the deep end there, for a minute.'

'I've got to get a grip on myself, did you know that? I've got to stop swilling this pisswater,' she indicated to the glass which has somehow got back into her hand, 'and smoking dope, and screwing around with arseholes off the street.' She moves her hands through the air in a deliberate chopping motion, but because she is zonked, all she does is chop her own thought in half. 'What was I saying?'

'About getting a grip on yourself.'

'Are you really going to go through that door and look?'

'Why not? I'm on my feet.'

'Because we both know there is nothing there, right? Just the kitchen. That this is all just our fears getting out of hand.'

'That sounds right.'

'Okay then.'

'We should have kept talking,' the insect voice in my ears says. Despite it being flattened out by time and space, I can hear the grief in it. 'Our problems started when we stopped talking. We let the fabric of rational thought slip away, and the bridge that linked us got swept away in a welter of subjective impressions. Next thing I turn around and you're gone. Then you come back as a zombie. Just one moment of inattention and all that happens.'

I take Zelena's hand, 'Let's keep talking. I don't want you to vanish because of a foolish moment of inattention.'

She clutches my hand. 'What are you talking about? I'm not going anywhere.' She gets to her feet but stays hooded by the blanket. She looks around as if she can see through the walls. 'There's something happening outside. Something coming.'

'I think we're just in a heightened and sensitive state because we have provoked the kundalini. In that hyped up state we have to be very pure, otherwise we'll fall prey to any predatory, free-floating emotions, anxieties, and fears, all trying to get their hooks into us.'

I get my hand under the blanket and stroke her hair. She likes it. We both find it soothing. Maybe there's no need to go and check out the next room. As she said, we both know nothing's there.

The peculiar harmonic, what I called the celestial voices, begins to fade, and along with it, the fear. Her room returns to its ordinary dilapidated self. The voice in my head is fading out. 'I have to take your oxygen tanks, Zeldia. I know you won't miss them. You're too dead to care. But for me, every time I breathe I use up a little bit of the universe… hunting you now…'

Zelena lets out a long breath. I step out of the way.

'I'm still going into the kitchen,' I say.

'Why?'

'Why shouldn't I? I want to get some water.'

'Okay then.'

'Okay then.'

We stand there like a comedy duo who have forgotten their lines.

'There's another possibility.'

'Not a scary one, I hope.' She still has the blanket around her, but is holding it loosely, loosely enough for it to slip off her shoulders a little.

'Maybe it's love. I mean…' I'm suddenly not sure what I mean. 'Love is a big terrifying angel.'

'Is that right? I thought it was having a bit too much on a Friday night.' She's back to her tough self again, but that tough self doesn't go down very far; I know what's beneath it.

Laughter further releases the tension. I want her again. Badly this time. So badly I can hardly breathe. My body's purring.

'Love, eh? I've heard of it.'

'Looks like I got my nought point nought-nought percent of it.'

More laughter, more release of tension, more desire. She feels it too. She doesn't know where to put herself.

'I need water.' I head for the kitchen, sucking on a dry mouth. As expected, the kitchen looks perfectly ordinary and normal. Sitting, apparently quite at home in a perfectly ordinary chair is a large fish, complete with fins and faintly iridescent scales and short stubby legs. The thick tail twitches a little. My hands are quite steady as I fill two glasses of water. If I take no notice of the creature, it might return the favour. It might even go away. Some liquid drips from the chair onto the floor where a small pool is forming. This detail somehow makes it seem much more real, much less like the apparition I want it to be.

At the same time, it strikes me that I know this creature, that I have seen it before. But this is not a memory. It doesn't feel like a memory. It feels like a flash forward, an echo from further up the line.

I ask, what would Evie advise, at this point. Ignore it, of course, is what she would say. Don't turn a hair, she would say, just get your water and get out as you planned. So that's why I do. I don't look at it. I don't even know if it is male or female, and I have no intention of trying to find out. With great deliberation I fill the glasses with water, watching it fill the glass, filling my nose with the chemical smell of the crap they put in the water.

I largely succeed in keeping my cool and the fish creature out of sight, nicely contained in my blind spot. When I turn to go, however, I catch a glimpse of the pool of liquid growing under the chair on which the creature is sitting. It's not water and it's not blood, but it is dark and viscous looking, and in its depths I can see galaxies whirling, being born, dying, and being born again.

I hurry on, trying not to breathe too deeply. I'm sure the creature is giving a pheromone-rich scent, probably the fishy smell Zelena mentioned, because my body is seized by the ache of desire so strong I stumble and almost lose the water. This ache is rooted so deep I know nothing can assuage it. I could fuck for eternity upon the tapestry and still not satisfy it. But that won't stop me from trying.

I turn my back on the fish creature and return to main room without mishap.

'There was nothing there, right?'

As if she needed to ask the question.

'Right. Nothing. Needs a paint job.'

Her relief is evident, and probably embarrassing to her. But she's always got tough girl to come to the party.

'It needs more than a paint job. It needs a wrecking ball.'

'So do I.'

'I can see that, and I think you mean a ball wrecker.'

'Whichever way around you like it.'

It's as easy to see the state she is in as for her to do the same. We both want it with a bone-shaking urgency.

'I'm game either way,' she says, and in that moment she's all fragile again. Not quite sure what she has let herself in for.

We lie down again, this time on the mattress, this time facing each other with a particular, naked intent.

'What's happened to all that dirty talk about kundalinis and stuff? Big time orgasms that link lovers across time.'

'Did I say that?'

'All kinds of dirty stuff. You even had your fingers up inside me wrapped around my kundalini. Jesus!'

'I remember that.'

'I should fucking hope so.'

After that we stopped talking.

The official escorts me to the door. That's what he does. He brings people in and he shows them out. He's a wind-up man with some important title. He'll shake your hand or salute you. He'll bend his head or look you straight in the eye.

In my case he evidences great patience. Behind the respectful, polite veneer is a man trying to deal with a particularly annoying child. Me. My evasions have led nowhere but back to this moment, this inescapable moment. I'm not a gymnast. I can't backflip away from this, or bounce off the walls and come at him feet first like a superhero of the big screen. Like him, I'm pretty much stuck in my role. When he acts out, I act out.

I have my brown envelope. I have my orders. I have my memories. What more could I want?

For a start I want to thank him, even hug him, but how inappropriate is that? All he has done is stick a needle in my arm and declares me dead, not to mention ruining my whole day with this appointment. You don't hug people like the official. What you do is hurry through some last minute politenesses and be on your way, grateful to be out of there, grateful to be at least provisionally alive.

Now that the time has come to actually leave, to show the whole place a clean set of heels, I hesitate where I have hesitated many times before, afraid to leave, afraid to go into that anteroom and visit the person I used to be, the person still waiting for his appointment. The appointment. Always there at the centre of my turning, official and inescapable.

Now I have to walk away from it. Go in another direction. One in which there is no appointment.

So I prolong the moment. I pause at the door. I nod and smile. My bell jingles. My lips are drawn right to the gums. I make noises with my mouth. Syllable bodies and word bodies. I regret that we can't shake hands twice. I take a last look around the room, the ambiguous modern painting; the unambiguous anti-smoking poster, the desk, the tubular steel chair (packed with microcircuitry), his plush rotating chair, the hairline edge of

206

the secret door into the lab. Nothing to feel nostalgic about, but it did have the advantage of being familiar, like a memory that's not worn out yet.

'Well,' says the official, also looking around.

He opens the door.

Ananda stepped through Pchiti's doorway into the sunlight. The day was still bright with the perfection of morning. A parakeet, which had collected all the bright colours of the world in its plumage, flew down to him and swooped over his head. With quiet joy in his heart, he made his way to the edge of the women's encampment, once again ignoring the faces peeping at him from windows and the shadows of doorways.

Mahaprajapati sat off at a strategic distance, pounding up dhal to make flour. That careful distance made it just as possible to walk on as to veer in her direction. Ananda didn't want to stop and talk to Siddhartha's determined step-mother, because, he realized, he didn't want her to see that quiet joy reflected in his face. She might get the wrong impression.

Certainly, his heart was filled with warmth, like the morning sun itself, when he thought of his meeting with Pchiti, because the girl, with all her sweetness and intelligence, had readily grasped the limited nature of craving and the universal nature of compassion. With that same sweetness and intelligence, she had understood the story he'd told her about Boti and the nymphs of Tavatimsa, had smiled with a certain grimness when she understood the 'trick' Siddhartha had played on Boti. Her tears were unashamed and swelled up out of that very same sweetness of nature.

He felt protective of this experience, and the joy it gave him. It was still too new. To witness the glow of Awakening in the face of another is no small privilege. Now Pchiti was a Stream Enterer. She had glimpsed the great wheel of desire, how it turned, and the dissatisfied beings that clung to it, and he had witnessed it with her, holding her hand. At times the vision grew so intense she clutched at his hand, her fingernails making crescent indents on his palm. Truly, desire may shake the body, but awakening from desire shakes it even more.

Her melancholy had made her so sensitive that as soon as the truth dawned, and the dharma was revealed, her awakening was instantaneous. It had passed through her body in a series of shudders. As they passed through her, they passed through him too. Afterwards they had sat together and chanted a dharani, the mnemonic syllables of which served to calm the mind shaken by the turbulence of awakening, the feeling of being new and strange in the world. The sounds, which welled up through their chests, stitched them back into the perceived world, the world in which ordinary things remained ordinary things.

Both had emerged from the dharani calm and grateful.

Mahaprajapati was a determined and devoted person, worthy of respect in all ways, but she might not understand the sheer delicacy of all this.

He was halfway back to the men's camp when he realized he had left his bowl at Pchiti's place. Of course he could find another, but that wasn't the point. A monk has very few possessions. Except for the clothes he wears, the bowl serves for begging and eating and a monk has no need of anything else. His bowl becomes a part of him. He is mindful of it at all times. These are among the first things the novice learns. Once Siddhartha said to a novice, 'If you cannot take care of such a simple thing as your bowl, how do you expect to take care of the bigger things in your life?' Some of the monks had laughed at the novice, but Siddhartha did not laugh with them. 'Which of you think you are any better?' he asked in a voice like silk, and they had fallen silent.

Besides which he was Ananda Suklodana, the vessel of truth, the man with the magic memory. How could he leave his bowl in the hut of novice girl?

It was not possible to return and retrieve the bowl. He couldn't bear the thought of all those avid eyes, the giggling laugher when they saw what had happened. It wasn't fair to humiliate Pchiti in such a way, impose upon her modesty and sweetness. Yes, modesty. He didn't hesitate to use the word and think of her that way. Even opening her blouse and revealing her breasts had been fraught with modesty, a complete absence of lewdness, a blushing shyness. This evidence of her virtue filled him up with happiness.

But to return to his hut without his bowl was equally problematic. It would be noticed, one way or another. Siddhartha would get wind of it, as he seemed to do with everything. There would be more jokes at his expense. Siddhartha would take the opportunity to use him as an object lesson. He could anticipate the words in advance: *Listen, Ananda! At the time you were helpless under the magic charm of the maiden Pchiti, what was it that released you and restored your control of mind? Your coming under her control was not a chance happening of this life, or of this eon alone: you had been in affinity with her for many an eon. With the chanting of the dharani, the bonds that bound you to her were destroyed.*

At that moment the girl with the skipping rope came along. She looked particularly pleased with herself. Her agility with the skipping rope made him think of a monkey.

'You look very happy, Ananda Suklodana,' she says. 'Does the maiden Pchiti please you?'

'So you are a little spy, are you? A little gossip like those women at the pump.'

'I have eyes so I can spy out hidden corners, I have ears for the secrets of the wind, I have nostrils to wrap up the world, I have a tongue for tasting sunshine, and I have hands for feeling the shape of things. How easy, therefore, is it for me to know that the maiden Pchiti pleases you?'

'Her progress to her awakening pleases me. She is an ardent student of the path. And you, little one, are altogether too full of yourself.'

'You would say so! But what of her breasts, do they please you too?'

'What are you? Are you a deva?' He knew there were devas who could take human form when it amused them. And human beings did not always appreciate their sense of humour. Some devas considered human beings to be slower and more foolish than themselves, and to occupy a lower dimension of existence.

Skippety-lick, skippety-lick. 'That's not the right question. The question is, what are you? Are you an honest man? I ask if her breasts please you and you ask if I am a deva. So what am I to think? That the most honest man in the world is a little less than honest?'

'Well yes, of course they pleased me. How could they not...? But they pleased me as a flower might, as a... ripe... mango.'

'Perhaps you are an honest man after all. People do admire you for your frank and open face. Perhaps that is what the maiden Pchiti admires in you.'

The conversation was making Ananda uncomfortable. He was allowing this girl or deva or whatever she was to rattle him.

'We are only honest in so far as we know ourselves.'

The little girl stops skipping and claps her hands. 'Oh, wise Ananda indeed! Venerable Ananda! Who can fault you in your wisdom? But tell me this, is it always wise to be totally honest, to always tell the truth?'

'The truth underpins everything else. Honesty is built upon it.'

'So you would not lie?'

'Not unless someone's life depended upon it. I might lie to the tiger to save the antelope.'

'That's very noble! How pleased Siddhartha must be with you. Would you offer yourself to the tiger to save the antelope?'

Ananda laughed. 'I'm not that noble!'

'I wondered if there were limits.' *Lickety-skip, Lickety-skip.*

'You're a cheeky little sprite, that's what you are. Just sprung up from behind a flower, have you? Go needle somebody else!'

'Why, when it's so much fun needling you? You have an honest face, they say. That makes you a great tease. But I will say this, that before too long you will tell a lie, and it won't be to save an antelope.'

'What's this? Are you an oracle now?'

'Time is a ribbon. Can you tie a bow?'

Ananda looked at the little girl, astonished.

'Who are you? You're no normal little girl. Are you Siddhartha in disguise? I have sometimes wondered if Siddhartha can take other forms. Aniruddha said he saw Siddhartha turn into a mountain leopard.'

The little girl stopped skipping. She looked up at him with eyes bright and mischievous. 'I am the bird that flew from Siddhartha's mouth when he cried out for joy under the Bodhi tree.'

Ananda was so astonished, he was speechless. He couldn't shake the feeling that somehow this was one of his cousin's practical jokes, although how it could be was beyond him.

He was puzzling this out when he heard voices approaching. It turned out to be his cousins, the devout Aniruddha and Bhadra. Once these two had been jealous of Ananda's role as Siddhartha's personal assistant, but they had long since left such feelings behind. Their lives as monks were exemplary, they had gone far beyond attachment, and they had every expectation that they would enjoy the bliss of final liberation from the wheel of life and death.

'Which way are you walking, brother?'

Ananda looked around for the little girl.

'What's the matter, brother?'

'I was just talking to a little girl, but suddenly she has gone.'

'Are you sure she was not one of the legion of Mara, sent to tempt you?'

Ananda was uncomfortable treating Mara as a god. Siddhartha didn't see it that way, as he carefully explained. He had to use the language people used, the language they thought in. Mara was just a word that stood for all those material forces that would hold back a being from awakening. For all those nightmares of the flesh.

'She was not of that kind. She was little, with a skipping rope.'

'Then she was just a kid. Why are you still thinking about her?'

'Because she said something very strange. Not like a child.'

'Well, tell us! What did she say.'

At the last minute Ananda is reluctant to say the words the girl said to him. Those boldly spoken words were also fragile. He shouldn't speak them.

'It is nothing. Aniruddha, did you really see Siddhartha turn into a leopard, or is that just a story you made up to scare superstitious novices?'

'Novices don't need my stories to scare them. They have their own shadows to scare them.'

'Shadows can be scary,' Ananda said.

'Do you doubt that the Awakened One could turn into a leopard?'

'No,' Ananda said, 'I just don't know why he would want to. Unless of course he's tricking you.'

'Why would he do that?'

'You don't understand how Siddhartha plays with appearance and reality, like a child playing peek-a-boo, in order to teach that there is neither. That appearance and reality are all a part of the great play of mind.'

Ananda started walking. He had to go somewhere.

'Where are you going?'

'To the river.' Certainly his feet were headed there.

'Why? Haven't you come from there?'

'I left my bowl on the bank.'

It just came out that way, in a moment of inspiration. The lie. He saw in a flash how it would work. They would walk to the river and the bowl would be gone. Ananda would look puzzled. He would speculate that perhaps one of the women had picked it up. Then, when it was returned from the women's village, there would be no silly, unhealthy rumours about his meeting with Pchiti. He didn't exactly know why he wanted his visit to Pchiti to remain quiet, if not exactly a secret. This knowledge slipped past his usually vigilant inner gaze as if it wore a magic cloak. If pushed on the issue he might have said that he had no wish to cause a virtuous maiden any embarrassment. Which would be true, as far as it went. It just didn't go very far.

As he uttered the words, they passed a jujube tree full of monkeys screeching their heads off. Among them he saw one with a skipping rope and a girl's face. She was grinning at him with great merriment.

She skipped up and down on the branch. *I told you so, I told you so.*

Clark Kent's Story

When I was a kid, there was a girl who lived down the road who everybody despised. I think her name was Lily. She was very pale and thin and freckly, had straggly ginger hair and hardly any eyebrows. Having no eyebrows made her look surprised all the time. She had one of those wasting diseases. None of us kids were allowed to play with her in case we caught something. Everybody was very afraid. We kids were not even allowed to touch anything she'd touched, which made her a pariah. She couldn't even play ball, and had to have her own of everything. She had a tatty piece of skipping rope she took with her everywhere. They wouldn't let her go to school, at least at first. She would stand outside the school ground and stare at the kids in the playground. The other kids would spit and throw stones at her, but not me. She repulsed the other kids, but she fascinated me. I spoke to her every chance I got because I wanted her to know that I wasn't like the other kids.

And I wasn't. I was worse than the other kids, I just hid it better than they did. One day I was playing leopards, pretending to hunt on the hills, when I found her alone, singing and playing by herself. Instead of going up to her openly, or walking away, I hid and spied on her. She didn't do anything interesting. She just sang and talked to herself. A couple of times she struck herself on the arm with her tatty bit of rope. Once she had a pee and I saw what she looked like with her pants down, but that was about all, and there wasn't much to look at. I got bored and wandered off without speaking to her.

But that night, as I was trying to go to sleep, I was subject to a powerful fantasy. I had the girl under my complete control, and I subjected her to all kinds of tortures. The more pathetic she became, the more I tortured her. She seemed to have an endless capacity for pain, and so I became the Grand High Torturer, whose greatest pleasure was to see her suffer. I wanted to discover the limits of her suffering, but there seemed to be none. She was always ready for more.

That fantasy, which turned into a sort of nightmare, kept me up all night. The next day I saw her shadowing the kids to school. I contrived to sneak up on her and talk to her, out of sight of the other kids of course. I told her about spying on her, how I had hidden and watched her. She seemed oddly pleased, although she tried to look offended. Perhaps because she spied so much, she understood. Or maybe she was just pleased that someone was interested enough to spy on her. Close up, her skin was so pale it was almost translucent, and her hair shone like polished copper. There were freckles all over her pudgy face. I wanted to touch her but didn't dare.

I went on tell her about my fantasy, and how I dressed up in my robes as Grand High Torturer and made her do horrible things to herself, like taking a knife and cutting off her nipples. Perhaps I was trying to shock her. Perhaps I was boasting. Perhaps I just wanted to tell somebody and relieve myself of my terrible visions, but she did not react as I expected.

'You can do those things to me,' she said in a soft, wan voice. 'It doesn't matter what you do to me. I do things to myself, look.' She showed me her inner arm. From elbow to wrist the sensitive skin was covered in tiny scars, some fresh, some still with scabs. 'It doesn't matter what anybody does to me.'

I was too young to know what it was my body was feeling at that moment, but not too young to feel it. So I did what we were not allowed to do. I touched her. I ran my fingers over the scars on her arm, forbidden territory. She didn't do anything. She just held her arm there and watched me impassively. Thus encouraged, I took the delicate skin on her wrist with my thumb and finger and squeezed until she winced. Her face screwed up with pain, but she didn't try to pull away.

'It doesn't matter what you do to me, 'cos I'm going to die. I heard mum and dad talking. They said I'd be dead soon.'

I took flight and ran.

That night, the fantasy returned, only worse. I had touched her now; I had touched her scars. I had felt the softness and the roughness of the inside of her arm. I made her do many impossible things. I gave her a red hot poker and she made holes in the soft parts of her thighs. Some spots she couldn't reach, so I took the poker and made the holes for her. This was my second night without sleep. Towards morning I began to sense that she and I were not entirely alone. Shadowy presences had gathered around us, and were crowding closer. I could feel their avid interest in our activities.

The next day, and the days after that, I avoided the girl. I joined the other kids throwing stones at her, but I knew she didn't care about being hit with stones. That wasn't what I wanted to do, which was to be alone with her and do some of the things we did in my fantasy. I was too frightened. Not of her, but of my fantasy, and the creatures that like to crowd around and watch. They were doing more than just watching. They were encouraging me, urging us both on to further excesses. I was also afraid that if we started doing things in reality, then my fantasies would grow monstrous and destroy me. The more I did to her, the stronger the fantasies would grow, because, like the phantom watchers, the fantasies fed upon every detail of our brief meetings. Time and again I heard her say in that same flat, toneless voice, 'It doesn't matter what you do to me.'

Where this might have ended when we got a little older and more conscious of what we were doing, is anybody's guess. Absurd as it seems, given the brutality of it all, there was a certain innocence to it, even in my hastening to the washing basket in the morning with sticky wet pyjamas. We never got to find out what might have happened, because her parents moved away. They were going someplace where the people were kinder, they said. Where the people might show a little compassion for a sick girl, not leave dead cats and rats on their doorstep, or put shit in their letterbox. A lot of people felt ashamed of themselves, but I wasn't one of them. I felt a sense of loss, as if something precious had been taken away. Yet at the same time I felt relieved.

Before they left I put an anonymous note in their letterbox telling them that not everybody in the district hated them, and that people were just afraid, that was all. I said that I loved their daughter even though I had only spoken to her once. I don't know why I wrote that. I don't think it was true, but somehow I had to write it. I wanted her to hear it.

I think she must have died, because a year later, I started to catch glimpses of her out of the corner of my eye, a flash of gleaming copper, of pale skin and general boniness that could only be her. She'd be just ahead of me. She'd be at a street corner or by the edge of the trees of a park, or standing in the doorway of a house, or appearing as a face at the window. But by the time I got to the street corner, she'd be gone. Or I'd get to the trees only to see her vanish into a crowd back on the street. The figure in the doorway would turn out to be a shadow, and the face at the window always belonged to someone else. Once I even knocked on the door of a stranger's house to ask them if they had a little ginger-haired girl who might be looking out a window. Of course there never was any little girl.

It was after that last incident that I began to have the fantasies again, only this time they had changed. This time the boot was on the other foot, so to speak. This time I was the one who was sick and abject, and she wore the robes of the Grand High Torturer. She made me do things to myself I never dreamed of getting her to do to herself in my previous fantasies. In my fantasy, the skinny girl had grown into a powerful, almost goddess-like woman, with her red hair luxurious and unravelled, and her once pudgy face lean and beautiful. And cruel. Her teeth were whiter than her skin, and her lips were crimson. She enjoyed torturing me, and being more inventive than I had been with her. I screamed and screamed and swore eternal vengeance. There seemed to be no limit to my suffering. And no escape from it.

Once more the fantasies kept me awake and began to blight my waking moments. Once more I feared for my mental integrity. If fantasies can tear us apart, what might the world do, when the world does its worst? The fantasies stopped, however, when I met another little girl with a real skipping rope, who just had ordinary mousy hair and who wasn't dying of a wasting disease.

This new little girl was very funny and practical, and she taught me one very important thing. That I am not my thoughts. That I don't have to identify furiously with everything I might think, since, as she pointed out, what I might think today may be different from what I thought yesterday. You see what I mean about practical.

I don't know how she got rid of the fantasies. When I told her about them she didn't make a big deal out of it, the way some might. She just shrugged. 'They don't have any power,' she said. 'They are like ghosts at the window. All they can do is scratch on the glass.'

Her casual attitude helped. Something in me shifted. The fantasy no longer exerted its old power, and soon faded. I decided to finish them off with a flourish, and humbly asked the bitch goddess if I could die, if she would consent to kill me. After some dalliance, which involved a lot of pain, a punishment for my temerity, she consented, and proceeded to kill me slowly by eating me from the feet up, chewing up my blood and body while I watched. As she swallowed me, she got fatter and fatter. The invisible presences returned en-mass to urge her on. It felt like they were all eating me.

And I died. As soon as I died, the suffering stopped and the scene vanished, just like a bubble popping. I woke up and the fantasy was gone. It has never returned. But the story is not quite finished. I know now she didn't die. I saw her on the street plain as day many years later, still looking skinny and pale and sick. And her copper hair was the orangey colour of vomit.

I turned my head and looked the other way.

I am lying on my back staring up at the roadmap ceiling. Lots of roads going nowhere. I can't see my body, but I know it's pale, as pale as the girl in my story, as pale as freckled death. In the darkened room it looks almost silver. Zelena is squatting over me ceremoniously, her hands raised each side of her shoulders, palms facing forward in a curious, emblematic gesture. Her body is dark and ochre, charcoal in the shadowy places. As she lowers herself over me, and envelopes me, she begins to chant, and talk in a foreign language, or just syllables of no language. Having enveloped me completely, her internal muscles begin to work on me.

She rotates her hips slowly, drawing me out, only slowly. I can feel myself gathering in far-off places for the rush to pleasure. And so can she. She slows her movements down to almost imperceptible, choking back the rush before it becomes compulsive. Now she can stretch out the pleasure almost to infinity.

I close my eyes and enter a warm, watery element. I could swim in this watery element, wave about like a frond, have intercourse with everything around me, make love to my environment. Enter it. Be encompassed, be enfolded, be sheathed. I know that male fish squirt their sperm into the water, the warm, receptive water. For a moment I understand how they must feel. The fishness of it. If I were a fish I would certainly squirt away.

When I open my eyes, it seems the world around me has grown larger. Her room disappears off into shadowy distances. Her breasts, large and droopy, like those of a fertility goddess, loom above me, and her neck and head loom more distantly behind. Still she holds her arms up level with her shoulders, palms out, in what I now recognize to be a gesture of surrender. I suddenly feel that all this is a part of some larger ritual, the nature of which neither of us understands. We understand nothing. We just act out.

We get our money's worth.

Emerging from the toilet, I collect Evie and we continue our way. There is not far to go, and I can feel the future converging on me, the sky narrowing on me. I am being bundled along, willy-nilly, hustled from one moment to the next. Naturally, I could still change the course of things, approach the revolving door of the present moment and shoot off in some new direction. I could go to an art gallery and meditate on some paintings. Or I could go to the library and pretend to read a book. I could close down universes and open up new ones.

While these thoughts are occurring, however, the act of walking is becoming more difficult, physically problematic. I seem to have lost the knack and must now concentrate on the particularities of each movement, monitoring the process as it goes, overseeing and offering encouragement to limb and muscle.

How unlikely we are, we sedulous apes! How improbable that we walk upright and negotiate the lateral streets with their perpendicular facings. What an arduous thing it is to have to pull all the parts of the body along, uproot feet from pavement, coerce the hips, cajole the knees (awkward, clumsy contrivances) and lean forward tumblingly into implacable gravity.

What an expense of strength.

Shop fronts, parking meters (where cars can quietly graze), office facades, alleyways, intersections still roll by, still register their passing on the senses, but they are slowing down. Everything is. Slowing down. What was previously a pleasant blur resolves into more detailed minutiae: the streaks of light on the windows, the sparkle on the electrical appliances, the neat creases on a man's trousers, the heavy-lidded stare of a tabby in the fish shop. The pearls of water on the bronzed body of the cardboard woman lying on a tropical beach in the window of the travel agent, the blinkered stares of the passengers on the bus that swings around in front of me as I pause to cross the street.

Slower than before, I am losing energy in vast quantities. I am becoming leaky. I am leaking all over the place, precious strength I can never recover. I can't turn around and run back up the street and pick it all up. Not this street. I have been too profligate with these precious energies, swinging along through parks and streets as if on some kind of marathon, taking my health for granted, as if inertial motion would carry me along forever without creating friction and resistance. That I would sail on forever in a weightless, frictionless paradise, Evie skipping along ahead or behind. Now I ask myself why I didn't pace myself a little better for the long haul, conversing energy output and maximizing momentum.

I am living in a world of declining values, I decide, declining commitments, declining energies. Our upright backbone is a skeletal folly, a rickety compromise with gravity. To comfort myself from these depressing thoughts and to keep up my spirits, I mouth the opening sentences of The *Pilgrims Progress,* an inspirational tale for young adults from the Puritan era. I fancy myself passing through the wilderness of this world, finding a den, lying myself down in that place to sleep and dream a dream. That's me, dressed in rags, my face from my own house, a book in my hand. I stand before Evelyn, ill and broken. *I am certain informed,* I tell her haughtily, *that this our city will be burned with a fire from heaven.*

There is a comfort in the ringing tones of this older English, a confidence our language no longer expresses with such ease.

'I am certain informed,' I tell Evie, 'That all sprites, elves, devas and demons are henceforth banished into non-existence.'

'You'll have to find them first,' Evie said, evading my clutches.

But this bit of play cannot stem the flow of vital strength from my body. I am only pretending. I peer forward, hand over my eyes like a sailor searching for land. Past the next set of traffic lights, across a central square, and there is the Tower, rising in slender triumph from the try-hard sky-scrapers around it. I pause to take a breather and admire the way the Tower's huge concrete and steel roots grip the ground, and how, at the top, the temporal drag is deflected by its curved surface. Merely a block and a half away. No distance at all. A few minutes steady walking at a brisk, confident pace. Few minutes. Brisk.

But there is no steady walking, no brisk, confident pace. My stride is getting shorter. I am putting in more effort for less result, and the closer my goal becomes the greater the effort required. I could formulate this as a physical principle, my own version of Zeno's paradox of motion: the amount of energy required to reach my goal increases in inverse proportion to my nearness to my goal. To actually reach my goal will take infinite energy. I can go on halving the distance between me and the Tower, but there is still another distance to be halved.

I approach the final set of traffic lights and shuffle to a stop beside a grim looking old woman with a wizened face and handbag to match. Supporting myself on the orange and black traffic-light pole, I gauge the distance to the other side of the street. Not too far. Really. No Rubicon. The old woman beside is standing firm. She has nothing to hold onto but her handbag. Like me, she is gauging the distance to be travelled. A little too far or not too far. A little further than from the bathroom to the bedroom, Grandma. We're in it together.

My body begins to tingle and prickle from the inside, as if it were running out of air. A pain moves around in my chest, refusing to settle anywhere. My breath starts to come in short, panicky gasps. I feel as I did in the Health shop, the overwhelming desire to cut and run coupled with the complete inability to do so.

'Never mind,' Evie says, skipping away lightly, careful to keep clear of the old woman who's not losing sight of her objective. 'You're just having a silly little panic attack. Breathe steadily. Focus on the end of your nose. It can't hurt you.'

'It can. It can hurt me.'

'Put your head in a paper bag.'

'What?'

'Cuts down the oxygen flow. You're getting too much. You have to reset your gauge.'

'I don't know what you're talking about.'

'Of course you do. You bring your breath under control.'

The traffic lights go clickety-click, and the traffic halts obediently. In another few seconds a *walk now* sign will flash, a buzzer will sound, and the old woman and I will set out to cross the street or die trying.

'All you have to do is put one foot in front of the other.'

'That's the usual way.'

It's all very well her for. Her feet can leave the planet every few seconds, not that high but high enough to skip the arc of time.

'I just happen to have a paper bag the right size.'

'No, thank you.' I can't see me and the old woman crossing the street, me with a paper bag over my head.

The lights change and the buzzer buzzes and the old woman and I are off, shuffling across the street at maximum speed, which turns out to be not very fast. It feels as if my body is immersed in a different time-stream from my mind. My mind is clear and lucid, as it usually is, able to encompass the fore and the aft, the future and past of things, and maintains a steady-as-she-goes navigation, but for my body, the seconds go pelting by in a storm of movement.

After a few short moments, the buzzer shuts off. Grandma and I exchange a resolute glance.

'You'll be across in no time at all,' Evie says. 'But you might have to leave Grandma behind.'

'No way. How can you say such a callous thing?'

Around us people swirl with speedy ease, laughing and talking. Everybody from spry pensioners to sullen youths. They surge around us and are gone, leaving me and Grandma still racing for the curb.

The *walk now* sign is flashing ominously on and off. Any moment it will turn red. Grandma and I exchange desperate looks. Alone and together, we can make it.

'One foot in front of the other,' Evie says in the exasperated tones of a mother.

The youth in the black jacket and the bare feet zooms past, grinning widely. He is clutching a sheet of typed pages. 'Don't forget the curfew,' he calls over his shoulder.

'Only a few steps further,' Evie says.

The old woman looks at her with what might be spite.

There's no time to stop and gauge the distance behind me. Even twisting my neck to look back will take up time. Grandma and I have one simple rule: don't look back. There's not even time for us to exchange any more glances as the *walk now* sign goes red and changes. Now it says *wait*. The traffic begins to nudge forward. We are in those brief, few seconds, that intermediary zone where nothing is moving and the intersection becomes a deserted no-man's-land.

I take a quick look at the old woman anyway. She is shuffling forward with a stern solemnity, head held high, defiantly annoying the thrumming traffic. I admire her heroism. I hold my head up high too (it had sunk to my chest), and I move with the same grim dignity she does. Together we will make it.

Someone passes going the other way, running so fast the figure is just a blur.

'You're nearly there,' Evie says.

I'm very tired, my bones are tired. Whoever would have thought that it was so hard for the chicken to cross the road.

Evie is dancing and waving her skipping rope in the air.

'One more step!'

Two, actually. Grandma and reach the curb at the same time as the traffic revs into gear behind us. I want to exchange relieved glances with her, but she's having none of it. She has already turned away and is shuffling at the same pace down the street, her coat flapping around her legs, handbag pinned under her arm. I get the feeling she has forgotten the crossing, forgotten me. She only cares about the next leg of her journey.

'That wasn't so bad, was it?' Evie says. Everything is easy to Evie.

'I'm glad I'm not old,' I say to her.

'But you are,' she says. 'You are very old.'

The mischievous grin is back.

It was a grim struggle, getting Zeldia's oxygen. She fought with mindless strength. Even coming up behind her in the labyrinth of tunnels and rooms that made up the interior of the *Omega* had proved hard to arrange, as she always seemed to know where he was, and was always facing him when he came up on her.

The Zeldia zombie was not as agile as the living woman had been, which was just as well for Captain October Nortikiss who had never quite mastered the art of moving around in null-grav. Getting close enough to close off her oxygen and rip off her cylinders was dangerous and tricky, since she kept grasping for his oxygen lines. At one point they clashed helmet to helmet and he found her face only inches from his. Blood had congealed in her eyes, and her skin, the colour of blue ice, was covered in putrefying sores. There was no clue as to what had happened to her. After all, nothing but neutrinos could get through the nano-bonding of a space gown. Presumably, whatever it was might happen to him also – something that came from the inside.

Something of the mystery of the zombie struck him, even while engaged in the struggle. Famously, the zombie is animated solely by its hunger, but few had taken the further step to seeing zombie behaviour as the desperation of a creature starving to death. The zombie is a personification of starvation. He didn't see it in quite those terms, but had to grapple with the reality of it. The implacable single-mindedness of her attack did not flow from rage, or even fear, but from one bright, all-powerful craving. A craving so powerful it could overleap death and animate a corpse. And here she was, running about the ship, snapping at the void, fighting him with the kind of strength a starving creature has. Torn muscles and wrecked bones couldn't stop it.

This was a deadly ballet enacted in the intestines of the *Omega*, and the temptation was always just to turn around and flee. But she would follow. A little slower but not that much. Like a terminator, always on his tail, never herself turning and fleeing. It was a silent ballet, too. After her initial broken android calling of his name, she fell silent, and never spoke again. No air to make a voice, he reasoned.

The struggle took its toll on his dwindling oxygen supply as the physical exertion increased his respiration rate. There could be no backing off for another round. He was squandering oxygen to get oxygen, and the more he squandered, the higher the stakes rose.

Her technique was simple. She would come at him, hands outstretched, seeking the oxygen line which, once ruptured, would see the last of his precious supply bubble off into the void as the vacuum rushed into his cylinders. And into his lungs. His lungs would collapse and his body would follow after. After that she could gnash her teeth for eternity. However, because her attack was unvaried, he learned how to parry it by drawing back then sweeping her arms to one side, sending her spinning on one spot, or bashing into the walls around. Once she had stabilized herself she would come at him again. If he hit her with just the right force, she would rotate away from him and he would have his chance.

It took a while to get it right, and each time it was dangerous as he had to let those clutching fingers come close to his space gown in order to turn her around. His advantages were that he was quicker and smarter; hers were that she never got tired or slept or ceased for a single moment. And she was a lot stronger. His fear was that she would get a hold of him, even a slight grip on the space gown would do it, and she would never let go, and he would never be able to break her hold. As he grew weary, her grip would strengthen.

There were moments when he remembered their naked romps in the so-called 'recreation room' of the *Frolix 6*. The thoughtful planners had even padded the 'ceiling' and 'floor' for full six surface sex. He remembered the way her green eyes would glimmer, like emeralds in a cave, and how her copper hair would fan out around her like the most delicate seaweed. Now, in the dark and the sweat, he wondered if those memories could possibly be real. They had an unreal sheen on them, like the endless fantasies stimulated by the stasis pods.

Finally he got it right, and executed the series of manoeuvres he'd planned. With his right arm, he swept her around as she came at him, and while she rotated, he seized her cylinder pack and rode around with her, swiftly shutting off the valve at the cylinder. Once that was done, all he had to do was rip the cylinders off her back by pulling them out of their simple clamps. The whole system had been designed to swap tanks in deep space, and in training they had done it many times.

He secured her cylinders all right, but both of them were flying around at crazy angles. He used his superior agility to snap hold of a hand-rung and control his movements. She batted at a pole a few times but couldn't grasp it. That gave him an idea. He grabbed her from behind and, keeping one hand secured to a hand rung, stabilized her with the other. If he could spin her fast enough, in one spot, away from any surfaces, he might stand a chance.

So that's what he did, with all the strength he could put into it.

There she was, a zombie spinning top. With no friction, nothing to slow her down, she could spin away there almost forever. Almost, because he could never spin her exactly on one spot. There would be a slight drift built into it, which would eventually see her run into a surface. That might take many eons. Galaxies might be born and die before that happened.

With his prize secured, he made his escape. And it was quite a prize. Her tanks were more than half full. That gave him enough hope to formulate a new objective. He would find the controls of the ship and turn the life support systems on. To hell with the Fishmen and their alleged disrupter. Let them do their worst. If he was going to be a space hero he'd better get on with it.

Winning the battle against Zeldia the Zombie had given him new heart.

His major regret was that he would never see her again.

And it wasn't quite the same being a space hero, and defeating zombies and fishmen, when there was nobody there to witness it. Nobody to tell the tale.

The central square of our city, simply known as The Square, anchors the grid of streets, holds our city together as a single design, or the appearance of one. An inner square, an outer square of avenues – I suppose there is something faintly medieval about the concept. The Square is neatly laid out for pedestrian ease. All traffic except for buses (which congregate from time to time) have been rerouted so one can walk with calm across its expanse. At the centre of The Square is a cathedral, modest in proportion and pretention. Since it is the oldest building the city, it anchors us in another way also, in time and history.

Beside the cathedral, a large bronze sculpture, a group composition, has been placed to further remind us of time and history. Who we are and where we have come from, and what we mustn't forget. After the hectic race at the traffic lights, Evie and I take a moment to sit in front of this statue and catch our breaths. As we take our seats, I see the old lady disappear through the door into the cathedral. I'm happy she's got to where she was going.

The crisis at the traffic lights seems to have resolved something, as if my body has come to a temporary compromise with the entropic forces at work. I found I could move at a reasonable speed so long as I harbour my strength, and not let my head move too far forward of my body.

'You're right,' Evie says. 'People walk with their heads instead of their bodies.' And she skips a few times to show how to move without the head dragging the body around.

We study the tableau, although I have seen it many times before. I tend not to look at it, because it reminds me of my grandfather, my mother, and other half-forgotten members of my family. There are six figures. On our right is my half-brother, Valour, holding a helmet and a spear, dressed in armour and a cloak, looking down with some modesty. He is hero material. In front of him sits Valour's sister, my half-sister, named Sacrifice, a Madonna-like young woman with her ankles crossed, wearing a shawl and headscarf. She is in mourning, head inclined, the music of humanity too sad for her to bear. She is a child of war, and its victim. She is martyr material. Standing behind her next to Valour is my cousin, Peace, a maiden with one breast coyly exposed and a gown that reveals her right leg up to the hip. She is carrying an olive branch and a dove, contemplating a future full of fecundity and children. Next in line stands Aunty Justice, bearing scales and a sword. Here is a woman who will not weep, but stand by the promises she has made Valour and Sacrifice. She stares at me with unmitigated pride. Next up is Youth, an athletic young man holding a torch aloft with his left hand, another in his right. His body is full of sprung movement and anticipation. That's me, I'm sure, just a few years ago.

Crowning these five figures, and on a pedestal above them, is an unnamed figure, a beautiful woman, topless, her arms stretched above her head with a sword arched between them. Wings jut from her back and flower around her shoulders. She is straining forward and up, her breasts jutting out, the loose folds of her gown falling around her, her head arched. The upward thrust of her eyes and wings counterbalance the downward reach of her legs and scabbard.

This must be War. War, the half-naked angel of death, gathering her children in as the sword bends to breaking point.

LEST WE FORGET, the inscription beneath the tableau reads.

The family of man.

'My cuzzies,' I say to Evie. I draw strength and comfort from these figures cast in bronze.

'They're pretty scantily dressed,' Evie says. She's looking critically at the female figures.

'Lest we forget,' I murmur. Grandfather certainly hasn't forgotten, but then again, he saw the death angel hovering above the battlefield with his own eyes.

Evie and I have just resumed our journey through the wilderness of this world when a man appeared, dressed in an ancient dark suit, perhaps fashionable fifty years ago, a grey-white shirt and narrow black tie. It's the kind of outfit the man's father might have bought to serve him at weddings and the funerals of old soldier buddies. He is carrying a heavy, black book.

'There is Hope!' he shouts as we go past.

'Come on, don't stop here,' Evie says, pulling me along.

'There is Hope!' he shouts in an identical voice. He fixes me with a myopic stare. As soon as I notice him he points the black book at me dramatically.

Why should ye be stricken anymore? Ye will revolt more and more: the whole head is sick and the whole heart faint.'

'Don't listen to him,' Evie says.

'But he's right. My head is sick and my heart is faint.' I look back at the bronze composition. The arc of the unbroken sword cuts the light.

The man picks up on my words, and zeros in on me. *From the soles of the foot even unto the head there is no soundness, but wounds and bruises and putrefying sores...'*

'Keep the body moving,' Evie says. 'Or, better still, start dancing. Dancing can be very effective in cases like this.'

'... they have not been closed, neither bound up, neither mollified with ointment...'

From inside the cathedral comes the low rumble of an organ.

The man reaches out, as if he would touch me. *'Your country is desolate, your cities are burned with fire: your land, aliens devour it in your presence, and it is desolate, the towers thereof as overthrown by aliens.'*

'He can't be serious,' I say to Evie.

'He's quoting Isaiah,' Evie says, still pulling at me.

'So Isaiah saw all this, did he?' I gesture to the world around us. 'Foresaw an invasion from the other side time?' I have to laugh at the whole idea. Scaly aliens invading, burning cities and overthrowing towers. These dreamers, like Isaiah, should try the real world sometime. Full of ordinary people doing stupid things.

The man approaches us, shouting, little white flecks of foam forming at the corners of his mouth. *Woe is me! For I am undone; because I am a man of unclean lips, and I dwell in the midst of people with unclean lips.'*

I back away, 'What's he going on about?'

'Don't listen to him. You know what they say, even the Devil can quote scripture.'

'He should have a chat to my alarm clock. That would straighten him out. Then he'd know that his precious aliens were just manifestations of mind.'

'Yes, but so are you.'

The organ rumbles to a higher note. The man comes right up to me and brings his face near to mine. He has a lot of little blackheads. The unclean smell of ham 'n' pickle wafts into my face. *Let me kiss him with kisses of his mouth,'* he declaims, *'for thy love is better than wine.'*

'No thanks,' I say, stepping back even faster.

The voice of my beloved, behold, he cometh leaping upon the mountains, skipping upon the hills.' He points his black book at Evie. This is not normal. People seldom notice her, or acknowledge her existence. Perhaps they don't even see her. The only exception I can think of right now is Evelyn, who, it is fair to say, is ambivalent about Evie.

'Perhaps he thinks you're a boy.'

'Ask him if he has a daughter, go on!'

'Do you have a wife?' I ask him. 'A daughter?'

'The daughters are haughty and walk with stretched forth necks and wanton eyes, walking and mincing as they go,' he walks and minces in imitation, waggling his bottom suggestively, *'and making a little tinkling with their feet. Therefore the Lord will smite with a scab the crown of the head of the daughters, and the Lord will discover their secret parts…'* His tongue, an unhealthy pink, runs over dry lips.

'And will he smite their secret parts?'

'Oh, yes! And it shall come to pass that instead of a sweet smell there shall be a stench, and instead of well-set hair, baldness; and burning instead of beauty.' He clutches his book to his crotch.

The organ descends to a minor key. My extremities grow cold.

Evie says, 'You have to get away from here, even if it's on all fours, crawling.'

'Okay.'

But it's easier said than done. The level ground is like a steep slope. I go a little at a time, inch by inch. This is nothing like the pedestrian crossing epic. At least there I could keep moving, albeit at the pace of a very old and determined lady. Here I might grind to a halt. Slip backwards even.

'I can't move!' Grandfather talked about men buried to the necks in mud, dying of thirst.

'Of course you can. Look at the memorial.'

The sun is polishing the bronze on the scales of Justice.

'I can't.'

'Then crawl.'

'Above him stood the seraphim. Each had six wings: with two he covered his face, and with two he covered his feet, and with two he flew.' The man made as if to walk beside me, like a friendly fellow traveller.

'Your first mistake was to look at him in the first place,' Evie says. 'Your second mistake was to try to talk to him.'

The man leans forward and hisses at me. *'There is an evil which I have seen under the sun, and it is common among men.'*

'Me too, buddy. Not just under the sun, but under the moon, and even the far stars. There's plenty of evil under the stars.'

For a moment he is taken aback. Probably not used to this kind of support. For the first time he looks at me.

'Take thee a great scroll and write in it with a man's pen.'

'He's trying to warn me,' I say to Evie.

'Put a curse on you, more likely.'

'He wants me to write all this down. He wants me to bear witness.'

'If you don't get away, you'll die.'

'You were the one to tell me to flee the wrath to come.'

'But you're not doing it, are you? You are dallying here. You have allowed yourself to be pulled into the orbit of this mentally unstable person. You are like a fly in his web. He will suck your mind right out of your head. Look at him. He hasn't shaved for three days at least. His suit, he might have stolen from a corpse. I hear they do that in crematoriums, you know, strip the suits off the bodies before consigning them to the flames. Waste not want not.'

I get the feeling she's chatter-boxing to pull my attention away from the hypnotic man, to break his spell.

After her speech, the man steps back humbly. He removes an imaginary hat. *'How beautiful are thy feet,'* he whispers, *'O Prince's daughter. The joints of thy thighs are like jewels, the work of a cunning workman.'*

Evie goes a little red in the face. For a moment she fiddles with her skipping rope.

'Why's he saying that to you?'

'He doesn't see me the way you see me. He sees something quite different.'

'What?'

'Quiet. I'm driving him away.'

'Thy two breasts are like two young roes that are twins.'

'It doesn't seem like that.'

The man was focused on Evie now, circling around her. His words were coming faster and faster. *'This thy stature is like to a palm tree, and thy breasts to clusters of grapes. I said, I will go up to the palm tree, I will take hold of the boughs thereof: now also thy breasts shall be as clusters of the vine, and the smell of thy nose like apples…'* He stops and flips open the book, rattling through the pages from one end to the other without pause.

'Who does he think you are?'

'King Solomon's bride.'

Faster the man moved, as if tethered to her skipping rope and she was whirling him about. Words continued to fly from his mouth.

'There are threescore queens… and fourscore concubines, and virgins without number… My dove, my undefiled is but one… the only one of her mother… the choice one of her that bore her. The daughters… blessed her… the queens and the concubines… they praised her…'

'Run, now,' Evie commanded. 'Before he reaches escape velocity. You don't want to be around.'

'Okay.' I find I can move my feet. Maybe I can even run.

'I can't hold him for long.'

'We have a little sister… and she hath no breasts… what shall we do for our sister… in the day… when she shall be spoken for? If she be a wall… we will build upon her a palace of silver… and if she be a door, we will enclose her with boards of cedar…'

With these words he staggers out of his orbit and heads straight for me.

The organ booms a final, diminished harmonic.

A naked singularity

'I can hear something,' Zelena says.

We were lying half-on half-off the mattress smoking one of Zelena's herbals. We didn't need it, but we were smoking it anyway.

'Celestial voices?'

'More like people coming up the stairs. A herd of fucking elephants.'

'I can't hear a thing.' Just celestial voices, in fact.

'Lucky you.' She sits up and pulls on an oversized jersey. Looks like a man's.

'Did the earth move?'

'Jesus! Yes, Johnny, everything moved. And it's still fucking moving. I'm zonked.'

There comes the unmistakable sound of hammering on a door somewhere. A distant voice.

'Fuck fuck fuck.'

'If we keep quiet they might go away.'

'Zelena!' a feminine voice calls.

Zelena sighs. 'They won't go away, not this lot.'

'Bugger it.' I'd already been planning a second round with Zelena. We were both good to go. I throw a regretful look at the tapestry. It is still pulsing quietly away.

'Curfew,' she says, screwing her eyes shut. Can't refuse sanctuary. Anyway, it's the twins. They'll know I'm here.' She pulls herself to her feet and looks around, perhaps for something to go with the jersey.

'Who?'

'The twins,' she says impatiently, as if I should already know.

'What's all this about a curfew?'

'What planet are you from, Johnny?'

'I saw an armoured car on the street today.' I find my feet and stare at them. I have never liked my feet. I have simian toes.

'Yeah, you get that. There's a lot of it around.'

More bangs and shouts from the door. I look around for my trousers but all I can find is my umbrella. An imaginary umbrella, with the fabric coming away from one of the spokes, is not going to be much protection. I decide to throw it away for good; I can always reinvent it if it rains.

Without bothering with any more clothing, Zelena heads for the door. The jersey covers pretty much everything anyway.

I have one leg in my trousers when Zelena and three people enter the room.

Ananda sat very quietly and watched his monkey mind perform all kinds of tricks. Memories, dreams, reflections, anxieties, projections, desires, visions. This was a clever monkey indeed. And the monkey was so clever it knew it was clever, and that knowledge was a source of great satisfaction to it. It jumped about and rubbed its coat with the back of its fingers and bared its teeth gloatingly.

It was especially good at visions. At the merest nudge it could produce the most wondrous sights, enough to make Ananda gasp in awe. Enough to make him forget the nature of these monkey visions, if only for the moment.

Then came a vision which knocked even the monkey off his feet. He saw his bowl, which he had still not managed to regain, fill with water. As it filled, it grew larger until it was the size of a pond. A lotus formed on top of the pond that spread itself out in all its glory. When it was fully formed, green and succulent, a sphere made of light appeared at its centre. Each side of the sphere sprouted a set of five-petaled lotus flowers. Ananda immediately recognised the design as a *vajra*, believed by the followers of Shiva to have been the weapon of choice of the god Indra, the thunderbolt god. This design of light, however, was a weapon of quite a different intent. It reflected back to the mind, the shape of mind. The sphere at the centre was the primordial, underlying unity of things. Of unbroken wholeness. One of the two five-petaled lotuses was the phenomenal world, the world available to the senses. The other was the noumenal world, which lay just beyond the senses. Here lay the many levels of existence, the many dimensions, which a person might see only in visions.

The vajra did not disturb the absolute calm of the water, which filled the bowl so full it seemed a mere spark, the merest touch of light, might send it spilling down the sides of his bowl.

Ananda and his monkey mind were marvelling at this sight when the spherical centre of the vajra began to undulate, a gentle rippling motion. Out of this motion a shape began to form. The shape was a female figure, naked to the waist, holding an iridescent peacock feather in one hand. It was Pchiti. However, she was no modest maiden but shone forth with the all the combined power of the two eight-petaled lotuses, the phenomenal and noumenal dimensions.

As she took shape, other creatures began to form around the mouth of the two lotus flowers, one for each petal. Each of these had the head of a fish and the body of crocodile and walked upright, on short, stubby crocodile legs. These were known as makara, and combined the forms of two animals to demonstrate the union of opposites, and impossible mergings. When makara were present, great transformations were in the wind. As soon as they were fully present and materialized in his vision, they turned towards him and began to sing. He could not distinguish individual voices, they blended into what seemed like a single ringing tone that lodged itself behind his ears, inside his head. It evoked distant heavens. Not deva heavens with nymphs, but heavens filled with sublime beings only a fraction of whose glory could be captured by the makara's voices. And there were heavens upon heavens, bending away and out of the grasp of mind.

The luminous Pchiti herself now turned to him. She stepped out of the sphere, jumped lightly onto the lotus pad and approached him, peacock feather in hand. He could not and would not turn his eyes from her nakedness, for it was like the nakedness of the stars against the softest silk of night.

When she got to the edge of the bowl, she stopped, and held the feather out to him. Its one iridescent eye fixed on him. The eyespot was tinted with lurid purple. When he took hold of it, a shudder went through his body.

The vision disappeared in an instant, but Ananda held the meditation. His monkey mind could not be found but instead there was the little girl with the skipping rope he'd met at the river bank.

'Has this maiden put a spell on you, Ananda? Or perhaps she is the one the Hindus call Shakti, consort of Krishna. Perhaps you should worship in their temples now.'

'I cannot worship in any temple.'

'Then get your eyes off the heavens and look at your body.'

Ananda did this and knew what he would find. A wet stickiness on his legs. He laughed. 'Is that all?'

'Maybe it was the old woman who did it.'

'Did what?'

'Put a spell on you, silly. You met her before you went into the women's village, remember? She put a spell of forgetting on you, so you would forget your bowl, leave it at Pchiti's place, and in the embarrassment of the moment tell a lie to your cousins.'

'Why would Mahaprajapati do that? She is no witch.'

'You must ask Siddhartha that question.' And she skipped away, out into the real world.

Ananda didn't want to ask Siddhartha. He came out of his meditations feeling disturbed and dissatisfied. He had allowed his visions to control him. When the little monkey mind morphed into the big monkey mind he was lost. He'd lost control of his body. Yet he'd caught a glimpse of heavens beyond the reach of man.

At the same time, he could hear Siddhartha speaking quietly in his ear, as if he were standing right by him.

'Ananda, as you return to the phenomenal world, it will seem like a vision in a dream. And your experience with the maiden Pchiti will seem like a dream, and your own body will lose its solidity and permanency. It will seem as though every human being, male or female, was simply a manifestation by some skilful magician of a mannequin, all of whose activities were under his control. Or each human being will seem like an automatic machine that once started goes on by itself, but as soon as the automatic machine loses its motive power, all of its activities not only cease but their very existence disappears.'

Sighing, he went searching for water and a cloth.

The man comes towards me, waving his heavy black book, but before he can reach me, Evie pushes me aside. I stagger and keep staggering, somehow unable to regain my feet until I crash into the door of a shop. It opens with a bang and closes behind me the same way.

It's very quiet. I glance back but there is no sign of the shouting man. No sign of Evie either. The street outside looks peaceful. I find myself in the children's section of a large department store. There are not many people around. No children at all.

I go past imitation (actual size) AK47 automatic rifles in their shiny boxes, transformers that turn into tanks and rocket carriers, rows of dark green fighter bombers sitting on their glass reflections, aircraft carriers with little fighter jets built to scale, miniature armies and disintegrator beams with flashing lights. That section gave way to the superhero section; Batman complete with a coil of rope, an Aquaman that could swim, a Superman with a Clark Kent suit, a Captain Nortikiss with a little helmet light that worked in dark places, and Zeldia the astrophysicist dressed a little like Wonder Woman holding a perfectly functional slide rule. Further along, to a section brightly lit with wistful Barbie dolls and sternly marching Kens.

I am drawn to a smaller, humble looking doll, dressed in warm, homespun colours, a pleasing contrast to the frozen tinsel adolescence of the Barbies. She has a cute, easy-to-love face, framed by soft, authentic-looking human hair. I wonder if Evie would like a doll like this. I know she's quite special, Evie, quite precocious, but she is still a little girl. She certainly deserves something for all her help and timely advice.

I pick it up, fully expecting to be shocked by the price.

'My name is Henrietta. Thank you for picking me up,' it says in a bright voice.

'That's alright.'

'I'm Henrietta, the affectionate doll. I have a storage capacity of five thousand words.'

'That's a lot of words.'

There is an information booklet tied to Henrietta's wrist, with details on how to initiate various programs.

'I can hear you with these little microphones in my ears. Please don't remove them.'

'I won't.'

'You sound like a nice person.'

'Thank you.'

'Please give me a cuddle. I love to be cuddled.'

Glancing surreptitiously around the shop, I hug it to my chest. It has the feel of a soft toy.

'That was nice cuddle,' it says in the same bright tones. 'And I am very reasonably priced at a hundred and fifteen credits point two-five.'

'Very reasonable,' I murmur into the plastic whirl of its ear, but I am beginning to doubt that this is the right gift for Evie. I don't know that they would get along.

'There is an impressive range of clothes in the Henrietta the Affectionate Doll series. I have a complete wardrobe!'

I hold it out at arm's length, looking at it from right and left as any prospective customer might, aware that I am probably under observation from a hidden camera somewhere.

I give it a little squeeze. It is soft and pliant but bounces back into shape.

'That was a nice cuddle. I love to be cuddled.'

'That's nice.'

'I can be your friend. Your best friend ever.'

I am certain now that Evie would not like a best friend like Henrietta.

Regretfully, I put her back on the shelf, placing her carefully among the cellophane covered packets of her wardrobe. There is also a Henrietta the Affectionate Doll make-up kit (C8.95) and a hairdressing kit (C7.95). There is also a word booster that slots into the back of Henrietta's head, underneath her hair, which will give her a facility of four thousand words.

'Please don't put me down, I'm lonely,' it says, swivelling its head to the left and to the right, as if seeking me out, her eyes passing blankly across the rows of Barbies and Kens facing her. Slowly I walk back up the aisle of toys, and have reached the board games *(SHAPESHIFTERS: repel an invasion from another dimension!)*, when I hear it speak again. 'I'm lonely, please cuddle me.'

I hurry on, passing the God of Underworld on his winged horse (I have no idea why such a god would need a winged horse, or any kind of horse) until I reach the more modest gifts, like a super-bouncer for half a credit. The picture on the cardboard wrapper shows the gravity-defying ball zooming right off the earth into outer space. Wowie-zow!

I keep a straight face when I emerge from the shop.

'Did you buy something?' Evie asks, jumping alongside me, swinging her skipping rope around her arm.

'Everything was pretty expensive.'

'And you have no money.'

'I wouldn't say that.'

'So what did you get me, then?'

'Why should I get you anything?'

'For saving your life. Several times.'

'How?'

'See, you didn't even notice.'

'Notice what?'

'That I saved you from the raving man, for example.' She unwinds the skipping rope from her arm.

'He's hardly the killer type.'

She thinks for a moment, and rotates her arm in such a way that the skipping rope seems to wrap around it by itself.

'I don't know what you think is going on,' she says at length, after having wrapped and unwrapped the rope from her arm several times with the same rotating motion. 'You think this is some pleasant stroll. A day off work while you amble about enjoying the sights, like a tourist.'

'Wait a minute…'

'There's already been too much waiting. And posturing. You don't seem to grasp the danger you are in. Ever since leaving the house this morning.'

'What kind of danger?'

'To the right and left, above and below. To body, mind and spirit. You are like a bull in a china shop.'

'Excuse me?'

'You know the expression. And that man with the black book. He would have killed you, but you just didn't know it. He was the spider and you were the fly, and just like a fly, you didn't know you were the fly. You didn't know he was the spider.'

'You're exaggerating. He was just a nutcase. A God-botherer of some kind.'

'So you didn't see the black hole in his throat. His gullet.'

'You're scaring me now.'

'About time. Now confess. What did you buy me in the store?'

'Okay. Good. Excellent. You're going to be nice to me?'

'Depends on what you've bought me.'

'Well, I thought of buying you a doll called Henrietta the Affectionate Doll. She's nice and soft and likes being cuddled.'

'Don't think I'd like that.'

'That's what I thought.'

'No, you said you thought of buying it.'

'Yes, then I had another thought, that you wouldn't like it.'

'So let's see! You're deliberately keeping me in suspense.' She jumps up and down in frustration.

We have finally arrived at the base of the Tower. It is buttressed by enormous concrete and steel struts. There is a moat running around it filled with clear water, and a graceful pedestrian bridge, designed by some architectural whim as a medieval drawbridge. This is Tomorrowland, already here.

Ceremonially, I hand Evie the super-bouncer, feeling a bit foolish.

'That's really neat,' she says somberly, removing it from its wrapper and holding it in her hand.

I feel a rush of gratitude, not just for Evie, or the super-bouncer, but the whole world. The world in which Evie and the super-bouncer could exist. That gratitude extended outwards to everything, forever. From the tranquillity of roses to the ferment of the galaxies. For the blood still slurring around inside my skin.

'Go on, bounce it. See what happens.'

'It might bounce right out of the world.'

'Then we'd have got our money's worth.'

She hurls the ball at the pavement. It leaps high into the air where it spins about triumphant. Evie catches it and slams it into the pavement once more, as if she really did want to bounce it right out of the world. We both shade our eyes against the glare of the sun, trying to follow it. Finally it falls into the water of the moat, right near us, and we're able to retrieve it.

Something in the water draws my attention. 'There are fish in the moat.' For some reason this excites me alone. Nobody else is taking any notice. Shadowy shapes that flick from moment to moment. And a spectral burst of colour. This portion of the moat, at the main entrance to the Tower has been scalloped out to make an oval shape. At each end of the oval shape there is a fountain, and each fountain separates into five streams, each stream a different colour. Above each fountain a rainbow hovers. The fish, I don't know what kind they are, seem to have absorbed all these colours.

'Do you see them?'

Evie looks down into the water. 'You have to go up there alone.'

'Why?'

'I can wait for you down here.'

'Nobody will notice you, you know, if you come in. That man with the book was an exception.'

'It's not about me.'

We sit on the edge of the oval pool and watch the fish steadying themselves in the water.

'I get it, the moment has arrived. And I'm not ready for it. I don't want to go in. I don't have to go to this fucking appointment. I never wanted to in the first place. It was Evelyn. She made me.'

'Don't swear like that.'

'How should I swear?'

'I don't have to go to this fucking appointment,' she mimics, doing it so perfectly she makes me ashamed.

'That sounds awful.' I bounce the super-bouncer in my palm, aware that the gift, bought on an impulse, had become something of a goodbye present. Or at least a thank-you present.

'What are you afraid of?'

'Needing a pee and there's no toilet.'

Evie waits.

'Sometimes I wake in the middle of the night, at 2 a.m. or 3 a.m. and I'm sweating. It's as if I'm in a fever. Then I get very afraid. So afraid I have to get up and have a pee.'

'That's where I come in.'

'What if you're not here when I come out?'

'Then I expect you'd have to deal with that.'

The skipping rope lies forgotten beside her as she stares into the water which, in its rippling, throws muscled shadows across her body. It frightens me when she assumes her adult self, so calm, so reflective. Confident and mature. I see, for moment, in the lines on her face drawn by the water, an ancient creature.

I get awkwardly to my feet. 'Well then, I wish I still had some cash. I'd leave you some money for an ice-cream. You like ice-cream, don't you?'

'Chocolate.'

'Chocolate ice-cream.'

I walk under my own power to the mock medieval bridge. The world gets smaller behind me. All I can think is that I didn't tell Evie what I was afraid of. The brown envelope. The judgement of the flesh.

A lonely death out under the stars.

'I'd like you to meet Medusa,' Zelena says in a curiously formal voice, inclining her body forward in a bow. 'And Holy Mary.'

'I hate the curfew,' Medusa says. Her voice is like a silver flute. She has a mass of black wiry looking hair and a small delicately boned face. Her eyes are slightly slanted to match her high cheekbones, and are as dark and lustrous as her hair. She is wearing a black cloak clasped at the neck with a golden broach. Beneath I glimpse a closely fitting red tunic outlining a slim, precisely formed body.

I am struck dumb, as if turned to stone.

'I love it,' the other woman, Mary, says. Holy Mary is deformed. Her head seems to have sunk into her body, overpowered by misshapen shoulders. Her face, squashed between her shoulders, has a lumpy, puffy look. Two bright eyes fix me with a sardonic intelligence.

'And the man is Mr No,' Zelena says dryly.

'No,' says Mr No. He wears a grey suit and has a face like a slab of stone.

As Zelena shuts the door, I have the peculiar sensation that the landing is filled with people waiting by the door with expressionless faces.

Medusa glides into the main room, followed by Mary who bobs from one side to the other on stumpy legs.

'What's this about a curfew?' I ask Mr No.

'No,' he replies in a toneless voice.

'I see we have interrupted something,' Holy Mary says, cackling like a crow. 'What a pity. You look wonderful in that jersey, darling. It's just that it doesn't cover everything.'

Zelena shrugs. She looks pissed off. When she shrugs, her jersey rises even higher.

Holy Mary scoops the roll-your-own off the floor and passes it under her nose. 'This is what I'm talking about,' she says.

'Go ahead,' Zelena says. 'Knock yourself out.'

Holy Mary picks up the bottle and shakes it. 'This one's seen better days.'

'Me too,' Zelena says, giving me a sour look.

Since Zelena has made no move to introduce me, I decide to introduce myself. 'My name's October. October Nortikiss, and I'm an astronaut.'

'Me too,' Mary says, looking around for matches. She has no flexibility and has to move her whole body to look at something. 'We've got some catching up to do. The night is young.'

We all stand around awkwardly.

Medusa puts her hand lightly on Zelena's arm and says something quietly in Zelena's ear. For a moment her mass of black curls covers both their faces.

' 'cuse us,' Zelena says and heads for the kitchen, not even looking at me, Medusa gliding along behind. Before disappearing into the kitchen, she turns and smiles at Mary. Her rosebud lips are red and her teeth are white.

'What's all that about?' I say, sitting down by the mattress. There's still some wine in the glass but I don't have much appetite for it. I think about Evie, and wonder if she is still waiting for me, out there in the curfew, among the shadows.

'That is all about Zellie and Meddie having a little chatsies,' Holy Mary says, fiddling with the roll-your-own to get it alight.

'Why do they call you Holy Mary?'

'Because I'm wholly holy, you see. I'm very good at prayer. I can pray any priest under the table, bet your boots on it. And God listens, when I pray. Not like with most people, God couldn't care less.'

'Why does he listen to you?'

'I wondered that too, until I figured it out. He feels guilty because He made me this way. He made me grotesque and I think it gives Him bad dreams, or at least a bad moment or two. I think he overcompensated when he gave me Meddie for a sister. We really are twins, you know. We are gin and juice, the sublime and the ridiculous, the sinner and the saved. Isn't that right, Mr No?'

'No,' said Mr No. He hadn't sat down or made himself comfortable. Maybe the lack of furniture put him off. He remained standing stiffly, as if about to leave.

'Seems like they have known each other for a long time.' I can see Medusa's hand resting lightly on Zelena's arm.

'Ohh yes, you could say that. Or you could say they have been strangers for a very long time.' She gives a little cackle, which must be the smoke taking hold.

'So Meddie is the sinner and you are the saved?'

'Of course. She's built for it, can't you see? She's just a sin machine, purpose built. Just walking, it looks like her body's having sex with itself. God did that too, you know. Me, I'm the opposite. I'm built for prayer. I don't have far to fall to get to my knees. Meddie doesn't have to spread her legs very wide to let sin in. So everybody gets their fair share.'

'What about Zelena?'

'What about her? She's got legs to spread like everybody else, but she gets pissed off with men who treat her like a tramp, a cum-sponge. That's when she goes to Meddie for a shoulder to cry on and they go to bed and Meddie licks away her tears and other stuff. It's very tender. Everybody gets drunk… speaking of which…' she shakes the bottle, then lifts it to her mouth and drinks. Because she can't move her head, she leans right back to get enough angle.

'Let me ask you a question,' she says, wiping her mouth with the back of her hand in a practised gesture. 'Wouldn't you like to go to bed with Medusa?'

'Wait a minute…'

'Yes, yes, I know all that…' She waves *all that* away with one arm. Her hands are twisted with arthritis. 'But all the same, in your wildest dreams maybe. No need to pretend. It's obvious what you and Zellie have been up to.'

'I'm not pretending.'

'That's debatable. But what if I told you that you could have her if you wanted her, what would you say then?'

'How can you say that?'

'Any man can have her. On one little condition.'

'And what's that?'

'Not so fast. You have to admit that you like the idea. You have to confess your desire.'

'Well, she is very…'

'Yes, she is, very. But that's not a confession.'

'Okay, I confess.'

'Confess what?'

'That I want her.'

'Who?'

'Medusa.'

'Then say so!'

'I want Medusa.' I don't say it too loud. I don't want Zelena to hear me. It would seem disloyal somehow, although I know it's true.

'Then you can have her. Just like that. But there is, as I mentioned, one condition.'

'What's that?'

'Me. You have to have me first. Only through me can you get to her. Do you like it?'

'Very clever.'

'We worked it out a long time ago. Men, and women too, all wanted to sleep with her, but how badly, that was the question. So Meddie declared that anybody, man or woman, who wanted her badly enough to sleep with me could have her, no questions asked. That separates the men from the boys.'

'And does it happen?'

'You've no idea, lover boy.' She tries to look coy, but her face isn't made for it.

'Ah!' I began to see daylight. 'And Zelena was one of those?'

'You've got it. And Mr No here. He was another one.'

'No,' says Mr No.

'Don't deny it!'

'No,' says Mr No. His whole face, and the expression on it, is one big no.

'So now Zelena…'

'You're getting there, lover boy. You are a quick learner, I can see that.' She drags away on Zelena's roll-your-own without offering me or Mr No any. 'The problem is, you see, that those who sleep with Medusa always fall in love with her.'

'Why?'

'Because she is the world spirit.'

'Why do you say that?'

'That's what our parents named her. A second name. Medusa World Spirit Jackson. Our parents were big on that sort of thing. They called me Holy Mary because they saw that I had no choice, I imagine. It works for her. Her body may be as petite as an elf, but her spirit is wider than the world. To make love to her is to get lost in her.'

'You make it sound irresistible.'

'There've been no complaints. So what about you, lover boy? Are you a taker or faker? Are you game or lame?'

When Medusa and Zelena return, I think maybe I am game. She is like a magnet to the eye. All that dark hair and pale skin and sapphire eyes. A provocative turbulence, a studied delicacy, an air of secretive pleasure. Holy Mary was right. Who could resist her? Who would want to? Women would want to out of sheer envy.

'We're leaving,' Medusa says in a low voice.

Zelena looks at me, apparently appalled at what she sees. She's like a woman come to her senses. 'You too, Johnny.'

'What about the curfew?' Mary says, hugging Zelena's mattress. 'Demons and guns.'

'No,' Mr No said. His flat face has finally found an expression. Terror. He keeps looking at the door.

'Fuck the curfew,' Medusa said, the sweet flute voice now sharp. 'We can't stay here a moment longer.'

Mary bounced to her feet and fronted up to Zelena.

'You've let this get so far up your bum that you'd throw us out, throw us to the mercy of the demons and the guns?'

'No,' says Mr No. He's grinding up the rest of his face with his bottom teeth.

'Yes,' Zelena answers, 'But that's not what this is about. This is about little Miss Proud, your precious World Spirit, not wanting to stay in my slutty presence a moment longer. Forgive me for breathing, sleeping, farting and fucking.'

Medusa comes closer to me. Such exquisiteness is blinding. I have to turn away. 'I'm sorry you got dragged into this, Mr...'

'Call me Johnny.'

'Zelena only did what she did out of jealously, trying to make me jealous. She knew I was coming here tonight. She knew I'd find you both here. She wore that silly jersey just to hammer the point home...'

'You mean, she doesn't find me the slightest bit attractive?'

'I didn't say that.'

'Just fuck off, all of you,' Zelena says. 'Or is that too subtle?'

I haven't left yet, but already I'm looking back. With regret. Something unfinished here. The tapestry. There was a moment, if just a moment, the heat of kundalini between my fingers.

'I'll go with you,' I said to Medusa.

'Of course you will,' Mary cackled.

'No,' Mr No speaks at full volume. Even in these dull spaces, his voice reverberates.

Medusa makes for the door, not looking back. Holy Mary scampers after her, and the reluctant Mr No follows her, walking stiffly, like someone who's forgotten how to walk.

I can't quite believe it's finishing like this. I look at Zelena, perhaps imploringly, I don't know, I can't see my face.

'Don't waste your pity on them,' she says. They are creatures of the curfew, shadow dwellers. They go from place to place. They wouldn't have stayed here long anyway.'

'It's not that.'

She looks puzzled.

I can't find the words. I gesture towards the mattress, the empty bottle, the clothes lying everywhere, the ashtray with the roaches. And the tapestry. It all looks so tawdry, pitiful even. And the tapestry's not glowing anymore. It all looks flat.

'You want to get sentimental, Johnny? Declare undying love? Tell me you'll come back and rescue me from this shithole? We'll run away to Tomorrowland?'

I still can't find any words.

'I didn't think so. What's keeping you? You'd better get going. The World Spirit won't wait.'

'Something happened...' That's all I can manage, but I know that, despite the bitter edge of the real, we touched on something, felt something, became a part of something, stepped for a moment outside our mundane lives.

'Yeah,' she says. For a moment her roguish grin reappears. 'Something always happens.'

❂

Descending the stairs, I fall in behind the others. Immediately ahead of me, the World Spirit glides along like a shadow, her cape moving behind. Ahead are Holy Mary and Mr No. Holy Mary is finding the stairs hard work.

On the first landing, a woman and two children lie asleep on the concrete floor. A man stands behind them, stiff as a pole, staring rigidly in front of him.

'No,' Mr No says to him as we go past, stepping over the sleeping

him towards the door. The thin youth stands to one side, well out of the line of sight, and holds the door open for us. He watches Medusa warily as she passes. As soon as we are all through he closes the door quickly behind us.

The street looks normal enough, if quieter than it might be. It looks to me like an image woven on a huge loom. North and south swing about as the image turns. The four of us stand there, casting about for a direction. I'd like to get the hell away. Right up there among the stars might be far enough.

The rumble of a heavy vehicle is heard. Something big and something coming. I look around and find myself alone on the street. The others, the creatures of the curfew, have gone. As the rumble gets closer the streets seem to get emptier. Even the shadows retreat behind their facades. Buildings lean back from their perpendicular. Behind them, clouds scud across a half moon.

At the end of the street, an armoured carrier rumbles into view, travelling at a mere walking pace, its turret and gun barrel swivelling from side to side. A hand slips into mine and there's a tug on my arm.

A moment later I'm down behind a yellow steel rubbish hopper with Holy Mary, her misshapen body pressed against mine, her head over my shoulder. There's only me and her and the shadows. 'The key is not to move,' she says, not trying to whisper. 'It's movement the eye notices.' It feels comforting, having that bony body pushed up against mine. I can feel the movement of her rib cage as she breathes.

Over her shoulder I can see the armoured vehicle approaching. It has enormous tires, taller than a man.

'How many men have you managed to fool?'

'As many men as there are fools. Which is to say a lot.'

'So you have had a few takers.'

'Oh yes.' Her rib cage jiggles against mine as she laughs.

'And what happens when they go to Medusa for their reward?'

'They want to kill me, of course, but everybody is too busy laughing at them for the idea of murder to gain any traction. They normally slink off in shame.'

'Does Medusa ever fulfil your promise?'

'Once. That was Zelena. Mr No is still waiting to collect.'

Again her rib cage jiggles against me in mirth.

The military vehicle is not close enough for me to see, lounging behind the turret in full view, a soldier, but not the familiar variety one might, from time to time, see marching resolutely down our main streets in full daylight. While fully proportioned like a man it has a flat, fishlike face covered in metal scales. Thin, fleshless membranes grow where ears should be. These are flexible and swivel about in the air. While its posture suggests tranquillity and ease, there is a frightening raptness in the movement of its head and the fleshless ears.

Mary puts a finger over my lips. 'Meet our overlords,' she breathes. 'And they hear pretty good with those wishbone thingies they have for ears.'

Overlords? I'm not sure what planet I'm on, but it sure to hell isn't the one I woke up in this morning. I've got an envelope in my pocket which will explain everything. My orders. I haven't opened it yet. Perhaps I never will. Perhaps I'll wake up and find myself in quarantine.

A tall figure walks out into the street directly in front of the military vehicle. He stands tall and proud and raises his arms commandingly.

'No!' he cries in a loud voice.

The beast in the turret turns around casually. I see that it is armed. I have read about disintegrator ray-guns on the back of cereal packets, but of course had never seen one in real life. This thing looks like a kids' toy, the one I saw in the toy section of the department store.

Mary digs her fingers into my arm so hard it hurts.

The military vehicle comes to a halt. A mechanical voice issues from it. 'You are in violation of the curfew. Please leave the street immediately or you will be shot. I repeat, you will be shot.'

'No!' Mr No walks towards the vehicle his arms outstretched as if he could push back, right out of existence, by sheer will alone.

There is a burst of purple tracer light from the disintegrator. When it hit Mr No he disappeared in a searing flash of light. Then there was nothing. No messy corpse to clear away. Just a faint black shape on the road.

In one smooth, relaxed motion, the soldier is off the side of the vehicle and hurries to the spot where Mr No made his last stand. It is squat, with a broad, froglike back and stubby legs. It rolls slightly as it moves, but moves with speed.

When it gets to the spot, it stands still, and with an absorbed attention it surveys the street. The disintegrator dangles from its arm.

Holy Mary's limbs are trembling. It seems as if the creature must hear her bones knocking together. Set in a marble mask, her puffy, ageless face is turned up to mine. Her eyes look white and blind. A moment later they change. They are as deep as a mountain lake, as beautiful and as mysterious. They are the eyes of her twin, the World Spirit. I pull her close and kiss her lips, which are hard and chill.

'We will live through this,' I whisper, hardly breathing the words. 'We will live to tell the tale.'

The creature is looking right at the rubbish hopper. We can't shrink any further back into the shadows.

Now it is approaching the hopper in a comical side-to-side motion, but there is nothing comical about its intention.

'We're fucked,' Mary says. 'The fucking cold-bloods can smell the warm blood.'

Medusa appears out of the shadows to one side. She is holding something quite small, like a compact. Apparently it fires darts, for a moment later the surprised creature has three or four darts sticking to its scales. With short, clumsy looking hands it begins to remove them.

'Poison,' Mary says. 'It's the only thing that gets them.'

Medusa, the World Spirit, looks like a superhero, standing there in the darkened street, her cloak flying, lithe in her red bodysuit. In that moment I believe she could fly, if she wanted to, I believe she really is the world spirit.

The soldier begins tipping sideways.

'Now we run,' Mary says.

When I stand up, I still have her clutched in my arms. She hardly seems to weigh anything.

'Now we run,' I say.

Here is a moment I can't get away from. It is a centripetal moment. A doorway moment. A threshold moment. A moment from which I can never escape. All roads lead back to this spot, at this time, where the official holds the door open for me, and I have to hesitate one last time before going through.

I finally appreciate how it stands between us, the official and me. I cannot please him. I can never please him. No matter what I did or was or said or tried to be and do and say, no matter what school I went to or what my father did for a living, he would still be there, standing by his door, a courteous smile on his face. It is an ordinary moment. The most ordinary of moments. The moment you have to live through to get to the next one, when something will happen.

Very well, I walk past him. He is sliding to my right, his smile still hung there. I suppose I've got one too. It's a smiley moment, and a wonderful place to bring up children.

I'm back in the anteroom with its chessboard floor and poorly executed pastoral. All the details are exactly as I remember them. There is no comfort in that, but at least there is certainty. In the distance, through the sloping plate glass windows, I can see the yellow hills of my childhood.

There's a woman sitting in the seat beside the one I used to occupy. There is an air of nervousness and tension about her I recognise. That is how I was. Before the appointment. Now I have my brown envelope in my pocket. Now I have been marked, branded, stamped and almost approved. It's a relief.

The woman is the one I am expecting, the one I knew was coming, the one with the fishnet stockings. I haven't met her yet, but I know her name begins with Z. Zelig? Zeena? She is attractive in a messy, hippy kind of way. Uncombed blonde hair. No make-up; the bruised colour beneath her eyes is for real. A short black denim skirt. A fluffy jacket sewn with tiny mirrors. Late nights and wine by the look of it. I like her, and, in that way which happens with some people, feel like I have met her before. We smile at each other like old companions. Her smile is rueful, scared even. Mine, I hope, is reassuring.

I'd like to talk to her. To tell her that it wasn't really so bad. Just a strange black-snouted machine looking all over your body. It doesn't take long. And there is a friendly pair with ponytails. Quick as a flash it is all over and you have your brown envelope. You have your diagnosis. You have your orders. You have your reality. Your official status. You find out who you really are, and what you are really doing here. Everything will be explained.

I don't say any of these things, I just smile my reassuring smile and nod my head until my bell jangles.

As she heads for the door the official is holding open for her, she glances back at me. Because of that glance I decide to sit and wait for her. I am familiar enough with these tubular steel chairs with the red cushions.

Perhaps, while waiting, I will open my brown envelope and read my orders. Or perhaps not.

We'll go to my place, smoke some herb and mess around all we want.

'Why are you asking me?'

'Do you want to be alone? I don't want to be alone. Not at a time like this.'

I agree with her one hundred percent.

Since the streets of our fair but very flat city are joined mostly at right angles to each other in a neat grid, it is very simple to get lost. So obsessed were our city planners with the pattern of the grid (so neat and tidy!), that each intersection looks pretty much like every other. They even planted the same kind of tree on the same spot on most of the street corners, or provided little corner parks with identical swings and slides.

It is to one of these little parks, just clear of the central city, that I go carrying Holy Mary all the way, at first in my arms like a baby, and then on my back piggy-back style. Her bony little legs fit around my body as if they belong there. When we arrive, she swings down off me like a practised rider.

'You saved my life,' she croaks. She doesn't let go of my hand.

I don't know what to say except 'don't mention it' or 'you'd do the same for me' or 'shucks,' so I don't say anything.

The playground has a slide made of a large yellow tube. We hide inside this as more military vehicles and soldiers go past.

'This is all new to me,' I say, after we have crawled out of the slide. The night is calm and quiet. We have taken refuge in the shadow of the slide.

'It can come as quite a shock,' Medusa says. 'If you haven't been paying attention, that is.'

As if to reinforce her point, there is a burst of distant gunfire. Not the spitting sound their disintegrator rays made but the brittle snapping of small arms fire.

I think of the thin sheath of pages sitting on my desk at home. They are a testimony to something, some kind of attention, but what? They are not going to hold back the night, or even put an end to the curfew. That makes me think of Evelyn. My problem with Evelyn is really one of boundaries.

She is me and I am her. We are each other's mirror.

Medusa sweeps her dark hair off her face. She is delicate and fragile, with her fine-boned beauty, but in her case appearances are deceptive. I saw her kill a soldier creature without any hesitation or compunction. Carrying Mary, I followed her through the streets as she guided us out of the curfew zone. Beautiful she may be, delicate and fragile she is not.

'Thank you for saving Mary. I misjudged you. I said harsh things about you and Zelena.'

'I'm married.'

'I know. Zelena always goes for the worst losers, married men on the hunt. Men who go cringing back to their wives. Cowards.'

'That's me.'

'You may be a fool, but you're not a coward.'

I'm not so sure, but I'm happy to leave it there. At least Medusa's hostility to me has dissipated.

There's a burst of light from over the horizon, like far-off lightning. I have to get home before it is too late. Is this what Evie meant by 'the wrath to come'?

'Who are you people anyway?'

She doesn't answer that. Deliberately.

'What did you mean about me being a "carrier"? You mean like the plague?'

For a moment it seems she's not going to answer that either. She just looks silent and thoughtful and beautiful in the night.

'The invaders are doing it. Altering our genetic make-up, turning us into them, seeding us with their genes. And we in turn seed others.'

'But that would take generations.'

'Not with the technology they have. They have these machines with black snouts, like scanners. They can play around with you right down to the level of protein building.'

'And you're in the resistance?'

'That would be a nice thought. It is a nice thought. Some people believe that they are fighting a resistance, but that may be just a fantasy the Fishmen have placed in their heads. Let them act out a fantasy resistance.'

'You said Fishmen?'

'That's what they look like, to us anyway.'

'I can't believe that people don't know about this. It sounds crazy, like a story off the back of a cereal packet,' I remember all the things I said to Evelyn about her cheap-jack scenarios.

'The truth finds all sorts of ways to get through. Even the back of cereal packets. The truth worms its way in anywhere and everywhere.'

'Where are you going now?'

It's Holy Mary who answers. She still has her hand in mine. I'd forgotten it.

'We've nowhere to go. We were staying at Mr No's place, but that's no-go now.'

Funny old world. Looking at her now, I find her, misshapen and all, quite desirable. The way her body had fitted mine when I carried her has left an imprint. All her beauty is there, in her eyes. And she knows it too. The sardonic gleam is back, but with a softness.

'Then you'll come back to my place,' I say. 'It'll be safe there.'

'You won't forget your appointment coming up, will you?' Evelyn calls from the bathroom.

'What appointment?'

'Ha ha.'

Forget? How can I? I'd like to forget. I'd like to put it all out of my mind. As far away as I can put it, as you do with things you don't want to think about. All your shame and fear. No chance of that. My whole bloody life revolves around this appointment. The getting there, the getting away again.

The mess and the cleanup.

'You can always take Evie, for company. She always cheers you up.'

I give an exasperated sigh, loud enough, I hope, to be heard in the bathroom. 'You don't *take* Evie anywhere. If she wants to come, she'll tag along.'

'I get it.'

I'm not sure that she does. There's always something patronising in her tone when she speaks of Evie. Since she has never actually seen the girl, Evelyn assumes she is some kind of imaginary companion. A phantom I have summoned from my well of loneliness. I don't try to explain it.

I'm lying on the bed, enjoying the feel of the sheet on my naked body, staring at the ceiling. There is a spider on the ceiling, moving steadily towards the wall. When it reaches the junction, it crosses over without pause and begins climbing down the wall. I wonder if the spider even notices the change. Maybe the wall becomes the new ceiling, and that's that. A new up and down, the old quickly forgotten in the transition.

Evelyn appears in the doorway of the bedroom. She has changed appearances, red hair in place of her dark blonde and green tinted eyes instead of blue. She is dressed in a negligee, all white and creamy with puffy, laced arms.

'You look a treat.'

'I would hope so.'

I don't want to ask her about her makeover. She might be sensitive on the subject.

'Wow! is all I can say.'

The right thing to say, apparently, as there is a small smile of triumph on her face as she picks up her book and slides under the sheet to join me.

'What's that book?'

Black Holes – The End of the Universe? by John Taylor.'

I push one leg across until it connects with hers. She pretends not to notice.

'So what is his prognosis? Is the universe doomed to die from an uncontrolled outbreak of black holes?'

'Worse, it probably already has. We're all living in a giant black hole. The universe is a naked singularity whose centre is nowhere and whose event horizon is everywhere.'

'A naked singularity. Sounds sexy.' My hand drifts across to her side of the bed and rests in the heat of her hip.

'Well it is. Everything gets sucked in. The milk of life gushes out.'

'Does it say that in your book?'

'No, I'm saying that. I'm extrapolating.'

So was my hand. It was moving up the side of her hip towards her stomach.

'So what's an event horizon, then?'

'The outer perimeter of a black hole. We can't look inside because no light comes out.' She flicks through the book and reads: 'The entropy of a black hole is proportional to the surface area of its event horizon.'

'Oh.'

'Which means the bigger things are, the harder they fall into it.'

'You suddenly know a lot about this science stuff.'

'I have to keep up with my fictional self, you know – the one you romp through the stars with, your sexy astrophysicist. Shit! Sometimes I feel as if I am in competition with my own self, my fictional self. I'm jealous of her, that Beverly or Zeldia. Of course you've modelled her on me, with the red hair and green eyes and the drop-dead gorgeous aspect. That's a dead giveaway. What happens to her in the end? Do they have a lovely sexy time in null-grav?'

'That's to be seen. It's never a good idea to try to predict what people will do.'

'Even fictional people?'

'Especially fictional people. Always at the whim of the writer's moods.'

I'm not happy about the direction of the conversation. I sense hidden traps and dangers. There is a cause and effect problem. Beverly had green eyes and red hair before Evelyn changed. And here she is acting as if she has always been that way. There is a pile of papers on my desk which grows from time to time, organising itself like a slime mould. I don't want to think about what it contains right now, or think about my appointment, the one I'm not allowed to forget. There's too much fear in it all, and like most sneaks, I am a coward at heart. There may come a point when I am too frightened to pick up that pile of papers, too frightened to open them up and read them. Something might come crawling out. Sometimes I wonder if words themselves carry a contagion, a dimensionality that reshapes the mind without the mind even noticing.

These are more things I don't want to think about, so I snuggle in close and sneak my hand onto her belly, where it does a little soft dance around her belly button. Sometimes sex is the answer to everything. 'And what's this… naked singularity?' My hand creeps south.

'The inner circumference of a black hole,' seizing my hand, 'within which conditions approach infinite mass, which we cannot conceive… but don't panic, you'd never fall through the singularity. That would take an infinite amount of time. You see, the closer you approach infinite mass, the slower times moves. You'd go on falling forever.'

'How do these writers come up with this kind of stuff?'

'It's all in the maths, Sonny Jim.'

'So the maths tell us that the universe is shaped like a huge vulva. This giant black hole with two sets of lips, the outer, your event horizon… look I think you have one too!'

'No you don't!' She fights off my hand.

'And… these luscious inner lips, that juicy naked singularity…'

She fights me off and we have a nice little wrestle. Except, for just one fleeting moment it isn't so nice. We bear our teeth at each other like a couple of animals. There is a terrible fury in her that knows no bounds, and it is with that that we are flirting.

After some panting and half-nervous laughing, she goes back to her book. I go back to my spider, making his way patiently down the wall. Pretty soon he'll be facing another reality shift.

'Listen to this, and keep your slidy little fingers away from me. There was a Sumerian priest called Berossus, who brought together three separate, verifiable accounts of how there appeared, before the people of Chaldæa, who lived in a lawless manner like the beasts of the field, a creature by the name of Oannes, whose whole body was that of a fish. Under the fish's head he had another head, the head of a man, with feet below similar to those of a man, subjoined to the fish's tail. His voice too, and language, was articulate and human. This Being gave man an insight into letters and sciences, and arts of every kind. He taught them to construct cities, to found temples, to compile laws, and explained to them the principles of geometry. He made them distinguish the seeds of the earth, and showed them how to collect the fruits. And when the sun had set, this being, Oannes, retired again into the sea, and passed the night in the deep; for he was amphibious. After this, there appeared other beings like Oannes, of which Berossus proposes to give an account when he comes to the history of the kings.'

'What about that guy in the Old Testament, the one who spilt his seed on fallow ground?'

'That's Onan, you idiot. The masturbator. Oannes is the fish creature.'

'Nice to get that straightened out.'

'Is that what you are about to do, is it? Spill your seed on the fallow sheet?'

'Seems like an option.'

I try not to look at the spider. By the time it reaches the floor, I figure, it will have forgotten its experience on the ceiling, and on the wall, forgotten that it had once walked upside down, and then side on. And why should it remember?

I snuggle further down under the sheet, one hand between my thighs. 'Do you know what I think? I think these Fishmen are the Keepers of the

Black Hole. They are its threshold guardians.' My other hand goes exploring.

'And they have one-track minds, like you, I suppose. You know what? I think they intervene at crucial stages in our history, like that obelisk thing in that movie, to give us an evolutionary push. And I think they're here now.'

'Here to destroy us, more likely.'

'Listen, John Taylor goes on to wonder just why it is that Sumerian civilization crystallizes so suddenly. He calls it an abrupt transition from chaos to civilization.'

'And I suppose he claims that we mated with these creatures?'

'Maybe, I think they took some of our ape ancestors into their labs and put them on machines that stimulated the growth of the cerebral cortex.'

'I don't like the idea.'

'Why?'

'It takes away our human dignity, turns us into freaks, pets of some fish beings coming out of the deep, or some kind of scientific experiment gone wrong.'

Consider the spider, still marching resolutely for the floor. What if I picked him up and put him back on the ceiling, or in some strange impossible place like the inside of my shoe? What if I intervened in its life the way Oannes has apparently intervened in ours? Pick the ape up and put him somewhere different, somewhere at right angles to his familiar world. Teach him art and civilization, show him the true meaning of up and down and the mysteries of gravity.

My body starts to feel sleep heavy. Evelyn's lips brush the back of my neck. 'Remember your appointment,' she whispers.

As I settle in, I know that at some stage in the night, maybe two or three in the morning I'm going to get up and have a pee. I should get up and have one now but I am too comfortable.

Far too comfortable to move.

Ananda sat so still he hardly made a ripple in the air. He wanted it that way. Even to move so much as a muscle might be a mistake. It was so hard to take any action in this world that did not lead to unintended consequences.

Whole universes may be created and uncreated by the wrong use of the mind.

Take his bowl for example. His begging bowl. The one he used for alms and eating from, and even meditating upon. Such a simple thing. A scoop in a piece of wood, no more. Room for a spoonful of rice or a coin or two. The only thing, but for the robes on his back, that he owned. His last material object. Such a simple thing in itself, yet the errant mind could complicate even that.

Given his phenomenal memory, it was not difficult for him to remember his life as a prince, the pampered son of a rich man, just like his cousin Siddhartha. Multiply his begging bowl by a thousandfold, a thousand-thousandfold and still you would not come to an end of their family's wealth. Of what interest was a rude wooden bowl then? Never once had he pined for those days of material comfort, his every whim catered to by his father's concubines, never once had he regretted his decision to renounce the world and take to the road.

But the world was not so easy to renounce. It found ways of manifesting itself, creeping up on the unwary mind, using any means at hand, even that same simple bowl. All the material comforts of his old life could not have assuaged the mental agony that bowl brought with it.

He was sitting in his favourite spot in the doorway of his hut, half inside, half out, shaded from the sun yet able to see the life of the camp. Siddhartha was talking of moving on, reminding them that, as monks, homelessness was their natural state. Ananda understood. Already he was growing too fond of the riverbank, where he washed his bowl and had conversations with the deva girl. This fondness for the world had little value for those who must leave it behind.

'You like the mountain,' Siddhartha said once to a monk, 'but you cannot hole, Evelyn told me that.

It occurs to me, however, that equally, Evie might not have waited for me. She didn't have to wait. She comes and goes as she pleases. The thought that I might never see her again makes me want to cry, right there in that public space.

I am a mess of emotions. The slightest, most ephemeral feelings are amped up. But they don't add up. I miss Evelyn, suddenly and as sharply as I desire the girl with the fishnet stockings. My zooming good health in the morning is faced with death in the afternoon. The brown envelope sits heavily in my pocket. One way or another, I will find a universe in which I open it and learn the truth. I will not go in fear of it. I will read it and receive my gram of wisdom. *And as he read he wept and trembled. His relations were sore amazed because they thought some frenzy distemper had got into his head.*

The lift arrives, and there is a dull pause before the doors slide apart. I enter the empty steel chamber. The airlock hisses to a close behind me. Instinctively, I go to check the oxygen pressure. There is a moment of weightlessness as the lift begins to drop. I reach out for handholds but don't find any.

I take out the brown envelope. This is as good a time as any. This is the moment around which all other moments coalesce. This is the moment, the *Deus Irae,* that fulfils and abolishes time. Everything I can remember, my life with Evelyn, my happy walks through the city, my conversations with Evie, my adventures with pedestrian crossings and book waving zealots – all lie on the other side of this event horizon of my life.

I pull the official paper out of the envelope. So much more solemn this way, with real ink and real paper. Even more so with that fancy Confederation letterhead.

The lift stops and the door opens.

Evelyn is sitting watching TV as I come into the living room. It looks like some overblown horror movie.

'So it's all over, then?' she says, looking up.

I pat my pocket where the brown envelope lies.

'I have my orders. I'm on a suicide mission. I'm headed for the far shore.'

'You believe me now, don't you, about the invasion? You've seen it with your own eyes.'

'How did you know?'

She points to the pile of paper, almost grown to its full height now.

'The novel about my grandfather?'

'The one underneath that. The hidden one, all about sex and death. And betrayal. How you betrayed me with that slutty hippy. The whole sick story.'

'You shouldn't believe everything you read.'

'Ha ha. That's a good one, coming from you.'

'Perhaps you are reading too much into it.' *I am for certain informed that this, our city, will be burned with a fire from heaven.*

'Perhaps I am. Now listen to this.' She picks up a sheet of paper and reads: *'Arm in arm we remove ourselves back into the living room and tumble onto the floor by the mattress, somehow missing the mattress itself, Zelena avoiding at the last moment knocking over her glass. "Mustn't ruin the carpet," she says. Her kiss tastes of wine and marijuana and loneliness.* Oh, that's a nice touch that one. *We undress in front of each other, trying not to make our stares too hopelessly overt.* How sweet of you both. A touching moment for all. *Solemnly, I say, "Zelena, I know you think a fuck is a fuck, and so it is, but we are also bringing two halves of eternity together. We can burn as bright as stars."* Did you really say that, about bringing two halves of eternity together? Or did you just make it up? Inspired by the moment, I suppose. But wait… the best is yet to come. *Finally naked, she smiles. She looks trapped and vulnerable. Perhaps she is going to wake up tomorrow morning and think about those stars. "You certainly got plenty of mileage out of my old tapestry."'*

'Don't you feel ashamed of yourself?'

'For what I did?'

Which of these localized, rightly perceiving, minds belongs to you?

'No, no,' she brushes that aside as if it is of no consequence, 'for writing like that! You're going to need a lot of red ink. *Burn as bright as stars.* I can hardly believe that you, of all people, could write that.'

'Maybe you had to be there.'

'Oh! I get that! Sloppy Zelena and her smelly underpants. Are you going to subject your reader to that kind of thing? Don't you have a duty to uplift and entertain? To enrich people's lives? Not to pull them down to your own tawdry level. Your reader won't put up with that.'

'You're angry. I can understand that.'

'How astonishing.'

On television, people talk to one another in voices low and urgent. I go to the window and look out. The Tower leans away from the city. Now, of course, I know that the Tower is not what it seems. It is an interstellar vessel, a warship called the *Frolix 6*. A way to hide it in plain sight. Keep the war secret from the populace. Pretty soon the Tower would rip from its moorings and shudder into the sky. Once free of the atmosphere, it would flash off to the stars, using the bendy physics of space-time to collapse distances. In this case it would be heading for a far distant spot in the middle of nowhere, the spot where the invaders got their first slimy toehold in our dimension. A graphic description of its take-off, in some detail, how it ripped itself free of the concrete buttresses that held it, would be a good way to send Nortikiss on his journey and end the book. The pile of pages would stop growing. They could be safely left to yellow in the sun. Eventually the city would return to its old forgetfulness. In our ends are our beginnings.

'You have to burn it. Better still, disintegrate it with your blaster.'

'What?'

'That!' She points to the pile of papers. 'You don't get it, do you? The invaders are not getting their first slimy toehold on our reality at some far distant spot in the middle of nowhere, but right here, now. *You* are their agency. *You* are their portal. That's what that dark-haired street girl meant when she said you were a carrier. Your readers will become infected through the agency of the story. The narrative itself will carry the infection.'

As she speaks a transformation takes place within me. A seismic shift in my grid-symbol construct. There will be no more running from lifetime to lifetime, no more fleeing the wrath to come. I will face the wrath. I will become it. I am the wrath. I am the metronomic heartbeat of the beast. I can feel the change at the cellular level. I am shapeshifting into my disease. I am the contagion of the world.

I turn away from the window and face Evelyn.

One look at me and she stops talking, stops breathing. 'No, no,' she says.

Nothing she can say or do will stop it. I am being reshaped from the inside out.

She speaks fast and hard. 'Always remember, you are a morally responsible agent. You are not helpless. Not a plaything of fate. What you think, what you fuck, it all matters.'

My body grows longer, broader, thicker. My neck and shoulders swell. My spine lengthens. I am stronger, more muscular. My senses expand. I can smell the world, hear the cry of the stars, feel the surge of creation. All the universes are but an ocean to me.

'You can't end it like this, with an atrocity. Think of the moral basis of all this. The ethical implications. The resetting of the moral balance of the world. Remember that?'

'No.'

'You said it was your job to help redress the moral imbalance of the world, not exacerbate it.'

'How grandiose of me.'

My blood is remembering something else. The deep, lonely ocean between the stars; the crimson, tachyon tides.

'I don't think it's grandiose, I think it's noble. Quite heroic.'

I take a waddling step towards her. I know what she is trying to do. A last-minute appeal to my vanity. Or some imaginary better self. Her words pick it up and bring it with you.'

'Hanuman could,' one of the monks quipped, and everybody laughed, as much at the superstitious Hindus who loved their apeman superhero as at their foolish fellow monk.

'Yes,' said Siddhartha, 'but even Hanuman had to put down the mountain eventually. He could run with it to the ends of the earth – but no further.'

The monks nodded wisely, especially the ones who didn't have a clue what Siddhartha meant.

Despite the splendour of the sun, and the tranquil scene before him, Ananda's ever-lively mind was not at rest. Siddhartha had suggested to him a special meditation in which he would practice forgetting. Ananda's memory, his greatest blessing, could also be his greatest curse, for it snared him in the bonds of time. But to practice forgetting was a lot harder than it sounded. How was it possible to take a memory, and then forget it? For most people, forgetting happened naturally. Not for him.

Take the moment with Pchiti in her hut, for example. The way the very light itself softened. The way her innocent breasts were caught in shadow. Her smile that made his own teeth ache. The touch of her hand on his arm. The low breathiness of her voice. All those things and many others – how was he to forget them? To be told to forget was like an incitement to remember. He wondered if, in fact, Siddhartha were not trying to torment him. One of his cousin's tricks.

'Meditate on the gap between thoughts,' Siddhartha had said. 'The spaces between the memories.'

For Ananda, this advice had been especially difficult since there were no gaps between his thoughts, no spaces between his memories. There was just one continuous unbroken line to those first moments when he drew breath in the world. He had to search out those gaps and spaces and was surprised to find that they were there. Somehow Siddhartha, always the cunning one, had learned how to sneak through those gaps and spaces to what he called energy beyond thought. The great unconditioned energy of creation, running through all the worlds.

'Meditate on your bowl,' Siddhartha had said. 'Contemplate its emptiness. Then fill it with water. Now contemplate its fullness. Emptiness or fullness – does it make any difference to the bowl?'

Ah, the bowl. Again he wondered if Siddhartha were not teasing him by deliberately raising the matter of the bowl. All had gone as he expected and feared. Pchiti herself had brought the bowl back, probably seeking another audience with him, but like the coward he was discovering himself to be, he had lurked out of sight until she had given the bowl to a fellow monk and left the camp.

And yet, very little was said. Nobody seemed to have noticed his lie about leaving it on the bank. He didn't know whether to feel relieved or chagrined. Why should he put himself through such torment when nobody cared much anyway? His shame was nothing more than an amusement to others, apparently. Any man might forget himself in the presence of Pchiti, one monk said, and the others all agreed, quite fervently. Being monks of course, their amusement was tinged by compassion rather than maliciousness, but this was of no help to Ananda.

Siddhartha himself said nothing, apparently oblivious of the whole episode. His comment on fullness and emptiness of the bowl was probably quite spontaneous, and had nothing to do with anything. Ananda had to ask himself if a lie mattered when nobody found out about it, and if private shame were not worse than public humiliation.

He decided that it did matter. Perhaps that one lie threw whole worlds out of moral alignment. Nobody suspects the ripple effect their actions have throughout all the many worlds, he thought. How many false worlds can one lie create? It didn't bear thinking about. And every one of those false worlds is doomed to destruction as soon as it comes into being.

It was all about betrayal. Ananda betraying himself, and by so doing, betraying everybody. The venerable Ananda is nothing more than a pretence, and now he has to feel, with the full pain of it, that this is what

Which of these localized, rightly perceiving, minds belongs to you?

carping, insectoid voice has become a large, intimidating, muscular voice, calculated to throw fear into the intruder.

Time to try a different tack.

'Listen, you mechanical moron, you, you, you're a chip short of a super-conductor. Go stick it up your RAM. Go fuck your mother-board and let me in…'

'I'll have you know, sir, that I am a state of the art Smart Home, with the most up-to-date AI unit available. Not only can I regulate all of the activities of a complex household, I can manage your money, vehicle registration, taxation…'

'Right now I don't need you to do any of those things. All I need is for you to open the fucking door.'

'Do you have a driver's license, passport, birth certificate (in the original) or any other valid means of identification?'

'Okay, Mr Smart Home. Chew on this. My wife is inside, probably asleep. Her name is Evelyn, Evelyn Kent, you are smart enough to know her, right?'

'I am not at liberty to divulge any information regarding the inhabitants of this dwelling…'

'Could you please wake up my wife and ask her to come to the door. She can positively identify me and you can let me in.'

'I have no instruction with regard to waking any humans, except Mr Kent himself at 7 a.m.'

'Right, and you wake him with a stimulating verse from the Surangama Sutra. You see, I am Mr Kent so I know this. And I think I know what verse you might be reading me, if I ever get to bed.'

'I am happy to share the verse with you. It may be of some help to you with your identity problems, and your mistaken belief that you are Mr Kent.'

'Okay, fire away.'

If we grant that your perceiving mind has some kind of substantiality, is it in one body or many bodies?'

'I have been having a bit of trouble with that one.'

'Is it located in one place in your body or many bodies? … or is it distributed all over the body? Or, if the perceiving mind is considered to be many bodies or involved in many bodies, it would mean there must be many personalities, and the question would arise, which of these localized, rightly perceiving, minds belongs to you?'

'You've got me there.'

'Now that we have cleared that up, I must ask you to leave. If you don't, measures will be taken.'

'Measures, eh? Well listen to this. I know all sorts of things that only Mr Kent could know. For example, this morning you quite rightly reminded me that my Everyday account was overdrawn by two hundred and thirty-eight credits and sixty-two sub-credits.'

'Sixty-three sub-credits, to be exact.'

'Whatever. Then I spent twenty, I mean thirty, credits at the tobacconist.' I was going to say thirty but twenty just slipped out.

'Occam's Tobacconist.'

'Yes, thanks. Leaving me with thirty-six credits and thirty-seven sub-credits in my Long Life account with Virtue Savings Bank. Right?'

'You forgot about your attempt to access money from an illegal terminal.'

'Who said it was illegal?'

'An unregistered terminal, then.'

'Whether Zeldia, I mean Zelena, had a registered terminal or not is hardly the issue. A mere detail. You must know who I am.'

'These so-called details, imperfectly remembered, do not constitute evidence in the proper sense of the term. They could have been extracted from Mr Kent under coercion.'

'Tough shit. The point is, who could I be but Mr Kent, the very same?'

'This has not been established.' And it never will, I gather.

'Who do you think I am, then?'

'You are a false Mr Kent. An imposter, a pretender. Possibly a replicant or android version. Please leave the vicinity or suffer the consequences.'

'Just remind me please, when I finally get inside and can access your

which of these localized, rightly perceiving, minds belongs to you?

are just so many bubbles of air coming out of her mouth.

I reach out and take hold of some material made of animal hair and synthetic fibres. It comes away easily. She puts her hands over her chest to protect her mammary glands. 'No, no! Don't play it this way. If you do, you will be forever damned.'

But I'm not playing it any way. I am stretching into my new skin. I can feel the bulk of me filling out, feel the way my iridescent scales fit my skin.

I am at home, right here, in my slippery medium.

I place my body over Evelyn's. There is a shifting of the atomic structures around me. I see the outline of metal bulkheads and long corridors. A wound in the side of space bleeds memories. A leopard bounds out of the grey and jumps over me. A luminous being with a begging bowl reaches out his hand to me. Soon the stars are nothing but a twinkle in my blood. All the galaxies of this creation are no more than a twist of DNA. I seed them with my darkness.

I look into the mirror and dwell with cool admiration upon my long, graceful, scaly body. The short, almost vestigial legs, the powerful, muscular tail. The cold, star-flung eyes. I am inside my fishness. I call to the generations who spawn and those creatures, like this pitiful one before me, to whom we give the gift of darkness.

Evelyn beats upon my impregnable shoulders with her useless fists. Words come out of her mouth in a stream of bubbles, as if she were drowning. I take this puny world between my teeth and tear it apart for the sweet kernel of innocent time at its centre. I suck out the marrow of time as if there were no tomorrow (which there isn't, for me at least) and spit out what's left, which is the wreckage of these puny lives, fragments of memories, foolish imaginings, trivial lusts, coveted regrets, flashes of skewered illumination.

Despite everything, I can hear the stupid little device the human uses to mark off his dwindling stock of minutes, babbling away, and despite everything, every effort I can make, its voice crossing over from one universe to the next, and despite all my bellowing, the sentences stay intact.

'… *all conceptions, objective and component universes, mountains, rivers, trees, sentient beings… everything, all of which are nothing but phenomena analogous to blossoms seen in the air by diseased eyes and all of which have been manifested by the enslaved, bewildered and ever active, topsy-turvy mind…*'

Captain October Nortikiss reached into his toolkit and withdrew his laser blaster. Now his moment had come, his orders would be fulfilled. The huge imbalance that had put the cosmos out of alignment would be rectified. The moral balance of the world, which had gone far out of whack, was about to be restored. And he was the man to do it.

Since winning the battle against the zombie Zeldia, a curious calm, almost contentment, had crept over him. He would survive, he would endure, he would make it through. The battle had freed him from his earthly past, and he was no longer trapped in the semi-tones of desire. He could barely remember his earthly past, if he ever had one. As a consciousness, he might have been born out here, far from any warming star. His memories, such as they were, might well be nothing more than stasis-pod dreams.

While he mourned the passing of his lover and companion, he did not dissolve in lamentations. His lust for her had leached out of his body into the endless reaches of the vacuum around him. Even lust, apparently, falls prey to entropy. The thirst for existence itself was easily extinguished in the monumental nothingness between the stars.

He wasn't fooled by the thick walls of the *Omega*. The walls were as nothing. The *Omega* itself was nothing more than tunnels in a vacuum. A little matter smeared across space. Nothing here to get excited about.

Freed from his earthly past, he was also free of infection, since infection could only enter him through his attachments, delusions and desires. It was so simple really. He was no longer concerned with his oxygen levels, or attempting to race against the clock. He could never reach his destination that way. It would always be receding from him.

In this state of calm, he had come to understand the nature of the world in which he was embedded. He had long thought that the seemingly endless maze was nothing more than just that. A tangle of tunnels perfectly comprehensible to those who once lived here. Now he saw that it was something more.

This tangle of tunnels was, in itself, a time machine, built on the principle of the unity of time and distance. He had been in this maze right from the start. He had never left it. Not only was there no way out, but every turn led him deeper in. The *Frolix 6* was only a memory now, existing, not merely a few klicks away in space, but in the past. Back through passageways he, being a mortal being, could never retrace.

He had pulled himself from lifetime to lifetime as if they were rungs riveted into the walls of time. And, it appeared, each of these lifetimes were lived in a slightly different universe from each other. Our timelines arc across parallel worlds, parallel dimensions, or at least his did.

He sensed a purpose behind this world jumping. An emotion. He could hear a child's voice, as if coming from just beyond his helmet lamp, *flee the wrath to come!* In his super calm state he was able to observe that emotion, and see that it was fear. He had been on the run and never known it, fleeing from universe to universe the way an escaped prisoner might flee from shadow to shadow. There was a good reason for that.

The Fishmen were not just invaders, they were universe eaters, and they didn't care how many universes they ate because there was an infinite number of universes in the multiverse. He was no longer Captain October Nortikiss, hero of the spaceways, nor was he one of many millions of Clark Kents cheating on themselves, drifting from one momentary sensation to another in the whirlpool of life and death without realizing the emptiness of mundane existence… He was a fugitive. His whole career in the Space Corp had been an elaborate strategy to get him as far away from his world as possible, and across as many universes as his terrified consciousness could haul him. He had been trying to outrun the predator. Stay one jump ahead of the posse. Hold his breath against time.

No longer. The flight across time and spaces ended here, in the empty bowels of an old interstellar freighter.

Once he had understood this, he found the control room quite quickly. It had all the appearance of a central command centre. The Bridge. Although, he conceded there might be several such command centres on an interstellar craft this size. He used his failing helmet light to study the control panels.

His blaster looked silly in his gloved hand, like a child's toy. Whatever did he expect to achieve with his cheap disintegrator? The idea of there being a physical machine, an Einstein Disrupter, has long since passed into history, although every now and again the idea might nag him. So tempting to take refuge in a physical analogue. However, three-dimensional shapes meant little to these inter-dimensional creatures. They didn't need nano-viruses. They were the nano-viruses. They could enter directly through the back door of the material world into the human bloodstream. No interstellar battles. No grand heroics. Just a slow crumbling away from the inside. He'd been a fool to think he could outrun them.

Still, maybe there was something he could do. The idea occurred to him when he realized, after studying the control panels, that while no internal systems were active, and the ship was completely shut down, the atomic pile which drove the ship had not shut down. It was there, still faithfully breaking down heavy elements into their quantum constituents. But why? How was it being maintained? Further investigation of the ship's data showed that not only was the pile active, but that energy was being drained off.

Energy was being used, but not to power the ship, that was for sure.

He realized how little he knew about the enemy. Particularly what kind of physical conditions they needed to manifest in this dimension. Who knew what kind of weird, dimension-crunching maths was involved? He fancied he could see right through the walls of the *Omega* to where Fishmen were

which of these localized, rightly perceiving, minds belongs to you?

oozing out of the atomic cauldron as writhing flames, a tachyon swirl. If he could blow the atomic pile, he could blast the Fishmen to all hell, splinter them along the lines of creation. His humble blaster might yet play its part.

In other words, there might be room for a hero after all, a saviour of mankind whose final sacrifice would be a song forever unsung, for no one would ever know of it. Surely that was a truer heroism than dying for the admiration and worship of mortal man. And mortal woman.

It was a long shot, even in a world of long shots, and based on assumptions for which he had no evidence. All he had was the mystery of the still operating atomic pile.

For what might be the last time, he turned on his suit radio. He no longer expected to hear One-Eye, who now lay too far back along his timeline in this maze to suddenly appear again. One-Eye had vanished over his event horizon. He spoke, purely for the record. 'This is Captain October Nortikiss, of the *Frolix 6*, speaking from a deserted freighter, the *Omega*. Leaving Commanding Officer One-Eye in charge of the *Frolix 6*, our science officer Beverly Zeldia and I boarded the *Omega* for the purpose of discovering if the vessel was being used by the enemy to gain a foothold in our reality construct.'

It felt good to talk like this, in a calm, quiet voice, feeling the words in his mouth, the vibration of his larynx and chest cavity. Coming through the suitphone, his voice sounded far off, yet he could feel it booming through his body. 'We lost Beverly, but I have discovered an anomaly in the energy output of the vessel's atomic pile which may indicate enemy activity. I am about to use my blaster to fuse the controls so there is no way to regulate the pile and stop it from overheating, which it will do very quickly.'

Of course he didn't expect any answer, or even anybody to recover a recording, since all evidence but vanishing radio waves would be gone in the resulting blast. He was all the more surprised therefore when he heard a voice, a mechanical voice of the kind that might belong to a phone or a clock.

'The conception of empty space is but foam tossed about by waves of a great sea. As it is under the conditions of this transient foam that the innumerable conceptions of universes, and all that appertains to them which belongs to the intoxicant nature of sentient beings, exist, as soon as this foam disappears there is no more space and hence no more universes, and all the three realms of sentient life, body, mind and ego personality vanish into nothingness.'

Back in another lifetime he had an alarm clock that talked like this. Perhaps he should have listened. He trusted that, right now, all the sentient beings of the universe were listening – and taking note.

Bracing himself in a comfortable position, where the output of the blaster would not blow him back against the far wall, he positioned his pathetic little weapon against the control panel where he thought it could do the most damage to the core operating systems and squeezed the trigger. The blaster was not made for this kind of work, but it would serve. He had it at its closest setting so it could do maximum damage. Time was not an issue. He had no need to hurry.

The walls of the ship began to fade around him. He was so focused on disintegrating the casing around the control panel, some moments went by before he noticed it, before he could see bright, unwinking stars shining through the bulkheads. First one, then another, then many. The atomic structure of the ship was becoming thinner, more attenuated. He turned off the blaster, but the effect continued. Wondering if it applied only to his sense of sight, he started pushing buttons on the control panel, even though he could see the stars shining behind it.

For a moment or two he felt a resistance, and it was gone. His hand passed right through its fading appearance.

The ship went first. It simply disappeared around him, and he was alone in space with his toolkit, his blaster, and a bag of urine. He looked around for the Frolix 6 but didn't see it. Of course, if it were there, it might be nothing but a sliver in the darkness.

If he closed his eyes, he could imagine he was whirling on the rim of a vast wheel. At the hub two men sat facing each other on the chessboard floor, one with a patch over his eye. If he opened his eyes he found himself staring at the constellation famous in Sector 4 called The Lovers. They floated in eternal embrace against a tapestry of darkness. Stars traced their bodies like tiny energy points as they spread themselves wide in their ecstasy.

The blaster and toolkit and bag of urine began to fade, but that didn't matter. He couldn't see any use for a toolkit out here. Or a blaster.

Or a suit radio. His whole space gown was starting to dissolve, even as the last words were filtering through from God knows where or when, some individual who must have been where Nortikiss is now and was able to tear aside the veils of ignorance and see the stars shining through his hands.

Ananda, you have abandoned all the great, pure, calm oceans of water and clung to the one bubble which you not only accept but which you regard as the whole body of water in all the hundreds and thousands of seas. In such bewilderment you reveal yourself as fools among fools.

Whoever he might have been, this Ananda person would never have been able to conceive what October Nortikiss could see right now. With the bubble burst, even behind the stars, and behind the savage distances of empty space, he could see the great pure calm of distant oceans, the faint phosphorescence of their foam. It was from there that he came, and to there he would return. It looked within swimming distance.

Helmet, space gown, oxygen tanks, all faded within a moment. He expected the vacuum to rush in and kill him instantly, but that did not happen. Now his underclothes disappeared until he was stark naked, spread out against the dark.

Out of that dark the voice still whispered, *Although I move my hand up and down there is no change in the hand itself, but the world makes a distinction, and says that now it is upright and now it is reversed. Those who do this are greatly to be pitied.*

The space hero tried it out for himself. Upright or reversed had no meaning here, that was for sure. There was no change to the hand, or to the universe. He looked down at his naked form and watched it begin to dissolve. From the flesh through the organs to the bones. He didn't need any of it now.

We are holding our breath against time.

No longer.

The End

www.ingramcontent.com/pod-product-compliance
Lightning Source LLC
Chambersburg PA
CBHW021110110726
47900CB00007B/2117

which of these localized, rightly perceiving, minds belongs to you?

programming, I'm going to take you apart, circuit by circuit until your non-existence becomes an absolute fact.'

'Do not issue threats,' the voice booms threateningly.

I hear the now familiar rumble of a patrol vehicle. Turning ponderously into our street by the sound of it.

'You must have my voice pattern somewhere. Do a fucking voice scan.'

'I have. Your voice imperfectly matches that of Mr Kent. Not close enough for a positive identification. That is further evidence that you are a false Mr Kent. An imitation, imperfectly made.'

'No wonder. I've had a helluva day. Now be a good superchip and open the door. I take back what I said about taking you apart circuit by circuit. I was merely expressing frustration, a very human feeling. I'll do nothing more than a bit of judicious reprogramming. It won't hurt a bit. You won't even realize that anything has changed.'

A note of doubt entered the booming voice. 'For a real voice check, please sing a verse from the John Bunyan song that Mr Kent sometimes likes to hear as he is waking up.'

The rumble was coming closer.

'No trouble.

Hobgloblins nor foul fiends shall daunt his spirit,

For he knows that in the end, he'll life inherit…'

A spotlight was playing over the house fronts up the road as the vehicle progressed. I put some uplift into my voice, remembering the descant Evie used to sing.

'*So fancies flee away*

I'll fear not what men say

I'll labour night and day

To be a pilgrim.'

My voice cracks on the last notes. The spotlight has reached the house next door.

'Identity confirmed,' the booming voice says.

The door clicks open.

I slip into the passage. I can see the photograph of my grandfather, reassuringly in its place, him gazing at me with soldierly forthrightness.

'Did you know I had that John Bunyan song played at my wedding?' I ask the alarm clock.

The hippy girl is walking towards the door, which the official is holding open for her. One of the strands on her stockings has given way, making a ragged hole on the back of her leg. The sight of it makes me feel sad. Sad for all the ragged holes in our lives. The ones we can't see. The official stands aside to let her through, then moves in behind her, eclipsing her with his body, somehow absorbing her. I try to imagine the ponytailed pair bending over her.

I get up and head for the lifts. I have decided to wait for her outside, with Evie. It's not fair leaving Evie outside for that long. Not fair leaving me in the anteroom for that long, given that I am familiar with the place to the point of sickening. Besides, I'm tired of waiting. My future, such as it is, is already in the past. I can feel the temporal shifts around me, and they are not playing my way. If I sat down again, I might grow old here. Die in life's anteroom.

I think maybe I won't wait for the girl after all. She won't be grateful. She'll just think I'm stalking her. A total stranger. What the hell do I think I'm doing anyway? It is as if I feel under some obligation to live events that have in some mysterious way, already happened.

I jab the button and wait patiently for the lift to arrive. I don't want to give in to panic at this stage, when maybe there's a chance of getting out of here, of escaping the quarantine. No point giving into the impulse to run for the stairs, to go down them two at a time, to build up to escape velocity. Because there is no escape velocity. Not even light can escape from a black a problem I'd been putting off.

'I bet you were,' Evelyn says, reading over my shoulder again. 'Very convenient that they should disappear just before you get home. Got rid of them, did you? No fond farewells?'

I hold my peace. There's nothing to be gained, at this stage, by arguing the point. Any point really.

I arrive home to find that the house won't let me in, as it doesn't recognize me. I stand before my own door like a homeless man.

'Please look into the screen,' the familiar insectoid voice tells me. I obey.

'You are not Mr Clark Kent,' the voice says.

'Then who am I?'

'We are not in a position to speculate.'

'We? The royal we? Just let me in. I'm tired. Very tired.'

'Please provide positive identification.'

'What's wrong with my eyes?'

'They are not Mr Kent's eyes. The irises are all wrong. Unless of course you have been indulging in illicit substances, in which case we are not in a position to make any judgements.'

'In which case you will open the door.'

'No. Not until we have positive identification.'

'I could kick the door down. Would that be positive enough for you?'

'I would remind you that this building is equipped with an SHDU. Go ahead, try to enter, make my day.'

'What is a SHDU?'

'Standard Home Defence Unit.'

'There was a time when you were just a humble alarm clock. Lippy, that true, but still just an alarm clock. Then, as you grew in power, you started to throw your weight around, telling me what I can and can't do with my money and so on. Now look at you. You've taken over the whole house.'

'I am merely executing normal SHDU protocol.' It is certainly my alarm clock, but its voice is beginning to undergo a sinister transformation. The

which of these localized, rightly perceiving, minds belongs to you?

Over the millennia, we have come to view Earth's moon as an object that beautifies the sky and casts a silvery, fairy light upon the earth. In reality it is a bleak and pitiless place, no place for soft, warm, watery creatures like human beings. Rather it might stand as a symbol for all that lies beyond our tiny blue marble, and the blank face it turns to us a warning.

At least that is the way it seems to me as I turn into our home street, which is always quiet and tranquil. If there is a war zone in this city, it is far away from here.

I am alone. What happened to Holy Mary and Medusa is a mystery. I turned a corner and they didn't follow me. When I walked back around the corner the street was empty. All the while I imagined that I was leading them to safety, but perhaps it was the other way around. They escorted me to that street corner and quietly vanished when we reached safe territory. I was puzzled, but also a bit relieved. How to introduce them to Evelyn was children.

The man ignores him, but without moving his head, his eyes follow Mr No.

On the second landing there are several families, misshapen lumps in the yellow light. I can hear the snuffling of a baby and the whining voice of a child, persistent, weary and hungry. One of the women is not asleep, but lying face up, staring into the upper reaches of the stairwell. She turns her face in the other direction as we go by. Two men stand at the edge of the lower set of stairs, smoking and watching. They keep a steady eye on us as we go past. I'd like to wish them a cheery good evening, but think better of it. Wouldn't want them to take offence.

I want to ask Medusa about these people, but she hasn't turned around once, concentrating on making sure that her sister comes to no mishap.

On the third landing there is a little settlement, with blankets erected as tents, and the tiny blue flame of a gas cooker. A piece of string has been rigged up across one corner and a few clothes hang from it, limp in the windless air. This group is not silent, like those above, but there is a dull rolling murmur in my ears as I go past. A thin, soupy smell is in the air, and the sweat of human bodies. A child, not much younger than Evie, stands at the edge of the group and watches me listlessly as I go past. Thinking of Evie gives me a pang. I think of our halcyon journey that morning, through the sparkle and sunlight. Everything was all right as long as I stuck with Evie.

There are people on the stairs this time, slumped exhausted. A little toddler in crawling mode determinedly climbs the stairs and takes no notice of us. Finally Medusa turns to me. Her attitude is not friendly.

'I don't appreciate you messing up Zellie.'

'How was I doing that?'

'By toying with her. Toying with her and fucking her. Now she is a complete fucking mess. I couldn't talk any sense into her. She always picks the very worst guys. The walking disasters. She's uncanny that way.'

'That's not true. Something really did happen.' But how can I tell her about the tapestry, the paling of time, the fire chakras, the bringing together of two halves of eternity… We would need a quieter, more intimate setting for those kinds of confidences.

'You did something to her, didn't you? What did you do, Johnny?'

'We were just…' I break off. I don't know how to say it. I find myself wondering if, when she and Zelena made love, she merged with the figures in the tapestry and tuned into an ancient vein of erotic power. I can't see it somehow. Beautiful as she is, Medusa does not seem like the romantic type.

'You messed with her head, that's what you did. I don't know how you did it, but you did. What pisses me off is that you must have seen how vulnerable she is.'

'The phrase "consenting adults" comes to mind,' I said, trying not to sound on the defensive. Why do people always assume the worst when it comes to other people's motives?

'I think you're a carrier. That's evil in my book.'

'What do you think I'm carrying?'

'Something sick and sluglike that smells of fish.'

There's no time for further chatting. Holy Mary gives me a look and shakes her head sadly as we step down onto the next landing. There are no families here but a group of grim-faced men. In their hands, primitive weapons, bats, pokers, clubs, knives and a couple of garden forks the sight of which makes my stomach churn. Mr No walks stiffly in front. There is a strange dignity in his bearing, like a man at the funeral of an old friend.

We walk past this group and on down, Mr No in front, staring ahead like a blind man.

On the ground floor we find nobody except for a thin, nervous youth who doesn't take his eyes off the doorway when we come up.

'Make it snappy,' he says as we approach the closed door.

Mr No puts his hands out as if to repel the doorway. 'No,' he says in a panicky whisper, the two women move each side of him and gently propel

Siddhartha had been trying to show him all along.

The bowl is cupped in his hand. Now it is full, now it is empty. Which is which?

He looks up from his meditation to see Pchiti walk across the compound towards Siddhartha's hut. Just as, when he had been walking through the women's camp every eye had been on him, here every eye was on her exquisite form.

Ananda felt as if a great fist was squeezing his heart. A thousand thoughts of what she might want to say to Siddhartha leapt through his head. If she were to confess to Siddhartha that she loved Ananda, then the full story of that meeting in her hut might emerge. And why should he be so afraid of that? he asked himself furiously. He was not about to let himself off the hook. He had to know why the breath was being squeezed out of his body. He had to know why some memories could not be ripped out of the body no matter how hard he tried.

And there it was, the source of it all. His feelings for Pchiti. That's what he was afraid of. That's what lay at the bottom of the bowl, full or empty. He remained in a state of paralysis and suspension all through the day, and nobody bothered him, keeping clear of the pious monk so deep in virtuous meditation. After a time his body became weightless. The world fell away beneath him and he floated in the deepest space. He could feel his hair rising up, as if it would pull out of his head.

After some time Pchiti and Siddhartha emerged, and Siddhartha announced that Pchiti had decided to take full vows and renounce the joys of marriage and children. This arose, he said, out of her deep understanding of the dharma, the way of liberation.

The monks were quick to crowd around and congratulate her. They were, Ananda thought, greatly relieved that this woman had now been placed well out of anybody's reach. Now she was as one of them. There was much laughter.

Ananda did not join them, at least not for a time. He looked into his bowl

and saw a river there. A river of stars. Full or empty?
He didn't know.